PRAISE FOR S

"Susan Stoker knows what women want. A hot hero who .... save a damsel in distress . . . even if she can save herself!"

—CD Reiss, *New York Times* bestselling author

"Irresistible characters and seat-of-the-pants action will keep you glued to the pages."

—Elle James, *New York Times* bestselling author

"Susan does romantic suspense right! Edge of my seat + smokin' hot = read ALL of her books! Now."

—Carly Phillips, *New York Times* bestselling author

"Susan Stoker writes the perfect book boyfriends!"

—Laurann Dohner, *New York Times* bestselling author

"These books should come with a warning label. Once you start, you can't stop until you've read them all."

—Sharon Hamilton, *New York Times* bestselling author

"Susan Stoker never disappoints. She delivers alpha males with heart and heroines with moxie."

—Jana Aston, *New York Times* bestselling author

"Susan Stoker gives me everything I need in romance: heat, humor, intensity, and the perfect HEA."

—Carrie Ann Ryan, *New York Times* bestselling author

"Susan Stoker packs one heck of a punch!"

—Lainey Reese, *USA Today* bestselling author

DEFENDING ZARA

DISCOVER OTHER TITLES BY SUSAN STOKER

Mountain Mercenaries Series

Defending Allye
Defending Chloe
Defending Morgan
Defending Harlow
Defending Everly
Defending Zara
Defending Raven (July 2020)

Ace Security Series

Claiming Grace
Claiming Alexis
Claiming Bailey
Claiming Felicity
Claiming Sarah

Delta Force Heroes

Rescuing Rayne
Rescuing Aimee (novella)
Rescuing Emily
Rescuing Harley
Marrying Emily
Rescuing Kassie
Rescuing Bryn
Rescuing Casey
Rescuing Sadie (novella)

Rescuing Wendy
Rescuing Mary
Rescuing Macie (novella)

Delta Team Two Series

Shielding Gillian (April 2020)
Shielding Kinley (August 2020)
Shielding Aspen (October 2020)
Shielding Riley (TBA)
Shielding Devyn (TBA)
Shielding Ember (TBA)
Shielding Sierra (TBA)

Badge of Honor: Texas Heroes Series

Justice for Mackenzie
Justice for Mickie
Justice for Corrie
Justice for Laine (novella)
Shelter for Elizabeth
Justice for Boone
Shelter for Adeline
Shelter for Sophie
Justice for Erin
Justice for Milena
Shelter for Blythe
Justice for Hope
Shelter for Quinn
Shelter for Koren
Shelter for Penelope

Stand-Alone Novels

The Guardian Mist
A Princess for Cale
A Moment in Time (a short-story collection)
Lambert's Lady

Writing as Annie George

Stepbrother Virgin (erotic novella)

DEFENDING ZARA

Mountain Mercenaries, Book 6

Susan Stoker

Published by Montlake, Seattle

www.apub.com

Amazon, the Amazon logo, and Montlake are trademarks of Amazon.com, Inc., or its affiliates.

ISBN-13: 9781542017138
ISBN-10: 1542017130

Cover design by Eileen Carey

Cover photography by Regina Wamba of MaeIDesign.com

Printed in the United States of America

DEFENDING
ZARA

Chapter One

"They're beating the crap out of them! We've got to *do* something!" Gabriella exclaimed.

"We can't go out there yet, they'll just turn on us," Mags said patiently, but she had a worried look in her eye.

Personally, Zara wasn't sure if they should go out and help the two men currently getting the shit kicked out of them. Growing up the way she had, in the poor barrios of Lima, Peru, Zara had learned to always take care of herself first. Everyone and everything else took second place to her innate need to survive. But she couldn't help feeling awful about the men being thrashed just yards away.

It was the middle of the night, and the women had watched from afar as a pair of soldiers from the Peruvian military prepared to raid one of the houses with a team of men from the United States.

Once upon a time, Zara might've done whatever she could to gain the attention of those Americans . . . now all she wanted was to run away and stay safe.

But because she liked and respected Mags, the leader of their ragtag group, she stood her ground behind the women huddled around the door of the shanty and watched two Americans get beaten up by a gang of bullies who lived in the barrio they all called home. No one outwardly defied those men, though Mags and their group did what they could to silently and secretly resist them.

But the fact that the men had begun to steal children to sell to Roberto del Rio, the notorious and ruthless leader of the biggest sex-trafficking ring in Peru, had changed things. Mags wasn't going to stand for that. No way.

Pushing her short brown hair out of her eyes, Zara absently made a mental note to cut it soon. It was getting too long, and the last thing she wanted was for someone to look at her and realize she was a woman. As it was, with her short hair, slight build, breasts bound tightly to her chest, and short stature, they saw what she wanted them to see. A dirty, poor teenage boy named Zed. She'd worked hard over the years to cultivate that image, and while Mags had somehow seen through her disguise in a heartbeat, most people didn't take a second glance at her.

Which was how Zara liked it. And how she'd managed to survive the last fifteen years living on the streets and in the barrios of Lima. She could barely remember her life before. Didn't want to remember it. That life was gone for good. *This* was her life now.

"They're running away," Teresa whispered in Spanish. "Something must've scared them."

"Are they still alive?" Gabriella asked.

"I don't . . . Wait, yeah. The one closest to us just moved his foot," Teresa said.

"Okay, we have to be quick." It was something everyone already knew. This wasn't the first time they'd gone out of their way to help some poor soul who'd had the misfortune to be on the receiving end of the brutal gang's attention. "We'll grab the first guy, bring him back here, then Zed can load him up while the rest of us go back to get the other one."

"Why don't we just leave them there?" Bonita asked.

That was what Zara wanted to know, though she'd never voice it. The injured men were strangers. They weren't even from here. They weren't from the barrio, so why put their own lives at risk for them?

"Because they're here trying to help," Mags stated firmly. "They obviously don't know the men from the military are corrupt. They don't know that their mission was likely to fail from the start, simply because those soldiers are pocketing money from del Rio. If one of these men was yours, a *good* man who was fighting against the evils of the world instead of working for Satan, would you want them to die like that?"

All of them were silent in response.

Zara had spent a lot of time with the women around her. She trusted them. They all knew suffering intimately.

Maria was twenty-nine and from Mexico. She'd been married off when she was fifteen and had fled her abusive husband a few years ago. She had ended up penniless and alone in Peru, and Mags had taken her under her wing.

Bonita and Carmen were thirty-two and thirty-five, respectively. They'd both been sold when they were only twelve years old by their own families to Roberto del Rio. They'd been "retired" from del Rio's service for five years or so, and had spent most of that time with Mags.

Gabriella was the youngest of their group at twenty-one and had grown up in the barrio, much like Zara. She'd managed to avoid being "recruited" by del Rio, but only by sheer luck and because Mags had done her best to keep her hidden from the scouts who frequented the area. Teresa was from Brazil and had been with them for around six months. She'd been "fired" by del Rio and left to fend for herself.

Interestingly enough, *no one* knew Mags's story . . . but it was obvious she'd suffered the most. She was friendly to their motley crew and did her best to help others, but she never talked about herself or how she'd ended up being the sort-of den mother to a group of broken and desperate women.

Everyone shook their heads at her question. If the Americans were "good men," as Mags had put it, then no, they didn't want them to suffer at the hands of the barrio's meanest bully, Ruben, and his mob.

"Right. On the count of three, we'll all go out and drag that first man back. Teresa, you're responsible for getting rid of the drag marks so if the gang comes back, they don't know where he went. Zed, you get the ambulance prepared."

Zara nodded and turned toward the contraption they called an ambulance. It was actually a rickety old bicycle that had been hooked up to an equally old-looking box on wheels. It had a hinged lid with strategically placed items on top. Cans, pieces of wood and scrap metal, trash . . . anything that would make someone who glanced at it not look twice. But under that hinged lid was an empty box, large enough to carry a human being through the back streets and barrios of Lima.

It wouldn't pass a thorough inspection by the police or military, but at a glance, it looked like a giant pile of garbage. Zara made sure the rubbish on the lid was secure, and she tested the connection from the box to the bike. The last thing she wanted was for the thing to come unattached while she was on her way to the doctor.

Zara had met Daniela Alvan through Mags. She was in her mid-thirties and the closest thing the barrio had to a doctor. She'd helped more women than Zara could count, and her specialty was midwifery, but she regularly stitched up the wounded, treating knife and gunshot wounds. Daniela was discreet, and she lived in a small house near the barrio Zara had made her home. It had actual brick walls and running water, both of which were luxuries most in the area didn't have.

Daniela had often allowed "Zed" to help her, running errands and allowing her to watch and assist as she treated patients. As a result, Mags now considered Zed their little group's personal doctor.

But they both knew the men who'd been beaten would need more assistance than Zara could give them. So she would take them to Daniela, who would make sure they weren't bleeding internally, and then they'd return them to their American friends so they could get the proper medical treatment they most likely needed.

But the first aim was to get them away from the area. Away from the gang that hated any and all outsiders and would come back to make sure they were dead—once the danger from whatever had spooked them had passed. They'd search every hovel until they found them, which was why Zara was making sure their "ambulance" was ready to go.

Within seconds of checking the wheels on the decrepit bike and trailer, Zara startled when the women burst back through the door. They were dragging a man who looked like he was dead already. His head lolled backward and his eyes were shut.

"Drag him to the trailer," Mags ordered.

It took four of them to move him, and Zara had no idea how in the world she and Daniela were going to be able to get him out of the trailer by themselves, but she couldn't worry about that right now. She and Mags held the trailer steady while the others struggled to get the man's unconscious body up and over the lip of the wooden box. He was tall and muscular, which made their job all the harder.

When he was finally inside, Zara looked down at him in consternation. They'd been able to carry two people in the trailer in the past, but the American was huge. Zara estimated that, when standing, he'd tower over her by at least a foot. Even after they'd arranged him on his side in a fetal position, it was obvious his companion wasn't going to fit in the small space that was left.

"Ruben and Marcus are coming back this way!" Bonita hissed. She was peering between the wooden slats through a gap that served as a crude kind of door.

"Which means Eberto, Alfonso, and the rest of the gang will be back before too long," Gabriella said, something they all knew.

"Shit," Mags muttered under her breath. "There's no time. We can't go out and get the other American. Zed, you ready?"

Zara nodded. She took one last look at the injured man at the bottom of the trailer. He had brown hair and day-old scruff and had been stripped of his shirt, pants, and shoes by the men who'd beaten him. He was wearing a bloody and torn undershirt and a pair of boxer shorts.

Something about seeing the man in his underwear made her feel sorry for him, which was an unusual feeling for Zara. She did her best to stay as far away from men as possible. She'd learned a long time ago that they were nothing but trouble.

But seeing this American so badly hurt, knowing it was up to *her* to get him help, made her anxious. She could take him straight to his American friends, but she suspected the two corrupt soldiers would promptly blame her for his condition and arrest her. And who knew if they'd actually help him?

No, her best bet was to get him to Daniela. She could make sure he wasn't going to die, then they'd figure out what to do with him after that. Maybe she'd warn him about the kind of men his team was working with. Everyone in the barrios knew many of the bastards who worked in the First Special Forces Brigade in the Peruvian military were corrupt, working in cahoots with del Rio and anyone else rich enough to pay them to look the other way when something illegal was going on. How they regularly ran sweeps of the barrios and beat anyone who dared speak back to them or look at them sideways.

The lid was lowered and the women fussed over the items camouflaging the box. When they were satisfied that it looked like nothing more than a heaping pile of trash, they stepped back.

Mags approached Zara as she climbed onto the bike. She reached out a hand and squeezed Zara's shoulder. "Be careful," Mags said in English.

When Mags had found "Zed" five years ago and discovered that, once upon a time, English had been her primary language, she'd made it her mission to help Zara practice it every day. She'd taken Zara under her wing and given her the first sense of family and safety she'd had in a decade. There wasn't anything Zara wouldn't do for Mags, and if she wanted her to relearn English, that was what she'd do.

Zara nodded.

"Stay with Daniela as long as necessary," Mags ordered. "Don't come back here until we know it's safe. While del Rio is snatching up younger and younger boys and girls, people who look as old as teens are still disappearing. Understand?"

"Yes," Zara said succinctly. She didn't talk much. Had discovered a long time ago that she learned a lot more by listening. And because she'd learned Spanish by ear, she felt self-conscious speaking it, despite being fluent.

"Report back when you can, and use your own judgment about returning the man to his friends," Mags said. "Also . . . while we have no idea what kind of man this one is, try to remember that they're not *all* bad. There are some noble and kind ones out there."

Zara nodded, even though she wasn't sure she believed the older woman. She'd seen the worst humanity had to offer. She'd seen men literally steal food out of the hands of babies, push older men to the ground as they crossed a street. And, of course, there was the rampant corruption in the police and military forces that were supposedly there to protect the citizens of Peru.

A niggling memory in the back of her mind tried to push forward. The memory of a man whose arms were the safest place she ever remembered being. A man who smelled like aftershave and soap, who could make her giggle, and who beamed with pride when he smiled down at her.

But the second those memories tried to creep in, Zara ruthlessly shut them out. That part of her life was gone. There was no use remembering it or wishing for something she could never get back.

"Go on now, and remember not to rush. If you do, you'll draw attention to yourself. Just go slow, stop every now and then to pick up something off the ground. Act like nothing's wrong and no one will look twice at you. And Zed?"

Zara looked up at Mags in expectation.

Lowering her voice, Mags said, "I'm proud of you."

Zara's chest felt tight. She could count on one hand the number of compliments she'd received in the last fifteen years. And coming from Mags, a woman she admired and looked up to, those words meant a lot.

"Thank you," Zara said gruffly.

"You're welcome," Mags said, then took a step back and turned to Gabriella. "Make sure the coast is clear to go out the back."

The other woman nodded and headed to the back of the shack to look out the other door. Apparently seeing none of the gang members lurking around, she pulled back the piece of metal blocking the exit and nodded.

Zara took a deep breath and pushed on the pedals of the bike. It was tough to get going, since she was towing more than two hundred pounds of human flesh behind her, but once she did, Zara kept her head down and her eyes up. She navigated the rough dirt paths of the barrio and didn't seem to breathe until she left the slum behind and was on the concrete sidewalk outside the walls.

She wasn't in the clear, though. She had to stay sharp. All it would take was one policeman getting a little too nosey, and both her life and the life of the man in the trailer behind her would be worth less than nothing.

Breathing slowly and trying not to do anything that would bring attention to herself, Zara slowly pedaled toward Daniela's house. She hoped the man behind her was all right. That he wouldn't wake up and freak out, exposing them both and probably signing her death warrant. In his condition, he likely would have trouble lifting the lid on the trailer, as it was secured with a small hook, but he could yell out. And if he really tried hard enough, he could probably break the hook and flip up the top.

She'd be hauled off to jail for kidnapping, and who knew what would happen to him.

With that thought in mind, Zara took the risk and pedaled just a little bit faster.

Chapter Two

Hunter "Meat" Snow moaned low in his throat. He couldn't remember being in this much pain . . . ever. Oh, he'd had his share of moments as a Delta Force operative in the Army where he'd been tortured, but generally he hadn't been beaten up by a dozen men at one time.

He remembered going to help Black along one of the streets in the barrio, but they'd both quickly been overtaken by a gang of men determined to punish them for some unknown slight.

The last thing Meat remembered was looking over at his friend and praying their teammates would find them sooner rather than later.

No, that wasn't true. The *very* last thing he remembered was lying in the dirt and trying to breathe when a bunch of shadowy figures appeared above him. He'd tensed in preparation for another beating, but instead they'd grabbed hold of his arms and begun to drag him off. The pain of the movement had been enough to render him unconscious.

And now he was . . .

Where was he?

Meat tried to roll over onto his back, but realized he couldn't. He was in some sort of container. He could feel movement. Every bump felt like a knife to his ribs, and his shoulder was on fire. His head was throbbing, and he couldn't see. Had he been blinded?

Turning his head, Meat was relieved to glimpse a sliver of light coming from above him. So he wasn't blind, thank God. But where was he, and what was happening to him?

He could hear car horns honking and people speaking in rapid-fire Spanish, but since he couldn't understand the language, he had no idea what was being said. Meat realized that he wasn't handcuffed or tied, and it seemed weird to take someone captive but not immobilize them—though his captor's idiocy was to his benefit, so he wasn't complaining.

With one hand, he pushed up on whatever was above him, but wasn't really surprised when it didn't move. What he *was* surprised by was the severity of the pain that went through his body. It was enough to make him see stars, and he had to close his eyes and pant a bit to help alleviate the agony. It was more than obvious he wasn't going to be able to physically fight his way out of whatever box he'd been put in. He just had to wait the situation out. Assess things, then make plans to get back to Black and the rest of the team.

Lying on his side in the box was excruciatingly painful. Every breath felt as if nails were being driven into his side. Meat knew he probably had a couple fractured or broken ribs as well as a dislocated shoulder. He felt nauseous, which meant he most likely had a concussion too. But it was his ankle that worried him the most. He could fight with broken ribs and a concussion, but he wouldn't get far on a bum ankle.

Just then, his body was flung slightly forward, and his shoeless feet slammed against the box. There was loud shouting, and the box he was in teetered from side to side for a moment before steadying.

Meat didn't hear much of anything else, because when his feet hit the wall of the box, it felt as if his ankle had taken a hit from a sledgehammer.

Gasping for breath and feeling light-headed, Meat fought against losing consciousness, but it was no use. There was only so much pain he could take, and he passed out once more.

Zara swore under her breath. She'd been thinking too much about the man behind her and had almost ridden out into the middle of an intersection. The last thing she needed was to get run over with her illegal cargo.

She ignored the people yelling at her from their cars as they passed, and tried to control her breathing as she waited for the light to turn green so she could cross the street. She was almost at Daniela's neighborhood, and while she wouldn't look too out of place there, riding her bike and pulling a trailer seemingly filled with trash, she also didn't blend in as well as she did in the slums.

Daniela wouldn't know she was on her way, but it didn't matter. She'd take in Zara and the patient without any issues.

Pedaling around to the back of the house, Zara climbed off the bike and opened the wooden door in the fence. She pushed the bike through, then carefully closed the door behind her. She steered the bike between two beat-up old cars and left it there for the time being. She quickly ran to the door and knocked.

For a heartbeat, Zara thought maybe Daniela wasn't home, but she breathed a sigh of relief when the doctor finally opened the door.

"Got a patient for me today, Zed?" Daniela asked in Spanish.

Zara had no idea if Daniela knew she was a woman and not a teenage boy, but she hadn't offered up any explanations, and the doctor hadn't pried.

Nodding, Zara turned back to the bicycle. She shifted a few things around on the trailer, then unhooked it and lifted the lid.

Her heart lurched when she saw the man lying so still inside. For a second, she thought he was dead, but then she saw his chest rise and fall with a labored breath.

Closing her eyes in relief, Zara was having a hard time understanding why she cared so much. First of all, the man was a stranger. She'd never set eyes on him before today. And second, he was a *man*.

All her life—well, in the last fifteen years—she'd done her best to stay away from men. But there was something about *this* man, something inexplicable, that made her want to get closer instead of push him away.

Daniela was busy unhooking the trailer from the bike when Zara finally got herself together. She and the other woman had done this several times, and together they pulled the trailer inside the small, clean house. Daniela got a pallet ready on the floor while Zara stood over the trailer, staring at the man. When the doctor was satisfied with the makeshift bed she'd made, she instructed Zara to kneel on the floor and help guide the man's unconscious body as she literally dumped him out of the trailer.

The way the man's body flopped out of the box wasn't exactly graceful, but there was no way the two of them could've lifted him out gently and placed him on the pallet. Zara did her best to protect his head from hitting the floor, and once he was out of the trailer, she quickly worked with Daniela to straighten him out and place a pillow under his head.

He looked even bigger stretched out on the floor in the small treatment room Daniela had set up. His face was white, and a nasty gash on his head was still bleeding sluggishly. Ruben and his gang had done a number on him, and Zara once again felt sorry for the unknown American on the floor.

It was an odd feeling. After what had happened to Zara . . . to her *mother* . . . she couldn't remember a time when she'd felt sorry for *any* man. Hatred and disgust, yes. Satisfaction when they got what was coming to them, yes.

But feel sorry for them? No.

But this man had done nothing more than try to help kids who were destined to end up in Roberto del Rio's clutches. Something Mags and the rest of their group also tried to prevent.

"Do you know his name?" Daniela asked, bringing Zara out of her musings.

She shook her head.

"Well, I have a feeling he'll probably be waking up before too long." Lifting his eyelids and peering at his eyes, she said, "He's got a concussion, and guessing by the shoe prints on his T-shirt, probably a few broken ribs. I need to examine him, and your job is to keep him calm. Think you can do that, Zed?"

Zara looked up into Daniela's eyes and nodded. They'd done this before. Zara would hold the hands of wounded patients, stroke their faces and hair to calm them, make sure they didn't jerk away or otherwise try to get up.

She had a feeling it would take more than a little hair stroking for this man to stay down.

She carefully picked up his hand, noting that his knuckles were split and bleeding. She felt strangely proud that he'd obviously gotten in a few licks of his own before he was overtaken by Ruben's gang.

As Daniela started her examination to determine exactly how badly he was hurt, Zara studied his face. His eyelashes were long for a man, and she wondered what color his eyes were. She'd failed to notice when Daniela lifted his eyelids. His nose was bent, and she guessed it was probably broken. He had the beginnings of a beard, and his hair was a tad bit too long, falling over his brow. His shoulders were wide, but his chest tapered down to a slender waist. He had large biceps, and his fingers were long and slender. Zara also saw the edge of a tattoo on his inner arm peeking out from under the sleeve of his T-shirt.

All in all, he was very good-looking. She might avoid men like the plague, but she could still appreciate a handsome guy when she saw one. And this wounded soldier lying helpless in front of her was definitely beautiful.

Zara was startled out of her inspection of him when his eyes popped open and stared up at her.

Gray. His eyes were a pale gray with streaks of blue. They were unique and fascinating. Even though they were full of pain, something in their expression instantly drew her in. Made her want to know this man. To know all the secrets he might hide from the world.

His hand tightened on hers to the point of pain, but Zara didn't let it show. She kept her expression blank, a look she'd perfected over the years. The less others knew what she was thinking and feeling, the better.

"Where am I?" the man demanded in English.

"Talk to him," Daniela ordered. "Keep him calm."

Zara's mouth opened and she tried to speak, but she couldn't think of anything to say. Most of her life, she'd spoken only when asked a direct question. She wasn't exactly a conversationalist. And even though he *had* asked her a question, she wasn't sure what to tell him.

His eyes narrowed as he stared up at her. "Where's Black?"

Zara knew her English skills had suffered over the years, but even though she understood his words, she didn't understand what he meant. She stared down at him and furrowed her brow.

"My friend. Where's my teammate?"

Ah. She shrugged. She wanted to tell him Mags and the others had rescued him too, but since Ruben and his friends had started to creep back out, they probably hadn't gotten the chance. She hoped his other teammates had intervened, but she had no idea what had happened after she'd ridden away.

The man frowned, then inhaled sharply when Daniela manipulated his right ankle. He lifted his head and winced even as he glared down at her.

"Sprained," Daniela told Zara. "Badly. I don't think it's broken, but he shouldn't be walking on this for several days."

"Shit," the man swore. "What'd she say? Can you understand me? I don't know Spanish . . ." He sighed. "This sucks," he muttered. "I'll have to tell Gray he was right when he said it would do me good to learn a foreign language."

Zara sympathized with the man. There was a time when she hadn't understood Spanish either. And it had been extremely scary and frustrating. She squeezed his hand and said quietly, "She said it's probably sprained. Not broken."

The man's gaze whipped up to hers—and it seemed as if he could see into her soul at that moment. "You speak English."

Zara nodded slightly.

"What's your name?"

She hesitated. For the first time in fifteen years, she considered offering someone the name she'd been given at birth, but knew she couldn't. Especially not with Daniela right there.

"Zed."

The man frowned. "Zed? But that's a boy's name."

Zara nodded again and didn't take her eyes from his.

The frown grew. "But—"

Daniela interrupted whatever he was going to say by explaining what she'd found in her initial exam. "It's my guess he's got a few broken or cracked ribs. A concussion, possible broken nose, dislocated shoulder, and, of course, that ankle is messed up. He'll have quite a few bruises and scratches, but overall he was very lucky. What happened?"

Zara explained what had happened back in the barrio. When she mentioned the American team had been trying to rescue a group of boys Roberto del Rio had targeted, Daniela's face turned hard.

"As much as I hate the corrupt politicians and police officers who run this city, I hate *that* man even more."

So did Zara. Every woman and child in the slums of the city knew of Roberto del Rio. He had not one ounce of empathy in his entire body. He took what he wanted, when and where he wanted, and if anyone dared get in his way, he simply killed them. The military and police knew what was going on in that big mansion of his, and yet they didn't do anything about it because del Rio greased their palms with more money than they could legally make in a year.

It was sickening and depraved, and there wasn't a damn thing anyone could do about it.

"What's she saying?" the man asked, looking between her and Daniela.

Zara didn't answer as Daniela continued speaking. "I'm guessing he's going to want to go back to his friends soon, but with his injuries, he's not going to get far. He's going to need to stay here for a few days."

Zara winced. He wasn't going to like that, and she couldn't really blame him. Turning to look down at him, she asked, "What is your name?"

"Meat," he said without hesitation.

Again, Zara figured her English was just rusty, even after all the practicing with Mags. She had to have misunderstood him. That couldn't really be his name. Her brows furrowed as she tried to search her mind for what he really meant.

"It's really Hunter. Hunter Snow. But everyone calls me Meat. It's a nickname."

Ah, *that* made sense. But then Zara couldn't help but wonder why he'd been labeled with such an odd nickname. She wanted to ask why, but with the way he was painfully squeezing her hand, she figured now wasn't the time.

"She says that your ankle is hurt. And your head, ribs, and shoulder too. You'll have to stay here until you're better."

He was shaking his head before she'd finished speaking. "No, I need to get back to my team. To Black. They've got to be worried about me. Give me a phone. *Now.*"

Zara turned to Daniela to translate Meat's request, but he moved before any words could leave her mouth.

He sat up and wrapped his good arm around her neck, yanking her backward and holding her against his chest. The move had to have hurt, but his hold was tight.

Zara's hands instinctively grasped his arm, and she dug her short fingernails into his skin, but he didn't even seem to flinch. She could feel his fast breaths against her neck, but despite his obvious fear and anger, she didn't believe her life was in any real danger. Yes, he had his arm around her neck, and she knew without a doubt he could easily cut off her air. But he didn't.

Daniela was yelling at the man, telling him to let "Zed" go, but since Meat couldn't understand her, the words were useless.

"Tell her to bring me a phone," he ordered. *"Teléfono!"*

Daniela was shaking her head even as Zara began to speak. "There's no phone here. No phone lines. The government tore them down."

"Then a cell phone," Meat growled. "Everyone has a cell."

Zara shook her head as best she could in his grasp. "Maybe in America. Not here. They're expensive. Look around you. Does this look like a wealthy house? It's not. You're in the slums. The barrio. Only people working with the corrupt police and military have cell phones. The rest of us spend our days trying to find enough to eat and staying away from those who want to do us harm."

It was the most she'd said in a really long time, but she wanted him to understand. To know she wasn't lying to him.

"Why am I here? Where am I?" Meat asked.

"Ruben and his gang were going to come back and kill you. They'll search every home in the barrio to find you. Finish what they started."

"Why not take me to my team? They would've protected me."

Zara swallowed hard. She wasn't sure whether he believed her about the cell phones, but he'd probably have a *really* hard time believing the military they were working with in Peru were dirty. "The men they're with *wouldn't* have."

Meat was silent after her statement, and Zara wasn't sure if that was a good sign or not.

Daniela took the opportunity to speak to Zara, low and urgent. "Hit him hard and fast on his bad shoulder, Zed. He'll let go and you can get away from him."

Zara knew she was right, but she couldn't make herself do it. She should. Meat had sat up and was holding her against him awkwardly. She not only had access to his hurt shoulder, but she could also slam her elbow into his ribs or kick his ankle to make him release her.

Instead, she remained stock-still. Giving him time to think about her words.

"You're saying the First Special Forces Brigade is crooked?" he asked, some of the ire gone from his tone.

Zara nodded as best she could. "Probably not all of them, but most."

"Fuck." Meat's arm loosened around her neck. Still, Zara didn't move. "My friend? What happened to him?"

"I don't know," Zara admitted. "Mags was going to go get him, but Ruben returned."

"Mags?"

"My friend. She's kind of the leader of the people I call friends."

"I need to know," Meat said, and Zara could hear the emotion in his tone. "He's got a woman back home. She'll be devastated if he doesn't come home to her."

Something within Zara softened. She didn't trust men, not after what had happened fifteen years ago—and what she'd seen since—but something in Meat's tone made her remember the way her father used to care for her mother.

How he'd pleaded for *her* life, not his own, on that day so long ago.

"I'll find out for you," she said quietly. "But if there was any way for your friend to be saved, Mags will have figured it out."

"I don't trust this Mags person," Meat retorted.

Anger stirred in Zara's chest. It had been a long time since she'd allowed herself to feel any kind of emotion. "*I* do. And she will."

She felt more than heard Meat sigh against her back. She felt his arm relaxing around her at the same time Daniela moved. She'd obviously gotten tired of watching and waiting, and now she leapt into action.

Daniela karate-chopped Meat's ankle, and he roared in pain, immediately letting go of Zara. But instead of grabbing her again and using her as a hostage, he did something she didn't understand.

He pushed her *away* from him.

And instead of lunging forward and slamming his huge fist into Daniela's face, he tried to get away from her. But he didn't move fast enough.

Because of situations with previous patients who'd been out of their heads with pain, she wasn't about to back down, more than willing to defend herself and Zara.

She hit his ankle again, and Zara watched as Meat gasped in pain, then his eyes rolled in his head, and he fell backward.

Zara could only stare as Daniela stood, her chest heaving with adrenaline. "Are you all right?"

She nodded.

"Good. I'm sorry. I didn't expect that. Come on, help me get him back into the trailer, and you can dump him in the nearest barrio."

Zara gasped in surprise.

"Come on! Don't just sit there, help me."

Zara found herself moving in front of Meat, blocking Daniela from touching him again. "No."

"What?"

"He's hurt. He won't last an hour in his condition if we leave him out there. He wasn't hurting me. Just holding on to me as he tried to make sense of his situation."

Daniela studied her for a long moment, then finally sighed. "I'm not thrilled with this, Zed. If he hurts you, remember I said I told you so. I don't like being threatened."

Zara nodded. She understood that, but she'd counted on Daniela's innate need to help others. She was relieved she hadn't been wrong.

"Fine, then help me clean his wounds. The last thing he needs is for them to get infected. We'll splint his ankle, put his shoulder back into place, and we'll have to make sure to wake him up every hour because of his concussion. I don't have any painkillers for him, so he'll just have to go without until he's well enough to stand up on his own. We'll get rid of him as soon as possible. I'm guessing two or three days."

Zara's heart lurched at hearing that, though she couldn't understand why.

Meat was a connection to a past she didn't really remember, didn't *want* to remember. She didn't understand why she felt *anything* about him or his situation. Especially when she had no doubt that, as soon as he was able, he'd go back to his friends and America.

Chapter Three

Meat woke up yet again in excruciating pain. But this time, he was more aware of what had happened and where he was. He kept his eyes shut after he woke, trying to get as much information about his situation as he could. He'd been stupid, underestimated the Peruvian doctor.

He'd also been strangely distracted by the doctor's English-speaking helper.

He'd said his name was Zed, but the name didn't compute with what Meat's senses were telling him. Yes, he was short and skinny, like a teenage boy would be. He had short, messy brown hair and an attitude that would make him fit right in with most teenagers back in the States.

Meat had initially been confused when he'd heard the assistant's name was Zed—but his suspicions were confirmed when he'd put his arm around the kid's neck.

When Zed had been pressed against him, Meat had known beyond a shadow of a doubt that *he*, in reality, was a *she*.

Even though she was covered in dirt and wearing a T-shirt three sizes too big and sweatpants that covered every inch of her legs, he'd known.

He wanted to open his eyes, stare into hers, and flat-out ask why she was pretending to be a boy, but he kept very still, taking in as much information as he could before letting anyone know he was awake and aware.

He heard the doctor talking, and then felt what he instinctively knew was "Zed's" hand against his forehead. She was cleaning his face with a washcloth. She didn't talk much—he'd noticed that about her even in the few moments he'd spent in her presence—but her voice, when she *did* speak, also gave her away. It was low, but not low enough for most young males. Her English was only lightly accented, and he wasn't even sure she was a native Spanish speaker.

Nothing about her added up, and she had his curiosity piqued, to say the least.

Realizing that he wasn't going to find out any new information by listening, since he didn't understand Spanish, Meat pretended to slowly wake up. By the time he opened his eyes, both Zed and the doctor were standing across the room from him. They'd obviously learned their lesson about getting too close.

"I need to get out of here," he said softly.

He saw Zed look at Daniela before turning back to him. "You're too hurt. Daniela says it'll be about three days before she thinks you'll be well enough to fend for yourself."

"Three days? No fucking way," Meat said with a shake of his head. "Just drop me off near my team, and I'll be fine."

He saw Zed's eyes narrow, and she crossed her arms over her chest. Meat's gaze dipped, and he wasn't surprised to see nothing. He'd felt the bindings around her body. He wondered if it hurt to make herself look as flat as a boy.

"Stand up and walk across the room to prove that you can do it, and I'll take you back."

Meat stared at her, wondering if she was telling the truth. Deciding to call her bluff, he nodded. He sat up very slowly and scooted until his back was against the wall behind him. He brought his good leg up and pressed his hands against the crumbling plaster.

Pushing to his feet, Meat swayed. He closed his eyes, trying to get his equilibrium back. His head was pounding so badly, blackness threatened to overtake him. Taking two deep breaths, he managed to beat it down.

When he opened his eyes, he saw both the doctor and Zed still watching him.

The doctor, Daniela, looked smug, and Zed looked nervous. She was chewing on a plump lower lip and wringing her hands in front of her now.

He very slowly moved his right leg forward to take a step—and the second he put weight on it, he crumpled to the floor.

His ribs and shoulder screamed in pain, and he couldn't stop the vomit from moving up his throat. He puked on the floor, then stilled in a combination of embarrassment, pain, and frustration.

"I'll clean it up," he heard Zed say softly, but he didn't see her come toward him until he felt her hands on his shoulders.

"Come on, shift over to your butt. That's it. Now lie down. I'll help you."

Knowing he'd probably just made his situation worse, not better, he gave himself over to her care. He allowed her to assist him, and he lay there quietly as he tried to overcome the excruciating pain in his head and ankle and ribs.

He was aware of Zed cleaning up his puke and was ashamed that he couldn't do anything to help. But she didn't rail against him. Didn't tell him she was disgusted or in any way make him feel bad for what had happened.

When she was done, she moved his pallet over to where he lay and got him settled once again. Meat finally opened his eyes and looked around the room. Daniela was nowhere to be seen. It was just him and Zed.

He needed answers, and she was the only one who could give them to him.

"Tell me your real name," he said quietly.

"Zed."

He shook his head. "No, your *real* name," he insisted. "I'm guessing most people don't look twice at you because of how you present yourself, but it's obvious that you're no more a 'Zed' than I am a 'Huntress.'"

She blinked. Then licked her lips, her eyes dropping from his.

"I know you have no reason to trust me, but I'm not going to tell anyone. It's not a secret that I'm not happy to be here. But I don't hurt women or children. Period." He stared at her and hoped like hell the sincerity was coming through.

After several minutes, when he didn't think she was going to say anything, she surprised him.

"It's Zara."

"Zara what?"

She blinked again in surprise.

"What's your last name?" Meat pressed. He wasn't sure why it was so important she shared that with him, but somehow he knew it was.

"Layne."

"Zara Layne. It's pretty," Meat told her.

She didn't blush or look away. Instead, she said, "It's just a name."

"I'd ask why you don't use it, but I think I have a good idea."

She didn't take the bait and explain, so he continued. "I'm guessing life isn't easy out there. Especially if you're a woman. You're slight, so it's easy to pass as a boy, but I bet those who bother to get close to you know, don't they?"

She shrugged.

"Thank you for trusting me with that. I won't make you regret telling me." He moved slightly and winced as he jostled his ankle.

"Be still," Zara admonished.

"I hate this. My friends will be frantic to find me."

"The military men you were with . . . they knew about the boys."

His eyes narrowed. "Knew? What do you mean?"

"We've seen them in the barrio before. They pay for the children. And if the parents don't want to sell, they take them anyway. I wouldn't be surprised if they paid Ruben to attack you and your friend. It wouldn't look good if Americans found out the truth about what they are doing."

Meat's mind was whirling. Their handler, Rex, had been working with the Peruvian military and police for a while, and the intel they'd had on this raid had been solid. But if what Zara was saying was true, it made sense why everything had seemed to go sideways once they were in the country.

The men who'd been with them on the raid hadn't seemed to know much about the barrio they were going into, hadn't been very forthcoming about how many boys were suspected to be in the hut when they got there. Things had changed so much from minute to minute that the entire team had been extremely uneasy. But because they were already in Peru, and had the approval of the government, the team had decided to go forward.

And the two Brigade members hadn't seemed worried at all from the start. They'd been laughing and joking right up until the moment they'd entered the decrepit home.

Not only were there boys inside, but women too.

Rex and the team had heard about corruption in the police forces in Peru, but they hadn't suspected anyone from the First Special Forces Brigade.

They certainly hadn't expected to be caught smack-dab in the middle of a big fucking mess.

Zara and her friends hadn't hurt him, and she'd said they'd planned on helping Black too. She'd gotten him out of the barrio. At least, he assumed they weren't there anymore, if his memories of being jostled and traveling inside some kind of box were anything to go by.

And she and Daniela had bandaged up his ankle and cleaned his cuts and wounds. They hadn't given him medication, but he believed them when they said they simply didn't have any. He wasn't about to lie around for three days, but for now, he couldn't do anything with his head and ankle in the shape they were in, so he would have to put his trust in these women.

"If you're telling the truth, I owe you and your friends my thanks." Zara simply nodded.

His eyes closed, but then he forced them open again. "I need to know about Black."

"I'll try to find out."

His eyes closed again, and with a herculean effort, he pried them open one more time.

"Gray's wife should be having their baby any day now. He won't leave if I'm missing. He'll miss the birth. Arrow's wife is also expecting. She still has about a month and a half to go, but the stress of him being away could make her go into early labor. Chloe and Everly are probably worried, too, and Harlow will be frantic when she hears about Black being attacked. They're my friends, Zara. My brothers. I can't stand the thought of them worrying about me."

"Sleep," Zara said softly. "I'll wake you up in an hour to make sure you're okay because of your head."

"Please," Meat pleaded, not ashamed that he was begging. "I need to know my friend is okay . . ."

The last thing he remembered was Zara's hand clasping his own and squeezing.

After what seemed like two minutes, but was probably an hour, Meat was abruptly woken with a hard shake to his good shoulder.

Expecting to see Zara, he was surprised to find Daniela standing over him. She was holding a knife at her side, and it was more than clear she didn't trust him.

She said something in Spanish, then held up her free hand with three fingers sticking up.

"Three. *Tres*," Meat told her.

She nodded, then backed away from him toward the doorway.

"Wait!" he said, and pushed up on an elbow, wincing when even that small movement made bile move up his throat. He forced it down and asked, "Where's Zed?"

But Daniela didn't answer, simply left him on the floor to wonder if he'd said something that had made Zara flee.

Meat wasn't sure how much time had passed, but every hour, Daniela roughly shook him awake and held up a hand, demanding he tell her how many fingers she was holding up before leaving without talking to him further, not that they could understand each other.

He wished he had his watch so he'd know how long he'd been lying on the floor in the house, and how long Zara had been gone. He knew it had to have been at least ten or twelve hours, because when he was woken this time, it was well after sunrise, perhaps late morning.

And Zara was at his side once more.

She'd gently nudged him awake—unlike her friend, who hadn't bothered trying to be kind when she'd tended to him. Meat was so happy to see her, so happy to be able to talk to someone, that he smiled. "You came back."

She nodded and pulled out a bottle of water, two candy bars, and a plastic jug. The food and water looked amazing. Meat hadn't realized how hungry he'd been until that moment. He frowned at the jug, wondering what it was for, when Zara spoke.

"Toilet."

She wasn't blushing and didn't seem embarrassed that he'd have to pee in the jug, and she'd have to dispose of it for him. But thinking about it, Meat realized that if she'd lived in the barrios for any amount of time, nothing probably shocked her.

Relieved because he *did* need to pee, he reached for it. She handed it over, then stood and walked out of the room, giving him privacy. Thankful for that, Meat quickly took care of business and set the jug aside.

She returned in minutes and carried the container away. She returned shortly and placed the now-empty jug near him. She sat next to him and held out the water and candy.

"Where'd you get these?" he asked.

She stared back, saying nothing.

"Have you eaten?"

For the first time, her gaze fell from his, and she nodded.

Her stomach growling at that exact moment wasn't the only thing telling him she was lying.

He held out one of the candy bars. "Here. Take it."

She looked at him in disbelief, and Meat disliked the shock on her face. "Hasn't anyone given you a candy bar before?"

This time, she didn't take her eyes from his as she shook her head.

"Well, there's a first time for everything," Meat said as lightly as he could. But inside, he was shaken. He knew poverty existed. Had seen his share of it around the world. But the barrio had shocked even him. He didn't know how Zara had gotten her hands on the candy or water, but he made the immediate decision to eat the bare minimum. She and Daniela probably needed the food and water way more than he did.

"I'll get better food tomorrow," she said between bites.

"It's fine." And it was. He'd gone days without eating in the past, so he wasn't too worried. He was more concerned about his ankle healing enough that he could walk on it. His head was feeling better, but still wasn't one hundred percent yet. At least he could sit up without vomiting. He'd take that.

They sat together eating their candy bars in silence. Finally, Meat couldn't stand it anymore. He was more than curious about the young woman sitting next to him. If what she'd told him was correct, she'd literally saved his life. For that alone, he wanted to know everything about her.

"So, Zara . . . tell me about yourself."

Chapter Four

Zara froze. She wasn't ready to talk about herself. Hell, she *never* talked about herself. It was safer that way. But she didn't want to get up and walk away either. For some reason, she felt comfortable with Meat.

It made no sense, really. But then again . . . she was tired. Tired of constantly looking behind her. Of having to scrounge for food. Of trying to stay under the radar. She was way too practical to live her life wondering "what if," but at the moment, talking to Meat, she felt her guard lowering.

She still wasn't going to talk about herself. Not yet. She'd only known this man for hours. But she could put his mind at ease. "I went back to the barrio and found out about your friends today."

His eyes widened and he sat up straighter. He leaned toward her eagerly. "Yeah?"

Zara nodded. "Mags said that right after I left with you, the Americans came and got the man you'd been with."

Meat sighed in relief. "Thank God! Did you get a chance to tell them I was all right?"

Zara bit her lip and shook her head.

Meat frowned.

At his expression, she found herself wanting to explain. "The Special Forces Brigade members are still with them. We can't risk talking to the Americans. It would bring attention to ourselves. Bad attention." Zara wasn't sure Meat understood. "The best thing is to not be seen," she said. "If they see us, they'll start asking questions, and we won't be able to help others like we do now."

Meat looked at her for a long moment before he finally nodded. "I understand."

"Mags said she would try to get a note to them. But hopefully you will be healed enough to leave soon, and it won't be necessary."

"I wondered where you had gone today," Meat said. "I hadn't expected you to do that for me."

"You were worried about them."

"I was. But still. How far did you have to travel to get back to the barrio where you found me?"

She hesitated. The last thing she wanted was to get Daniela in trouble, or for Meat to get too curious. The less he knew, the better.

Before she could think of a good answer, he spoke.

"Never mind. I'm learning that there're a lot of things I'm better off not knowing, right?"

Zara nodded.

"Have I thanked you yet?" Meat asked.

Zara looked at him with what she knew was probably another shocked expression.

"I guess I haven't. It's obvious you know this area much better than I do. Black and I weren't expecting to be jumped like we were. I appreciate you and your friends stepping in to help us, especially considering the amount of danger it obviously put you in."

Zara licked her lips and said nothing.

"You haven't asked what we were doing there."

She already knew about the boys they'd found, but shrugged anyway.

"My friends and I are part of a somewhat secret group. We're called the Mountain Mercenaries. We've made it our mission to rescue women and children from those who would do them harm. The wife of our leader, Rex, disappeared years ago, and he suspects she was kidnapped into the sex trade. He's never stopped looking for her. In the meantime, he's dedicated his life to helping others like her, who are taken from their homes and families.

"We were working with the government on a human-trafficking sting. We were told there were several boys on the verge of being sold into the kind of life no child should ever know exists. Our intel was good . . . but when we got here, things got all fucked up. We should've pulled out of the mission immediately, but decided to go ahead with it. That was our mistake."

Zara stared at Meat. She and the others had already deduced the Americans were there to try to save the children, but they hadn't known anything about their motives. They'd wondered why a group from the United States would care about what happened to a bunch of poor barrio kids. And it was obvious that Meat *did* care. He cared about a bunch of children he'd never met.

For just a moment, Zara wondered what her life could've been like if Meat and his friends had been around when *she'd* needed them.

But the second she had the thought, she dismissed it. She didn't know how old Meat was, but fifteen years ago, he probably wasn't in the same line of work he was in now.

Then something else he'd said registered, and she explained, "A lot of the military is corrupt. Not all of the soldiers, but many. Money is scarce here, and it's hard to hold on to morals when your family is living in filth and starving, so some start working for the drug cartels. Or del Rio. The men your friends are with are not good. I told you already that they help del Rio find women and children for his sex houses. Recently, they've begun looking for much younger children. I suspect the reason everything went wrong is because they were trying to make sure you *didn't* succeed."

Meat didn't blow her words off. Didn't tell her she must be mistaken. He simply grimaced. "That makes a lot of sense. Can I ask a question?"

Zara nodded.

"Are my friends safe? I know they won't leave without me, and they're probably working with the military to try to find me. If they're in danger from these corrupt men, I need to get back as soon as possible, even if it's not healthy for me."

Zara's respect for Meat increased tenfold.

"They should be safe," she said with conviction. "They're after women and children, not strong men. And not Americans. They may have paid Ruben and his friends to intervene beforehand, to try to disrupt your mission of rescuing the children, but if they did, that clearly didn't happen. Mags said that after the raid the children were reunited with their parents and moved to a group home in Lima somewhere. But del Rio and the military members under his control won't want you guys here any longer than you have to be. They want to get back to their regular routine."

"And what's that, exactly?" Meat asked.

Zara shrugged. "Intimidation. Taking children from their mothers to give to del Rio. Keeping the honest police off the trail of the people working for the drug cartels. Taking women off the streets to replenish their numbers in the sex houses."

Meat leaned forward, and Zara heard him inhale sharply. It was a reminder that he wasn't anywhere near full strength, that his ribs were still very painful.

He put his hand on her leg and asked with uncanny insight, "That's why you dress like you do, isn't it? And why your hair is so short, and why you bind your chest."

She was alarmed at how easily he'd seen through the disguise she'd worn like a shield almost her entire life in Peru. She panicked for a second, wanting to run away and hide. To get away from Meat's piercing gray eyes that seemed to see right through her.

"Don't panic," he said, as if he could read her mind. "Your secret is safe with me. I'm impressed, actually. Not everyone would be able to pull it off, although I'm surprised anyone can be around you for more than five minutes and not know you're a girl. How old are you, Zara? Sixteen? Seventeen?"

She slowly shook her head.

"Eighteen?"

"Twenty-five," she admitted quietly.

Meat sat back and stared at her in shock. "Seriously?"

She nodded.

"Wow. Okay, now I'm even more impressed. How did you learn English? I've noticed that not many people speak it in the barrio."

Zara considered what to tell him. She *wanted* to spill her guts. Mags had encouraged her to find out if the American would help her. She wanted to tell Meat everything, to ask if he'd help get her back to the United States, but she wasn't sure she could handle possible rejection. Not from him, and not after all this time.

She'd fantasized about going to America, but that was all it had ever been—a fantasy.

Deciding to take baby steps, she said, "I was born there."

Meat looked confused. "Where? The barrio?"

"No. America. I lived in Colorado."

"*Seriously?* Holy shit! That's where me and my friends are from! Colorado Springs. Where were you born?"

"Denver," Zara whispered. Goose bumps had risen on her arms, and she knew she was breathing too fast. This couldn't be a coincidence . . . could it? For so long, she'd been lost and abandoned. She hadn't completely agreed with Mags about helping the Americans . . . but maybe, just maybe, this was fate.

Meat opened his mouth to say something, and at that moment, Daniela burst into the room and told Zara that she needed her help with a patient.

Zara immediately stood up, but Meat grabbed her hand. It must've hurt, but he didn't let go. "What's going on?"

"Someone's here to see Daniela. Needs a doctor."

"I want to continue our conversation. I want to know more about you."

Zara felt butterflies in her stomach at his words, but she ruthlessly tamped them down. He lived in America. Had tons of friends and had no clue about the harsh world she lived in. She wasn't a good person. And even if she did get up the nerve to ask him to take her back to the United States, what would she do there? Where would she go?

Life in the barrios was all she knew. At least here, she had Mags and Daniela and the other women.

"Zed!" Daniela called out from the other room.

Zara pulled her hand out of Meat's and turned away from him.

"If I can help in any way, let me know," Meat called after her. "I'm a medic, and even if I can't stand up or move all that fast, I can still advise you."

She nodded and forced herself to turn away from him. The longer she was around Meat, the more she liked him. He was a good man— that was easy to see.

Zara wasn't exactly surprised to find the heavily pregnant woman standing in Daniela's living room. She had a small child at her side, a girl probably around four or five. The woman was panting and telling Daniela that she'd been in labor for almost twelve hours, and that something was wrong. The baby wasn't coming out.

Zara also wasn't surprised the woman had managed to get herself to Daniela's home. There really hadn't been any other choice. It wasn't as if they could pick up a phone and call for help. She didn't know where the woman's husband was, probably out begging for money or searching for work—if she even had a husband. It was the way of life in the barrio.

Daniela got the woman settled on a sheet in the middle of the living room, as the room they usually used for birthing was currently occupied by Meat. The little girl sniffed and looked scared to death.

She'd probably been watching her mother struggle to bring her brother or sister into the world for hours now.

Not giving it a second thought, Zara took hold of the girl's small hand and led her toward Meat's room. He was sitting up and staring at the doorway when she entered.

"What's wrong?" he asked urgently.

"Her mother is here to give birth," Zara said. "Can you watch over this little one?"

"Of course," Meat said without hesitation, holding out his hand.

Zara led the child over to Meat and told her in Spanish that Meat was a nice man, and he would keep watch over her while she and Daniela helped her mom.

"Meat?" the girl asked.

Zara smiled. "It's a nickname."

She nodded. "Like how Mamá calls me *Bonita* but my real name is Natalia."

"That's right," Zara told her. "*Bonita* because you're a beautiful little girl."

Natalia giggled, then sobered as she asked, "Is my mamá going to be okay?"

"Daniela is going to do everything she can to help her."

The little girl nodded.

"So you'll stay here with Meat?"

She nodded again.

Zara turned to Meat. She knew he'd been watching her very closely as she'd spoken with the little girl. "Her name is Natalia."

He nodded. "I'll take good care of her. Go on, go help Daniela. We'll be right here waiting."

Zara didn't have a lot of opportunities to thank anyone. People here didn't go out of their way to help others, simply because they were so busy trying to keep their own heads above water. But she felt immense gratitude toward Meat at that moment. "Thank you."

"You don't have to thank me for doing the right thing," he told her. "Go on, we'll be fine."

Nodding, Zara turned back to the doorway. She couldn't help but look behind her before leaving the room. Meat was leaning toward Natalia. He was wincing as if the movement hurt, but he didn't call her back and say he was in too much pain to help. He patted his chest and said, "I'm Meat." Then he pointed at her and said, "You're Natalia."

The little girl nodded, and the last thing Zara heard before getting preoccupied with the young woman trying to give birth was the little girl's soft giggle.

Chapter Five

Meat was exhausted, and both his ankle and ribs were throbbing. His shoulder felt pretty good, though; the ache from having it put back into place wasn't very concerning compared to his other injuries. He also had to relieve himself, but he stayed stock-still as he leaned against the wall of the room and kept his eyes glued to the doorway. He had no idea how much time had passed, but it had to have been hours.

He'd done his best to keep Natalia occupied, playing a game where he said a word in English and she told him what it was in Spanish. They'd gone through numbers, colors, and body parts. Meat couldn't say he was any more fluent than he'd been a few hours before, but he'd half fallen in love with the small child now sleeping in his arms. She'd begun to get tired, and since there wasn't a bed in the room and he was sitting on the pallet, she'd crawled into his lap, put her head on his chest, and fallen asleep almost immediately.

She wasn't very heavy, but even the slight weight against his ribs was painful. Meat ignored the way it felt as if he had a baby elephant resting on his chest and concentrated on the noises he was hearing from the other room. It was frustrating to not know what was happening, to not be able to help. He was accustomed to being *useful*. To helping out in emergency situations. But all he could do was listen to the three women speaking Spanish in low tones and the occasional moan from the woman who was trying to give birth.

He was half-asleep himself when he felt Zara return. He didn't even question how he knew she'd entered the room; he just did. Night had fallen, and the only light in the room came from beyond the door. Zara was silhouetted with her body blocking the light, and Meat could practically see through her threadbare shirt and pants.

"How is she?" Meat asked quietly.

"Resting," Zara replied, keeping her voice low.

"And her baby?"

Zara shrugged. "It'll be touch and go for a while, but we got him out. He was breech, but I got him turned around, and they're both resting right now."

As her words sank in, Meat gaped. "*You* got him turned around?"

She nodded.

"How?"

Zara held up her hands. "I've got small hands. I was able to reach inside and physically turn him. It's not ideal, and very painful for the woman, but it worked . . . this time."

Meat was blown away by her matter-of-fact words. Back home, when a woman had a baby in breech position, she was brought to the operating room to have a C-section. But Zara had literally used her own two hands to reach inside the woman's womb and physically turn the baby so it would have a chance.

My God, the more he got to know Zara, the more she impressed him.

But he could also see the toll the work had taken on her.

"She shouldn't be on top of you like that. It has to hurt," she lightly scolded, nodding to a sleeping Natalia.

"I'm fine," Meat said, the aches and pains he'd fixated on earlier now seeming superficial after what the woman in the other room must have gone through.

"Let me take her to her mom," Zara said, as she stepped into the room and reached for the sleeping child.

"As long as you come back when she's settled," Meat said, keeping a hand on Natalia's back until Zara agreed.

She stared at him for a long moment before nodding. She grabbed the empty container he'd used earlier that day and placed it by his side. "You can take care of business while I'm gone. Is there anything else you need? I can go out and find you some aspirin if you need it. Or something stronger. How's your ankle? Does it need to be rewrapped?"

Meat shook his head in exasperation. There was no way he was going to say anything that would make Zara head out at this time of night to get him a fucking aspirin. "I'm good," he said, letting go of Natalia as Zara picked her up.

They looked at each other for a long moment, something passing between them. A kind of comradery that hadn't been there before he'd willingly looked after Natalia while Zara and Daniela helped the little girl's mother give birth. Before, he'd been just another patient, but now it seemed more like they were a team. Working together toward a common goal of helping another.

He liked that. A lot.

Zara turned and headed for the doorway with the little girl, and Meat took care of his bodily needs while she was gone. He very slowly stretched out on the floor. It hurt, but also felt pretty damn good after sitting up against the wall for so long. He gingerly rotated his ankle, wincing at the pain that shot up his leg, but decided that, while it hurt, it didn't feel quite as painful as it had the day before. Within a couple of days, Meat thought he'd be able to put weight on it, and the second he could, he'd be gone. Back to his friends and getting the hell out of the country.

Zara returned a few minutes later and grabbed the container he'd used and once again disappeared through the doorway. She was back within a minute, the container empty.

"Good night," she said softly.

But before she could leave once more, Meat reached out and snagged her hand in his. She tugged at it in surprise, which sent a shaft of pain through his ribs. Meat ignored it.

"Stay here tonight," he said.

When she hesitated, he simply added, "Please?"

He watched as she took a deep breath, then nodded. She slowly got to her knees and lay down next to him on the hard floor.

"That doesn't look comfortable," he ventured after a moment.

She shrugged. "I'm used to it."

Her words made him scowl. Without thought, Meat reached out and put his arm around her shoulders and tugged her into him. She came willingly, but he figured that was more because she didn't want to hurt him than out of any eagerness to be near him.

He urged her to put her head on his good shoulder. She was stiff and awkward next to him, and Meat wanted nothing more than for her to relax. "You're safe, Zara," he told her. "I'm hurting too much to do anything more than lie here next to you. I'm not going to pounce on you in the middle of the night. You have to be exhausted; it's tiring saving a life."

He heard a small, amused snort leave her mouth, but he felt her give in a smidgen.

"That's it. Just relax." He wanted to ask her more about her life in the United States. Ask how she'd come to be in Peru, enduring the life she was currently living. Then he thought about how reliant he'd become on his computers. If he wanted to know something, he simply looked it up. Without electronics, he had to rely on getting information the old-fashioned way . . . by asking. He wasn't the best communicator, but there was something about watching Zara slowly open to him, trust him, that made every little scrap of information he found out all the more satisfying.

"If I hurt you, let me know," she mumbled.

"You're good," he reassured her.

He felt it the moment she fell asleep. She'd been holding herself tense against him, but the second she went under, her entire body relaxed. And nothing had felt better than that trust.

Meat had never been one to cuddle with the women he slept with. Then again, it had been years since he'd even *been* with a woman. He'd been so preoccupied with the Mountain Mercenaries and busy with the behind-the-scenes computer research, he hadn't had time to go out and woo someone. He'd never been a one-night-stand kind of guy—that just seemed gross to him. But lying with Zara in his arms reminded him of what he'd been missing.

Was this how his friends felt with their women? This sense of calm? Of rightness?

Shit. He needed to get his head out of his ass. He knew next to nothing about Zara Layne. Only her first and last name and that she was born in Colorado and apparently helped out the local doctor. That was it.

But the more he tried to remind himself he didn't know her, the more he realized how wrong he was. He might not know the common things, but he knew she was a good person. Down to her dainty little toes. She did her best to protect others, like him and Natalia, and she didn't ask for anything in return for that help. She was loyal to her friends and disgusted by the rampant corruption all around her. She would give up food for someone else, even if she was starving. She was quiet, but that didn't mean she didn't pay attention.

With every hour he spent getting to know her, his intrigue grew.

For the first time in his life, Meat hoped he wouldn't heal too quickly. The faster his ankle got better, the sooner he'd be leaving.

Then he had a crazy thought. If Zara had been born in the States, she was an American citizen.

What was preventing her from going back?

She couldn't really want to *stay* here in Peru, could she? Living in abject poverty, scrounging for scraps of food? She was an adult—he still couldn't believe she was twenty-five; with her hair cut the way it was and her chest bound, she easily looked to be in her early to mid-teens—so she could leave without having to ask permission from a parent.

Feeling excitement about the fact that maybe he'd have more time to get to know the woman in his arms, Meat closed his eyes. He was getting used to the pain, or maybe it just wasn't as bad.

As much as he enjoyed sleeping with Zara, he had to get better as fast as he could and get back to his friends so they could all go home. Gray needed to be with Allye when she had their baby. Meat would feel horrible if Gray missed it because they'd been looking for his sorry ass.

Every time Meat woke up that night, he panicked for a split second, thinking Zara had left him, but then he'd open his eyes and realize she was right where she'd been since he'd fallen asleep. Her head resting on his shoulder, her arm now lightly around his belly.

They were both sweaty, and he needed a shave and to brush his teeth, but there was no way Meat was letting her go. She felt too good next to him. Too right.

Chapter Six

Gray ran a hand through his hair in agitation. They'd moved their operation from the barrio to a nearby motel. It wasn't exactly up to most Americans' standards, but no one on the team cared. They were too worried about Meat.

Black had been beaten badly by the group of men who'd jumped him and Meat in the barrio. And Gray and the other mercenaries were pissed that the two Peruvian military men they'd been working with hadn't seemed all that concerned about finding those responsible. They'd been more eager to bust in doors, scaring the shit out of the residents who lived in the poor neighborhood.

It was Ro who'd brought it up after Meat had been missing for almost two days. They'd all been exhausted after looking for their teammate for a second entire day, with no luck. The team had said their good-nights to the additional members of the Brigade who'd joined the group after Meat had disappeared, then had gathered in Gray's motel room.

"Is it just me, or were those guys more interested in leering at the women and throwing their weight around than actually trying to talk to the residents to get information about Meat?" Ro asked.

Gray sighed in relief at his friend's words. "Thank God it's not just me thinking that."

"I get wanting to make sure your authority is recognized, but it seemed they were more interested in scaring the shit out of everyone, kids included, than actually aiding the search," Arrow agreed.

"Meat couldn't have just disappeared," Ball said in frustration. "Someone had to have gotten him out of there."

"I'm sorry I didn't see more," Black said from the bed. They'd stuffed him with all kinds of painkillers, and he still looked extremely rough. But besides a sprained wrist and some hellacious bruises, he was going to be all right. Apparently his head was stronger than they would've guessed.

"Not your fault," Gray told him. "But Ball's right. Someone saw something, and my guess is they're not going to tell us with our military friends hovering nearby. Not that I can blame them. This mission has stunk from the moment we landed in Peru, and I'm beginning to understand why."

"Corruption," Arrow concluded.

"Exactly. Which is going to make finding Meat even harder."

"Can we ditch our escorts?" Ro asked.

Gray shrugged. "We could, but it's probably not a good idea. It was made very clear when we entered the country that we were to stay with them at all times. I'm surprised they left us alone in this shitty motel, if I'm being honest."

"We should go back to the barrio and start asking questions tonight under cover of darkness," Ball said.

"As much as I want to, none of us are fluent in Spanish—which I'm going to set about changing the second I get back to the States. It's ridiculous that between us, none of us can speak or understand it. Anyway, we could head to the barrio tonight, but I have a feeling we'd just scare the residents instead. Not only that, but we're supposed to be working with the government. Rex asked us to do our best to cooperate and not do anything that would piss them off."

"Which is ironic, since I suspect some of their own soldiers are working with the very people we were sent here to stop," Black said from his place on the bed.

"Right," Gray said. "If any of us knew Spanish, I wouldn't hesitate to go back out there and knock on every door and find someone to talk to us. It pisses me off, but I'm afraid for the time being, we're just going to have to play nice and wait until the morning."

"You talk to Allye?" Arrow asked after a moment.

Gray sighed. "Yeah. She said she's been having some pain, and the doctor said she thinks it's a precursor to the baby coming."

"Shit," Ball muttered.

"If you want to head home, we'll stay and find Meat," Arrow offered.

Gray closed his eyes for a moment, overcome with love for his brothers-in-arms. Opening them again, he looked at Arrow. "What would *you* do if it was Morgan?" They all knew Morgan was almost as pregnant as Allye. She had about a month and a half to go in her pregnancy, however.

"I know what I'd *want* to do, but I also know she'd tell me to keep my ass here until I found Meat and brought him home," Arrow said.

Gray nodded and snorted out a breath. "Sounds like the exact conversation I had with Allye earlier."

"Meat wouldn't want you to miss the birth of your first child," Ro told Gray.

"I know, but here's the thing . . . ," Gray said. "I can't stop thinking about how we found Morgan. She'd been missing for a year, and no one was even *looking* for her. I can't imagine leaving here without Meat. He *knows* we're looking for him. Just as I'd know if it was me. I can't leave without him. As a SEAL, I was taught we simply don't leave a man behind. Ever. And even though Meat wasn't a SEAL, it still applies."

"Then we need to hurry up and find him," Arrow said definitively.

The others nodded their agreement.

"Rex has been poring over satellite images and hasn't seen anything out of the ordinary," Gray informed everyone. "He's got some stills of the men in the street beating on Black and Meat, but pictures from the satellite are only taken every thirty seconds. In one photo, Black and Meat are lying in the street, and in the next, it's just Black. So whatever happened occurred within thirty seconds."

"Fuck. There has to be more," Ro complained.

"There might be, but we all know Meat's our resident hacker and computer expert. Rex is no slouch, but when push comes to shove, Meat's the master," Gray said.

"Besides, it's not as if there are any surveillance cameras to hack into out here," Black said.

"Everything about this place isn't sitting right with me," Ball said softly. "And it's more than the corruption. It's the gang that attacked Black and Meat. It's the way the women won't look anyone in the eyes, how they cower away from us when we try to talk to them. It's the abject poverty and how no one in the military seems to give a shit."

"We can't change a culture," Ro pointed out.

"I know, but the Brigade's behavior goes against everything we stand for," Ball said. "We've spent years trying to give women and children a better life. I understand that there are still way too many places in the world where men think they're superior to women and will do everything in their power to stay on top of the food chain, but it fucking pisses me off every time I see it."

"My brother, Lance—you guys remember, the photographer?—said the same thing when he was down here accompanying that film crew," Black said from his place on the bed. "They were doing a documentary on prostitution, and when he got back, he said it was one of the most depressing things he'd ever seen and done. That there was a defeated vibe from all the women. Unlike in the States, where some women actually choose to sell themselves, the women down here don't have a choice. They're either sold by their own parents or forcibly taken from their homes and told they can leave when they've worked off a debt."

"A debt that never existed in the first place," Gray mumbled.

"Of course. Lance also said there were a lot of foreign women caught up in prostitution here. Some didn't even speak Spanish. He and his crew weren't allowed to talk to or film any of those women, though. Every time Lance got a glimpse of one, she'd disappear into a room or be shuffled out of sight by one of the johns. He said some of the women looked American, but without speaking with them, he couldn't be sure. The name del Rio was mentioned a lot, and I looked into it. He's apparently *the* man down here. He's got the most control over the sex trade, and he has everyone who's anyone on his payroll."

There was silence in the room after Black's statement. Everyone lost in their own thoughts. Finally, Gray said, "We'll just have to do better tomorrow. Take some cash. Maybe if they won't talk to us out of the goodness of their hearts, they'll talk with an incentive. Lord knows the people here need money. I'm not leaving until we've got Meat. We haven't ever left anyone behind, and we're not about to start now."

One by one, the other men agreed with Gray. Ro and Arrow left to go to their room next door, while Ball settled onto a pallet on the floor. No one said a word, but Black, Ball, and Gray definitely weren't sleeping. Too much had happened, and they were too worried about their friend and teammate.

The third day went about the same as the one before, as far as the search inside the barrio went. No one knew anything, and no one had seen anything. The military members had been just as asshole-ish as they'd been the previous day, as well, and hadn't cared that they were scaring the residents, who might've been more help if they didn't feel so threatened.

Even with Gray offering money to anyone who might help them find Meat, they'd gotten nowhere. But Gray got the definite feeling some of the people in the area knew more than they were saying. Especially those who lived on the street where Black and Meat had been beaten. Gray supposed he couldn't blame them for being wary, but it was frustrating as hell.

The only thing that made Gray feel even the slightest bit of hope that they'd see Meat again had happened near the end of the day. They'd been inside one of the hovels on the street where Meat had last been seen, and the military member who'd been with him and Ro had stepped out. There were two women inside who'd sworn up and down they hadn't seen, heard, or known anything about a missing American.

The second their escort had left, however, one of them had said in broken English, "Maybe someone took friend to doctor. He come back when better."

Gray had opened his mouth to ask for more information, but their escort had stuck his head back into the hut and barked something in Spanish to the women. They'd nodded and immediately turned their backs to Gray and Ro, and had begun to sweep the floor as if their lives depended on it.

Sharing a look, the mercenaries had been frustrated, but it was more information than they'd gotten all day. The woman hadn't confirmed someone had taken Meat to a doctor, but that was the implication.

Hoping like hell the woman hadn't been fucking with him, Gray had followed Ro out, but before he'd left, he'd placed the money he'd been trying to bribe someone with all day on a small shelf near the door.

Once again, that night they met in Gray's motel room to update Black on the search, since he'd still been laid up in bed. Gray and Ro told the others what the woman had said, and they all agreed that since they'd found neither hide nor hair of Meat in the actual barrio, the woman's suggestion had merit. At least they hoped so.

They had little hope of finding him on their own, though. There were hundreds of acres of destitute areas like the one they'd been searching. Not to mention the houses outside of each walled barrio. If someone had taken Meat out of the barrio, it would be like looking for a needle in a haystack. All they could do was wait, and pray that Meat would be brought back to them. Or, if he was being held hostage, that he'd find a way to escape.

Chapter Seven

Three days had passed since Meat had been brought to the doctor's house. Night was falling on the third day, and while he wasn't feeling up to going toe-to-toe with another gang, he was feeling much better than he had even a day before. He hadn't seen much of Zara today, but he hoped she'd return soon. He couldn't communicate with Daniela, and while she was nicer now, she didn't exactly seem overjoyed to have him there.

Meat had woken up this morning with Zara in his arms. He was actually surprised, as he'd figured she was probably an early riser, like himself. It wasn't until Daniela had banged her hand on the entryway that Zara had jolted awake. She'd blushed when she realized where she was, and said something to Daniela, who disappeared, leaving them alone.

She hadn't said much to Meat, just mumbled about having to go, and before he could stop her, she'd left.

Meat had spent the day gently and repeatedly moving his ankle to try to get his range of motion back and to help it heal faster. His ribs still hurt like hell, but he'd had broken ribs in the past and did his best to ignore that pain. The bruises all over his body throbbed, and every now and then a feeling of nausea would make him dizzy. He slept a lot, as the house heated up quickly in the afternoon sun, making him drowsy.

By the time he woke up next, the sun was setting and he was starving. Meat knew his time being immobile and helpless was almost over. Tomorrow, he'd see how well he could bear his own body weight and think about getting out of wherever he was and back to his teammates. Moving at night would be better, as he could blend in, but it would also be more dangerous. He wasn't an idiot; he knew moving around the poorest sections of Lima in the dark wasn't exactly smart, but since all he had on was an undershirt and a pair of boxers, he wasn't dressed for slinking around in the daylight.

His thoughts were interrupted by Zara's return. She was still wearing the same large T-shirt and dirty, beaten-up sweats she'd been wearing when they'd met, but seeing her standing in the doorway made him wonder yet again how anyone could mistake her for a boy. Her hair was short, yes, but her hips were a bit too wide to be male, and her daintiness also made her look feminine.

Her cheeks were flushed. From exertion or the heat, he couldn't tell, but it made him think about how she might look after being thoroughly ravished.

She stood there staring at him without a word, and finally, Meat realized she had a plastic bag in her hand. It was stuffed full.

"What do you have?" he asked, nodding toward the bag.

Zara shuffled in and shrugged. "I found some stuff for you today. You might not like any of it."

Meat had no idea what she'd gotten for him, but he knew without a doubt that whatever it was had taken her all day to acquire. He didn't want to think about how she'd gotten the items, but he'd be happy for whatever she'd scrounged up all the same.

"Well, come over here and let's see what you have."

She nodded and moved closer. Meat hoped there was food in the bag, but he wasn't holding his breath. He could go another day without anything to eat; he'd gone longer on some of his past missions for the

Army. Daniela had brought him water throughout the day, so he was good there.

Zara put the bag down and bit her lip as she stared at him.

Meat patted the floor next to him. "Sit, Zara. You look tired."

She blinked at him in surprise, and Meat wondered if anyone had ever looked out for her before. Worried about her. He guessed probably not—and that made him both sad and pissed off.

She slowly sat as Meat peered into the plastic bag. His eyes widened as he pulled out the first item. It was a black T-shirt, new, with the tags still on it. Next was a pair of jeans, again with the tags still on them. She'd also gotten him brand-new socks and a pair of slightly worn, but not tattered, sneakers. The size on the jeans was about right, and the shoes would be a little big, but he could stuff newspaper or something in the toe to help that.

At the bottom of the bag was a can of soda, an apple, something wrapped in wax paper, and another candy bar.

He looked up at her in surprise. "Where'd you get all this?"

Zara shrugged again.

He wasn't going to let it go. "Seriously, the clothes are brand-new. You said you didn't have any money, so how'd you get them?"

"I went to Miraflores, the tourist area, and begged," she said with a tilt of her chin, as if daring him to judge her for it.

Meat was floored. He couldn't think of anything to say, and apparently she took his silence for disapproval.

"The tourists are more likely to give money to a homeless boy than anyone around here. Besides, no one in this area *has* any money to spare. I had to guess on your sizes. I hope they fit. I didn't think you'd want to be walking around in your underthings when you leave. And you have to have shoes." She shrugged again. "I bought the hamburger with the last of the money I got, and I stole the other food." She stared at him defiantly.

"Stole it?" Meat asked, hating the thought of her putting herself in a position where she might've gotten caught. But surprisingly, he wasn't put off by it for any other reason. Of course stealing was wrong, but he'd seen enough of how people lived here in the last few days. He'd be a hypocrite if he got all judgmental on her, then accepted her gifts. Especially when she was going out of her way to help him.

"Yeah. I'm good at it. I wouldn't have gotten caught, if that's what you're thinking. The tourist shops are always crowded and busy. It's easier than taking stuff from a local store around here. Pickpocketing would have been even easier, but by the time I'd begged enough money to buy the clothes, it was getting dark, and most of the tourists had already locked themselves behind their hotel doors."

Meat's head was spinning. He couldn't remember a time when he'd been so surprised by someone. He was jaded, had seen just about everything humanity had to offer, but right now, he couldn't do more than stare at the slip of a woman in front of him.

She started to stand up and said, "Sorry it took so long. I know you've got to be hungry."

Meat's hand shot out and closed gently around her biceps before she could get up. "Stay," he said, in a tone much gruffer than he'd intended.

She looked at him a little fearfully.

"I've been alone with my thoughts all day. I could use someone to talk to," he pleaded.

After a moment of indecision, she settled back on the floor next to him with her legs crossed.

"You must be tired after being on your feet all day," he said.

She shrugged.

"Did you get something for yourself to eat?"

She shook her head.

Now Meat wanted to lecture her. Tell her that she had to take better care of herself, but he knew he'd be out of line. She'd clearly done an amazing job of taking care of herself in this harsh environment already, and she didn't need him preaching.

He opened the candy bar and tore it in half before holding it out to her.

She looked from the candy to his face, then back to the candy, but she didn't reach for it.

"Go on," he urged. "The least I can do is share the meal you worked so hard to get."

"It wasn't hard," she protested, still staring at the chocolate but not lifting a hand. "Lots of people feel sorry for me when I beg, and I'm actually quite good at stealing."

He didn't doubt her. And if she was trying to put him off, it wasn't working. All she was doing was making him more impressed by her resilience. He waved the chocolate back and forth. "Please? Share with me?"

Licking her lips, Zara finally reached for the candy. They ate in silence, and Meat knew he'd never forget how amazingly good that chocolate tasted. He opened the hamburger, and even though he had brief second thoughts about eating it cold for sanitary reasons, he also tore it in half, and once again handed a portion to Zara. This time she only stared at the food for a heartbeat before reaching for it.

Their fingers brushed . . . and Meat swore he could feel that touch long after they'd finished the hamburger.

They shared the apple as well, and after he'd taken a long sip of the warm soda, he held out the can to her. She shook her head.

"Why not?" Meat asked.

"It's full of sugar," Zara responded.

Meat couldn't help it; he chuckled. Then he was laughing so hard he had to put a hand over his ribs to try to control the pain the laughter was causing. But he couldn't stop.

Luckily, Zara's lips were pulled up into a grin. She might not know what he was laughing at, but at least she hadn't bolted from the room.

"I'm sorry," Meat said when he had himself under control. "I shouldn't laugh. You're right. This shit is horrible for you. But with all this"—he waved his hand around them—"I wouldn't think you'd be that picky when it came to what you ate and drank."

For a second, he was afraid he'd gone too far and offended her, but she simply gave her signature shrug. "Growing up, my parents told me that soft drinks were bad for me. I guess I always remembered that and have steered away from them."

Her words struck Meat hard. "Your parents?" he asked softly, before he quickly chugged the rest of the soft drink. She was right—it wasn't healthy in the least—but he needed the calories, and the caffeine gave him a much-needed boost.

"Chad and Emily Layne."

When she didn't volunteer any other information, Meat realized he was going to have to ask anything he wanted to know. Moving slowly so as not to startle her, he put the trash from his odd dinner aside and reached a hand out to rest it lightly on her knee in support. "Where are they now?"

"Dead," Zara said, with no inflection in her voice.

Meat flinched. "How? And when?"

Zara looked up at him then, and he'd never seen such sorrow in someone's eyes. It was as if she'd lost them only yesterday, but he had a feeling it had been long ago. He didn't think there was any way Zara's parents would've left their daughter to fend for herself in the barrios of Lima the way she'd obviously been doing. Not if they could help it. Obviously, he didn't know the Laynes, but if they'd come to this country on vacation with their daughter, it wasn't likely they would've left her there on purpose.

"They were murdered fifteen years ago while we were walking back to our hotel in Miraflores after dinner."

Meat could only stare at her in silence for a moment. "You were with them? What happened to you?" he finally asked.

Zara shrugged and dropped her eyes. "The men took me with them because I could identify them. They apparently didn't have the guts to kill a ten-year-old kid, so they dropped me off in the middle of the night in one of the barrios . . . and I've been here ever since."

Chapter Eight

Zara held her breath and waited for Meat's reaction to the story she'd told only a couple other times in her life. The other people she'd opened up to when she was younger hadn't understood her, or simply thought she'd come up with a new angle to beg for money, telling her to go home.

But she hadn't been making it up, and she had no home to go to.

If Meat didn't believe her, it wouldn't really matter. She'd continue doing what she did every day, helping Daniela and doing her best to eke out an existence in the barrio with Mags and the other women.

What was harder for her to dismiss was the pull she felt toward Meat. He was the first person in a very long time, other than Mags, to look at her like she was a real person. The tourists usually just looked past her, or tossed down some money and continued on with their fun vacation. The other residents of the barrio were too concerned about their own struggles, finding food and remaining unnoticed themselves, to care about anyone else.

Zara hated begging for money but had known she'd never be able to steal the clothes he needed, so she'd spent all day sitting outside the tourist shops trying to look as pathetic as possible so people would give her money. And they did. She'd spent every cent on the clothes and resorted to stealing most of the food.

She had no idea if Meat would actually believe her, or pat her on the head and give her false sympathy before turning over and thanking his lucky stars he was leaving soon.

"Tell me more," he said after a long moment.

Zara bit her lip, trying to decide what she wanted to tell him. When she'd gone back to the barrio to find out about Meat's friend, Mags had told Zara everything she knew about Black, then said in no uncertain terms that if the opportunity arose, Zara should tell the American her story. She'd insisted this could be Zara's chance to get back to where she belonged. Back to the States.

But Zara wasn't sure she belonged anywhere anymore. She'd made the streets of Lima her home. She had only a fourth-grade education, was penniless, and wasn't sure any of the relatives she vaguely remembered would want anything to do with her. She wasn't a kid anymore, and she'd been out of America longer than she'd been in it.

At least here, she was needed. Zara and the others helped the local kids, did their best to keep them out of the clutches of men like del Rio and Ruben in the barrio.

But something in Mags's tone had gotten to her, and sitting on the hard concrete, begging for change, she'd fantasized about going back to Colorado and finding her relatives overjoyed to have her back.

That, and hot showers and tables full of food.

Zara didn't know if Meat would believe her story. Didn't know if he'd be able to help her return to America. Wasn't even sure it was possible, considering she had no identification, no proof she was who she said she was. She had literally only the clothes on her back. But like Mags had said, if she didn't try, it *definitely* wouldn't happen.

So she took a deep breath and started to tell her story. The whole story, for the first time in fifteen years.

"I was ten when my parents decided to come to Lima for vacation. I wanted to go to Disney World, but they thought it would teach me more if we came here. We were staying at a hotel in the Miraflores area.

I don't remember what it was called, but I remember the huge tub in the bathroom and how the water in the shower came from little holes in the ceiling rather than a showerhead."

She shook her head at the odd things she remembered.

"We'd gone out to dinner one night, and I guess we stayed too long. Everyone knows not to wander around after dark, even in the upscale, touristy area. I remember I hated my dinner. I complained and pouted throughout the meal. My dad scolded me, told me to stop acting like a four-year-old. I was mad at him, mad at how they sat at the table laughing and drinking wine when I just wanted to go back to the hotel and eat some of the candy they'd bought me earlier that day."

Zara took a deep breath, ashamed of how shallow she'd been back then. She'd been completely unprepared for the life that was ahead of her.

She felt Meat's hand resting on her leg and was surprised to realize it didn't creep her out that a man was touching her. He wasn't groping her, wasn't looking at her with lust in his eyes. Even looking like a boy, she'd been subjected to the lustful glances and touches of men who thought they had the right to fondle her and say whatever they wanted, simply because she was homeless and alone on the streets.

"Go on," Meat encouraged softly.

Her throat felt dry. Zara hadn't talked this much in a very long time, but she nervously licked her lips and continued. "I was walking a couple paces behind my mom and dad. I was still mad at them and knew they thought my little temper tantrum was amusing. They were talking about the boat they'd chartered for the next day and how fun the outing was going to be, when two men appeared out of an alley we were passing. They dragged my mom into it and covered her mouth so she couldn't scream. My dad did his best to get her away from them, but he was stabbed before he could do much more than plead for her life.

"I didn't know what to do . . . maybe I was in shock. So I just followed them into the alley. I'm not sure the men even knew I was there, or that I'd been with my mom and dad at all. They left my dad's body at the end of the alley in the shadows and dragged my mom farther into the darkness. She was trying to struggle, but the guy had his hand over her mouth, and she couldn't do much of anything. She was small, like me. She was no match for them.

"The second guy finally noticed me, and he grabbed me. He held his hand over my mouth as the other guy raped my mom. Then they switched places, and the second guy also raped her. When he was done, my mom's eyes met mine . . . and I saw the relief in them. That it was over, that they'd leave now and we could get some help."

Zara stopped and closed her eyes. That moment would always be imprinted in her mind. She could see everything as if it had happened yesterday. She hated going to Miraflores, knew exactly where that alley was, but since that was where she got the most money while begging, she went down there anyway.

She hadn't realized she'd been clasping her hands together until Meat took one of them into his own. He didn't say anything, which she was glad for. Now that she'd started this story, she just wanted to finish it. To tell one other person what had happened that fateful night that had changed her life forever.

"But instead of leaving, the guy who'd just raped my mom . . . he took out a knife and slit her throat. She didn't have time to say or do anything—it was *so* fast. He left her there on the ground, her pants around her knees, and even though I didn't understand Spanish at the time, he obviously wanted the guy holding me to finish me off. But apparently he had a weird sense of honor or something, because he refused."

She gave a little snort. "Murdering a man and raping and slitting a woman's throat was fine, but killing a kid was taking things too far. They argued, and I guess neither wanted to be the one to kill me. So they took me with them. I was scared out of my mind. I had no idea what their plan was. I realize now how lucky I was. They could've sold me to someone like del Rio, but they didn't."

When she paused for a long moment and didn't continue, Meat asked, "What *did* they do, Zar?"

Zar. She liked that. It was much better than the name Zed, which she'd picked out years and years ago when she realized it was better to pretend to be a boy.

When she felt Meat's fingers gently squeeze her own, she decided to finish her story as quickly as possible. "They drove for what seemed like hours, but I know now was probably only about thirty minutes. They pulled into a barrio much like the one where you were attacked and literally pushed me out of the car. They yelled a bunch of stuff at me, probably threatening to come back and kill me if I told anyone about what happened, then they left. It was pitch-dark, and I had no idea where I was."

"Shit, Zar."

Yeah. Shit. "I was terrified. I couldn't understand what anyone was saying, and no one could understand *me*. I managed to find a hiding place along the back end of a concrete-block wall in that barrio. There was tons of trash and pieces of extra concrete piled up against the wall, and I basically burrowed a space under it all until my body could fit inside. I hid there for days, hungrier than I'd ever been in my life and terrified that one of the big, scary-looking men who roamed the barrio would find me. Sometimes I came out at night and stole scraps of food, but for the most part, I lived in that hole for weeks."

"God, Zara. Was anyone looking for you? What about your relatives back in the States?"

Zara shrugged. "I don't know. I didn't speak Spanish, and it wasn't as if there were televisions playing news in the barrio. I was scared to death that if I did tell someone, the men would come back and kill me. After a while, it actually seemed not so bad anymore. I had my own little space, and no one bothered me much. I eventually cut off my hair because it was so dirty and gross, but more because I saw how girls got a lot more attention than boys. Bad attention. I wanted everyone to leave me alone, and that seemed the best way to do it."

Meat's gray eyes bored into her own. "What were your parents' names again?"

"Chad and Emily."

Meat nodded. "I wish I had my computer with me right now, but I swear to you, Zara, I'm going to do everything I can to find your people, if you have any, and let them know you're alive and well."

She nodded, feeling an emotion she hadn't felt in years almost overwhelm her.

Hope.

"But aside from that, I want to take you back to America. There's no doubt you've done the best with what life has thrown at you, but you don't belong here, Zara. Will you let me help you get home?"

She stared at him in disbelief. Mags had urged her to ask Meat if he would help her get in touch with the American embassy and plead her case. She'd tried it once before, but the guards had taken one glance at her—in her dirty clothes and looking like a street urchin—and escorted her off the property. They hadn't wanted to hear her story, hadn't even given her a chance to prove she wasn't lying.

But Meat believed her. She hadn't even had to tell him the few things she remembered from her childhood in the States to try to convince him.

Misinterpreting her silence for reluctance, Meat did his best to talk her into going with him.

"I'm the computer expert on my team. As soon as I can get my hands on my laptop, I'll be able to pull up any information available on your family, who I'm sure will be overjoyed to know you're alive and well. You're a United States citizen, and even if we have to give them blood so they can do a DNA test, Rex'll be able to expedite that so we can get a passport and get you out of here."

"You make it sound so easy," Zara whispered.

Meat chuckled. "It's not, but my friends have connections. Rex will take care of things from his end, and we'll keep you safe until we're out of here."

"King?" Zara asked.

When Meat looked confused, she explained, "*Rey* means 'king' in Spanish, but I think it's *rex* in Latin."

He chuckled. "I have no idea how you know that, but you're right. He's kind of in charge of the team. He vets the missions we go on and has connections everywhere."

Not sure about this king person, Zara bit her lip.

Meat leaned close and slowly brought his hand up to her face. He tugged her lip free of her teeth and gently ran the backs of his fingers over her cheek.

Zara stilled. She'd *never* experienced the kinds of feelings that were coursing through her body right now, as Meat touched her. They were scary and exciting at the same time. She wasn't sure if she should lean into him or pull away. So she did neither, just sat frozen, trying to process her emotions.

"Zara?"

She looked up at him.

"Will you come with me? Back to the States?"

Could she? Was she brave enough to take a chance?

She nodded once.

Meat beamed. "Good. Will you take me back to my friends tomorrow?"

A million excuses came to mind about why she shouldn't. He still had a concussion. His ankle still wasn't healed. It would be better to go at night when there would be fewer people around.

But she'd heard the anguish in his voice when he'd said his team would be worried about him. That his friend was probably missing the birth of his first child. And she could hear the longing for him to be reunited with them. Hadn't she felt the same way when she'd been taken from her parents? Like she'd do whatever it took to get back to what was familiar?

"Yes," she told him after a beat, liking that he didn't try to rush her. That he always let her think through things without pressuring her for a quick answer.

"Thank you," he said simply. "It's late, you have to be tired. Will you lie next to me again tonight?"

Zara nodded. She *was* tired. Exhausted. From the stress of being back in Miraflores, of begging for money, of worrying she'd be caught when she stole. Of telling Meat her story, and possibly having him dismiss what she'd said, like others had before him.

She slowly lay down, and just like before, Meat pulled her into his side. She rested her head on his shoulder and carefully wrapped her arm around his belly. "How are your ribs?"

"Cracked," he responded immediately.

Zara rolled her eyes. She had a feeling he'd downplay his injuries. She'd been in his position before. Well, not exactly, but she'd been hurt in the past and still had to keep on living her life, so she understood. He wasn't going to let his ribs or head or ankle keep him from getting back to his friends.

She worried for a moment about the logistics of returning Meat to the barrio. It would be tricky, and they'd have to come up with an explanation as to where he'd been and who had helped him. There was no way she was going to expose Mags and the rest of the women, or Daniela, so they'd have to devise a believable story.

She also didn't think he'd be able to walk all the way back to the barrio, so she'd have to use the bicycle and the hidden storage compartment again, which Meat probably wouldn't like. She'd also have to hide the bike somewhere so the military men didn't see it. She'd snuck him out when it had been dark. Now there were more military members around because of Meat's disappearance, and she didn't want them figuring out how they were able to smuggle people—including children—out of the barrio right under their noses.

"Stop thinking so hard," Meat said quietly.

"I can't," Zara told him honestly.

She felt more than heard his chuckle. "We can worry about all the what-ifs tomorrow," he said firmly. "Rest."

For only the second time in the last fifteen years, Zara fell asleep feeling safe. The first time had been the night before, when she'd slept in this same position with Meat.

She knew it was dangerous, that she shouldn't rely on anyone, but for just a moment, she wanted to be weak. To let someone else worry about roving bands of men looking for trouble, or the corrupt police, or someone who wanted to steal what little she'd been able to acquire for herself.

As if he could read her mind, Meat said, "Sleep, Zara. I won't let anything happen to you."

Chapter Nine

Meat wasn't happy.

He hadn't really remembered much about how he'd gotten to Daniela's house, but when he'd seen the small wooden box disguised as trash that he was supposed to get into, memories came rushing back. The pain. The confusion. The darkness.

Now he was back in that box, being jostled as Zara towed him through the back alleys and streets of Lima toward the barrio where he'd last been seen. He hated not being able to see what was going on. Not being able to protect Zara. Which was ridiculous because she was obviously the expert here on her home turf.

He hadn't slept much the night before, thinking about all the things that needed to be done to get Zara back to the United States. His fingers itched to get on his computer. If what she said was true, and he had no real reason to distrust her, the press back in the States was going to have a field day.

Her life would change in a big way, and things would be extremely hectic and probably confusing for her for a while. But Meat wasn't going to abandon her. Not only did he owe her a debt he wasn't sure he could repay, for saving his life from the gang in the barrio, he was drawn to her. She was unlike anyone he'd ever known. She was resilient. Strong. Shy. Kind. And all of it together was irresistible.

Meat felt the bicycle slowing down, and he tensed, not knowing what to expect. He heard lots of childish voices around him, and giggling. Not sensing any danger, he peeked out the small hole Zara had shown him before she'd shut the lid.

Zara had climbed off the bike and was talking and laughing with a group of children in ages anywhere from around five to twelve, at his best guess. She made a point to talk to each one, and they were smiling at her. After a few moments, she said something to the group, and they all waved at her and ran away. Meat saw a look of sadness on her face before she turned and climbed back onto the bicycle.

He realized in that moment how big a deal it was going to be for her to leave. She'd been on the streets since she was ten. Fifteen years. Scraping to get by, making friends with others in the same situation. Looking after those more vulnerable than herself, like the group of children he suspected she'd just said goodbye to. He might be able to rescue *her*, but how many others were being left behind? Not necessarily American citizens who were kidnapped and left to die, but just kids in need in general?

Forcing himself to concentrate on where they were going, Meat tried to shake off his depressing thoughts.

Zara had explained that when they got close to the barrio where she hoped his friends would still be, she'd hide the bike, and he'd have to walk the rest of the way in. He was all right with that. The clothes she got him mostly fit, except for the shoes. His ankle was still sore, but he'd wrapped it that morning as tightly as he could. He'd walked farther in more pain in the past. His head only slightly throbbed now, and thankfully the nausea he'd been experiencing was gone.

Getting Zara to wherever the team was staying would be trickier. The Brigade would still be assisting his friends, and they'd probably not take kindly to Zara showing up with him and finding she'd basically kidnapped him. Meat had no idea where his friends had been staying or how they were getting around the city, but he and Zara had discussed several possibilities on how to keep the military team from seeing her. He'd also promised that if nothing worked out, he'd return for her.

And he would. No way was she spending one more night alone in the barrio where she'd already spent fifteen years. The thought of her sleeping on the ground was abhorrent.

After another five minutes or so, Meat felt the bike slow again. He watched as Zara got off and pushed them into an alley. She waited for a minute or two, then finally lifted the lid on the box. As they'd discussed, he quickly climbed out, breathing a sigh of relief. But the alley they were in smelled disgusting, so he nearly choked on the large breath he'd just taken.

When he'd controlled himself, Meat helped Zara hide the bike amid the garbage. Finished, he stood back, impressed because anyone walking by wouldn't have any idea there was a bicycle and trailer hidden there.

"Your friends will be able to find it?" he asked, wanting to make sure. The last thing he wanted was for this obviously important and necessary mode of transportation to be lost to those who needed it most.

Zara nodded. "This is a usual hiding place for it. And Mags knows, if I don't show back up, to come looking for it. That I went with you."

Her explanation made sense, and he was impressed with how well she and her friends had worked around the obstacles they faced in their everyday lives. His chest swelled with something that felt like pride.

Meat had no idea why this slip of a woman affected him so much. He'd just met her a few days before, but she'd managed to impress the hell out of him. Despite that, he still wanted to be the one keeping her safe from anything and everything that had hurt her in the past.

Stockholm syndrome? He didn't think so. Yes, she'd basically kidnapped him, but he knew now that she and her friends had done so with the best of intentions. They hadn't chained him up, and he could've left the doctor's house at any time. He wasn't sure how his friends would see the situation, but Meat didn't care. He felt a connection to Zara that he hadn't felt toward anyone.

"How is your ankle? Can you walk all right?" Zara asked.

Meat nodded without thinking about it. He knew he didn't have a choice. He couldn't lean on her, because it would look weird for a grown man to be leaning on what everyone assumed to be a teenage boy. It would bring unwanted attention. He didn't look like the badass American soldier he thought he was, not with his scruffy clothing and his three-day-old beard and greasy hair.

"Remember to call me Zed," Zara muttered as they headed down the alley toward the street.

Meat's senses were assaulted when they finally got to the street and began walking toward the barrio. Rapid Spanish voices rang out all around him. The smell of garbage and smoke from fires filled his nose. He'd been in the barrio before, but knowing that this was where Zara had lived for so many years made the area seem even more depressing.

The sun felt good on his face, but he could feel the sweat dripping down his temples and soaking through the shirt at the small of his back. The hair on his arms stood straight up, and Meat felt naked without any kind of weapon. He was out of his element and didn't like it one bit.

Then a thought struck him.

How would he feel if he was *ten years old* and had been dumped here like a piece of unwanted trash? Would he have been able to survive like Zara had?

He doubted it.

His admiration went up another notch. It was one thing to hear her story when they were sitting in a relatively safe place; it was another altogether to see the world she'd conquered through his own eyes.

"Okay, we're coming up to the back entrance. There are two military guys there, probably on the lookout for you. Remember the plan?"

"Yes," Meat said, not in the least offended that she'd asked. They'd gone over it at least ten times, but she had a lot more to lose here than he did. He wanted to reach out and take her hand in his, but didn't dare. "Be careful out there, Zara," he said softly. "No matter what happens in the next thirty minutes, remember that I'm on your side. I'm going to help you."

"Don't panic if things get crazy," she responded. "It's just the distraction."

Meat nodded.

He heard something to his left and craned his neck to look. Seeing nothing, he turned to reassure Zara one more time—but she wasn't there. One second she'd been by his side, and the next she was gone.

Taking a deep breath and trying not to worry, Meat approached the break in the wall that surrounded the barrio. The military men looked up in disinterest, but the second they saw him, they shot to attention.

One immediately reached for the radio on his side while the other stepped up to him. "Hunter Snow?" he asked.

Meat nodded. "That's me."

Within minutes, it seemed as if there were a dozen men from the First Special Forces Brigade surrounding him.

Three days ago, he would've felt comfortable and relieved to be in their presence, but after learning about the rampant corruption, and how most of the residents of the barrio were scared of the military, he was anxious to see his teammates.

The Peruvian men talked among themselves, and just when Meat was wondering what was going on, out of the corner of his eye, he saw a commotion.

Turning, Meat couldn't keep the huge smile off his face.

Running at full speed toward him were Gray, Ro, Arrow, and Ball. Black was following them as fast as he could, but it was obvious the man was suffering from his own injuries.

Turning his back on the military members standing around, Meat started toward his friends.

Gray was the first to reach him, and he engulfed him in an embrace without an ounce of self-consciousness. Meat's ribs protested the movement, but he barely felt the pain.

The others joined their huddle immediately after, and Meat had never felt more relieved in his life. For a while he hadn't been sure he'd ever see these men again.

And once more, thoughts of Zara snuck into his consciousness. How she'd probably dreamed of this exact kind of reunion with her own relatives, but had been denied. It made him all the more determined to bring her back to the loving embrace of the family that *had* to have been in agony, wondering where she was all these years.

Everyone stepped back when Black reached them. Meat turned to him, and the two men hugged for a long moment. Black was the first to pull away. "You look like shit."

Meat laughed, then groaned as he put an arm around his middle. "Fuck, that hurts. And I'm guessing if I looked in a mirror, I'd look a lot like you."

"Actually, since we've been able to shave and you haven't, you look more like the abominable snowman," Arrow quipped.

Meat couldn't even muster up the energy to care that he was dirty, probably smelled awful, needed to brush his teeth, and had a three-day-old beard. It felt so good to be back with his friends, he didn't give a shit how much crap they gave him about his looks.

"Where have you been?" Gray asked the question Meat knew everyone probably had on their minds.

"Later. I assume you haven't been staying here?" Meat asked.

"Hardly," Ro snorted.

"Fuck no," Arrow said.

Glancing behind him at the military men hovering nearby, Meat lowered his voice. "You been driving yourself here to look for me or what?"

Gray's eyes followed Meat's, taking in the Brigade. Then he said quietly, "We've got our own vehicle, but we've always got eyes on us. Why?"

Meat wasn't surprised. "I'd love to get a shower and get off my feet," he said, loud enough for the men nearby to hear. Then, quieter, he said to Gray, "I've got a friend I need to accompany us back to wherever we're staying, and it needs to be on the down-low."

Bless Gray, he didn't even blink. He simply nodded and muttered, "We need a distraction then."

Meat opened his mouth to explain he didn't think that would be necessary, that his "friend" had it covered, when there was a loud commotion somewhere in the near distance. Several people began shouting at once, and then Meat heard a gunshot.

Half a dozen of the military men ran toward the sound, which seemed to be coming from a couple alleys over from where they were standing. Three others ran toward where the Mountain Mercenaries were huddled up, reuniting and talking.

"We must go. Now! It's not safe."

Meat couldn't help noting that the men didn't seem concerned for the many women, children, and elderly who were scurrying around, trying to get to the dubious safety of their huts and shacks in the barrio. But he kept his thoughts to himself as he and his teammates hurried toward an exit in the fence about a hundred yards from the one he'd entered minutes before.

Gray was at Meat's side, and as they approached a black van, he whispered, "Where's your friend?"

"I'm not sure," Meat said.

Ro opened the door and put a steadying hand on Meat's side when he started to climb inside the vehicle.

A pair of dark blue eyes stared at him from the floor between the second and third rows of seats.

More relieved than he could say that Zara was already there, he scooted into the third row, putting himself between her and the door.

He had no idea how she'd known which vehicle they'd be traveling in but assumed one of her friends in the barrio had seen the Mountain Mercenaries get out of the van when they'd arrived.

To his teammates' credit, even though they couldn't have missed Zara, they didn't say a word about their stowaway. They simply piled into the van, with Ball shutting the door once they were all in.

"We've got two rooms at the closest motel," Gray said as he slid behind the wheel. "We usually park in the gated lot behind the building. The military doesn't follow us in, since they aren't staying there. They've posted a van full of guards outside, though, supposedly for our own safety."

Meat nodded, distracted. Outwardly, Zara seemed calm and collected, but he could feel her body shaking against his leg, and she was holding on to the material of his pants with a white-knuckled grip. She gasped at hearing the military had guards watching the team, but didn't say anything.

"You have info on our military friends?" Ro asked Meat.

"I don't know for sure if they orchestrated me and Black getting beaten up, but they're definitely the reason this mission has been fucked from the start," Meat told his teammates. "Basically, they're crooked as hell and taking bribes from anyone and everyone. They were probably paid to try to sabotage the mission from the start, and when the locals decided we were easy pickings, they used my disappearance as a way to take attention off why we were here in the first place."

"Trafficking of the kids," Gray said solemnly from his seat behind the wheel of the van.

"Exactly," Meat agreed.

"And your friend?" Ball asked with a nod to Zara, still crouched down behind the seat.

"Zed's not a threat," Meat clipped.

"Didn't say he was," Ball said soothingly. "Just wondering what part he played in all this."

"I'll explain everything when we get to a safer place," Meat told his friends. All five nodded, and he sighed in relief. "Gray?"

"Yeah?"

"How's Allye?"

Gray's lips quirked upward, but Meat could see it pained him. "Good. Darby James was born yesterday, perfectly healthy."

"With a full head of hair," Ro added. "Complete with a white streak, just like his mama."

Meat lowered his head and took a deep breath. Pain filled his chest, and not just from his broken ribs. "I'm sorry, man," he said softly.

"Not your fault," Gray said firmly.

"Funny. It feels a hell of a lot like it is," Meat countered. "If I'd been smarter about everything, you wouldn't have missed the birth of your son."

"No, I shouldn't have run after the kid," Black said from the front passenger seat. "I fucked up by leaving my post."

Meat shook his head. "Any one of us would've gone after him," he tried to reassure his friend. He could tell Black was still beating himself up for his impulsive act.

"We didn't even find the kid," Black said. "We got jumped instead, and now the boy's probably lost and scared out of his mind."

"He's not," Zara said softly from her position at Meat's feet.

Tense silence filled the car at her words. Everyone turned to stare at Zara.

She seemed to shrink in on herself for a moment before sitting up straighter and squaring her shoulders. "His mother was scared she'd lost him to del Rio forever. They were reunited once the coast was clear and have moved out of the barrio to a different location. He's going to be a lot more careful from here on out. More aware of his surroundings, so he doesn't get snatched up by men on del Rio's payroll again."

When no one responded, she went on, "I'm not saying that Mr. Gray missing the birth of his child, or that Meat and you, Mr. Black, getting beaten up was a good thing. But the distraction allowed José to hide and get back to his mother."

Meat guessed Zara had learned about the boy when she'd gone back to talk to Mags and her other friends, while he'd still been down for the count at the doctor's house. He was glad for the boy, but still upset that Gray hadn't been there for Allye when she'd gone into labor.

As if he could read his mind, Gray said, "All the others were there with her. Chloe, Morgan, Harlow, and Everly. They didn't leave her side. Allye said the hospital staff was a bit taken aback by all the people who wanted to be in the room for the birth, but none of them would budge. So Darby came into the world surrounded by his honorary aunts and lots of love. And Zed . . . it's just Gray. Not Mr. Gray."

"I'm thinking I'd like to have this talk as soon as possible," Arrow said, studying Zara.

"What's the plan to get him inside?" Black asked. "He's small, but not *that* small."

"Think he'd fit in one of our duffels?" Ball asked.

"No!" Meat said. "We're not stuffing anyone into a fucking duffel bag."

"I was kidding," Ball mumbled, but Meat had a feeling he hadn't been.

"It won't be an issue," Ro stated. "Our shadows don't follow us into the parking lot. Gray can park on the back side of the motel. We'll all get out with your friend . . . Zed, right? . . . between us. He's so small, even if we *are* being watched, no one will see him. We'll go inside and upstairs like we usually do. No problem."

"We've been given two rooms. You and your friend can share with me and Ro," Gray said. "Arrow, Black, and Ball can share the other one."

Meat saw Zara shaking her head violently.

Without thought, he put his hand on her shoulder to calm her.

"What's wrong?" Ball asked, obviously seeing Zara's distress.

"If the military is paying for your rooms, they're probably bugged," she said.

Meat pressed his lips together. He didn't know if Zara was being paranoid or if she had a real reason to think that. Either way, he wasn't going to chance it. "I'll pay for a third room when we get there," Meat said. "You guys can take Zed upstairs. Once I get a key, we can use my room to talk."

Arrow leaned forward from Meat's right, studying "Zed" for another long moment, then looked back up at Meat. "It seems you have a lot to tell us."

He nodded. "I do."

"And you trust your friend with anything we might talk about?"

Meat nodded again. "Yes."

He held his breath. Generally, the Mountain Mercenaries weren't a trusting bunch. But with the addition of the women in their lives, they'd loosened up some. In their tight-knit circle, they shared almost everything. His friends might not know Zara was actually a woman, but they trusted Meat's instincts.

Then again, Meat had a feeling Zara wasn't fooling anyone. Arrow had a soft look in his eye that probably meant he'd figured out they weren't harboring a teenage boy, but a girl or woman instead. How in the world she'd managed to fool so many people for so long, Meat had no idea.

He hated to think about Gray missing Darby's birth, but Meat would apologize to his friend again later . . . and to Allye when he saw her. No matter what anyone said, Meat couldn't help feeling that if he'd managed to fight off the mob of men a little better, they'd already be home and Gray could've met his son by now.

Of course, that would mean that he wouldn't have met Zara, and she'd still be living on the streets. He was conflicted, and it was a strange feeling for Meat. The Mountain Mercenaries had had his loyalty for so long, it felt wrong to be glad things had gone down the way they had.

One look at Zara huddling at his feet seemed to make that feeling fade, however. He couldn't regret anything he'd done if it meant getting her home where she belonged.

Gray pulled into the gated parking lot and waved at the van of military personnel that had pulled into a spot on the street outside the parking area.

As if they'd practiced the maneuver, Ball, Ro, and Arrow formed a wall of flesh, disguising Zara as she stepped out of the van. She huddled close to Meat, and he put his arm around her as they walked toward the entrance. Black and Gray brought up the rear, concealing their stowaway from view of the soldiers on the street. Meat didn't dare breathe until they were safely inside the motel.

"I'll go get the third room," Ball said before breaking off toward the lobby. The rest of the group headed into the stairwell and started up.

Meat swore as each step caused stabs of pain in his ribs. His ankle was also throbbing. Walking was one thing; apparently stairs were something completely different.

He felt Zara's arm go around his waist, and she took some of his weight, just enough pressure off his ankle so he could successfully navigate the stairs without falling on his ass.

"Damn, do these stairs suck," Black complained.

Meat wanted to chuckle, but knew it would hurt too much, so he settled for nodding in agreement.

"Maybe if you did more than just lie there when a group of men decided to stomp on your chest, it wouldn't hurt so bad," Ro quipped.

"Fuck you," Black said with no ire in his tone.

God, Meat had missed these guys.

They walked down the hall to a room, and Gray opened it with an actual physical key, rather than the plastic cards they'd all gotten used to in the States. They filed in and stood awkwardly in the room, staring at each other. They couldn't talk, just in case the place was bugged.

Meat said, "I'm going to use the bathroom. Let me know when the other room is ready."

Then he put a hand on Zara's back and gently pushed her into the small bathroom. As soon as the door closed behind them, he turned on both the shower and the sink, knowing the sound of the water running would mask whatever they said if the bathroom had a listening device.

"You okay?" he asked, keeping his voice low.

She nodded.

"And your friends back in the barrio? They'll be okay after that distraction they provided?"

She stared at him for a long moment, and Meat wasn't sure what she was thinking.

"What?" he finally asked.

"Why do you care?"

Meat was nonplussed for a second. Why did he care? Did she really think he was that coldhearted? "Because they're your friends. Because they went out of their way to help me when they didn't have to. Because they could've been hurt."

"Sorry," she said softly. "I guess I'm not used to men helping me unless they want to somehow screw me over."

"Hear me now," Meat said seriously, putting his hands lightly on her shoulders. "I'm helping you because I want to. Because someone should've done it a long time ago. Because you've had the shit end of the stick for so long, it's about time you were treated fairly and got your just rewards.

"But most importantly, I'm helping you because I *like* you, Zara Layne. You fascinate me. I'm in awe of your strength and resilience. I hate what happened to you, but I'm so fucking thankful that you took a chance and helped me."

She blinked. "You like me?"

Meat couldn't help it. He laughed, then groaned as his ribs protested. "Yeah, Zara. I like you a hell of a lot."

She still looked baffled.

"Hasn't anyone ever told you that they like you before?"

"Not since I ended up here," she said honestly.

"Then I'll have to be sure I remind you every day from here on out."

"I don't think your friends like me."

"They don't know you."

They stared at each other for another long moment before Meat did his best to lighten the mood. "Hearing that shower is making me long to step inside . . . fully clothed."

Zara's lips twitched. "I can't remember the last time I had a shower. I don't think standing in the rain counts."

Meat's mood abruptly soured, thinking about the life she'd led on the streets. "If you can wait a few more minutes, you can take as long a shower as you want."

"How much hot water does this place have, do you think?" she asked, smiling.

Meat wasn't ready to be cheered up. "Hopefully a hell of a lot."

He watched as she searched for something else to say. "I'm sure your friends are going to want to talk."

"They can wait until you're ready," Meat told her.

"You never told me," Zara said, not looking up at him. "Why are you called Meat?"

"I was on a training mission in the Army. As a joke, someone made sure all our MREs—meals ready to eat—were vegetarian. We had four days in the field with only vegetables. I wasn't happy. I bitched about it the entire time. Said I was desperate enough to eat a horse to get some protein. The guys in my platoon started teasing me and calling me 'Meat.'"

Telling the story of how he got his nickname had never seemed all that embarrassing . . . until now. Bitching about having ready-made meals, which had at least two thousand calories apiece, seemed entitled and stupid after seeing how little the people in the barrios had. They'd probably kill to have those vegetarian MREs.

But Zara didn't berate him for being a thoughtless ass—she simply smiled again.

He opened his mouth to apologize for his ignorance, for not truly understanding how bad some people had it, when there was a soft knock at the door.

"Yeah?" he called out.

"Ball's back with the key to your room," Gray said.

"Be right out," Meat told his friend. He turned to Zara. "Ready?"

She shook her head, but said, "Yes."

Meat smiled at her. "It'll be fine. You'll see. And the good news is that Gray'll bring my computer."

"Your computer?"

"Yeah. I can't believe how badly I've missed it. I'm so used to being able to look things up at the drop of a hat. I want to look up your case and find out as much as possible. I also need to get in touch with Rex and get him started on your paperwork and documents to get you out of the country. We can't exactly smuggle you out of Peru like we smuggled you into this motel." He smiled at her, but she didn't smile back.

"What if you can't?" she asked.

"I can and I will," Meat returned. He held out a hand. "I'm not leaving you here. Now, come on. Let's go so I can properly introduce you to my friends, and you can get that nice long shower."

She nodded, and even though he could tell she was reluctant, she took hold of his hand, which made Meat feel ten feet tall. He swore to himself he'd do his best to never let her down. She'd been let down by so many people over the years—the men who'd killed her parents, the people who hadn't believed her—and he didn't ever want her to feel that way again.

Chapter Ten

Zara stood awkwardly in the middle of the room Meat had taken her to. She didn't want to sit on the bed and get it dirty. She was more than aware of how awful she probably looked and smelled. The motel room might not be fancy for these men's tastes, but to her, it was the most luxurious thing she'd been in since she was a little girl.

Just the thought of the clean sheets and towels was enough to make her hyperventilate. And a shower? A *hot* shower? Being naked in a place where she didn't have to worry about anyone storming in on her or stealing her clothes while she was preoccupied? That was heaven.

Meat had wanted her to shower before she talked to his friends, but there was no way she wanted to delay the inevitable. If they didn't believe her and kicked her out, she didn't want to have experienced the bliss of being truly clean, then having to go back out into the dirt and filth of the barrio. Besides, the grime covering her helped disguise her gender.

"Guys, I'd like you to meet Zara Layne."

She winced, not really expecting Meat to introduce her right off the bat by her real name, but when none of the men appeared shocked, she realized that they'd known she was a female probably from the get-go. She didn't understand why. No one ever looked twice at her. They always took her at face value. Saw her short hair, small stature, and just assumed she was a boy.

Each of the men nodded politely and respectfully. As if they were meeting in a formal setting and she was standing in front of them wearing a freaking ball gown or something. It was weird. She wasn't sure she liked having their complete attention like this.

"In case you didn't catch everyone's name in the car . . . this is Gray. His fiancée just had their baby, Darby. To his right is Ro. Then there's Arrow, Ball, and Black."

It was easy for Zara to remember Black, as he and Meat had matching bruises and scrapes from their run-in with Ruben and his friends in the barrio. She nodded back at everyone, not sure what she was supposed to say.

"Thank you for helping our friend," Ball said.

The others agreed, and Zara nodded again.

"Want to tell us what the fuck happened and where you've been?" Gray asked Meat.

Ignoring his friend's question, Meat turned to Zara. "You sure you don't want to get cleaned up while I tell them the entire story?"

For a second, Zara wanted to take the easy out Meat was offering. She didn't want to see the doubt on his friends' faces when he told them about her. She knew the story sounded crazy. How could anyone survive on their own in the barrio, much less a ten-year-old little girl? But she had, and she hadn't lied about anything she'd told Meat.

She lifted her chin and shook her head.

She couldn't interpret the look on Meat's face. She didn't have much experience with men. Didn't know if he was happy she was sticking around or upset with her. But when he reached out and brushed a lock of short hair off her forehead, she couldn't help but soften a little inside.

He turned back to his friends. "Right, so this is Zara. She's twenty-five years old. When she was ten, she and her parents were on vacation here in Lima. One night, her parents were murdered, and the killers took Zara with them. Apparently, they had some sort of crisis of conscience, because instead of raping and killing her, they dumped her in a barrio much like the one we've become familiar with. She's lived here ever since."

"She's American?" Arrow asked. Then he looked at Zara. "You're American?"

She nodded.

"Holy shit," Arrow mumbled, running a hand through his hair. "What are the odds?"

Zara was confused by that, and it must've shown on her face, because Black said, "When we were on a mission in the Dominican Republic a bit ago, we accidentally found a woman who'd been kidnapped from Georgia and was being held there."

Zara stared at him in shock. "Really?" she whispered. "What did you do with her?"

"We took her back home, and she and Arrow fell in love. Then he went and knocked her up," Ro said with a smile.

Zara was having a hard time processing what they were telling her. "So you guys, what . . . find lost Americans or something?"

All six men chuckled. "Not exactly," Meat told her. "I already told you that we've dedicated our lives to helping women and children. Along the way, some of us have managed to luck out and find women we've connected with in the midst of doing our jobs."

She looked from one man to the next. None of them were looking at her with disgust or suspicion. It was . . . weird.

"Anyway," Meat continued, "Zara and her friends saw what was happening with me and Black. They knew the mob of men would be back any second, so they came and got me out of there, and by the time they were ready to go get Black, two of the bad guys showed back up, and they lost their window of opportunity. Zara smuggled me out of the barrio to a doctor, where I stayed until I was well enough to get back. Had a concussion bad enough to knock me flat on my ass for the first day, and my ankle was also fucked up enough that I couldn't walk on it for a while."

"Why didn't you come and tell us he was safe?" Gray asked Zara, his eyes narrowing.

This was the look she'd been expecting. "Those military men you were with are on del Rio's payroll. They regularly patrol the barrios looking for women and kids to take back to him. I didn't want to risk the chance they'd turn on the rest of you . . . or my friends, who are still back in the barrio."

"What more can you tell us about this del Rio guy?" Ro asked. "We know some basics, but we want to hear any intel you can give us."

"He's . . ." Zara wasn't sure how to explain him. But she had to try. "He pretty much runs the sex trade in Lima. He controls and runs most of the brothels and is known for being completely ruthless. Women disappear all the time down here, and he even contracts outside the country to get foreign women too . . . whether they want to work for him or not. And he's been branching out, snatching younger and younger girls to work for him. Boys too." She saw the anger on the faces of the men. "He's evil, and no one can stop him."

"The police?" Ball asked.

Zara shook her head. "He pays them off. Same with the military. Not all of them, but enough. Many of the men you are working with get paid for bringing him kids and women from the barrios. Ones few people will care about or miss. No one but their friends and family, who don't have enough money to fight him," she said bitterly.

The room was silent for a while after her explanation, but it wasn't because they didn't believe her. At least she didn't think so. There was an undercurrent of anger, and it was obvious the men were trying to hold their tempers.

"Anyway, Mags, my friend and someone we all look up to and respect, didn't think it was a good idea to let you know about Meat right away, simply because you were always around one of the military men. We didn't know if they'd retaliate against the barrio in general, or tell del Rio about some kind of resistance. We weren't sure if you'd even believe us. Mags suspects the Brigade paid Ruben and the others to beat you up. If that little boy hadn't run away, and you guys hadn't followed him, they probably would've attempted something to draw your attention away from saving the others."

"Damn," Ro said, at the same time Black swore under his own breath.

"So what now?" Gray asked, looking at Meat.

"I get on my computer, find Zara's relatives, get in touch with Rex to help with getting her papers to get the fuck out of here," Meat said.

"One day? Two?" Arrow asked.

Meat shrugged. "As long as it takes."

"Wait, you can't—" Zara started.

The men either didn't hear her or ignored her. "I'll call Allye and tell her the good news that we found you, and let her know it might still be a few days before we'll be home," Gray said.

"Morgan still has a month and a half or so until she's due, although I'm sure not having me around to go shopping for her late-night cravings is driving her crazy," Arrow said with an indulgent smile.

"Chloe'll make sure she's good," Ro told his friend with a clap of a hand on his shoulder.

"Wait!" Zara said urgently. "You don't need to stay here with me. You should go home to your wives and girlfriends. I'll be fine waiting here."

"If you think we're abandoning you, you're wrong," Gray said in a firm tone.

Zara frowned.

"We aren't as naive as you might think," Ball explained. "We knew something wasn't right with this mission, but not to this extent, obviously. We'd already figured the men we were partnered with weren't exactly on the up-and-up. You and your friends did your best to save Meat and Black, and we don't take that lightly."

"If we'd known about you, we would've come for you," Arrow added. "No one—man, woman, or child—should be taken away from their loved ones and abandoned, but right now, you're our new mission. None of us are leaving without you."

For the first time in years, Zara felt tears threaten. She'd learned a long time ago that crying didn't help. In fact, there were a lot of people who enjoyed seeing tears because it meant they'd broken you. "I'm nobody," she whispered.

"Wrong," Meat said forcefully. "You're Zara Layne. You risked your life for mine, and I won't forget that. Ever."

"Me either," Ro said.

"Or me," Gray added.

The others all agreed.

"But I could be lying," Zara insisted. Not sure why she wasn't letting it go.

"Are you?" Black asked.

She stared at him. He was handsome. With his black hair and brown, piercing eyes, he could've been on the cover of any of the glossy magazines Zara had seen in Miraflores in the tourist shops. The bruises on his face didn't diminish his good looks in any way.

She didn't really care about how he looked. She'd come across many handsome men in the last decade who had black souls.

But she could easily see this man cared about his friend. And, for some reason, about her.

She shook her head.

Black nodded. "Right, then we're all staying until Rex can pull strings and get you a passport. We'll hole up here until that happens."

"What are we gonna tell the military?" Ball asked.

"We'll put Rex on that too. He's the one who was working with them. We've already told him that we thought some of the people he's working with are corrupt, but now we've got confirmation. He'll have to be careful, but he can help figure out how to get them off our backs," Gray said.

"We should probably change rooms, just in case the others are bugged," Ro suggested.

Gray nodded again. "While Zara and Meat get cleaned up, we'll work on that. Meat, you seem to be okay beyond some general pain, but I'd like to take a look at your injuries anyway, if that's all right."

Meat nodded. "Bum ankle, busted ribs, and the concussion, as I said earlier. Zara's doctor friend reset my shoulder. I wouldn't mind something to take the edge off, but otherwise I'm good."

Gray lifted his chin at his friend, then looked at her. "Zara? What about you?"

She frowned, not understanding the question.

He smiled. "You need any medical care?"

Zara wanted to laugh. She hadn't seen a doctor since she was about nine and had broken a finger at recess. She and her best friend, Renee, had been swinging in circles on the swings, and she'd gotten her finger stuck in the chains as they'd wrapped around each other. "No."

To his credit, Gray didn't push.

"I'll bring your duffel by when we're done," Ball told Meat. "Not sure what we'll do about Zara, though."

"I'm okay with what I've got on," Zara said quickly.

All six men looked at her as if she were insane.

"I mean . . . I'll wash them in the shower, and they'll be fine once they dry," she told them.

"I'll slip out and find something appropriate," Arrow said.

Zara hated the panic that tore through her, but the thought of putting on feminine clothes was abhorrent. She *couldn't* be a girl. It was too dangerous.

Meat turned to her and put a finger under her chin, so she had no choice but to look at him. "Trust us," he said softly. "Arrow isn't going to get you a big, poofy pink party dress, Zar."

She took a deep breath. Of course he wasn't. These men wanted to fly under the radar as much as she did. Especially after hearing how corrupt the people running the government were. She nodded.

"You hungry?" Gray asked.

Meat's stomach chose that moment to growl so loudly, there was no way anyone could miss it. Everyone chuckled, and even Zara had to smile.

"Guess that answers that," Meat said without an ounce of embarrassment.

"I can get something while I'm out shopping for Zara. I don't know what your situation has been for the last few days . . . Should I find something filling but bland, or go hog wild?" Arrow asked.

To her surprise, Meat turned to her. "What do you want, Zara?"

She immediately said, "Anything is fine."

Meat's eyes narrowed, and she wasn't sure what he was thinking. Then he turned back to his friend. "Filling but bland. And lots of candy bars. No soft drinks. Fruit and vegetables, if you can find them."

"Got it. I'll be back as soon as I can," Arrow said, not even blinking at the strange food request.

"Take your time. We aren't going anywhere," Meat told him.

Zara felt the pesky tears again. Meat had remembered that she didn't drink soda, and he'd obviously picked up on the fact that candy bars were her weakness. And it probably wasn't a good idea for either of them to gorge on rich, spicy food. She also couldn't remember the last time she'd had a full serving of vegetables. When she was a kid, she'd turned up her nose at anything green on her plate, but now, she'd kill to eat healthy vegetables with every meal.

The men started to leave the room, and Meat called out, "Gray?"

He turned after the others had left. "Yeah?"

"You'll bring my computer straightaway?"

"Be back in two minutes," Gray reassured him, and then it was only Zara and Meat left in the room.

"You go first," Meat said, gesturing toward the bathroom.

Zara hesitated. She didn't have anything to put on after she was clean, and even though she'd said she could put the clothes she was wearing back on, that was the last thing she really wanted to do.

Once again, Meat seemed to be able to read her mind. "I'll give you one of my clean T-shirts and a pair of sweats to wear until Arrow returns with something for you."

Zara bit her lip. She wanted to get in the shower more than she wanted just about anything—other than for her parents to be alive. But she didn't want to seem greedy or rude. "I wasn't kidding about wondering how much hot water this place has." She tried to make light of her situation. "It's been a very long time since I've been able to have a hot shower. Once I get in there, it'll be a while before I come back out."

Instead of laughing at her attempt at a joke, he frowned and stepped toward her. Zara held her ground and stared up at him; Meat towered over her. His broad shoulders blocked the overhead light. His scratchy dark-brown beard hid much of his face, but she could see the serious look in his eyes. "I don't give a shit if you're in there an hour, Zara. Take your time. Take all fucking night; it won't faze me."

"But I'm sure you want your turn," she protested weakly.

"And I'll get it. When you're done."

A momentary vision of them *sharing* the shower flashed through her brain.

Zara had no idea where that had come from. She'd pretty much thought she was uninterested in sex. She'd spent most of her adult life trying to avoid men and staying as far away from them as possible.

Yet here she was, alone in a motel room with a very good-looking guy.

She should be scared of him. Should be doing everything in her power to get away from him. But when he looked at her with respect, admiration, and tenderness, she couldn't seem to think about anything other than how big he was, how he'd be able to stand between her and anything or anyone who might want to hurt her.

It was crazy. Insane. But she couldn't stop her runaway thoughts.

"Okay," she said after a beat.

"Okay," he repeated with a smile. "While you're busy in there, I'll be out here seeing what I can find out about your situation and family. Is that all right?"

Zara couldn't speak. This man had done more for her in a couple of days than anyone had since she was ten. She finally nodded.

She wanted to explain that, fifteen years ago, her parents had little to do with her mom's family. That she remembered her maternal grandparents being cold and standoffish, and didn't really remember her paternal grandparents at all. Her dad had been an only child, and his parents had passed when Zara was young. But her mom had a brother, Alan. He was ten years older and kinda mean and someone her mother hadn't kept in touch with at all.

But she didn't say any of that. Maybe they were different now. Maybe losing their daughter, and her uncle losing his sister, had changed them. Maybe knowing their granddaughter was missing in a foreign country had spurred them to be more sympathetic toward others in general.

She wanted to know if they'd looked for her. If they still wondered what had happened to her—or ever had wondered at all.

But she couldn't open her mouth to ask Meat to find out. She was scared to know the answer.

Fifteen years ago, when she'd hidden in the barrio, terrified out of her mind, she'd stayed sane by convincing herself there was a massive search going on for her, and it was only a matter of time before the police would come marching through the barrio calling her name.

The first time she'd seen a police officer in the barrio, she'd come out of her hiding spot, eager to tell him that he'd found her. So ready to go home. But he'd raised and swung his baton when she'd gotten close, yelling something at her in Spanish.

Frightened, she'd backed away, tripping and falling, and he'd managed to smack the bottom of her feet with his baton. It had hurt. A lot. She'd run back to her hiding spot and didn't come out again for days.

Slowly but surely, she'd realized that the big search she'd envisioned in her mind hadn't happened. Or if it did, it hadn't made its way to wherever the men had dropped her off. It had been scary and devastating at the same time.

All these years later, Zara wanted to know if her relatives had organized a search. She wanted to believe they had . . . but could she live with the knowledge that they hadn't?

She straightened her spine. Of course she could. She'd made it this far on her own—she could continue to do just fine without them if it came to that.

"There's a lot going on behind those beautiful eyes of yours, Zara. I won't pry if you don't want me to, but after seeing the media circus that surrounded Morgan's return from the Dominican Republic, after she'd been missing for a year, I have a feeling your story will be even bigger. You were a kid when you disappeared, and somehow, against all odds, you survived. Everyone's going to want to know your story. We'll do our best to keep things under wraps, but the second Rex pulls his strings to get your passport and legal papers, word will get out. It's just how things are. I need to know what we'll be dealing with in regard to your family and your past. Okay?"

Zara nodded. She didn't want to be in the limelight. She'd done her best to fade into the background for so long, it was horrifying to think of herself in front of cameras or her image in the newspapers.

Meat reached for her hand and brought it up to his face. He pressed her palm to his cheek. Zara felt the scratchy beard on her skin . . . and wanted to know if the hair on his head felt the same way.

"You aren't going to be alone in dealing with anything, Zar. I'll be there. And the rest of the guys. And their women too. You'll see. You'll fit right in."

She wasn't sure about that, but didn't bother contradicting him.

There was a knock at the door, and Zara startled badly. Meat kept hold of her hand and did his best to soothe her. "Shhhh. It's just Gray with my computer, and probably my bag too."

She nodded, and he took one more long look at her before letting go of her hand. He walked to the door, taking his duffel bag and a backpack from Gray. He thanked him and said he'd see him and the rest of the guys later, when Arrow returned with food.

Meat closed the door, locked the bolt and the chain, then put the duffel on the bed. He pulled out a T-shirt, a pair of gray sweats, and a pair of socks. He then riffled through his bag some more and held up a small zippered bag. "There's a comb, shampoo, toothpaste, deodorant, and lotion in here. It's not exactly feminine, but I thought maybe . . ." His voice trailed off.

Zara's eyes widened at the offer. God, she hadn't used deodorant in forever. And real toothpaste? Bliss! She didn't even care that she didn't have a toothbrush. She could use her finger, just like she'd been doing for the last however many years.

"Thank you," she whispered.

Meat brushed off her thanks. He had no idea how much his actions meant to her. Clean clothes, a comb, deodorant . . . those were like a gold mine to people in the barrio.

"Go on. Take your shower. You're safe here. No one will come in and bother you."

Of course they wouldn't. Not with Meat guarding the door. And Zara had no doubt he would bar the door against anyone who might want to do her harm.

She picked up the clothes and toiletry bag and held them to her chest. There was so much she wanted to say, but she couldn't get the words out. She'd experienced small acts of kindness over the years, but nothing had touched her as much as what Meat and his friends had done, *were* doing, for her.

Nodding again, Zara turned and bolted for the bathroom. She shut the door a little harder than she'd intended and winced. She hoped Meat didn't think she was being rude.

She stared at the little lock on the doorknob for a long time.

She didn't need to lock it. Meat wouldn't walk in on her. She trusted him.

But still, she found her hand lifting and turning the small button all the same.

Trying to ignore the shame she felt at not completely trusting Meat, Zara put her bundle down on the sink. For just a second, she stared at the crisp, clean white towels hanging on the rack. She looked at the washcloths and down at the clean clothes on the counter.

She leaned over and put her nose into the fabric and swallowed hard at the smell of soap, detergent, and what she assumed was the scent of Meat himself. His very essence was woven into the fabric of the clothes he'd given her.

This was what heaven must be like.

Clean clothes, toothpaste, and hot water.

It had been a long time since she'd been this content.

And with that, Zara turned on the water in the tub, holding her hand under the stream until it got hot. Then she turned on the shower, pulled the curtain, and stripped out of the dirty, nasty, smelly clothes she'd been wearing for far too long, including the cloth she'd been using to bind her chest. Leaving them in a pile in the middle of the bathroom, she avoided looking at herself in the mirror, grabbed the small bar of soap from the sink, and stepped under the scalding-hot water.

Chapter Eleven

Meat sat on the edge of the chair at the small desk in the motel room, one ear tuned to the bathroom as he scoured the internet for information about the Layne family.

He'd heard Zara lock the door and honestly wasn't surprised. While he felt as if he knew her pretty well, in actuality, they didn't know each other at all.

His ankle and ribs throbbed as he scrolled through the search results, reminding him of how and why he'd met Zara.

Thirty minutes later, the shower was still running—and Meat sat back and sighed. What he'd found out about Chad and Emily Layne changed things. In some ways, what he'd learned made Zara's life easier, and in others, made it a lot harder.

The couple had been loaded.

Fifteen years ago, they'd been worth around ten million dollars. Now . . . that number had climbed to around twenty million. And if his nosing around was correct, Zara was the sole heir. She'd never have to worry about a safe place to sleep at night or having enough money to purchase clean clothes and a freaking toothbrush again.

But along with that money came headaches Zara had no clue about.

It looked like, upon her parents' deaths, the money had been put into a trust for Zara. She was supposed to have been receiving a monthly stipend upon turning eighteen, and she'd get the rest of the money when she was twenty-eight.

At one point, her uncle, Alan, had attempted to get his hands on the money, claiming Zara was deceased, but because her body had never been found, her parents' lawyer had fought him, and a judge refused to release the funds. Which was a smart move, considering Alan had been in and out of rehab and jail practically his entire life.

From the pictures he'd been able to find, Zara had been an adorable kid. Her brown hair was frequently mussed in the photos online, and her eyes seemed to sparkle with happiness. In short, she'd been happy and carefree. He didn't see any of that person in the Zara he knew, which was sad. He hated that she'd had to learn the hard way how unfair and hard life could be.

The thing that bothered Meat the most about his quick online search was the lack of press regarding Zara's disappearance. When her parents had been found murdered, there were a few articles about their missing daughter and speculation about what had happened to her, but that was literally it. There were no true-crime shows about the incident, no anniversary specials, no vigils on Zara's birthday each year, no updated sketches of what Zara might look like as an adult.

It was as if no one had cared that the little ten-year-old had disappeared into thin air, including her grandparents.

Compared to the ruckus Morgan's father had caused when *she'd* disappeared, the information on Zara was pathetic. It was heartbreaking, actually. Her paternal grandparents had died in a car wreck when Zara was five. But her maternal grandparents hadn't done any in-depth interviews about her disappearance. In the few pictures he'd seen, they'd appeared stoic. The only quote he'd found, from her grandfather, said that they'd told the couple not to go on vacation to Lima, that it was dangerous.

It was almost as if he was saying "I told you so," when he should've been putting together search parties for his missing granddaughter.

Meat vowed then and there to do whatever he could to help Zara reacclimate to life in the United States. Not to fail her in the way it seemed her grandparents had.

He had a feeling, because of her inheritance, people would be coming out of the woodwork offering to "help" her. And while she wouldn't come into the bulk of her money for another few years, she'd be getting a good chunk of back pay from the stipends she should've been receiving.

All in all, Zara was now a very wealthy woman. And with money came trouble.

When Meat heard the shower turn off, he glanced at his watch. Forty-five minutes. He smiled, loving the thought of Zara luxuriating under the hot shower. He didn't begrudge her the indulgence. If he'd lived the way she had, he'd take his time too.

Not wanting to risk using the motel's phone in case it was being monitored, Meat had a quick instant-messaging chat with Rex on a secure app they regularly used. Their handler had already spoken with Gray and was working on getting the documents Zara needed to legally leave the country. It would take a couple of days; even with his connections, he couldn't get a passport to Lima overnight.

Rex had been disgusted that he'd had to pay off a couple of Peruvian government officials to get it done, but after everything both men had learned about the corruption in Peru, neither was surprised.

Rex had asked if Zara would be willing to take a DNA test to prove she was actually Zara Layne, and Meat told him he had no doubt whatsoever she would. But he knew without a doubt that Zara was who she said she was.

Rex told Meat he was glad he had a hard head, and that he'd talk to him and the rest of the team when they got back to Colorado.

Meat had just pushed his laptop away when he heard the bathroom door open. Turning, he grinned when he saw the huge plume of steam rush out the door, followed by Zara.

The steam framed her, making it seem as if she were stepping out of a corny spaceship movie or something. Her short hair was wet and curled a bit over her forehead. Her cheeks were flushed, and his clothes were huge on her petite body.

Meat was moving before he even thought about what he was doing. He walked toward her, limping a bit, as his ankle hurt after the exertion of the day. He stopped in front of her, the fresh, clean smell of the soap she'd used wafting up between them, making him more than aware of how dirty *he* was.

He wasn't sure what he was going to say—if anything. He just knew that he was drawn to her. That he wanted to be near her.

"Feel better?" he finally asked.

She nodded and chewed on her lower lip.

He didn't know if she was nervous to be around him or if something else was agitating her. She looked so unsure, Meat wanted to take her in his arms and tell her everything would be okay. That he'd make certain of it. Somehow, standing there in her bare feet, wearing his clothes, she seemed more vulnerable.

Out on the streets, in her "boy" clothes, dirt on her face, she was in her element. She blended in and was perfectly capable of taking care of herself. But if anyone could see her right this second, they'd know she wasn't the teenage boy she'd pretended to be.

Meat's eyes wandered down her body for a split second, and he was startled to note she very much indeed had curves. She'd somehow managed to bind what looked like lush breasts, and while he couldn't exactly see much under the miles of cloth, there was absolutely no doubt that Zara was a woman.

She shifted in front of him, as if uncomfortable with his scrutiny. "I washed out my clothes, but couldn't put my . . . underthings back on because they're wet," she said in a rush.

Meat inhaled deeply, trying to get ahold of himself. He took a step back because he figured he was probably intimidating her, and that was the last thing he wanted to do. "I'm sure Arrow will find you appropriate underwear." He wasn't sure of that, and in fact, he didn't like the thought of Arrow picking out such intimate things for Zara. But that was ridiculous—first, because Arrow was completely smitten with Morgan, and second, Zara had to have something to wear under her clothes.

She simply nodded and hunched her shoulders forward, as if that would somehow hide her figure from him. Meat took another step backward, hating the idea of what she might've been through to make her so self-conscious and insecure about her own body.

Zara looked up when he moved again, and she frowned. "Does your ankle hurt?"

"Yeah," Meat told her honestly and without thinking.

Her frown deepened. "You shouldn't be standing on it."

He shrugged. "I'm not about to get on the clean bed until after I shower."

She looked up at him, and he saw some of her confidence returning. "Why do you keep backing away from me?"

Surprised she'd asked, Meat answered honestly again. "I'm making you nervous, and I don't want to crowd you."

"I'm not afraid of you," she replied, and Meat saw no signs of deception in her expression. His breath came out in one long whoosh.

"Good. Because I'd never hurt you, Zara."

"I know. You definitely had plenty of chances. Even that first night when you grabbed me around the neck, you made sure you didn't hold me too tight, and you never came close to cutting off my air. You might've had a concussion, busted ribs, and a bum ankle and shoulder, but I knew from the start that none of that would slow you down if you really wanted to hurt me . . . or leave."

She was right. There'd been something about her from that very first night that made him let down his guard and trust her.

"I'm sorry about that," he told her. "I wasn't sure who you or Daniela were and if you were going to hurt me."

"She *did* hurt you," Zara said. "She told me to hit your shoulder, that it would make you let me go, but I didn't have the heart . . . and I knew you weren't hurting me."

"Her actions were very effective," Meat said ruefully, remembering how painful the doctor's hit to his ankle had been.

"I'm sorry I took so long in the shower," Zara said, changing the subject.

Meat shook his head. "You're fine."

"It's just . . . it's been so long since I've been able to—"

"You don't have to explain anything to me, Zara. I don't care if you take hour-long showers for the rest of your life. You do what you want, when you want, and the hell with what anyone else thinks."

Her lips twitched at that. "Is that your life motto?"

Meat shrugged again. "Not really, it's just that I've seen firsthand how short life is. And after I got out of the Army and started working for Rex, I needed something to do with my free time. I started messing with wood and found out that I really enjoy making furniture. It relaxes me. Some men like to hunt or tinker on cars; I like working with wood. Taking a bunch of random pieces of scrap and turning them into a one-of-a-kind dresser or table is satisfying. It's not very sexy or exciting, but I don't care. If taking long showers relaxes you and makes you feel happy, then you should take one every day."

She stared at him so long after his attempt at setting her at ease, Meat began to feel uncomfortable. "I, on the other hand, don't enjoy taking that long in the shower. I guess it's because I feel too vulnerable in there, and because in the Army, we didn't have time to dawdle. And speaking of which, standing next to you makes me all the more aware of how badly I need to clean myself up. Arrow hasn't returned yet, but it should be soon. We can eat, and then I'll tell you what I found from my searches."

The uncertain look returned to her face, and Meat wanted to kick himself.

"Okay." She moved to one of the queen beds and sat on the very edge.

Meat stepped over to her and crouched down, mindful of his ankle. "What's wrong?" he asked.

"Did anyone look for me?" she whispered.

Even knowing he was filthy, Meat raised a hand and palmed the side of her face. Her skin was warm and smooth and slightly damp from both the steam in the bathroom and perspiration. He gently brushed his thumb against her cheek. "Yeah, Zar, they did. Not as long as they should've, and they didn't do nearly enough in my opinion . . . but they looked."

"Did they find the guys who were responsible for killing my parents? At least tell me they did, and they're locked up."

Meat hated to have to tell her. But she must've figured it out from the look on his face.

"They didn't, did they?" she asked.

He pressed his lips together and shook his head slowly. "There weren't any other witnesses, and it's not like they had any cameras in that part of town fifteen years ago. They didn't have anything to go on. I'm so sorry."

Zara sighed, then met his gaze and asked, "What now? I've got nothing, Meat. Do I go back to the States and live on the streets with the other homeless while I attempt to get my life together? I only have a fourth-grade education, no skills, and I can't imagine anyone would be all that excited to hire me with no job experience and with my background. I can probably get by with pickpocketing for a while, but with my luck, I'd get caught and end up in prison. Maybe I should just stay here."

Meat was shaking his head even before she'd finished speaking. "I can't say that it'll be easy to acclimate—I'd be a bastard if I tried to tell you that. But, Zara, you don't ever have to worry about being homeless again. One, because you can stay with *me* as long as you want. I don't have a huge house, but it's a nice cabin on a couple acres northwest of Colorado Springs. I've got two guest rooms and a spare room above my workshop, and you will *always* be welcome.

"But secondly . . . you also don't have to worry about where you'll live—or anything ever again—because you've got more money than I'll ever make in my lifetime."

Her brows furrowed in uncertainty.

"Honey . . . your parents had money. *Lots* of it. And you're their only heir. It's all yours. Well, not all of it, not until you turn twenty-eight. But enough that you can live wherever you want and take all the hot showers your heart desires."

She gaped at him as if he were speaking a language she didn't understand.

"I know it's a lot to take in, but you aren't alone anymore, Zara. And you can buy whatever you want, whenever you want. Clothes, food, a home . . . hell, a *couple* of houses. You don't have to work, and you can decide if you want to go back to school or lie around and eat candy bars all day. You're free, Zar. The life you've been living isn't the one you've been meant to live forever."

She didn't cry, didn't scream out in joy and dance around the room. She simply stared at him.

"Zara?"

"I'm scared."

Meat knew that. He could see it in the way her muscles were tight. How she sat stock-still. How her breathing sped up. "That's okay. If you want me to, I'll help you figure it out."

She immediately nodded.

The weird feeling inside him swelled up once more. He was glad she wasn't going to push him out of her life the second she got back to the States. He wanted to get to know her better. Watch as she learned to fly.

Eventually, he was sure she'd outgrow him. Get bored of his simple life on his small plot of land. But he'd do everything in his power to make sure she was ready to face the world when she *did* leave.

Brushing his thumb over her flushed cheek once more, Meat said, "I need to get cleaned up. I won't be long. Make yourself comfortable." Then he went to stand, and grunted in pain when the movement tweaked his ribs.

Zara was instantly there, helping him straighten.

"Thanks."

"That was stupid. You should be lying down," she chastised.

Meat couldn't help it. He grinned.

"What are you smiling about?" she asked in irritation.

"You. You're really *not* scared of me." It wasn't a question.

"Why should I be?" she asked, her hands on his waist as she looked up at him.

"Because I'm bigger than you. Stronger. A stranger. A man. I could name about a hundred different reasons."

"Most everyone is bigger than me," she retorted. "I cleaned up your puke, told you some things about me that I haven't told anyone else, and you didn't even flinch. You believed me when I told you my story and haven't given me any reason to think you'll suddenly decide to attack me. You gave me clothes to wear and didn't make fun of me when I took a really long shower."

Her voice lowered then. "You found me, Meat. Treated me like a human being, not an annoying bug you wanted to swat. I helped Daniela, but I sometimes felt like I was just getting in the way. You made me feel useful and needed for the first time in a long time. So no, I'm not scared of you. Scared of what's to come, yes . . . but not of you."

"Fuck, Zara," Meat said, his chest hurting from her words. "After I get cleaned up, can I . . . shit. Never mind."

"Can you what?" she asked with a tilt of her head.

"Nothing."

"Meat. What?" she asked again.

"I just . . . I'd like to hug you, but I don't want to overstep."

She was quiet for so long, Meat knew he'd fucked up. He started to take a step back, but Zara's hands tightened on his waist.

"I haven't hugged anyone since I was a kid," she whispered.

Meat's heart broke for her.

Then she continued. "I'd very much like a hug . . . but not until you change clothes. I can still smell that puke on you."

For a second, Meat wasn't sure how to respond. But when she grinned shyly up at him, he closed his eyes in relief and chuckled. "You gotta let go of me if I'm going to get that shower."

Her fingers tightened on him, but then she dropped her hands and shooed him toward the bathroom. "Well, go on, then. I might've saved you some hot water, but I'm not sure."

Meat made a quick decision to upgrade his hot-water heater back home. It didn't matter if she stayed with him for a day or a year. She'd have all the hot water she wanted if he had anything to say about it.

"Don't answer the door," he warned. "If anyone knocks, just ignore them. They'll come back later."

"What if it's Arrow with food?" she asked.

"I'll check with Gray when I'm done. Don't worry, you'll get your food," he teased.

"It wasn't *my* stomach growling earlier," she returned.

Meat chuckled. "Very true. Ten minutes and I'll be back," he told her. He grabbed the change of clothes he'd gotten out of his bag earlier and ducked into the bathroom. The mirror was still fogged over, and Meat was pretty sure he didn't want to see what he looked like right about now. He'd seen enough in the mirror in the other room. His face was bruised, and when he shaved off his beard, he knew he'd look worse. Maybe he'd leave the beard for now and take it off when he got back to Colorado and wouldn't have to be around people as much.

As he ran a hand over his face, he kind of liked the way it felt. Maybe he'd keep the beard even longer.

Zara had hung her shirt and pants over the towel rack, and they were slowly dripping on the floor. He'd move them into the shower when he was done.

But it wasn't her shirt or pants that caught his attention. It was the tiny scrap of black cotton underwear that made his heart clench. It had two holes in it that he could see, and the elastic was stretched out.

He was upset because those panties seemed to bring home to him just how hard her life had been. She'd had to claw and fight for everything. She should be wearing something lacy that would make her feel sexy and confident in herself and her femininity. But instead she'd made do with worn-out cotton panties. It made him sad and angry at the same time.

There was also a long Ace bandage hanging next to her pants. She obviously used it to bind her breasts, to flatten them to add credence to her disguise as a boy.

He wanted to shred it with his bare hands and throw it in the trash. Wanted to stomp out of the bathroom and tell her she never had to do that to herself again.

Instead, he took a deep breath and controlled himself.

He was proud of Zara for doing what she needed to in order to survive. What kind of underwear she wore made no difference in her daily life. But he had to wonder if she'd been hurt or assaulted in the time she'd been on her own. She likely had been . . . and the thought made him almost crazy. No one should have to be subjected to violence, but because he had such strong feelings about Zara, he especially hated that she had been.

He couldn't change her past, but he sure as hell could influence her future. No one would make her do anything she didn't want to do again. He'd make sure of it.

Quickly stripping off the clothes Zara had bought for him, Meat stepped into the shower, refusing to think about the fact she had stood in this exact spot, naked as the day she was born, not ten minutes ago. He picked up the bar of soap—again trying not to think about how it had recently been all over Zara's body—and began to clean himself.

The faster he got through his shower, the faster he could be near Zara again. Meat had never felt this . . . urgency and desire to simply get to know another person before. He hated to even spend ten minutes out of her sight, because that was ten minutes he wouldn't be talking to her. Figuring out her likes and dislikes.

Ignoring the twinges of pain from his body, Meat did his best to hurry through his shower. He had a hug he needed to give . . . and suddenly that was way more important than anything else.

Chapter Twelve

Zara had sat on the edge of the bed, afraid to touch any of Meat's computer equipment and not quite comfortable enough to completely relax. True to his word, Meat had taken just about ten minutes on the dot to shower and change.

When he came out of the bathroom, she could only stare. He wasn't wearing a shirt, just a pair of sweatpants that sat low on his hips.

"Sorry," he'd said when he emerged. "Gray's going to look at my ribs, and it's easier to just leave my shirt off for the meantime. If it bothers you, I can put it on."

Zara simply shook her head. Bother her? No, seeing his just-about-perfect chest wasn't a *bother*. He had a slight sprinkling of hair and not an ounce of extra fat on his body. The nasty bruises on his stomach and chest looked bad, but they didn't take away from the fact that Hunter Snow was built like a brick house.

They stared at each other for a long moment before a knock sounded at the door, scaring the shit out of Zara.

"Easy, Zar, I'm sure it's Arrow or Gray."

Actually, it was both. As well as the rest of his friends. Even Black was there. He immediately stretched out on one of the beds after Ro ordered him to get off his "fucking feet" before he fell over.

The men were gruff and blunt with each other, but oddly, Zara found she liked that. She was slowly feeling more comfortable around them.

Arrow placed two large bags on the floor by the bed and a third on the small table in the room. Zara was more interested in the smells coming from whatever was in that third bag than what was in the other two.

He immediately started unpacking the bag with the food—and Zara could only stare in disbelief. Where he'd found all that food in such a short period of time, around *here*, she had no idea, but her mouth immediately started watering.

He unpacked two containers filled with soup, several Styrofoam boxes with broccoli and carrots, and a final large container holding some sort of meat.

Zara barely heard what was being said around her; all her attention was on the food.

Arrow handed her one of the containers of soup and a spoon. Without pause, Zara took it over to a corner and slowly sat. She pulled her knees up and held her treasure close to her chest as she peeled the lid off. Fragrant steam rose from the soup, and she inhaled deeply. She stirred it, watching pieces of chicken and fresh vegetables float to the top.

Ignoring the spoon, she brought the container up to her mouth and took a tentative sip, not knowing how hot the delicious-looking liquid was. Her eyes came up—

And she froze when she saw all six men staring at her with varying looks of concern, anger, and sympathy on their faces.

She slowly lowered the soup and searched for something to say that would break the tension.

"It's all yours, Zara," Arrow said gently. "The rest of us have already eaten."

She had no idea if that was true or not, but she was ashamed of how she'd acted. She'd simply done what she would've if she'd been out in the barrio. Taken the precious food and backed into a small corner where no one could sneak up on her and steal her bounty before she'd had time to consume it.

Of *course* Meat's friends weren't going to take the soup away from her.

She closed her eyes and tried to pretend she hadn't just embarrassed the hell out of herself.

But Meat, being Meat, took the attention off her, putting it on himself. "Did you have any painkillers, Arrow? Because I could use a few."

"Of course. And yeah, you look like you've gone a round or two in the ring, that's for sure," Arrow told him.

"I think you look worse than me," Black observed.

"How do your ribs feel?" Gray asked. "Arrow picked up some wrap, which should help stabilize your core and take some pressure off."

The talk around her turned to Meat's and Black's injuries, and everything the latter had gone through over the last few days, and they all just let her be. At one point, Meat lay down on the bed, and Gray did a quick examination.

While that was happening, Ro mixed some of the meat and both veggies together in a container. He then walked over to where she was still sitting in the corner and placed the container on the floor next to her . . . along with a chocolate caramel candy bar. He didn't say anything, simply retreated to the other side of the room, where he leaned against the wall and turned his attention back to Meat and Gray.

It didn't take long for Zara to get full. This was more food than she'd seen at one time in months. Last November, she'd taken the bicycle and trailer to one of the charity dinners that had been offered close to Miraflores. She'd stuffed herself as full as she could, then taken as many leftovers as she could grab back to her friends in the barrio. Mags hadn't been there, but Teresa, Gabriella, Bonita, Maria, and Carmen had been overjoyed to see all the food. They'd sat in the darkness with only one candle lighting the hut, and had eaten until they'd all felt as if they were going to burst.

It had been a good day, but once the food was gone, the hunger inevitably returned, and the rough day-to-day life in the barrio continued.

Zara carefully put the lid back on the still half-full container of soup, and she brought that and the uneaten veggies and meat she hadn't been able to finish back to the table. Ball was standing there, and he took them from her, and Zara did her best to tamp down the feeling of regret that she had to give the food back. But he merely brought the containers over to what looked like a cabinet and opened it. It was a small refrigerator.

Zara sighed in relief. He wasn't throwing out what she hadn't been able to finish. She could still eat it later.

The thought of having food ready and available whenever she wanted it was a foreign one. There were few refrigerators in the barrio. And never any leftover food.

She appreciated that even though she had a feeling every man in the room was watching her, they did their best to make her feel as comfortable as possible. They didn't stare, didn't say anything about her food quirks. They simply continued to talk among themselves.

Meat had also eaten some food, and when he was done, Arrow brought Meat's uneaten food over to the fridge and stashed it as well.

"You talk to Rex?" Black asked Meat.

"Yeah." Then he looked up at Zara. "You ready to hear what's next?"

Her opinion of Meat rose at his question, and it was already pretty high. She'd been making decisions about her life for a long time now, and even though she trusted Meat, she didn't want him to just take over without giving her any say. She nodded.

He thanked Ball when he handed him his computer and opened it on his lap. He had his back to the headboard of one of the beds, with his legs stretched out in front of him. He'd put on a T-shirt, and Zara could almost picture him looking exactly the same way in his own house. Not that she knew what his house looked like, but he seemed comfortable in his own skin, and he'd obviously sat just like this with a computer in his lap in the past.

"Right—so, Zara's a multimillionaire," he said without preamble. "Her parents were loaded, and they left everything to her."

"Shit," Arrow said under his breath.

Zara looked at him in surprise. He was upset that she had money?

"Sorry, Zara. I'm happy that you don't have to worry about money, but this is gonna complicate things for you."

"Is it?" she asked.

He nodded. "When my Morgan returned to the States after being kidnapped, the press lost their minds. Everyone loves a feel-good story about someone being reunited with their family after disappearing. And Morgan had only been gone a year. You've been missing for *fifteen*. The press is going to hound you. They'll be relentless. And now, people are also going to come out of the woodwork asking for money. Telling you all sorts of sob stories about why they need it. Their kid has cancer, they're starving, they're homeless. Everything you can think of and more. They'll play on your emotions, use what happened to you to try to gain your sympathy and get money from you. It's gonna be hell."

Zara frowned. Well, shit, that didn't sound good at all. "I don't care about the money," she said honestly. "I'll just not talk to the newspapers, and no one will find out."

Arrow ran a hand through his hair but didn't say anything else.

"It's not that simple," Gray said gently. "They'll find out anyway."

"We'll run interference for her," Meat said from his spot on the bed. "We won't let her be harassed."

"Of course we'll look out for her," Gray replied, "but you and I both know they'll still get to her. You can't keep her locked up in a bubble. She'll be at the grocery store and someone will recognize her and harass her. She'll get hundreds of letters from people around the country begging for her help." Gray turned to address her. "You're going to have to harden yourself," he warned. "The stories you'll hear will break your heart. You'll probably want to give money to everyone and every cause under the sun. They'll try to make you feel guilty, like you're a terrible person if you don't donate."

Again, Zara wasn't sure she wanted to go back to the States. Maybe she could just take the money and get a house here in Lima. Far away from the barrios, in a nice neighborhood.

As if he could hear what she was thinking, Meat said to Gray, "Stop scaring her, asshole." Then he held out his hand. "Come here, Zara."

Without thought, she moved toward his outstretched hand. When she was close enough, he wrapped a hand around her waist and pulled her toward him until her hip hit the mattress. Meat looked up at her from his spot on the bed and said gently, "We'll figure it out."

We'll figure it out. Not *you'll* figure it out. His words made her calm.

"What about her family?" Ball asked.

Not moving his hand from around her waist, Meat said, "They're going to be an issue."

Zara's heart sank, but she couldn't say she was all that surprised.

"Her uncle, Alan, has been contesting the will and trying to get his hands on the money in her trust for years. Her grandparents don't seem to be all that interested in *anything* having to do with their missing granddaughter. I found an interview that was done about ten years ago, on the five-year anniversary of Zara's disappearance, and her maternal grandparents said they assumed she was dead, just like their daughter, and the money in the trust would be released to her closest living relatives when her twenty-eighth birthday finally arrived and she didn't come forward to claim it."

No one said a word. The men seemed to be holding their breaths, waiting for her reaction.

Zara looked at Meat and shrugged. "They never seemed to like me much when I was little. I was too loud, too annoying, too . . . childlike for them."

"You *were* a child," Gray said, clearly annoyed. "I haven't even met my son yet, and neither has my mom, but I know without a doubt that if something happened to me and Allye, and he was missing, she would move heaven and earth to find him."

"Not everyone is like that," Zara told him bluntly. She'd seen her share of horrifying things here in Peru. Mothers who sold one of their children so they'd have enough money to feed the others, men who beat the shit out of their wives because they were bored, grandparents who refused to have anything to do with their children or grandchildren because they felt they were beneath them. Nothing surprised her anymore.

"Well, they should be," Gray muttered. Then took a deep breath. "Right, so we'll deal with things as they come up. Zara is rich, and Rex is working on her documents to get her back in the country. We may need to set up at least one press conference so she can tell her story." He looked at her then. "The last thing you want is the press making up their own stories, or people who have no idea what they're talking about coming forth to explain what you're thinking and feeling. It sucks, but it's like a Band-Aid. Pull it off fast and get it over with, then you can concentrate on figuring out what to do with the rest of your life."

She didn't like it, but she hoped these men knew best.

"I've got a few extra rooms at my house," Gray told her. "You can stay with me and Allye if you want."

"You just had a baby," Ro said. "She can stay with me and Chloe—"

"She's staying with me," Meat interrupted before anyone else could offer their home to her. "That is . . . if she wants to."

Zara had never been so touched in her life. She'd gone from being essentially homeless to having these strangers offer to take her in. It was overwhelming and unexpected.

She realized that everyone was staring at her again. She panicked for a second, wondering why they were looking at her, then recalled Meat's words.

She apparently had enough money to live wherever she wanted, but the thought of living by herself, of trying to acclimate to a new life and world alone, was scary as hell. She nodded.

"What are you saying yes to, sweetheart?" Meat asked quietly by her side. "You've got a roomful of people who want to help you. No strings attached. The others"—he gestured to the other men—"all have women who live with them. That would probably make you feel comfortable, since you're used to hanging around with Mags, Daniela, and the other women here."

She stared at him, trying to read between his words. Did he already regret asking her to stay with him? It had taken her a long time to become friendly with Mags and the others. It was hard to make friends, especially with women, who always seemed to be more judgmental. Besides, what if the other women thought she was trying to steal their men? It had happened more than once in the barrio. Someone would take in a relative or friend who needed a place to live, and before long, the man was cheating on his wife with the newcomer.

"You said I could stay with you. I'd like that, if it's still okay," she told Meat.

He looked relieved, and that went a long way toward calming Zara. "Of course it's okay. But remember, I'm not that exciting . . . I'd rather tinker with my computer or make furniture than go out."

"He's not kidding," Ball said. "He's not exactly Mr. Social."

The others all started teasing Meat about his lack of social skills, but he didn't take his gaze from hers. He was intense, but Zara couldn't deny that she liked how he always seemed to know how she was feeling and what she was thinking. No one in her life, besides her parents all those years ago, seemed to understand her so deeply.

After a while, the guys got tired of picking on Meat and slowly began to disperse. Gray left first to go and call Allye and "talk" to his son. Arrow left next, saying he wanted to call his wife and make sure she was all right. Zara got the impression their marriage was recent, and Morgan wasn't quite due yet, but apparently Arrow was extremely protective of her and their unborn child, taking any chance he could to check on them.

Before he left, he nudged the bags he'd dropped on the floor earlier and said, "If anything doesn't fit, let me know and I'll go find you something else."

Zara had forgotten about the clothes he'd gotten for her. For now, she wasn't all that interested in looking at what he might've bought. The T-shirt and sweats she was wearing were extremely comfortable, and since she had no intention of leaving this motel room until she absolutely had to, she was good with what she had on.

The others left not too long after Arrow, saying they'd touch base in the morning to see what the plan was for the day.

That left Zara and Meat alone once more.

"You tired?" he asked.

Zara nodded.

"I'll sleep over here tonight. That bed is all yours," he said with a tilt of his head toward the other bed. "But first . . ." His voice trailed off as he put aside his computer and turned to face her. He sat on the side of the bed, which put her head higher than his. He held his arms out and asked, "Now that I don't smell like vomit anymore, how about that hug?"

He hadn't forgotten. Zara didn't know why she'd told him she hadn't been hugged since she was a kid, but when he'd come out of the shower, she'd actually been looking forward to feeling his arms around her. Then his friends had arrived, and she'd figured he'd forgotten about it.

But looking down at him now, she realized he probably didn't forget much.

Nodding shyly, she moved toward him. His legs were spread, giving her room to step between them. He scooted forward on the bed and slowly wrapped his arms around her waist.

Zara inhaled sharply when Meat laid his head on her chest.

She wasn't sure where to put her hands, so she loosely wrapped her arms around his shoulders. Even though he was sitting, he seemed to surround her. She could feel the heat from his thighs against her own legs, and even his breaths warmed her chest as he breathed in and out. He felt so strong, smelled fresh and clean, and his hair was still a bit damp.

Closing her eyes, Zara lost herself in the gentle touch of another human being. It had been so long since she'd felt this way. Safe. Content.

Fifteen years ago, her life had taken a drastic turn, which had knocked her sideways. It felt as if she'd just gotten another jolt, but this time it was a positive change. Hopefully.

One of Meat's thumbs gently and slowly caressed her back. Even through the cotton of her shirt, it felt like a brand. A good one.

Through some kind of miracle, Zara had managed to avoid being sexually assaulted. She'd lain low, pretending to be a boy, and had fooled just about everyone. She was a virgin in every sense of the word. Hadn't kissed anyone, hadn't been skin to skin with another person. Hadn't even touched herself much.

She hadn't missed it either. Hadn't wanted to get involved with anyone. She'd been too concerned about finding food and shelter to even think about boys or sex.

But standing there with Meat's arms around her, feeling safe, she thought about it for the first time ever.

What would it be like? How would it feel to have Meat's hands on her without anything between his skin and hers? Would he be disgusted by her breasts? Was she too lean, too boyish?

Zara was still feeling confused and unsure when Meat pulled back. His large hands rested on her hips, fingers almost spanning her entire waist.

She didn't understand why she was having these feelings now. Was it because he was helping her? Because she saw him as some sort of savior? She knew he was a good man. She was usually an expert at knowing innately who was good and who wasn't just by looking at them, but her radar could be broken because he'd been treating her so nicely. Maybe the hot shower, food, and shelter had swayed her, kept her from seeing his dangerous side.

As if he could tell she was panicking, Meat gently pushed her back a step and took his hands from her body. He shifted onto the bed and picked up his laptop. Without looking at her, he said, "Go on and climb into bed over there. I'm going to stay up and see what else I can find out about you and your family. We'll talk in the morning, Zara."

Feeling strangely bereft, and ashamed of her thoughts about Meat, Zara merely nodded and headed over to the other bed. She crawled under the clean sheets and lay stiff as a board. She'd offended him, and that hadn't been her intention. She'd just been unclear for a second about his motives. But she realized now he hadn't *had* any motives. He'd merely wanted a hug, and she'd somehow fucked that up.

Sighing, Zara shifted uncomfortably. The mattress was too soft. She was used to sleeping on the hard ground. The pillow put her head at a weird angle and made her neck hurt. But she knew she was supposed to like this. Normal people slept on soft mattresses and used pillows. She'd just have to get used to it.

Turning over on her side, putting her back to Meat, Zara stared at the wall in front of her. She was scared about going back to America. Mags had told her to tell the American the truth and beg him to help her. But now she wasn't so sure. Apparently she had no one waiting for her return. Her grandparents didn't care, and it sounded like her uncle only wanted her money. Lots of people would pretend to be nice to her to get that money. It sounded like hell.

Maybe she would wait until Meat fell asleep, get up, put her own clothes back on, and slip out. Go back to what she knew.

Her mind swirling in confusion and distress, Zara closed her eyes and waited for Meat to turn out the light and go to sleep, so she could decide what to do.

Chapter Thirteen

Meat knew Zara wasn't asleep when he turned off his computer and clicked off the light next to the bed. The hug he'd given her hadn't gone well, and he had no idea why. Something had happened in her head, and he didn't feel as if he had the right to ask.

He also didn't know what had woken him up in the middle of the night, but he knew immediately it had to do with Zara.

He quickly sat up, forcing back a moan at the pain the movement caused in his ribs. Looking over at the bed next to his, he saw it was empty.

He carefully swung his legs off the mattress with the intent of going to the door and chasing her down. The sound that woke him up had to have been the door closing behind her as she snuck out.

But he stopped when he saw the small lump on the floor at his feet. Zara.

She hadn't left.

She'd taken the comforter off the bed and dragged it to the opposite side of *his* bed, as far away from the door as possible. She'd made a pallet on the floor and was curled into a small ball.

His heart still racing from adrenaline, Meat carefully stood. He pulled the comforter from his own bed and got down on his knees. Very slowly, ever aware of his ribs, he lay down behind her, spreading his blanket over both of them. He wrapped an arm around her and cuddled his front to her back.

She didn't move, didn't turn over, but asked quietly, "What are you doing?"

"That should be *my* question," he returned.

"The bed's too soft," she said. "The pillow too."

Meat nodded. Of course it was. When you hadn't used either in fifteen years, it would be extremely weird to try to sleep on a real bed.

"I don't think this is going to work," she said sadly.

"Yes, it is," he countered immediately.

She shook her head. "I don't know how to be Zara Layne. I'm not that ten-year-old girl anymore. I'm Zed. Daniela's assistant, a pickpocket."

Meat tightened his hold around her waist. "You *are* Zara Layne," he insisted.

"I don't know who that is," she whispered.

"She's whoever you want her to be. I know this is hard. And I can't promise that from here on out, all things will get easier. Because they won't. But you don't have to change everything about who you are to be who you think you're *supposed* to be. You're more comfortable sleeping on the floor? Fine. Do that. Who cares? You want to continue to help sick people? We'll look into what it will take for you to volunteer at a hospital or something.

"My point is, you were able to adapt to become Zed. You excelled at it. You'll adapt to this too. And this time, you're not alone. You've got me and the rest of the guys to help you. And their women too. And you'll make new friends in the States."

"You make it sound easy," she replied.

"It's not. It'll be fucking hard," he said. "There will be times you'll wonder why in the hell you ever came back. You'll want to rail at the world and say it's not fair. But you're going to make it. I know."

"How?"

117

"Because you could've walked out that door tonight and disappeared again. You know the barrios way better than I ever could. I never would've found you. But you didn't. You stayed. You came over here and put *me* between the door and yourself. Deep down, you trust me. Even if you don't know why yet.

"I don't know why your grandparents or uncle didn't try harder to find you, and I don't particularly care right this second. What I do care about is that I *did* find you. Or rather, you found *me*. And now that you're here, I'll do whatever it takes to give you back the life that was stolen from you fifteen years ago. You just have to have the strength and courage to want it too."

She didn't say anything, but she didn't disagree with him either.

"We can't leave for another day or two. We'll stay here in the room and just talk. I'll tell you about Colorado Springs, about myself, about my friends' women . . . anything you want. I'll show you how to use the computer, maybe set up an email account for you, and we'll figure out our strategy for dealing with the press. We can even notify the lawyer who's been in charge of your trust and warn him that you've been found, so he knows to start preparing the necessary documents so you can get your money. This might be tough, but this time you aren't alone. Got it?"

She nodded . . . and he felt her scoot back a little to get closer to him.

Meat tightened his arm around her and closed his eyes. The floor bit into his hip, and his ribs definitely weren't happy about sleeping on the hard surface, but too bad. If Zara felt safer down here, he'd suffer through his own aches and pains to comfort her.

A minute or two went by without either of them speaking before Zara tentatively said, "I'm not the best reader. Will you help me understand the legal stuff I'm sure the lawyer will send for me to sign?"

"Yes."

"I'm not stupid," she said firmly. "But because I didn't have the chance to continue my education, there's stuff I don't know."

"Of course you're not stupid," Meat said, appalled that anyone would think that about her. It hadn't crossed his mind even once. She was wise beyond her years. She had street smarts that she'd gained the hard way. By necessity. "And legalese isn't my specialty either. We can get Rex to look at it, or we'll hire another lawyer to translate it for us."

She gave a little huff of a laugh. "I guess I can afford to do that now, can't I?"

Meat smiled. "Yup."

"You know what I want to do?"

"What?"

"Read Harry Potter. I've seen the books in stores and the billboards advertising the series, but I haven't ever had a chance to try to read it myself. I wasn't interested when I was ten, for whatever reason, and I'm sure it'll be over my head, but I want to try."

Meat had never been so impressed with someone. And her words made it all the more clear how much she'd missed out on over the years. "I'll send one of the guys out to find an English copy of book one tomorrow."

She shook her head. "No, I didn't mean right this second, just when we get to America."

"No time like the present," Meat told her. "We've got some time to kill, and believe me, you'll probably get very bored sitting in this room with me. It'll give you something to do other than stress about going back to Colorado and seeing your family again."

"Do you think they'll want to see me?" she whispered.

Meat wasn't sure. It wasn't as if they'd seemed to care that she was missing. But he didn't want to say anything hurtful to Zara either. "I think they'll be curious," he said after a beat. "They'll want you to prove that it's really you, and they'll probably have a lot of questions. So yeah, I think they'll want to see you."

"But will they want to see *me*?" she asked again.

"I don't know," Meat said honestly, understanding what she was asking. She'd be a curiosity. But would her grandparents really care about the person Zara was now? Would they welcome her back with open arms? He had no idea.

"Meat?"

"Yeah?"

"I'd planned on putting my own clothes back on and sneaking out tonight."

Everything within Meat rebelled at the thought, but he forced his muscles to stay relaxed. "When I woke up and saw your bed was empty, I had a feeling that's what you'd done," he admitted. "Why didn't you?"

"I was standing by the bathroom, and I looked back into the room and saw you sleeping. Your computer was on the mattress next to you, and I saw some of the trash from our dinner in the trash can. I thought about all you've done for me, and all that you've done for other women and children who have needed help . . . and I just couldn't do it. But you should know, I still want to. I'm not sure going back is the right choice. I don't think I'll fit in back in America. I don't fit in here either, but at least I know what to expect in Lima."

"If you had left, I would've gone after you," Meat admitted.

"You wouldn't have been able to find me," Zara confirmed with no ego. "I know the barrios too well."

"I know."

Meat felt Zara turn until she was on her back and looking up at him. He hadn't moved and was still on his side. He propped his head on his hand as he stared down at her.

"Then why would you bother looking for me?"

"Because you don't belong here. Your life was taken from you, and it wasn't fair. Because when the adults in your life, and the Peruvian police, should've turned over every rock to find you fifteen years ago, they didn't put in the effort. You're *worth* the effort, Zara. And . . ." He paused, not sure he should say what he was thinking, but deciding to throw caution to the wind. "And because even though I've only been in your life for a few days, I know, deep in my bones, that you're special. You're going to do great things, Zara Layne. I just know it."

He couldn't read what she was thinking; she simply looked up at him without blinking.

"And," Meat went on, "I like you, remember? You've snuck under my guard that I usually have up. I've helped rescue hundreds of women, but there's something about you that's different. You fascinate me, and I want to get to know you better. I want to know everything about you."

"I'm nobody special," she whispered.

"And that's why you *are*," Meat countered. "Most true heroes don't think they're anyone special either. Thomas Edison, Martin Luther King, Neil Armstrong, Anne Frank, Harriet Tubman . . . just to name a few."

Meat brought his free hand up and gently brushed her hair off her forehead. He couldn't see her very clearly, as it was the middle of the night, but dim light coming from a lamppost in the parking lot outside the window was enough to just make her out. He recalled how smooth her skin had been after her shower. Washing the dirt and grime off had made her literally glow, and he couldn't help but touch her now.

"I'm a true believer that everything happens for a reason. I don't know what the reason was behind your parents' being killed. Or you having to live the kind of life you've lived up until now. But I do know one thing—you've *already* done great things."

She shook her head. "No, I haven't."

"What about that woman at Daniela's? You probably saved both her life and the life of her baby. And those little kids who you stopped to talk to when we were on our way back to the barrio? And me . . . you and your friends saved me. I'm sure there are hundreds of other lives you've touched down here, and I have no doubt you'll do the same once we get back to Colorado."

Zara didn't say anything, simply turned back on her side in front of him. Meat relaxed against her once more. Neither said a word for a long while, until finally she asked, "Were you really going to come after me?"

"Yes," he said simply.

They didn't speak again. And it wasn't until Meat felt her body completely relax and heard her long, slow breaths, indicating she'd fallen asleep, that he allowed himself to close his own eyes.

He'd come close to losing her tonight. They both knew it. *He* knew she was strong enough to endure what was to come, but he hoped she'd figure it out somewhere along the way as well.

Chapter Fourteen

Three days later, Zara sat nervously in her seat next to Meat as they made their descent into Colorado Springs Airport. It had taken two days for Rex to get an American passport delivered to their motel. She had no idea what kind of strings he'd had to pull in order to get it done, but he had.

She'd learned a bit more about the mysterious handler for the Mountain Mercenaries, and although he'd piqued her interest, she was too busy thinking about other things to give him too much thought.

He'd told her the first thing she had to do when she got to Colorado was provide a DNA sample to prove she was the missing Zara Layne. She'd been surprised that she hadn't needed to do it to get her passport, but apparently Rex had some magic and managed to get the documents without that vital proof. She wasn't going to question it.

Meat had been in touch with the lawyer in charge of her trust fund, and the man had been understandably shocked. He'd refused to give any specifics to Meat, Rex, or Zara until he received proof beyond a reasonable doubt that she was who she claimed to be.

Arrow had done an amazing job of picking out clothes for her, and after he'd badgered her into telling him what she liked and didn't like from the first batch, he'd gone out and purchased a suitcase and clothes to fill it. She now had enough jeans, long- and short-sleeve T-shirts, underwear, bras, and socks to last her for years if she'd still been on the streets.

She'd also learned that Arrow thought he was some sort of comedian, because most of the T-shirts he'd purchased were the type tourists would buy. Shirts that said I LOVE PERU and one that had a llama on it, with a man dressed in traditional Incan garb, with the word PERU in big letters beneath them. Zara had never seen a llama in her life, and after she'd told Arrow, he'd merely smiled.

In fact, all the guys had been amazingly wonderful. Meat had obviously told Gray about her desire to read Harry Potter, because he'd shown up the day after her admission with a brand-new paperback copy of the first book in the series. Zara hadn't held a brand-new book since she was ten. The pages were crisp, and the cover was pristine. It was very hard reading for her, but she was doing her best to stick with it, and when Meat had seen her struggling, he'd offered to help explain any word she didn't know.

Zara had learned all about the women waiting back in Colorado . . . and was intimidated as hell by them. While the guys hadn't shared any specific details about their ordeals, it was obvious they'd each gone through hell. Zara wasn't so sure about meeting Everly, in particular. Police officers weren't high on her list of people she liked to associate with, but she couldn't imagine that Ball would be with someone who was corrupt, like almost all the cops she'd known down in Lima, so she'd do her best to give her the benefit of the doubt. Gray couldn't wait to meet his son for the first time, and Zara had heard so much about baby Darby that even *she* was anxious to meet the little guy.

But the person she most wanted to meet was Morgan. Her story seemed the most like her own, and Zara had so many questions for her.

When they'd left Lima, she'd been concerned about how in the world they were going to get her past the soldiers who were "looking after" Meat's team. The Brigade members stationed outside the motel had taken to parking in the lot, near the team's van. Maybe suspicious that the men hadn't left Lima immediately after finding Meat.

Whatever the reason, the team could no longer have just waltzed out of the motel with Zara. The Brigade would've noticed a strange woman with them. And they would've asked questions. Lots of questions. And while she hadn't been doing anything wrong, she'd still wanted to avoid the military at all costs.

The entire team had had a conversation the day before they'd planned to leave, brainstorming ways to sneak her out. It had been Zara herself who'd suggested hiding in a suitcase. Meat had vetoed the idea straight out, but the others had seemed to consider it.

In the end, it had been her choice—take a chance on the soldiers questioning who she was, where she came from, and why she was with the Mountain Mercenaries, or hide in a suitcase until they were in the van and on their way to the airport.

It had been an easy decision.

Zara had never been so glad for her small stature as she was when she'd been zipped into the rolling suitcase Ball had purchased. She'd supposed it wasn't any more claustrophobic than what Meat must have experienced in the back of the trailer she'd used to transport him to and from the barrio. It hadn't been comfortable, but it hadn't been entirely uncomfortable either.

She'd heard Meat and the others saying goodbye to a few of the soldiers and couldn't help but be thrilled she was getting one over on them.

Gray had placed the suitcase on top of their other bags in the small space in the back of the van, and the second they were safely away from their escorts—who'd been so glad to see them go they hadn't bothered to follow them to the airport—Gray and Ro had lifted the suitcase over the back of the third seat, opened it, and helped her out.

After that, getting through security and customs had been a piece of cake with her brand-new passport.

They'd flown first class to Dallas–Fort Worth, and even though she'd been nervous to go through customs in America, no one took a second glance at her. It was all somewhat surreal. She was used to being scrutinized carefully, mostly by shop owners who were afraid she was up to no good, so to be totally ignored was a novel feeling. One she liked.

But as they taxied toward the small Colorado Springs airport at the end of their journey, Meat looked out the window and swore.

"What?" Zara asked.

Instead of answering, he reached between the seats and poked Ball on the shoulder and pointed out the window.

"Meat, what's wrong?" Zara asked again.

He looked at her, and she didn't like the concern she saw in his eyes. "We thought we'd have a little more time before we'd have to deal with this," he told her.

"With what?"

"Look," he said, pointing to the window.

Zara turned and looked, and at first she had no idea what he wanted her to see. There was a large mountain peak that still had a bit of snow at the top that was absolutely breathtaking. She'd gotten so used to the barrios and slums of Lima that the sight of the beautiful mountains in the background let her know without a doubt that she was truly out of Peru once and for all.

Then she let her gaze wander lower . . . and saw what looked like dozens of trucks and cars, most emblazoned with numbers and letters, lined up along the road leading to the building they were taxiing toward.

She turned to look back at Meat and shrugged.

"It's the news media, Zar. I have no idea how they got word that you'd be here today, but they have."

Her eyes widened. They'd talked a lot about the media, and she wasn't sure she could deal with them right now. She wasn't ready.

She'd put on the nicest outfit Arrow had brought her, khaki pants with a short-sleeve dark-purple blouse. She was wearing a bra, which oddly felt more constricting than the band she'd been using to flatten her chest for years. She wasn't used to looking down and seeing her boobs, but she didn't have a reason to hide her gender anymore. It was scary, but she was very slowly getting used to it.

She still felt frumpy and dirty after traveling all day, though. Which was ironic, because she'd gone months without a shower when she'd been in the barrio, and just that morning, she'd taken another forty-five-minute shower and soaped herself clean at least four times. So she was in no way dirty like she'd been for fifteen years, but thinking about facing cameras and reporters made her cringe.

"We won't be talking to them today," Gray said from the seat behind her and Meat.

Zara had been so lost in her thoughts she jumped, and then turned to look at him. She felt Meat put his hand on her knee to help steady her and was surprised at how much his touch made her feel better.

"We need the proof of your DNA before you can think of making any kind of statement. The last thing you need to deal with is skepticism from the press. The FBI agreed to come out to Meat's house to interview you. They'll be waiting there for us. As we talked about, they'll take a swab inside your mouth to get your DNA, and they should have the results in about a day or two. You'll tell them your story, and that will be that. Okay?"

Zara nodded. "But what about them?" she asked, gesturing to the window.

"I should be surprised that somehow they found out about your return, but I'm not," Gray said. "We'll stay in the plane and be the last to leave. Black is on the phone with Rex, and he's already arranged for a car to pick us up. We'll walk by the reporters and just refuse to make a statement. It'll be fine."

"Why wouldn't he make arrangements for us to bug out a back door so she didn't have to face them at all?" Meat asked grumpily.

"We talked about this," Gray reminded his friend. "The more secretive we are about her return, the crazier they'll get. Zara needs to be seen. She doesn't need to smile and wave or anything, but simply seeing her won't actually be a bad thing. We'll just not say anything until we have proof in hand that she's the Layne heiress."

Zara looked from Meat's scowl back to Gray. She glanced in front of her and saw Arrow and Ball gazing back at her from between the seats. Across the aisle, Black was looking in her direction, and she had both Gray's and Ro's undivided attention from behind her as well.

She was surrounded by men who could certainly protect themselves with no problem, and who she was pretty sure would do the same for her. And they believed her. Not once had any of them expressed any doubt that she was exactly who she said she was. It was unbelievable, and it made her want to cry . . . even though she never cried.

"Ball and I will make sure everyone knows there may be a press conference at a later date, but for right now, Zara just needs some time to acclimate to her new situation," Gray said.

The pilot made an announcement that they were nearing the gate and to please not remove their seat belts until the plane had come to a complete stop and the seat belt light had been turned off. Zara turned back around to face forward and looked over at Meat. He hadn't taken his eyes off her.

"You okay?" he asked quietly. "Because if you'd rather, I'll call Rex and tell him to figure out a way to get you out of here without having to see *any* reporters."

Zara swallowed hard. He meant that. She could tell. "I'm okay," she said quietly. "I'm not ready to talk to anyone yet, but I can manage to walk by them. I think."

"Strong as fuck," he muttered, then moved his hand until he'd intertwined his fingers with hers.

Zara had no idea what was to come in the next ten minutes, but she knew Meat would be by her side . . . and somehow that made it less scary.

After the airplane door was opened, Zara sat quietly while the rest of the passengers filed out. Then Meat stood, and she grabbed her small backpack with her *Harry Potter* book and the snacks Meat had packed for her, just in case she got hungry. She wondered briefly what would happen with her suitcase, but figured Gray or one of the others would take care of it for her.

Ro and Ball went first and quickly disappeared in the crowd once they were off the plane. They were going to make sure a car was waiting for them, as Rex had promised. Meat had dropped her hand when they'd gotten up from their seats, and she missed the feeling of his large hand around hers. She didn't like being the center of attention at the best of times, and knew walking out in front of all the cameras was going to suck.

"You'll stay between us no matter what," Gray told her. "If anyone asks, we'll say we're your bodyguards. All you have to do is walk, okay?"

Zara nodded. She felt even tinier when the four men surrounded her. She almost wished they could hide her in the suitcase like they had when they'd left the motel in Lima, but she knew she'd have to face the press sooner or later and she'd only be delaying the inevitable. Meat was behind her, and every now and then she felt his hand rest on her back to help steer her, since she couldn't really see where she was going with Arrow at her front.

Once they started to approach the security area between the airline gates and those who didn't have tickets, they began to walk faster. Zara's heart pounded in her chest, and she did her best to look confident and sure of herself, when inside she just wanted to run and hide and not deal with this.

The second the reporters saw her, the noise in the small airport became almost deafening. Reporters yelled out questions, crowding in on them until Black, Meat, Gray, and Arrow were literally pressed up against her.

Are you really Zara Layne?

Why did you wait so long to come forward?

Do you know how much money you're worth?

Did you see your parents get killed?

Why did you stay hidden for so long?

Who helped you hide?

Were you raped?

What happened fifteen years ago?

Zara flinched as the questions kept coming. They were offensive as well as ignorant. It wasn't as if she'd been *hiding*. She would've loved for someone to find her and get her out of the barrio all those years ago.

And for someone to flat-out ask if she'd seen her parents get murdered? What kind of question was that?

Someone near them pushed forward a little too hard, and Black stumbled, knocking into her. Zara would've fallen sideways, but Meat's hand was there to steady her. When she was walking normally again, he didn't take his hand from her waist. Zara did her best to keep the frown off her face, but she wasn't sure how well she'd succeeded. She couldn't do anything other than look at the floor and hold on to her backpack for dear life.

After what was probably two minutes—that seemed like an hour—the doors to the airport swooshed open, and they were outside. The air was chillier and drier than Zara was used to, and it felt both strange and wonderful at the same time. A black SUV was waiting at the curb, and Arrow didn't hesitate. He wrenched open the door and scooted into the back seat. Zara was hustled inside after him, with Meat close at her heels. Ro was already in the front passenger seat, and the second the door was shut behind Meat, the driver took off, almost running over a cameraman who had stood in front of the car to get one last shot of Zara.

"You okay?" Meat asked.

Zara nodded, her mouth too dry to speak.

"That wasn't too bad," Ro said after a beat.

Zara stared at him in disbelief.

He turned around and chuckled at the look on her face. "Remind me to tell you about the press conference my Chloe had to participate in one of these days."

"No," Meat said immediately.

Ro simply grinned.

Meat leaned close and peered into Zara's eyes. "Seriously, are you okay?"

She nodded again and licked her lips. "Do people really think I was *hiding* all these years? That I didn't want to be found and rescued?"

He pressed his lips together. "Some probably do, yes, but they don't know you. Once you eventually tell your story, their attitudes will change."

Zara swallowed hard and tried to calm her racing heart. That had sucked. She definitely didn't like to be in the spotlight and dreaded having to do anything like that again.

"It'll be all right," Meat said softly, picking up her hand and threading his fingers with hers once more. "If we do a press conference, it'll be much less frenzied than that. There will still be lots of cameras, but they won't be chasing you down. You'll have more control. Promise."

She felt better that he'd said *if* there was a press conference, but she wasn't stupid. She knew she'd have to make a statement sooner or later. Oh, she could probably have someone else get in front of the camera for her, but she had a feeling if she didn't face the reporters, they'd hound her for months, maybe even years. It was better to just answer their questions so she could get on with her life.

They drove for quite a while before the SUV turned down a dirt road almost hidden among the trees alongside the country road they'd been on. They were jostled on the road for a while before Arrow griped, "You need to get this shit paved, Meat."

He chuckled and said, "I get fewer random people coming down here, with it being so shitty."

Zara hadn't realized they were on a driveway until they approached a clearing in the trees, and suddenly a house appeared in front of the car. It wasn't huge, but it wasn't a shack either.

"You live here?" she asked Meat as the SUV stopped.

"Home sweet home," he replied, then turned to get out. There were three other cars already parked in front of the house, making the area crowded with vehicles. And when an SUV carrying the other three members of the Mountain Mercenaries pulled up behind them, Zara just shook her head.

The second Meat got out of the car, men began exiting the other vehicles. They were all wearing dark suits, and even Zara could tell they were FBI. Meat hadn't let go of her hand, so she followed him closely as he ignored the men and walked up onto the small front porch. The men in suits followed, but Meat held up a hand, stopping them.

"Give us ten minutes," he said. Then, without waiting for an answer, he put a key in the lock and opened his door. He towed Zara inside and shut the door behind them. Then he went over to a panel on the wall and punched some of the buttons. He came right back to her and took her hand once more.

"I thought I was supposed to talk to them," Zara said softly.

"You are, and you will. But you need a little time to decompress after the airport. I thought I'd show you my home, and you could use the restroom and wash your hands and face before you have to tell your story again."

It was thoughtful. Very thoughtful, and Zara was more than grateful. The airport scene had rattled her, and she felt way out of her element. Having even ten minutes to not have to worry about saying or doing the wrong thing felt like heaven.

"Thank you," she told Meat.

"Come on. It's not huge, but it's home," he said, then proceeded to lead her through his house.

The bottom floor was completely open. The kitchen was off to the left as they entered the big room. The appliances were white, and there was an island with a long counter separating the kitchen from the sitting area. There were three barstools pushed in, and she wondered if Meat had made them himself.

"The kitchen could use some updating," Meat told her. "But I kind of like the look of the white appliances instead of stainless steel."

Zara had no idea what he was talking about. To her, the kitchen was perfect. It had been so long since she'd even been *in* a kitchen, it all looked outrageously expensive and over the top to her. She vaguely remembered the kitchen in the house she'd grown up in, but that had been so long ago she didn't recall too many details.

"Come on, let me show you the rest," Meat said, turning toward the large room behind them.

There was a huge sectional couch in the middle of the space, flanked by a big armchair, with a few other wooden chairs sprinkled around the perimeter of the room. A bookcase stuffed with books sat in a corner, and a huge television hung on the wall above a fireplace. Zara was immediately drawn to the bookcase, and she let go of Meat to walk toward it.

Books were the one thing she'd missed the most over the years. She'd been able to scrounge a few, but they were in Spanish, and the pages were usually half-missing or wet. She reverently ran her fingers over the spines of the books. She didn't recognize any of the titles, but she could almost imagine the wonderful stories contained within.

She closed her eyes, and a memory flashed through her mind of sitting on her dad's lap as he read to her. The story was long since lost, but the feeling of comfort and safety made her heart ache.

Hands landed on her shoulders, and Zara leaned back against Meat instinctually. It was surprising, but she felt that same comfort and safety around him. She knew it was probably because of what he'd done for her, and it was unlikely he'd ever feel anything other than a professional kind of concern for her, but she took comfort from him being there with her at that moment.

"You like books."

It wasn't a question. Zara nodded.

"Then we'll have to see about getting the rest of the Harry Potter books for you to read, as well as whatever else strikes your fancy."

"I liked reading when I was younger," Zara admitted.

"And if the way you've been going through *Harry Potter* is any indication, you *still* like reading," Meat said.

Zara nodded again and forced herself to turn away from the bookcase. She followed Meat through the house, almost overwhelmed by the size. This house would be a mansion back in Peru, and she couldn't help but think about how much Mags, Teresa, Bonita, and the others would love it.

Feeling sad that she'd probably never again see the women who had been her friends and helped keep her sane, she did her best to pay attention to what Meat was saying.

They went up the stairs to the second floor, and he showed her the master bedroom, the two guest rooms, and the two bathrooms. She asked him about the furniture, the beds and dressers, and he admitted that he'd made most of it. He was so nonchalant about it, but Zara couldn't help but be impressed with how pretty and sturdy everything was.

She didn't want their tour to end, but when they stood in the hallway outside the master bedroom, she knew it was time.

"Feeling better?" Meat asked.

Zara nodded. She was. He'd successfully taken her mind off the craziness at the airport. Of course, now she had to tell her story again, and probably answer more questions than Meat and his friends had asked.

"You're safe here," Meat said quietly. "Don't let them make you feel as if you aren't."

"If they don't believe me, will they take me away and arrest me?" she asked.

"No!" Meat said forcefully. Then, taking a deep breath, he said in a calmer tone, "No, they aren't going to take you anywhere. You're Zara Layne, and you haven't done anything wrong. They'll probably tell you not to leave the state until your DNA test comes back, but that's about all they can do."

Zara chuckled. "Where would I go? I mean, I grew up here and now I'm back, but I don't know anyone outside of Colorado. I don't have a car or a driver's license. I'm not going anywhere anytime soon."

"We haven't talked much about your childhood, have we?" Meat asked gently. "None of us wanted to bring up any hurtful memories."

"I had a good childhood," Zara admitted. "I haven't thought about it in a long time, blocked it out, but it doesn't hurt to think about it, now that I'm back here. I know now that we had money, but back then, I didn't think much about it."

"And you grew up in Denver?" Meat asked.

Zara knew they should go back downstairs and let the FBI investigators and Meat's friends come in, but she was enjoying this. Just the two of them talking. She had a feeling he probably was well aware of exactly where her childhood house was, since he'd done so much looking into her past, back in the motel in Lima. She nodded. "I think it was the Hilltop area back then, but I'm not sure what it's called now."

"It's still called that. I saw that your house was sold, and the proceeds from it and everything your relatives didn't want went back into the trust."

Zara sighed. It sucked that she didn't have anything to remind her of her parents. Not even a picture. But hopefully she could get something from her grandparents or her uncle. Surely they would've kept some knickknacks from her childhood home, wouldn't they?

"Sorry," Meat said, brushing his fingers against her biceps in a barely there caress before dropping his hand. "I didn't mean to bring up something so painful."

"It's not that. It's just . . . I feel kinda like it happened to someone else. I'm a different person than I was as a kid, and I keep thinking I should be more upset than I am."

"You've lived more of your life as Zed the Peruvian boy than you have as Zara," Meat told her. "Cut yourself some slack."

They heard a knock on the door downstairs, and Zara sighed. Looked like their time was up. "Meat?" she blurted before she could chicken out.

"Yeah?"

"I know I messed it up before, but do you think maybe you could . . . that I could have a hug before we go downstairs?"

"You didn't mess up anything, Zar," Meat told her, then opened his arms.

Without hesitation, Zara stepped into them.

This hug felt a lot different from their first one. Mainly because Meat was now standing, and he towered over her. Zara's head rested on *his* chest this time, and she could feel the steady thumping of his heart under her cheek as he held her close.

Neither said a word, but slowly, she felt the tension drain from her limbs.

It was unbelievable how much her life had changed in a week, but the constant throughout it all was this man.

Knowing she was getting too attached to Meat, that there was no way he could feel anything more than pity for the uneducated woman he'd found, Zara forced herself to let go and step back.

"Thanks," she said softly. "I needed that."

"Me too," Meat told her. "Come on, we better get down there before they get anxious enough to crawl through my windows."

For a second she thought he was serious, but then he smiled at her, and she chuckled. She wasn't worried about the DNA test; she knew she was who she claimed to be. But she was afraid of what came *after* that. She couldn't live in Meat's house with him forever, no matter how appealing that might sound. She had to figure out what to do with the rest of her life, and that part was overwhelming.

Deciding she could only take things one day at a time, the same attitude she'd adopted in the barrio, Zara followed behind Meat as they went down the stairs. The first step in getting her independence back was to talk to the FBI and tell them whatever they wanted to know. After that? She'd have to wait and see what happened.

Chapter Fifteen

Meat sat in one of the many chairs he kept around his living room for when the team and their women came to visit, stiff as a board as he listened to the FBI agents question Zara. He was so proud of her. She'd seemed so fragile in his arms, but after two hours of telling her story to the agents, she didn't even look tired or agitated in the least.

He knew it was all a facade. He could see her hands clenched together in her lap and the way she subtly shifted in her chair.

He knew the agents were aware of it, too, but they didn't seem to care. Probably too used to dealing with hardened criminals. Zara wasn't under investigation, and the FBI was simply trying to gather as much information as they could about a missing American and a decades-old murder case. But in Meat's opinion, they could have been more sensitive to her situation.

The first thing the agents had done was take the DNA swab from her cheek. The agent who'd swabbed her had packaged it up and left immediately, probably to expedite the processing at their downtown Denver office. Meat was glad. The sooner everyone knew for a fact who she was, the sooner she could get on with her life.

But Meat already knew who she was. She was Zara Layne. He wasn't an expert, but even he could tell from looking at the picture of a ten-year-old Zara that she and the woman sitting at his kitchen table were one and the same. They had the same blue eyes, the same little mole near the mouth. Her nose was still shaped the same, and every piece of information she'd told the agents about what she could remember of her life in Denver matched what he'd been able to find online . . . right down to the name of her elementary school, her teachers' names, and some of the kids she'd been friends with at the time.

Gray and the other Mountain Mercenaries had left a short while ago, except for Black, who'd refused to leave, since he'd been injured in the same incident as Meat had. They'd both told the FBI what they remembered about the attack in the barrio, and how if Zara and her friends hadn't interceded, they might both be dead.

"Why didn't you try to get help at any point in the last fifteen years?" one of the FBI agents asked—for the second time. He'd started out the interview with that very question, and Zara had told them calmly that she'd tried, but she was so young she hadn't known where to go or who to ask.

Zara had been doing so well up to that point, but he could tell that being asked the question again, as if the agent was accusing her of not trying hard enough to get help, broke the calmness she'd been trying to hold on to.

She'd been so patient, answering all their questions as well as she could. She'd even described, in as much detail as she could remember, what it had been like watching her parents get murdered. How she'd felt when she'd been hauled off and held tightly with a hand over her mouth as the killers had stuffed her into a car and driven away. How even when she didn't understand their words, she'd understood they would come back and kill *her* if she told anyone what happened.

But with that question from the agent, something they'd already asked, Zara was done.

She pushed back her chair and stood. She looked each of the agents in the eye, then said, "Why didn't I ask for help? I already told you this—I was *ten*. And I *did* ask for help, but no one could understand me, and frankly, they didn't care. When all you're worried about is finding food to feed your family and trying not to get killed, it's hard to give a crap about a lost little girl.

"I've told you everything I can remember. I *am* Zara Layne. Right now, I don't care if you don't believe me. *I* know who I am. And I'm tired. If you have any *new*, not-quite-so-offensive questions to ask me once my identity is proven, you know where to find me. But for now, I think I'm going to go upstairs to rest."

And with that, she lifted her chin and walked out of the dining room and up the stairs.

Meat wanted to give her a slow clap of approval as she left, but figured that wouldn't exactly be appropriate.

The agents weren't thrilled she'd ended their interview so abruptly, but since Zara wasn't under arrest, they had no choice but to pack up their things and leave. Of course, they gave Meat one last warning that Zara wasn't to leave Colorado Springs until her identity was verified.

After they'd left, Black said, "I like her. A lot."

Meat nodded. "At first glance, she seems fragile. Very young and scared to death. But deep down, she's strong as hell."

Black nodded. "Those men who attacked us weren't fucking around," he said, slightly changing the subject.

"No, they weren't," Meat agreed. He recalled how the mob in the barrio had known exactly where to hit to quickly render him unable to fight back. And how fast they'd stripped him of his weapons and his clothes. It was almost unreal.

"If they'd gotten ahold of us a second time, we wouldn't be here today," Black said.

Meat nodded.

"I didn't have time to think about much while it was happening, but when Gray and the others came and got me, and I came to, the first person I thought about was Harlow. How devastated she'd be if something happened to me."

Meat stared at his friend, wondering where he was going with this conversation. He didn't have to wait long to find out.

"I'm thinking about asking Rex to consider only stateside missions from here on out."

Meat was momentarily floored. But . . . what his friend was saying made sense.

"Gray missed the birth of his son. It was only because of Zara and her friends that you were found and I wasn't killed. During the search for you, we couldn't properly question anyone because we couldn't speak the language. The team has had some close calls before, and I don't think anyone thought too much about them. It was just part of being a soldier and a Mountain Mercenary. But now that we've all got someone waiting for us at home, I think things are different."

Meat nodded. He was still the odd man out. He wasn't married and didn't have a significant other, but he knew as well as anyone how close he'd come to death. "Have you talked to the others yet?" he asked.

Black shook his head. "No, but I'm thinking they won't argue. I know Arrow is worried about Morgan's pregnancy. She's been having some spotting and pains lately, even though she's still got about five weeks to go. Ro is worried about Chloe's brother's lowlife friends maybe deciding she would make a good target, even after all this time. Ball's got both Everly and her sister to worry about, and, of course, I'm always concerned about Harlow.

"I just think it's time. None of us are getting any younger, and one of these days our luck is going to run out. Sticking to domestic missions doesn't mean we won't be in danger, but honestly, I think we've got better resources to assist us, and if something happens back at home, we can more easily get here."

"If you're asking me first since I don't have a significant other, I'm in," Meat said. "After this last mission in Peru, and realizing how corrupt it seems everyone around us was, it's lucky we all came home with as few injuries as we did."

Black sighed in relief. "I'll talk to the others. See where they stand before we bring it up with Rex."

"You think he's gonna fire us all?" Meat asked, only halfway kidding.

"No. I think he's tired too," Black said. "His wife has been missing for a decade, and I think he's finally coming to the realization that she's well and truly gone. It sucks . . . but it's time to turn our attention closer to home."

"I agree," Meat said with a nod.

"Good. Now I'm gonna get home. I know Harlow is anxious to see for herself that I'm all right," Black said.

"You need any kind of painkiller before you go?"

"Naw. I took a couple not too long ago." Black glanced up the stairs, then back to Meat. "Tread lightly with her," he said quietly. "Even though she seemed to tell the agents everything she went through, I have a feeling there's a lot she left out."

"Yeah, I agree. But even if she didn't, I don't think we'd ever truly understand what she went through anyway. She was ten, Black. *Ten.* Practically a baby. The fact that she's alive and not needing to be institutionalized is a small miracle."

"Just don't forget that she's *not* a baby. She's a grown woman, and wise way beyond her years. In a lot of ways, she seems more mature than any of us. I'll call you soon about having that talk with Rex."

Meat nodded and gave Black a chin lift. After he left, Meat locked the door behind him and headed for the stairs. He'd clean up the glasses and miscellaneous items from the agents' visit later. Now, he wanted to check on Zara.

If he was honest with himself, he expected her to be in tears when he saw her. Extremely upset and emotional after her ordeal with the FBI.

When he knocked on the guest room door and opened it upon hearing her tell him to come in, he saw that she *was* upset and emotional, but she definitely wasn't crying. Zara was pacing the guest room with quick, angry strides. Back and forth from the window to the door, then back again.

When she saw him staring at her, she asked gruffly, "Are they gone?"

"Yeah, Zar, they're gone."

"Good," she spat. "I can't believe them! I mean, I understand they need to know my story to make sure I'm not lying, but for a second there, I thought they were going to take me to jail or something! I'm not the one in the wrong here, Meat. I'm the victim—although I hate that word. I prefer 'survivor.' I *survived* what happened to me."

Meat had never seen her so worked up before. So angry, so . . . forceful. "I know," he agreed quietly.

It was as if he hadn't spoken. "Seriously, how *dare* they question my actions? Do you know how many times I tried to get help? A lot! People either didn't understand me or didn't care. They had their own issues, and taking on a ten-year-old kid who was so obviously out of her element wasn't something they had the time or energy to worry about. I would've been an extra mouth to feed. No one could afford that.

"One day, not too long after I ended up in that first barrio, I decided I was going to walk back to Miraflores. I set out, determined to get to safety. I walked all day. *All day*, Meat. My feet were nothing but blisters on top of blisters because the cute little dress shoes I'd been wearing the night my life changed weren't exactly meant for hiking.

"I don't know where I ended up, but it wasn't anywhere near the 'nice' part of the city. I turned around, hoping to find my way back to that hole in the wall where I'd been hiding, but I was lost. *So* lost. It was getting dark, and I was scared. I saw a few people, but instead of taking pity on a poor little white girl, obviously out of her element, they made lewd comments. Said if I took care of *them*, they'd take care of me. One man even pulled his pants down and started rubbing his dick while trying to convince me to come closer! I'd never even *seen* a naked man before and was scared out of my mind!

"So I ran. With no clue what direction I was going, I just ran. I lost my shoes somewhere. Even though they didn't fit and were hurting my feet, *that* was the thing that finally broke me. I found a car and crawled under it, curling up next to the front tire, trying to get warm and hiding from everyone who wanted to hurt me."

"Jesus, Zara," Meat said, wanting to hold her. To comfort the poor, scared, lost little girl she'd once been. But at that moment, she looked like the last thing she wanted was a hug. She was *pissed*—and she looked glorious in her anger.

"Those FBI agents had no right to make assumptions like they did! They had no sympathy for the scared kid I once was; they only saw a woman who may or may not be lying. I know they have to consider it a possibility, because of the amount of money my parents left me, but it felt like they were condemning me for the actions of a *child*. It wasn't fair, and if that's how others are going to see me, I don't want anything to do with them!"

Zara was panting as if she'd just run a mile and glaring at him so fiercely, Meat couldn't help but be impressed. "You don't have to do anything you don't want to," he told her calmly.

She raised an eyebrow skeptically.

"I mean it," he said. "You don't want to give a press conference, you don't have to. Once the DNA results come back and prove you're exactly who you say you are, the FBI or cops will have no reason to talk to you again. And even if they want to, it's *your* decision if you want to give them another chance. You can hole up here in my house and ignore the world, if that's what you want."

Some of the anger went out of her rigid stance and expression, and her hands dropped from her hips. "Hiding sounds like heaven. Why are you being so nice to me? Is it because I saved you? I don't need your pity or gratitude," she said, still a little angry.

"I definitely don't pity you, but you have my gratitude whether you want it or not. You saved me. And I'm in awe of you, Zara. You're a survivor. A warrior. And I respect the hell out of you. When I think back to when I was ten, I know for a fact I couldn't have done what you did. All I was interested in was cartoons and food."

She swallowed hard and sighed. "You probably wouldn't have let the men take you away in the first place."

Meat shook his head and took a cautious step toward her. When she didn't back away, he took another. Then another, and he kept going until he was standing right in front of her. He gently put a finger under her chin and raised her head until she was looking him in the eyes. "You impress me so much, Zara. You went through something so horrifying and unbelievable, and yet . . . here you are. Standing strong, kicking ass and taking names. Don't let the insensitive questions and remarks from others who don't understand—will *never* be able to understand—get under your skin. You be *you*."

"What if I don't know who I am?" she asked softly.

"Then you take all the time you need to figure it out," Meat told her. "Now . . . you hungry?"

She nodded slightly.

"Then how about we go downstairs, and I'll make you an omelet or something?"

"Can you . . . Will you teach *me* how to do it?" she asked. "I obviously haven't had a chance to learn how to cook in the last decade or so . . . and I don't think cooking raw meat on a stick over a fire counts."

Meat refused to feel sorry for her. If she could laugh at herself, then the least he could do was laugh with her. "That might come in handy if we're camping, but I'd be happy to teach you what I know. Although, Harlow might be a better teacher. She's a chef."

Zara looked horrified. "No! I'd feel so inadequate next to her."

Meat shook his head. "She's a very good teacher, and she'd never make you feel deficient or bad about your skills or lack thereof."

Zara shook her head. "No. I want *you* to teach me."

Meat couldn't help but feel touched by her words. He shouldn't. He was just the most familiar thing to her right now. At some point, she'd realize that there were a lot more people out there way more qualified to help acclimate her to her brand-new world, but for the moment, he was enjoying it just being the two of them.

Without asking, and without thought, Meat pulled Zara into his arms. She didn't struggle or pull away, merely put her cheek on his chest and curled her arms around his waist. They stood like that for a minute or two before he reluctantly pulled away. "Come on," he coaxed, taking her hand in his. "Time for your first cooking lesson."

Zara Layne. Jesus. It was hard to believe she was alive. Everyone had assumed she'd been killed years ago, though her body had never been found.

She'd been kind of a mousy little kid. Not likely to take the lead in anything, content to hang back and follow. She wasn't pretty, but wasn't hideous either. She blended into the background.

Back then, her parents had plenty of money, but you couldn't tell to look at them. Most of the time they'd acted like it wasn't a big deal, and it probably wasn't—for *them*. When Zara had wanted a new toy, she'd gotten it. When she'd wanted a new dress, her parents had bought it for her.

Not everyone had been so lucky.

The person watched the news footage of Zara getting into a big fancy SUV, then talking head after talking head speculating on the Layne fortune . . . and couldn't help getting more annoyed by the second. More upset about how unfair life was.

Zara Layne wasn't the only one who'd had a hard life, but *she* was the one who'd ended up with a shit ton of money.

And why? She'd done nothing to deserve it. Any idiot could get lost in a foreign country. Yeah, her parents had been killed . . . big fucking deal. Everyone in the world had shit happen to them. Why was *she* so damn special?

She wasn't. But . . .

Maybe there was a way to get access to some of that money. Somehow?

It would take a little bit of time, some patience. And hopefully the men surrounding Zara on the news footage wouldn't be an issue . . .

But it didn't matter. Manipulating people—or outright scaring them—to do what you wanted them to do really wasn't all that hard.

Smiling, the person looked around the shitty apartment and thought about how great it would be to leave it behind. Not having to worry if the hot-water heater would work in the morning would be heaven.

Or wonder if a damn turf war would break out in the parking lot at any second.

Mexico . . . that sounded like the perfect place to live. Sun and fun and cheap drugs . . .

It would take some time to set up a plan, and there was no guarantee it would work, but with a little ingenuity and some patience, Zara Layne's money—at least some of it—could be used for something better than what *she* probably had planned for it.

Chapter Sixteen

Zara woke up on the floor of the room she'd been staying in at Meat's house and stared up at the ceiling. She still couldn't get comfortable sleeping on a mattress. It was nice, however, to have a clean carpet under her instead of the hard-packed dirt she was used to.

It was so quiet it was eerie. Life in the barrio had never been silent. There were always people talking, laughing, shouting; trucks driving by; horns honking; and in the near distance, the frequent sound of gunfire.

But here at Meat's house, it was so quiet Zara sometimes felt as if she were in another world altogether. The crickets would come out in the evening, and Meat complained about how loud they were, but to Zara, they were fascinating. She'd forgotten the sound. She'd forgotten a lot of things. Things most people took for granted. The sound of a toilet flushing. Of clean water coming out of a tap. The wind rustling in the trees. Birds singing.

She quickly got up and headed for the guest bathroom in the hallway. The master bedroom door was open, and she knew Meat would already be out in his workshop. She knew he wasn't up to doing much yet, not with his ribs still healing, but he was being very secretive about what he was doing out there, and Zara didn't feel like she knew him well enough to press him on the issue.

He was also a morning person, which suited her just fine. Zara had never had the opportunity to lazily sleep in. First because she was so scared and hyperaware of everything around her, then because the best chance for her to get food was in the mornings, before everyone was up and about. Sometimes she'd been lucky and gotten a place in line at a shelter; other times she'd been able to dig the stale and half-eaten bread out of the trash cans behind several of the restaurants a few miles from the barrios.

She still took extremely long showers, but Meat never complained. He even told her to take her time, that he had a huge hot-water heater that would accommodate her, and if it didn't, he'd buy one that would. Zara tried not to feel guilty, and she'd never take being clean for granted again. After more than a decade of having dirt under her nails, having her own body odor disgust her, she was going to take advantage of showering when and where she could.

Zara still didn't like looking in the mirror, but she forced herself to examine her body every morning. It seemed as if she was gaining a little bit of weight, especially with Meat taking great delight in teaching her how to make as many different meals as possible, but her hair still made her cringe. She'd hacked it off with whatever she could find for so long that it was a complete disaster.

Trying not to worry too much about it, Zara took her time in the shower, then got dressed in the clothes that Chloe had brought over. She was still too nervous to properly meet any of the men's girlfriends and wives, so instead of being gracious and welcoming, Zara had taken the clothes, thanked her, and then gone upstairs to her room and hidden until Chloe had left.

She couldn't really explain why she was reluctant to get to know any of them. They'd been nothing but nice, shopping for clothes for her, offering to hang out with her when Meat and the rest of the men got together for meetings having to do with the Mountain Mercenaries.

Maybe she was too afraid of being judged again. The disparaging attitudes of the FBI agents were still fresh in her mind.

The DNA results had come back two days after she'd arrived at Meat's house, and had proven what she'd been saying all along. She *was* Zara Layne. There was no doubt about it. She'd talked to the lawyer who'd been overseeing the trust her parents had left, and she'd already received her first monthly stipend just the day before. Twenty thousand dollars was more money than she'd ever seen in her life—and it wasn't even near what she was owed for the last seven years, which totaled well over a million. That would follow in the days to come.

Just the idea of having so much money at her disposal was unbelievable.

Meat had taken her into town, and they'd opened a bank account, where the rest would be deposited directly, and Zara knew she should be relieved that she had a means of supporting herself, that she wouldn't be homeless. But she still couldn't bring herself to get too excited about the money.

Today, her grandparents were coming to Meat's house to talk with her, and she was both dreading and looking forward to it at the same time. At first they hadn't wanted to travel from the Denver area down to Colorado Springs, even though it was only about an hour's drive. But Meat had told them in no uncertain terms that Zara was still recovering, and if they wanted to see their granddaughter, they needed to make the trip.

All in all, she had little to complain about. She had a roof over her head, and Meat was an amazing housemate, attentive, though he gave her space when she needed it.

But . . . Zara couldn't deny that she was lonely.

Even though she'd been on her own in Peru, she was never *truly* alone. Especially after she'd found Mags, Bonita, and the others. She missed talking to women who knew how she felt, who'd had the same kinds of experiences she'd had. Zara had no doubt Chloe, Everly, Allye, Morgan, and Harlow were nice, but she had little in common with them. Well, except for Morgan.

Zara wouldn't have minded sitting down with Morgan to learn how she'd felt when *she* came back to the States after her kidnapping, but she wasn't sure how to ask to speak to *just* Morgan without offending the other women. They were all very close, and the last thing she wanted was to piss them off.

After her shower, Zara chose to put on a pair of black slacks Chloe had brought over for her, instead of the jeans she'd been wearing most days. She also put on a feminine pink top instead of one of Meat's T-shirts, which she'd been wearing around the house. She felt uncomfortable in the more formal attire, the material of the top almost scratchy against her skin, but Zara tried to ignore it.

Doing her best to brush her hair and make it look somewhat presentable, she gave up when her too-long bangs kept flopping onto her forehead and the curls at the back of her neck stuck up a bit too much.

She went downstairs, and the first thing Zara did was check her email. Meat had set up two accounts for her—one for media inquiries and the general public, and a second private one for communications from her lawyer and himself . . . and anyone else she decided to share it with.

Every news source between California and New York had emailed her. She got upward of eighty requests a day for interviews, and journalists were constantly pleading with her to let them tell her story.

It was annoying and flattering at the same time.

Meat had offered to screen the emails on the public account, but Zara had refused. Information was power. That was how it worked in the barrios too. The more you knew about your enemies, and friends, the better off you were.

Zara had never heard of most of the people who'd emailed her, but she carefully researched each and every name, just to see what they'd already been saying about her and her ordeal. She knew at some point she'd probably need to give her side of the story. Some of the news stories she'd already seen were so sensational and so out there it was laughable.

One man claimed a "source" had told him Zara's parents were alive and well and hiding out in Colombia because the mob was after them. Another said Zara had been adopted by a wealthy Peruvian couple who worked for the government and kept her hostage in their house, and she'd just now managed to escape. A third claimed she was a spy working for the communists in Peru, sending top-secret information back to them so they could overthrow the United States government.

It was all fairly bizarre and ridiculous, but knowing who was saying what, and researching who wanted to interview her, gave her something to do.

This morning when Zara opened her emails, she had the usual outrageous number of reporters begging her to talk—but there were also two emails she hadn't been expecting in her personal account.

The first was from her uncle, Alan.

Zara,

This is your uncle Alan. I got your email from my mom. I'm glad you're alive. We didn't know what to think when you disappeared after my sister was killed.

Can we talk about the trust? You've been gone a long time, and I understand from what's been said on the news that you haven't been to school since you went missing, so all the ins and outs are probably confusing to you. I'm happy to sit down and explain what it all means.

In three more years, the money would've gone to me, and I could've done a lot to help out my parents and make sure they were taken care of in their golden years. You might not know this, but they've struggled recently, and it's only fair that some of that money go to immediate family.

There's enough money to share, and I know you want what's best for your family. I'm looking forward to explaining everything to you soon.

Alan

Zara read the email three times and *still* couldn't believe what she'd read.

How dare he act so condescending? Yes, she might not understand everything about how a trust worked, but for him to so boldly imply she was an idiot who needed him to "explain" it to her was offensive. He wasn't even being subtle about the fact he'd only emailed because of the money. If she was as penniless as she'd been in Lima, she had no doubt her *loving* uncle wouldn't even have bothered getting in touch with her.

She didn't remember Uncle Alan very well, but what she *did* remember was her mom remarking how he was always begging for cash, and how she knew if she gave it to him, he'd spend it on drugs. If he'd been into drugs back then, Zara was guessing he was still hooked. He sounded pretty desperate to get his hands on her parents' money.

Making a mental note to show the email to Meat later, Zara opened the other from an address she didn't recognize.

Zara,

I don't know if you remember me, but my name is Renee Heller. We were best friends in the fourth grade when you went on vacation and never came back. I remember you didn't really want to go all the way to Lima, but you didn't have a choice. You said you'd bring back a present for me, and I had so looked forward to playing on the school's playground when you returned, because no one liked to swing with me like you did! But you never came back.

I remember the day our teacher told us you were missing like it was yesterday. I didn't really understand, and for the longest time thought you had just moved to Peru.

I'm so glad you're home. I'm sure things are confusing and crazy for you right now, but I'm still living in Denver, and I'd love to see you at some point, if nothing else than just to catch up. I haven't really figured out what I want to do with my life yet. I'm currently working as a hairdresser, and while I like it, I can't really see myself spending the rest of my life cutting people's hair.

And to prove this isn't a scam, that I really am Renee, remember that time when we were in third grade and I spent the night at your house? We snuck out into your backyard with our pillows and blankets because we wanted to pretend we were camping. We told each other scary stories, and just as we were falling asleep, it started to pour. We were soaked and ran inside, but forgot our pillows and blankets. Your mom was SO mad the next morning when she looked outside and saw the soggy bedding in your backyard!

Anyway, I hope you get this email, and again, I'd love to catch up sometime. I'll leave my phone number, and you can always call me or just email me back.

Love, Renee

Zara immediately remembered Renee. They had been best friends when she'd gone on that fateful vacation to Peru. She vaguely remembered the conversation they'd had, about how it seemed they'd be apart forever, and how Zara had promised to bring Renee something "Peruvian" from South America. But she hadn't made it back.

Zara hadn't thought much about what the people she'd known had gone through when she disappeared. But now she thought about her old friend Renee and how confused she must've been when Zara just never returned. At least her parents' friends knew what had happened to them. Knew they'd been killed. When someone disappeared, there was just a void. The not knowing had to be just as tough, if not tougher, to deal with than an actual death.

While Zara hadn't planned on trying to look up any of her old friends, the thought of seeing Renee was appealing. She'd known her "before," and Zara had the urge to see if she and Renee could pick up where they'd left off. Yes, they were older and far different people than they'd been when they were ten, but she and Renee had been extremely close. Maybe they'd still click.

"Hey, anything new and exciting?"

Zara startled badly at Meat's question, not having heard him enter the house.

"You scared me," she told him with a hand on her chest.

"Sorry! I thought you heard the front door shut. Are you okay?"

Zara nodded. "Yeah. Just a little jumpy today."

"I figured you would be, which is why I came in from the workshop early. Any interesting emails?"

Zara shrugged, figuring she'd tell him about Alan and Renee later. She had to concentrate on getting through the meeting with her grandparents first.

"Are there any reporters that you like?"

Zara sighed. "I can't believe how *wrong* everyone has gotten things. It's as if, since they don't know the facts, they just make something up to have a story."

Meat nodded. "That about sums up the news business in our world today."

"Doesn't anyone care? I mean, do people really think that I hired a hit on my parents? When I was *ten*?"

"Probably not, but people will take notice and share the story just because it's so shocking. Some people still believe the world is flat," Meat said with a shrug.

Just then, they heard a vehicle pulling up outside. Zara's gaze whipped to the front door, then back to Meat. "Are they here already? They're early!" she hissed in a semipanicked tone.

Meat calmly walked over to one of the windows facing the front of the house and looked out. Then he turned back to her. "No, it's not your grandparents. It's a surprise."

Zara frowned. "A surprise?"

"Yeah, I've been working on something for you out in my shop, with help from Ro, since I'm still not healed. And this delivery will finish it off. Come here," he requested, holding out his hand.

Without hesitation, Zara shut the laptop and stood. She put her hand in his, and he walked with her to the front door.

Since returning, she'd discovered how much she'd missed skin-to-skin contact with another person. Over the last week, Meat had held her hand several times. He'd also hugged her every now and then. With each touch, Zara craved more. She loved sitting close to him on the couch while they watched the news, scoffing over the continued speculation about her reappearance. She enjoyed being with him in the kitchen while he taught her how to cook a steak the "right" way by searing it first, then finishing it off in the oven.

But she especially loved sitting in the backyard with him late at night and staring up at the stars. They were the same stars she'd looked up at so many nights, praying that someone would find her.

Now she *had* been found, and she was safe, warm, and mostly content back in her home state.

The truck in Meat's driveway said "Furniture Row" on the side. Meat shook the hand of one of the deliverymen without letting go of Zara's. "It goes upstairs, third door on the end," he told them. "And I'll pay you extra if you bring up the part that goes with it that's over there in the outbuilding." He pointed toward his workshop. "I've got a few cracked ribs that are still healing, otherwise I'd be able to carry it upstairs myself." The deliverymen agreed, and soon they were in the back of the truck getting ready to take inside whatever Meat had bought.

Zara had no idea what he'd purchased for her now, but when they were standing back in the living room, watching the men go up the stairs with a large box, then come back down to head out to his workshop to get whatever awaited out *there*, she said, "You don't need to buy me things, Meat. I can get whatever I need for myself now that I have money."

"I know I don't, but I think you're really going to like this."

That was what he always said. Whether it was a box of candy bars he'd picked up at the store or a T-shirt with a funny saying on it that he thought would make her laugh. He seemed to know her really well after only a week, even better than he had already, which almost scared her.

"I know today will be tough, so I thought I'd do what I could to try to take your mind off it for a while," Meat said.

Zara tried to tell herself he was only being nice because he felt responsible for her. That he wasn't doing all the kind things he'd done throughout the last week because he liked her in any romantic way.

As it was, she had no idea what all the feelings rioting inside her *own* body and mind meant. It was ridiculous to be twenty-five and still a virgin, and crazier still to have no idea what Meat was thinking when it came to her.

He held her hand a lot, was always touching her, was endlessly kind . . . but was that what men did nowadays? Was this a normal thing between friends? Or did it mean more?

She had no idea. Although, she knew that every time he touched her, goose bumps rose on her skin. She always woke up anxious to see and talk to Meat, and when they parted at night to go to sleep, she felt a little let down. She hadn't forgotten how good it had felt having him cuddled up behind her when they'd slept in the motel in Lima, and even at Daniela's. She'd felt safe and comforted and, for the first time, hadn't been scared to let a man touch her.

Zara was endlessly confused about her feelings for Meat.

And for the first time in her life . . . she wanted to kiss someone. But she had no clue how to go about making that happen.

Lost in her own musings, Zara hadn't realized the men were done hauling whatever Meat had made upstairs and were now waving goodbye. They shut the front door behind them, and Meat turned her to the stairs.

"Well, go on. Go check it out."

Zara looked at him before slowly starting up the stairs. Meat had let go of her hand, but she felt him walking close behind. She was nervous as hell to find out what in the world he'd bought, so she slowly opened the door to the room she'd been staying in.

Surprised, she stared at the new piece of furniture in the room.

The deliverymen had leaned the mattress that had been in there against one of the walls and had taken apart the frame as well. In its place was a smaller, lower bed they'd obviously assembled.

Zara looked from the beautifully carved headboard to the mattress and back to Meat. "I don't understand," she said. "That was a perfectly good bed. Why'd you get me a new one?"

"It's a futon," Meat said gently.

Zara frowned in confusion. "Okay?"

Meat smiled. "I know you haven't been sleeping on the bed, Zara."

She flushed. She hadn't wanted to say anything to Meat about the mattress being too soft or the pillows being too fluffy. She was still sleeping on the hard floor and was embarrassed as hell about it. She wasn't in the barrio anymore. She should be glad to have a soft place to sleep, but instead, she willingly crawled onto the floor each night because it was what she was used to.

"I wasn't spying on you," Meat told her. "I got up one night because I couldn't sleep, and I was headed downstairs to get a drink of water. When I passed your room, I saw the door was partially open. I went to close it, and I saw you on the floor. You should've said something, Zar."

She shrugged. "I'm sorry."

"No, don't apologize. I just want you to be honest. And while I don't care if you sleep on the floor or not, I *do* want you to be as comfortable as possible, and I know it can get drafty in the house sometimes. So I got you a futon. The mattress isn't as soft as those on a normal bed. I made a custom frame for it to bring it a little higher off the ground. There's an extra piece of wood under the mattress to make it a bit firmer as well. After you acclimate, we can remove the wood, then maybe add a foam mattress on top of the futon and under the sheet. Then, as you get used to *that*, we can switch out the mattress for something a little softer.

"But honestly, it doesn't matter if you need to sleep on the futon for the rest of your life. As long as you're comfortable and able to sleep, that's what's important."

Zara inhaled sharply, doing her best to keep the tears at bay. God, she hadn't cried when she'd been beaten up by a group of hungry men for the piece of meat she'd pilfered from a trash can. She hadn't cried the first time she'd cut off her hair, finally realizing she'd be safer pretending to be a boy. She hadn't even teared up when the small dog she'd befriended had disappeared, and she'd realized it had been caught and killed for food by a family of eight in the barrio where she'd been hiding.

But seeing the thought and effort Meat had gone to in order to make her more comfortable almost brought her to her knees.

"Go on. See what you think," Meat urged, pressing gently on her lower back.

Zara slowly walked toward the futon and sat on the edge. The bed was much lower than the other one, and her feet actually touched the ground when she was sitting. It was just the right height for her. She swung her legs around and lay flat on her back.

Closing her eyes, Zara realized it was perfect. It wasn't as hard as lying on the floor or ground had been, but she didn't sink down into the mattress either.

She turned her head and looked at Meat. He seemed anxious and concerned as he watched her test out her new bed.

"It's perfect," she said quickly, wanting to put him at ease.

"You don't have to say that to appease me," he told her. "If it's still too soft, I'll think of something else."

She sat up and shook her head. "I'm not lying. It's great. Thank you so much. I don't know what I—"

Meat moved faster than she knew he could, and his finger was covering her lips before she could finish her thought.

"Don't," he said, shaking his head. "You would've figured things out if I hadn't gotten hurt and we hadn't met. I know you would've. You were meant for greater things, Zara. And don't you forget it. Our experiences make us who we are. Yeah, maybe you would've been a different person if things hadn't happened the way they did, but I don't think I would've liked *that* Zara nearly as much. Did you ever see the movie *It's a Wonderful Life*, with James Stewart, before you went to Peru with your folks?"

"Is that a black-and-white movie with something about an angel and bells ringing?" Zara asked.

He nodded. "That's the one. George Bailey is having a hard time, and he wishes he was never born. An angel grants him his wish, and then he gets a glimpse into what life would be like for those he knows and loves if he hadn't been around. I believe down to my very bones that if you hadn't ended up where you did, things would've been very different for a lot of people, most especially me. But other than myself, I know you've already done things that will affect someone in the future that we don't even know about yet . . . I truly believe that."

Zara thought about his words. She wanted to dismiss them as just Meat trying to make her feel better about what had happened to her. But she couldn't help thinking about the woman in labor who she'd helped when Meat was at Daniela's. She'd literally reached inside that woman and turned her baby around. Daniela's hands weren't small enough to do it, and the woman might've died otherwise.

She thought about the many kids she'd helped over the years, giving them food she'd found or stolen. And even women like Bonita, Carmen, and Maria. She'd helped them countless times too.

Maybe, just maybe, Meat wasn't just being kind.

"You don't have to thank me, Zara. Just as you didn't want my gratitude, I don't want yours either."

"Then what *do* you want?" she asked, eager to hear his answer. Meat had gone out of his way to give her a place to live. To make her feel comfortable. To help her with her inheritance and improve her reading, to teach her to cook. He didn't make any demands on her and didn't seem concerned in the least about when she might be moving out.

"I want you to be happy," he said quietly, staring down at her with a look she couldn't hope to interpret. "To feel free to be who you want to be and do what you want to do. I want to give you back some of the years that were stolen from you and help you move forward."

Her shoulders drooped. Was that all?

As if he could read her mind, Meat slowly bent low and tilted her chin up with one finger. His head dropped—and Zara's heart went into overdrive.

She closed her eyes, praying she'd finally experience her first kiss.

Meat kissed her . . . but not on the lips.

She felt his lips caress her forehead gently before he pulled back.

Her eyes popped open, and she couldn't help but feel disappointed.

He studied her for a long moment, looking more serious than she'd seen him look since she'd met him. "I'm trying my hardest not to push you to do anything you don't want to," he said quietly. "But the more I get to know you, the more I like you. I'm attracted to you, Zara. But I don't want to make you uncomfortable. Just say the word, and I'll back off and never mention this again. We can be friends, and I'll do whatever I can to help you with the media, your grandparents, and finding a place to live. I'll be your biggest cheerleader and staunchest bodyguard."

"What if I don't want to be friends?" she whispered, not able to tear her gaze from his.

He frowned and stood up straight, taking a step back. "Then I'll still help you with whatever you need. But I'll ask one of the other women to come stay with you here until you can find somewhere else to live."

Zara panicked. That wasn't what she'd meant at all!

She stood and stepped closer to Meat. He stilled, and she took advantage of his indecision.

Feeling bolder than she'd ever been before, Zara rested her hands on his chest. She tilted her neck back so she could look him in the eyes. "I didn't mean that like you obviously took it. I have no idea what I'm doing here, Meat. I've never had a boyfriend. Never been attracted to anyone before, I was too busy trying to stay alive. But you make me feel things I've never felt.

"And it's not gratitude," she said forcefully. "I'm grateful to *everyone* for helping get me out of Peru. This isn't that. It's . . . more. Anytime

I'm near you, I feel as if I can fully relax. But at the same time, I feel weird inside, as if something about you gets my blood all worked up. I'm not explaining it well at all . . . but I feel a connection to you. One that I've never felt with anyone, and I have no idea what to do about it. I'm assuming writing a note and asking if you like me, and putting a big box with a 'Yes' and another box with a 'No,' asking you to pick one and give the note back, isn't exactly appropriate anymore."

Meat put one arm around her waist and pulled her into him. The other hand went around the back of her neck. Zara should've felt threatened, but she didn't. She relaxed into his body and waited to see what he'd say next.

"I'd check that 'Yes' box, Zar," he said softly. "You ever been kissed before?"

Zara knew she was blushing, but she shook her head tentatively.

"You haven't said, and I haven't asked, but . . . were you assaulted in Lima? Raped?"

"No," she said firmly. "And I'm not lying. It's why I cut my hair and pretended to be a boy. No one paid me much attention as a male, not like they would've if I'd looked like a girl."

"You definitely look like a girl, Zara," Meat assured her. "And I believe you. So, you're innocent . . ."

"I'm not innocent," she denied, not wanting him to think she didn't know anything about sex. "The barrios aren't exactly private. I've seen men with prostitutes. I've seen husbands make love to their wives. I've seen more penises than I probably should've by the time I was thirteen years old. No one thinks twice about whipping it out to pee whenever and wherever they want, no matter who's around to see."

Zara felt Meat's thumb brushing against her nape. "You're innocent," he said firmly. "You might've seen a lot, but if you haven't experienced a gentle touch or a kiss, or felt the connection two people can have while making love . . . you're still innocent."

She didn't know what to say, so she simply gazed up at him.

"I don't want to take advantage of you," Meat said with a frown. "The last thing I want is to start a relationship and, after a while, have you feel as if you're missing out. I should keep things friendly between us and let you see what you've been missing. Let you date, go out with different men, see what you like and what kind of man you're attracted to."

Zara's brows furrowed. "I know what I like, Meat. I like men who pay attention. Who buy candy bars just because they know I'll enjoy them. Who teach me to cook and don't laugh or make fun of me when I don't know the difference between a paring knife and a steak knife. Who can laugh at themselves when they mess up. Who stand back and let me have space when I need it, but are there for me when I want someone to talk to. Who don't interrupt me, and let me speak for myself to asshole FBI agents even when it's obvious I'm hurting.

"I don't want to go out with anyone else. I don't need to have a parade of men to choose from when there's already someone I admire and respect standing right in front of me. I'm not asking you to marry me. Just as you aren't promising me forever. But I'd like to think the feelings I have when I'm around you are special. I've never felt about anyone in my entire life the way I feel right now, in your arms. Maybe we aren't meant for the long haul, but for right now, it feels awfully damn exciting and right."

"Fuck. Innocent *and* brave. I can't resist that combination," Meat muttered with a tiny grin, before he leaned toward her again.

This time, Zara kept her eyes open and watched him get closer and closer. He stopped when his lips were a hairbreadth from her own.

"May I kiss you, Zara?" he asked, his warm breath wafting over her lips.

In response, Zara went up on her tiptoes and pressed her lips to his.

She had no idea what she was doing. She'd only seen her parents give each other small, short pecks on the lips, and she didn't think the brutal way she'd seen some of the men kiss the women in the barrios was appropriate either, but she had no idea how to proceed past this point.

Luckily, Meat did. The hand at her neck tightened, then moved to palm her cheek. He held her still as he took over. He brushed several light, teasing kisses over her mouth, then he briefly licked her lower lip, and she gasped in surprise.

He took advantage of her open mouth and slowly eased his tongue inside. He coaxed and teased until she shyly brought her tongue out to meet his.

Meat groaned, and it jolted Zara so much, she pulled back to stare at him.

He licked his lips, and she saw his pupils were dilated a little. She bit her lower lip and swore she could still taste Meat there. "Sorry," she said, a little unsure. "You startled me."

"It's okay," he soothed. "Best kiss I've ever had, hands down," he said reverently.

Zara scoffed. "I doubt that."

Meat rested his forehead against her own, and she closed her eyes, loving how intimate the gesture felt. "I can't promise not to fuck up in the future," Meat said seriously. "But I can promise to never deliberately do anything to hurt you. I'll bend over backward to give you what you need and want, when you need and want it. I'll never cheat on you, and I'll support you in whatever it is you want to do. I'll be here for you to lean on . . . and I'll give you all the kisses you want."

He pulled back. "We'll take this slow, all right? If at any time it's not working for you, all you have to do is tell me. Us being exclusive doesn't mean you have to live here forever. If you want to get your own apartment, I'll help you pick one out. You're not dependent on me for anything, Zara, understand? You've got your own money, and you're your own person. You've been making decisions about your own health and safety for a long time now, and you don't need a keeper or babysitter. I want to be your partner."

Zara breathed out a sigh of relief. She didn't need or *want* someone to make decisions for her. She wouldn't be good at taking orders. But it would be nice to be able to talk things over with someone. She'd been on her own for so long, had stressed over so many decisions she'd had to make, just knowing there would be someone there she could bounce ideas off was a dream come true. "I want that too," she told him.

The sound of the doorbell pealing startled Zara so badly, she jumped in Meat's arms.

"Easy, Zar. It's just your grandparents."

She looked up at him anxiously. "Already?"

"Yeah, but they can wait until you're ready and composed."

"We can't make them wait!" she exclaimed, trying to pull out of Meat's arms.

"Take a deep breath," he ordered.

She did as he said and immediately felt better.

"I'll go down and invite them in and get them something to drink. You come down when you're good and ready, and not a second earlier. Okay?"

As cowardly as it was, Zara nodded. She had no idea how this meeting would turn out. Her mom hadn't exactly had the best relationship with her parents, but maybe her murder, and Zara being missing for all these years, had somehow changed them too.

Zara hoped so.

Meat leaned down and kissed her briefly one more time before straightening. "I mean it, Zara, don't come down until you're ready."

"Okay. Thanks, Meat."

"Partners, remember?" he said, before turning and leaving her standing in the room.

Looking around, Zara's eyes landed on the futon once more. Meat had done something incredibly nice for her without hesitation. The bed was perfect. *He* was perfect.

Well . . . perfect for *her*.

Knowing she needed the few minutes Meat had so selflessly given her, Zara sat on the edge of the mattress and closed her eyes. She wasn't a poor, lost homeless kid anymore. She was Zara Layne, and the people downstairs were her flesh and blood. The only family she had left.

But if they didn't take her exactly how she was—then fuck them. She was done trying to fit in where she wasn't wanted. She'd done that for fifteen years. Enough was enough.

Knowing Meat would be with her was all the strength she needed to cut her grandparents out of her life completely, if it became necessary.

Zara did her best to clear her mind before going downstairs. She was still nervous, but not nearly as nervous as she'd been to admit to Meat that she liked him. That she was a virgin. And he'd believed her without hesitation. She knew not everyone would have. Meat was one of a kind . . . and for now, he was all hers.

Smiling, Zara concentrated on how his lips and tongue had felt, instead of on the impending meeting with her relatives.

Chapter Seventeen

Meat ground his teeth together and did his best not to say something he'd regret. These were Zara's grandparents, and he had no right to kick them out before Zara had even met them. But so far, they weren't exactly making the best impression.

Mr. Harper had immediately wanted to know how much money Meat expected for finding Zara. After he'd explained he didn't want the man's money, Mrs. Harper had curled her lip and made an insinuation under her breath that maybe he'd already taken his reward from their granddaughter another way.

As if that wasn't bad enough, they made it more than clear they weren't impressed with his house or anything about the decor. After sitting, Zara's grandmother offered a disparaging comment about his "rustic furniture" and how quaint it was. Her grandfather promptly looked bored and asked if Meat had anything to drink. It was only eleven in the morning, but somehow Meat wasn't surprised the man wanted alcohol already.

He was still attempting small talk, having reassured them that Zara would be down as soon as she was ready, when Mrs. Harper said, "She knew when we would be here, right? It's rude to keep us waiting."

Meat just about lost his cool and was seconds from telling her off when Zara entered the room. Her chin was up, and she didn't look the least bit intimidated to meet her grandparents, thank God.

"I'm sorry I wasn't available to speak to you as soon as you got here," she said, a hint of a Peruvian accent in her tone. Meat hadn't really noticed it before, but apparently when she got agitated, it was more pronounced. "I was otherwise occupied."

She walked up to her maternal grandparents and stood in front of them. Instead of standing to give her a hug, to say how thankful they were that she was alive and home after all these years, Mrs. Harper simply held out her hand.

Zara stared at it, but eventually reached out her own to shake it. Her grandfather did the same.

She turned to Meat and frowned as if to say, "What the hell?" and he did his best to keep his facial expression neutral. He was appalled by their behavior and already couldn't wait for this meeting to be over.

Zara sat on a chair next to Meat, across from the sectional where her grandparents were sitting.

"So, Zara, when do you think you'll be ready to move back up to Denver?" her grandfather asked.

Zara blinked in surprise. "What?"

"When will you be moving home? Of course, we had to sell Chad and Emily's house, but there's a guesthouse on our property you could live in," he said.

"It'll take a while to get you fixed up enough to be seen in public," Mrs. Harper mused. "Your hair is atrocious, so we'll have to get you some extensions. You'll obviously need more appropriate clothing as well."

Meat was incensed by Mrs. Harper's words. Zara was beautiful just the way she was. Yeah, her hair was a bit uneven, but it was a symbol of her strength, and exactly how much she'd endured and overcome. He actually liked her short hair.

"Why would I move back up there?" Zara asked with a tilt of her head, ignoring the rude comment about "fixing" her so she could be seen in public.

"Because it's what people expect," her grandmother said, as if it were the most obvious thing in the world.

Zara was silent for a long moment. Then she asked, "Did you even look for me? Wonder what happened to me?"

Mrs. Harper gasped and brought her clutched hands up to her chest as if in shock. "Of course we did! How can you even ask us that?"

"We put up a ten-thousand-dollar reward for your return," Mr. Harper added indignantly.

"But you didn't bother to go down to Lima, did you?" Zara asked. They both looked uncomfortable now.

"There wasn't any reason for us to go all the way down there," Mr. Harper answered defensively. "The police said they were doing all they could to find out who'd killed Chad and Emily, and to find you."

"Meat told me that you sold the house only three months after their deaths," Zara replied quietly. "You moved on without a second thought about what had happened to me."

"You have to understand," Mrs. Harper said. "We were being told that it was highly unlikely you were still alive. My daughter and son-in-law had been killed, and you'd probably been taken away to be raped and murdered. They said your body would never be found, that it was most likely in one of the huge dumps around the city."

Meat's hands clenched. *What the actual fuck?* Were these people really that heartless?

"Besides, even if you were found, it wasn't as if you could have lived in that house by yourself. The money from the sale went into the trust anyway," Mr. Harper added. "You'll still end up with the cash in the long run."

Zara closed her eyes for a second, and Meat wanted so badly to put his arm around her shoulders, but he sat as still as a statue next to her. These were her family members, and he had to let her take the lead in how to deal with them. Even if they were assholes, they were her blood.

"You think I *care* about the money?" Zara asked.

"Well, of course," Mrs. Harper scoffed. "Who wouldn't? We're not talking about a couple thousand dollars here, Zara. It's money your uncle Alan could've really used over the years."

"Yeah? For what? To buy more drugs?" Zara asked.

No one had anything to say about that.

"I'm so sorry my parents' money was inconveniently locked away so you and Alan couldn't touch it until I was declared dead, or until after I turned twenty-eight and didn't come forward to claim it. How disappointing for you that I showed back up when I did. Did you even think about me at *all* as the years went by? Wonder what I might be doing on Christmas morning? Give a thought to what I might be going through? Or did you just assume I was dead?"

They remained silent.

"Did you hire a private investigator? Beg someone from the FBI to look into my disappearance? Call the news outlets to keep my case in the public eye? Did you do *anything* other than call the Peruvian police the year after my parents were killed to see if they'd found me yet?

"You had the resources to raise absolute hell and do so much more than you ultimately did. Oh yeah—I know all about what you did and didn't do. I've made some pretty powerful friends of my own since I've been found. And I realize that's only been a week and a half, but *true* friends are made under the most extreme situations."

"Are you talking about *this* gentleman?" Mr. Harper asked, tilting his head to indicate Meat.

"Yes, I am," Zara told him.

"Did you know he's got less than twenty thousand dollars in savings?" her grandfather asked. "We had a private investigator look into him as soon as we found out you were staying here. Hunter Snow has no parents and no relatives. He only wants your *money*, Zara. There's no other reason he's being so accommodating. It's not like a relationship between you would ever work out. He's not even in the same social circles we are. Stop being so naive! It's embarrassing and unbecoming.

Now it's time for you to come home. Together, we'll do what we can to salvage your reputation and find you an appropriate husband. Someone who can overlook your past . . . how you've been living or anything you might've done to survive."

That was it. Meat was done.

He opened his mouth to lambaste the man, but Zara's hand clamping on his thigh kept him silent and seated.

"How much did you spend on the investigation into Meat, Grandfather?" Zara asked. "I'd bet my entire fortune that it was more than you spent looking for your missing granddaughter, wasn't it?"

When he didn't answer, she went on.

"And I don't care how much money Meat has. He's not being nice to me simply because of how many zeros there are in my bank account. The only people who care about that kind of thing are *you* and my dear uncle Alan—who was kind enough to email me to say he'd be glad to 'educate' me on how the trust worked . . . as if I'd believe anything he said."

Meat turned to stare at her. She hadn't told him that.

His mind whirled with things he needed to look up on his computer. He wondered how many other emails she'd received from people asking for money. He'd assumed she was only receiving email from the news outlets, but that had been naive of him.

Meat needed to talk to the others and make sure Alan Harper—or anyone else—wouldn't be a threat to Zara, now or in the future. He knew exactly how little money it took for someone to agree to kill someone else, and he'd be damned if Zara had survived everything she'd gone through to be taken down by someone in her own family.

"I don't know why you hate me so much, but I'm done," Zara told her grandparents. "Not only did you *not* care that I was missing or do anything beyond putting as little money up as you could for a reward, you haven't even bothered to ask me how I am! If I'm all right. Or inquire about where I've been and what I've had to do to 'survive,' as you so gently put it."

"We watch the news," Mrs. Harper said somewhat pathetically. "We know where you were and what happened."

"Do you?" Zara fired back. "Nearly *all* of the shit those reporters have said is dead wrong. I wasn't kept as a love slave for some drug dealer, and I wasn't some lawless punk making a living by robbing tourists!"

Two pairs of eyes stared at her blankly.

"Get out," Zara said as she stood. Meat stood alongside her and crossed his arms over his chest. "I don't want to see you again."

"But everyone expects you to come back to Denver!" Mrs. Harper protested.

"I don't care. You can tell your precious friends whatever you want to save face, but I'm done. I never understood why Mom and Dad didn't get along with you guys, but I do now. You're self-centered and snobbish and so concerned about your reputation and wealth, you couldn't give a damn about a lost ten-year-old who would've given *everything* she had if only someone had cared enough to search for her. *Really* search for her. You had your chance fifteen years ago to do the right thing, and you failed. Get. Out."

Mr. Harper opened his mouth as if to challenge his granddaughter's words, but Meat moved toward him, pointing toward the door and saying "Out" in a low, threatening tone.

The pair quickly stood and headed for the door.

On the way out, her grandfather turned to have one last word. "You haven't changed in fifteen years," he said icily. "Your parents were way too lenient with you. Let you wear what you wanted and run wild, and didn't bother to teach you the importance of your heritage."

"What someone wears has absolutely no bearing on the kind of person they are," Zara shot back. "Especially when she's *ten* years old. Jeez. Besides, look at *you*—you're wearing an expensive suit and a watch that costs more than the average Peruvian makes in a year, but you're still a bully and an asshole. Whereas some of the people I met who had literally nothing to their names were ten times the person you'll ever be."

Her grandparents turned and left the house without another word.

Zara stomped to the door and actually slammed it behind them. She stared at the closed door until they heard the sound of an engine starting up and a car heading down the gravel driveway.

"Zara?" Meat asked tentatively, not sure what kind of shape she'd be in.

"Fuck them," Zara said firmly when she turned to face him.

"It's okay to be sad," he told her.

"I'm *not* sad," she insisted. "I'm pissed. Seriously, how dare they come here and say mean things about you when you're the one who got me home? Meat, my parents were *nothing* like the assholes who just left. They were kind and generous, and you wouldn't know they were loaded just by looking at them."

"I know," Meat assured her, coming closer and reaching out to put his hands on her face.

"How do you know?" she asked, reaching up and grabbing hold of his wrists.

"Because they raised one hell of a daughter. If all they cared about was money, you wouldn't have survived."

Her face softened. "Yes, we were vacationing in Peru. But they never hesitated to give money to the homeless we saw on the streets. I think that's why they were targeted. Those men who killed them might've seen them giving money to someone, and wanted more. They had plans to donate to some sort of women's shelter while we were there too. I don't know which one or any of the details, but I heard them talking about it one night. They wanted to help those who weren't as fortunate. But they didn't get the chance. They were killed before the donation was made."

Meat leaned forward and kissed Zara's forehead. "I'm sorry your grandparents can't see what an amazing woman you are."

She shrugged. "I can't deny it hurts, but I've learned that our time is too short to dwell on the negatives. I've spent my life taking each day one at a time. I don't know what's in my future, so I try to stay in the here and now."

"You are one wise woman," Meat told her.

"Not really. Fourth-grade education, remember?" she said with a small smile.

"There's more to life than book smarts," Meat said. "And I have no doubt that you'll have your GED in hand before too long. And . . . I have to say, I like this new, outspoken Zara. Only a week and a half ago you answered most questions with a yes or a no and a shrug. Now you aren't afraid to say exactly what you're thinking."

"I think it's because I feel safe," Zara said solemnly. "I don't feel as if I have to be quiet and go unnoticed to blend into the background."

"Damn straight you don't. I like knowing exactly what you're thinking."

They stood like that in the foyer by the front door for a long moment. Meat with his hands on her face and Zara hanging on to his wrists.

Eventually, she looked away from him and asked, "Does my hair really look that bad? I mean, I know it's not stylish; I used to cut it with whatever sharp object I could get my hands on. It was more important for it to be short than to look nice."

Meat ran a hand over her short brown hair. "It could use some evening up, but honestly, I hadn't thought about it because I've been too busy being impressed by every other thing about you. If you really want to do something about your hair, I'm sure we can find someone to help you with it. There's a particular beauty salon some of the other women go to. We could book you a spa day, and you could get your hair done, along with a manicure and pedicure, if you wanted. A little pampering. But we've got something else we need to talk about right now."

She looked up at him. "We do?"

"Yeah. Uncle Alan?" Meat asked with a raise of an eyebrow.

Zara looked away again.

"And any other emails you might've received that could seem remotely threatening," Meat said. "I'm sure you know by now that I have the ability to hack into your emails and find out for myself, but I haven't out of respect for you. But, Zara, I will if you don't start talking to me. You aren't just a long-lost kidnapped little girl anymore. You're both rich and famous now. With that comes crazies who will do or say anything to get their hands on your money. You've seen firsthand what greed can do. The very last thing I want is for someone to snatch you off the streets and hold you for ransom. I can and will protect you, but I can only do that if I know where the threat might be coming from."

Zara took a deep breath and tilted her head up once more. "You're right. But Meat?"

"Yeah, Zar?"

"I hate being rich," she whispered. "I was scared, and life wasn't easy in the barrio, but I didn't often have to worry about people wanting to be my friend or hurting me because of what they could get from me. All I had to worry about was finding food and staying out of the way of the bullies and criminals."

Meat nodded. "Your grandparents were right about me. I've got some money saved up, but I'll never be a rich man, so I can't completely relate. But if you let me help you now, I'll do what I can to keep you away from the bullies and criminals here in the States as well."

"Thanks."

"Now, before we sit down with your email and you let me see each and every one that isn't simply asking for an interview . . . do you want something to eat?"

"Yeah."

Meat couldn't have stopped himself from leaning close and kissing her gently on the lips if his life depended on it. "I'm proud of you, Zara," he said when he pulled back. "I know some people probably expect you to be broken and damaged, but you aren't. You're strong, determined, and you have an innate sense of right and wrong. Your parents did an amazing job of raising you for ten years, and gave you the foundation you needed to become the pillar of strength you are today."

"I think that's the nicest thing anyone has ever said to me," Zara replied.

"It's true." Meat kissed her one more time, this time unable to resist licking along her lower lip to get just a taste of her before he pulled back. Her eyes were wide, and if he wasn't mistaken, he could see the pulse at the side of her neck beating faster than it had a second ago.

Meat wrapped an arm around her shoulders and pulled her into his side. "How about I show you how to make waffles from scratch?"

"You did that a few days ago."

Meat chuckled. "Then how about *you* show *me* how it's done?"

"Deal."

Meat was glad to see the smile on Zara's face . . . but he couldn't easily forget how horrible her grandparents had treated her. She'd seemed to blow them off, but he didn't know if she'd always be able to deflect those who wanted to hold her down, those who would disparage her and what she'd been through, and those who wanted to befriend her only because of her money.

Straightening his shoulders, Meat decided he'd do what he could to make sure she wasn't suckered in by any of them. He'd already been protective of her, but she really hadn't noticed since she hadn't left his house much. Eventually she'd figure out exactly *how* protective he could be. She might not like it, but tough. She hadn't had a champion for fifteen years—she had one now.

Chapter Eighteen

Later that afternoon, after they'd eaten, Zara sat at the table with the laptop Meat had given her to use, with him by her side, and showed him the emails she'd received.

There were tons from news reporters around the country begging for the opportunity to interview her. She had no desire to sit with a stranger and tell them *anything*. They didn't care about her; all they cared about were ratings. She wasn't so naive not to know that, so she'd simply ignored those emails.

There were also emails from people who'd found her private email address and had written begging for help. Those were harder for her to ignore.

Meat read the email from Alan and frowned. Then he reached for his phone and called Ball.

"I think we might have a problem," he said without greeting his friend after he answered.

"What's that?" Ball asked. Zara was sitting close enough that she could hear Ball's words even without the phone being on speaker.

"Zara's uncle. He sent her an email that has definite undertones. She doesn't have many good things to say about the man. If I had to guess, the uncle is pissed he's not going to get his sister's money, but he's trying to play it like he's magnanimously offering to 'teach' Zara everything she needs to know about the money left to her in the trust."

"Let me guess," Ball said. "He'll probably lie his ass off and take as much money as he can get."

"That's my assumption," Meat agreed. "I'm going to see what I can find on him as soon as Zara finishes showing me what other emails she's received, but I thought you might be able to check with Everly. See if the CSPD can put him on their radar?"

"Does he live here?" Ball asked.

"I don't know yet. I'm assuming probably Denver, though, especially since his parents are still there. They were just here, and they seemed to be on *his* side when it comes to the money."

"Zara met with her grandparents?" Ball asked. "How'd that go?"

Meat glanced at Zara, and she wrinkled her nose at him.

"Let's just say Christmas at the grandparents' house isn't exactly going to be a thing," Meat told his friend. "I just wanted to give you a heads-up and maybe see if Everly can do some looking into him. I've got the security system here at the house, and I'll know if someone comes down my driveway before they get here, but that doesn't mean he won't try to sneak in on foot or something."

Ball chuckled. "He'd be an idiot if he did that. Sneaking up on a former Delta man isn't exactly the best thing to do."

"I have a feeling he's not that smart," Meat said. "Emailing his niece to imply he deserves her money isn't exactly something a rocket scientist would do."

"I'll get ahold of the others as well," Ball said. "You'll let us know of anything else you find?"

"Yeah. I'm going to put a trace on Alan's cell phone just to keep an eye on him . . . but you didn't hear that from me," Meat said.

Ball chuckled. "Hear what? Tell Zara that Everly and the others want to come over and spend some time with her soon."

Zara lowered her eyes and studied her fingernails. She knew the guys' women wanted to come over and hang out, but she just wasn't sure she was ready for that. She didn't know why, exactly. Though she was definitely a little intimidated by them. They seemed to be way out of her league, and she didn't know how she'd relate to them.

"Will do. Thanks, Ball. I'll talk to you soon," Meat said.

"Later."

Meat clicked off his phone. "Why don't you want to meet the others?" he asked Zara as soon as he'd hung up.

Zara sighed. Figured he'd pick up on that. "I don't know."

"Can you try to explain it to me?" Meat pushed.

She glanced at him. There were so many things she hadn't talked about. Would *never* talk about. But she needed Meat to understand. "For so long, all I had to rely on was myself. When I was about twelve, I did meet a boy around my age. I'd been watching him for a while, and it didn't seem like he had any family, just like me. Eventually, I got up the nerve to approach him. We worked together for a short time. He would distract people on the street by break dancing—spinning around on his head and things like that—and when all the attention was on him, I'd walk through the crowd and pick their pockets. It was easy and exciting, and when we got back to the barrio, we'd split whatever I had stolen.

"Except that wasn't enough for him. Eventually, he wanted more. Said that he was doing all the work and he deserved three-quarters of the loot. I'd felt safer and had more fun with him by my side, so I agreed. We'd been doing this scheme for a few months when I got caught. A man grabbed my wrist when I had my hand in his pocket and almost broke it. Lifted me right off my feet. I yelled for my friend to help me, but he took off running. Didn't even look back."

"How'd you get away?" Meat asked, his hand coming down to cover hers on the table.

Zara shrugged. "I kneed him in the balls, and he dropped me. My tailbone hurt for weeks after that, but I ran faster than I ever had before. Back to the barrio. I found my so-called friend and asked why he hadn't stayed to help. He looked me straight in the eye and told me that I wasn't worth getting into trouble for. That he was just using me to get money for his father.

"It shocked me. First, I had no idea he'd *had* a father. But second, I thought we were a team. That he was my *friend*. Us against the world and all that. He scoffed when I admitted as much, and said that he knew I'd get caught sooner or later because my Spanish was shitty and I was too scrawny and weak."

"But that was a long time ago," Meat said gently. "Allye and the others aren't like that kid."

Zara sighed. "That's just one example, Meat. I don't make friends easily. It's hard for me to trust. Why would your friends' women even want to know someone like me? I'm weird, an introvert, would rather sit by myself in a corner than try to smile and pretend I'm having fun when I'm not. I'm not that smart, I'm too outspoken, and I have nothing in common with them."

"I think you're doing them *and* yourself a disservice," Meat said without any trace of irritation or exasperation in his tone. "Allye and the others have been through their own kinds of hell. They'd understand more than most how much you've been through. They won't push for you to talk about anything you don't want to, and they certainly wouldn't want you to pretend to be someone you're not around them."

Zara shrugged. "Is this going to be an issue for you? I mean, if I don't get along with them, does that mean *we* can't be friends?"

"Of course not," Meat said firmly.

"I'm not trying to upset you," Zara said tentatively.

"I know you're not."

"And I also know this is me just being weird. It was hard for me to make friends in the barrio, and if for some reason me and your friends don't hit it off, I know that'll be hard on you . . . and that's the last thing I want. I also know you'd never introduce me to people who would hurt me."

"I wouldn't," Meat confirmed.

"And I want to meet them. But I feel like I'm just not ready. I need more time. That's probably upsetting to you; it's obvious you care about all of them a great deal."

"I do. But I get it, Zar. You need to acclimate in your own time. And really, you've only been back in the States a little more than a week. Me forcing you to do something you aren't ready for will only be harmful in the long run. The last thing I want is to push too hard and have it backfire on me. You can meet them when you're ready. Okay?"

"Thanks. And for the record, I *do* want to get to know them, and let them know me. I miss my friends from the barrio, and I wouldn't mind making new ones here."

"You can never have too many friends," Meat said with a smile.

"I'm glad you think that way . . . because I *did* get an email from someone in my past, and I want to meet up with her."

Meat sat back in his chair and blinked at her in surprise. "What? Who?"

"Her name is Renee Heller. She was my best friend when I disappeared. She sent me an email. Apparently, she still lives up in Denver."

"Can I see the email?" Meat asked tentatively.

Zara nodded and pulled it up on the computer, then turned the screen to face him. She watched his face as he read it and couldn't tell what he was thinking.

When he was done, Zara said, "She said she's a hairdresser. She could probably fix my hair. I thought maybe I could invite her down here, and we could see if we clicked like we did when we were little."

"And you think it's really her?" Meat asked.

Zara frowned at him. "Of course. Who else would it be?"

Meat smiled sadly. "Someone else who wants to get close to you for a story. Or someone who wants to get ahold of your money."

Zara let out a rush of breath. "Oh," she said in disappointment.

"I'm sorry, Zar. I know this is hard. But you have to at least consider that this might not really be the person you knew when you were ten."

"I'm sure it's her," Zara explained. "I vaguely remember that sleepover she talks about in the email. How would someone else know about that? I also remember playing together for hours on the playground with her. I just . . . She's a part of my old life. The life I had when I was truly happy and carefree. If I can connect with even one person from that time, maybe it'll make me feel more normal. Like I can have a piece of the old me back. Then I think I'd be more ready to make brand-new friends. I know that sounds weird, but I can't help feeling that way."

Meat didn't agree or disagree with her right away. He simply studied her. Zara had no idea what he was thinking, but finally he asked, "Will you let me check her out before you meet with her?"

"What does that mean, check her out?" Zara asked carefully.

"Electronically. See what her bank account looks like, check out her work history, see if she's married, and what I can find out about her on social media."

Zara struggled with her conscience. On one hand, she liked that Meat was so protective of her, but on the other hand, it seemed invasive.

But what if Meat was right and this *wasn't* Renee? What if it was someone like that boy so long ago in the barrio, who was just using her for some nefarious purpose? She didn't want to be untrusting, but Meat had a point.

"Okay. But just because you might find something you don't like doesn't necessarily mean I won't meet with her. I've become a pretty good judge of character over the years, especially after that kid I befriended when I was twelve. I hope I'd be able to tell if she wanted money from me."

She knew Meat wasn't so sure, but he nodded anyway. "Deal. I'll share everything I can find out. I'd also like it if you would let me be there when you meet with her. And it's probably best if we don't meet here at the house. There's no need for her to find out where you're staying just yet. Okay?"

Zara nodded. She was all right with that. In fact, if she was honest with herself, she'd feel a lot better if Meat was there when she met with Renee. "Okay. Thanks."

"Now, what other emails have you gotten that I should know about?"

Zara and Meat spent the rest of the afternoon going through the hundreds of emails she'd received.

"How the fuck did all these people get your *personal* email?" Meat asked under his breath after they'd read an email from a woman in California who'd sent a dozen pictures of the burnt-out shell of a house, claiming it had burned down in the recent wildfires in the area. She'd tried to connect with Zara by saying she was now homeless, just like Zara had been in Peru, and how five thousand dollars would go a long way toward helping her rebuild.

"I messed up," Zara admitted regrettably.

"How?"

"I was reading this article about me, about what happened, and they'd gotten it all wrong. They didn't even care about getting the facts right! Anyway, I commented . . . and in order to comment, I had to leave my email address. I accidentally used the personal one you set up for me, instead of the public one. I didn't know the email would be published along *with* my comment," she admitted. "I didn't think anyone would even know it was me."

"Zara, the private email I set up for you has your name in the actual address. Why *wouldn't* they think that was you? At the very least, they would *hope* it was you and message you accordingly. This email has probably been shared far and wide by now, so there's no way I can do damage control. Even if I deleted it off that one post, it's too late."

"I know, I screwed up," Zara told him. "But . . . the good thing is that Renee was able to find and email me."

Meat sighed deeply. "Promise me that you won't send any of these people money," he demanded.

Zara glanced toward the screen. "Some of the stories are so sad, Meat."

"I know, but, honey, you have no idea if they're telling you the truth or not. I'm all about you donating money to people in need, but only if it's either to reputable organizations or if you're able to confirm a person's situation warrants it."

She nodded.

Meat brought a hand up and palmed the back of her neck. He pulled her forward until their foreheads were touching. "I love how tenderhearted you are. Honestly, it's a miracle you can still care about others after what happened to you. Don't change," he ordered gruffly. "I'd rather have you wanting to give money to every homeless person you see than become hardened and jaded and not care about anyone's suffering. I'll never stand in the way of you helping others as long as they're on the up-and-up. Okay?"

Zara liked the sound of that. Not that he thought she was gullible, but that he was talking about still being her friend in the future. "Okay," she agreed.

"And this goes without saying, but I'm going to say it anyway. If you receive any more emails or *any* kind of communication from your uncle, you've got to let me know right away."

"I will."

"Better yet, will you let me screen your emails for a while? I'd like to set up a third account for you, one that doesn't have your name in it this time. That was my mistake. You can use the new email to communicate with *only* those people you want to, like the other guys on the team, and hopefully, eventually, their women."

"And Renee?" Zara asked.

Meat nodded. "Yeah."

"Okay."

"How about using something like warriorwoman464 for your email?" he asked with a smile.

She rolled her eyes.

Meat pulled back, and his gaze went from hers to her mouth, then back up. "I'd like to kiss you again," he said quietly.

Zara simply nodded.

He leaned forward slowly, and the second his lips touched hers, Zara's eyes closed.

This time, the kiss wasn't chaste. He licked her bottom lip, and she immediately opened for him. How long they sat there kissing, Zara had no idea. All she knew was that she'd never be the same. She'd had *no* idea kissing could feel this good. And could make other parts of her feel like they'd come alive.

Meat didn't rush her, didn't completely take over the kiss. He showed her what to do, then let her explore and experiment. She nipped his lower lip and smiled when he groaned. When she sucked on his tongue, the hand behind her neck tightened, and he actually growled.

Zara shifted on the hard dining room chair and licked her lips when he pulled back.

He stared into her eyes for a long moment before smiling. "You might be new at this, hon, but you're a quick learner, just like you are with everything else."

He then kissed her once more, hard and fast, before pushing back his chair. "Come on. I've been sketching out a piece in the workshop that I want to start as soon as my ribs completely heal. Keep me company? You can read *Harry Potter* to me as I work."

Zara nodded eagerly, glad to leave the computer and the outside world behind for a while. Meat was very patient when she read out loud to him, never belittling her or making her feel stupid for not knowing a word or how to pronounce it. She was almost done with the first book in the series and was eager to move on to the next.

This was what she'd dreamed about late at night when she lay in the dirt, scared out of her mind. A place where she could feel safe and didn't have to think about where her next meal was coming from or if anyone would ever rescue her.

Meat had not only given her a place to relax and find herself again, but he'd started to make her think about things she hadn't even *dared* dream about. A family, a home, love.

As they held hands and made their way outside to his workshop, Zara thought about her friends back in Lima. Mags had been right. She didn't regret opening up to Meat and letting him take her back to America. She could only hope and pray that her friends were okay, and that they, too, would someday find security of their own.

Chapter Nineteen

Meat was beginning to worry just a little about Zara.

It had been two weeks since she'd met with her grandparents, and she hadn't left his home except for short excursions to the grocery store with him. He didn't really mind so much that she sequestered herself in his house; she'd only been there a few weeks. But he wished she was more interested in making connections with other people.

He'd taken her out a few times to drive an old Accord he had in his garage, and she'd seemed to enjoy that. They stayed on his property and basically just drove up and down his driveway, but she'd done well, and he knew she wouldn't have any issue when she got on the road. She wasn't quite ready to drive "for real" yet, as she put it, which he respected.

She'd plowed through the rest of the Harry Potter series and learned the joys of electronic books. Meat had ordered her a tablet, and she downloaded books from the library every chance she got.

He'd invited all the guys and their women over for a barbecue one evening, and while Zara had been polite and seemed to have a good time, she'd also been pretty quiet and hadn't seemed terribly enthusiastic about getting together with them again anytime soon. She hadn't ruled it out, but she hadn't encouraged a future meetup with any of the women.

Meat was happy to hang out with her himself. He loved doing so, in fact, but he wished she had more people to talk to. He was sure connecting with others would help her heal so she could really start living her new life in the States.

On the bright side, things between the two of them had been great. Amazing. Physically, they hadn't done more than kiss, but with every day that went by, things between them got deeper, more and more intimate. The other night, they'd spent about half an hour with Meat on his back, on the couch, Zara straddling his waist—but mindful of his ribs—while they made out. She might be a virgin, but she was quickly coming into her own sexually and discovering what she liked. And most of the time, what she liked was for Meat to let her explore.

He found that he couldn't deny her anything. If she wanted to see what happened to his nipples when she kissed them, far be it from him to tell her no.

He'd been monitoring the original email addresses he'd made for her, and she'd gotten a few more messages from her uncle, demanding she contact him about the trust—and each message seemed to get more and more pushy when she didn't respond.

She'd also received a few emails from nuts who said they didn't believe she'd been kidnapped down in Lima, and had accused her of murdering her own parents and hiding out for the last fifteen years.

Meat hadn't shared *those* with her, though. Every time she read or watched a report where someone claimed details about her that were so far from the truth they were laughable, she got increasingly upset. And he didn't want to add to her angst by sharing those ridiculous emails.

Zara had chosen not to have a press conference for now, deciding it wouldn't change anything that had happened to her, and hoping the furor over her return would die down if she ignored it. But it hadn't. It seemed the more time that went by without Zara telling her story, the more people wanted to know, and the more they simply made up what they wanted to believe.

And as much as Meat wanted Zara to get out more, to really start living instead of hiding out at his house, he wasn't so sure about her meeting with her childhood friend Renee.

He couldn't even put his finger on what bothered him about that situation. He'd thoroughly investigated her, and even had Rex see what he could find too. And what they'd found was exactly what she'd told Zara.

Renee Heller was twenty-five and had been in the same school and class as Zara when she'd disappeared, exactly like she'd claimed. She'd grown up in Denver, near where Zara had, and *was* currently a hairdresser. After graduating from high school, she'd worked at National Jewish Health hospital as an entry-level warehouse associate, receiving and delivering packages and shipments. But she'd worked there for only a few years before going to cosmetology school. She seemed to have an okay relationship with her parents, and she'd had a few boyfriends over the years.

She lived in a small studio apartment near the downtown area of Denver. The rent wasn't exactly cheap, but she paid it on time every month. She was tall and slender, with bleached-blonde hair, and was always impeccably dressed, based on her social media pics. Meat hadn't been able to find even one red flag that should make him leery of Zara meeting with the woman. She'd never been arrested and seemed to be a regular upstanding citizen.

But there was still something bothering him, and he couldn't explain the feeling.

Zara was happy to receive additional emails from her old friend, and they'd even begun talking on the phone. As much as Meat wished she'd make a connection with Morgan or one of the other women, like she seemed to with Renee, he wasn't going to let Zara know he was uncomfortable with her choice of friends, not when he couldn't find reason to be suspicious. She was an adult, even if she'd had an unconventional childhood, and could make her own decisions.

One night, he'd overheard Zara telling Renee how she'd sometimes had to resort to stealing for food. She didn't sound thrilled to be admitting it, and from the side of the conversation he could hear, Meat got the feeling Renee was hounding Zara for details on her less-than-savory experiences while in Peru, which bothered him. It didn't exactly thrill Zara either, if her tone was anything to go by.

Given the amount of time she spent on the phone with Renee, Meat wasn't too surprised when Zara came out onto his back porch and said that she and Renee had worked out a time and place to meet.

"Yeah?"

"Yeah. She has Thursday afternoon off. She said she could come down and meet me at Ted's Montana Grill in Briargate, just off Interstate 25. I told her I'd get with you and let her know."

Meat saw how excited Zara was for this meeting. There was no way he'd deny her, even though something still bothered him about Renee. "I'm happy to take you," he told her.

"Thank you so much, Meat," Zara said, then surprised him by straddling his lap. Because she was so small, she literally had to climb up onto the chair he was sitting in, and once in place, her legs were spread-eagle over his hips.

It was suggestive as hell, and it was all Meat could do to keep his hands at her waist to steady her and not touch her more intimately.

"I know you wish I'd be hanging out with your friends instead, but I have a connection with Renee that I don't have with the other women. I like them, but Renee *knows* me. Knows the person I used to be."

"She knows the ten-year-old kid you used to be," Meat countered. "So much time has passed since then. People change. You certainly have."

"I know," Zara said quietly, her hands resting lightly on his upper arms. "But when I talk to her, she reminds me of how I used to feel when I didn't have a care in the world. How much fun we had together."

Meat got it, he did, but he wasn't sure that was what Zara needed right now. She needed to make connections with people who weren't also reminding her of what she'd lost. She'd changed a hell of a lot since she was ten, and Meat liked who she'd become. "You're not going to be upset if I stay while you're meeting with her, are you?" he asked.

Zara shook her head. "No. And I'd like to introduce you to her. I mean, she's heard all about how wonderful you are."

"You tell her what I do?" he asked, concerned.

Zara nodded. "A little. I mean, she knows you make furniture, but I might've also told her that you used to be in the Army, and that you were down in Peru working on a case about exploited children when we met."

Meat nodded. "Let's keep it vague, all right? I know she's your friend, but typically, we don't go around sharing that we're a part of the Mountain Mercenaries or telling people what we do."

"Of course. I wouldn't put you or the others in danger. Besides, Renee wouldn't hurt a fly. She's a hairdresser, for goodness' sake. Oh . . . and speaking of which. If things go well, she said she'd be happy to do something about my hair." Zara grimaced. "It's getting more and more obvious that I did my own hack job on it. She said she could even it up. She offered to dye it if I wanted, but—"

"No!" Meat exclaimed, startling Zara, and she flinched back. "Shit, I'm sorry. I didn't mean to scare you. I just . . . I love the color it is now. It's unusual, just like you."

"It's brown, Meat. It's not unusual at all," Zara said wryly.

Meat's hand went to her hair, and he fingered a lock. "You have the kind of hair women spend their whole lives in a salon trying to achieve. It's brown, yes, but it's got shades of red hidden in there too. It's dark and deep, just like you. It makes your blue eyes pop, and the way it frames your face makes me think of a mischievous little fairy." When she kept looking at him with a frown, Meat sighed and dropped his hand. "I'm not that good with words, but your hair is beautiful.

Renee can style it for you and trim it, but honestly, don't let her mess with the color."

"Okay," Zara whispered. Then she leaned forward and shoved her hands behind his back and snuggled into him. "Have I told you lately how much I love the bed you got me?"

Meat inhaled deeply, loving her fresh and clean scent. He knew she was sensitive to the way her body smelled; he couldn't blame her, after spending as much time on the streets as she had. She'd begun to experiment with different kinds of soap. Morgan had sent over a whole box of fancy feminine shit she'd picked up at the mall, and Zara was currently wearing something that reminded him of a field of flowers right after a rainstorm.

"Yeah, Zar, you've mentioned it a time or two," he told her with a chuckle.

"Well, I do. And that pillow you bought for me is awesome. It's soft, but not too soft."

"Glad you like it."

"But you know what I like better?"

"What?"

She picked her head up and looked him in the eye. "Your shoulder."

Meat didn't know how to respond to that. He'd liked it a hell of a lot in Peru when she'd fallen asleep against him and had used his body as a pillow, but they hadn't repeated the experience since she'd been at his house. "Yeah?"

"Mmm-hmm. It's hard—not as hard as the ground, but not like a feather pillow either. It's also warm, and I swear I'm always cold. I have no idea how I'm going to make it through the winter here in Colorado. Once upon a time I loved playing in the snow, but after spending so much time in Peru, I think my cold genes have gone into hibernation or disappeared altogether."

Meat smiled at her and palmed the back of her head, gently forcing it back to his shoulder. He could feel the warmth of her body all along his; it made him hard, and he knew she could probably feel him between her legs. But after the first time it had happened, while she'd cuddled with him one night on the couch, she hadn't seemed to be bothered by his body's reaction to her.

Meat didn't respond. He simply enjoyed holding her. His ribs were healing nicely, and he felt only a twinge every now and then when he moved too quickly. Holding Zara definitely wasn't a hardship.

"Do you think Renee will like me?" Zara asked quietly after a while.

"Of course. She wants to meet with you, doesn't she?" Meat asked.

Zara nodded against him. "I just . . . I miss Mags and the other women down in Peru. I worry about them. There are days when I feel like I'm in a completely different world than they are, then I think about what they might be doing, what they may or may not be eating, wonder if they're safe from the police that patrol the area. And I feel guilty that I'm here, safe and sound. I kinda feel as if I've abandoned them. I think that's why it's been so hard for me to connect with Allye and the others. I almost feel like I'm cheating on Mags and everyone else. I know they wouldn't think that way, of course."

She sighed lightly. "After I meet with Renee, I'm going to reach out to Morgan and the other women again. I know it's important to you . . . and that makes it important to me too."

"I just want you to be happy, Zar. And Mags would too."

"I like to think so. When I get too down about what they might be going through in Peru, I try to keep in mind how amazing they are. Mags is super smart, and Gabriella grew up in the barrio, so she knows how to fend for herself. I just wish I could somehow share the safety and contentment I'm feeling with them."

Zara yawned against him, and he felt her sink even deeper into his body. It was dark outside now, and the crickets were chirping away. The air had cooled a bit, and the wind whistled through the trees on his property.

Meat knew things couldn't stay this peaceful forever. Zara would surely want to move out on her own to start her life again. His home was a temporary haven for her, one he'd let her stay in for as long as she wanted.

But the longer she stayed, the more he wanted her there—permanently. He liked listening to her read to him as he worked out in his workshop. He liked teaching her how to cook and drive.

He knew once she felt more comfortable with her surroundings, she'd blossom. He had no doubt she'd soon have her GED in hand and would move on to bigger and better things than living in the middle of nowhere with a retired Army guy and furniture maker.

Things with the Mountain Mercenaries had also been slow. Meat wasn't sure if that was because everyone was busy with their own families and lives, and Rex had taken notice and backed off the assignments, or what. He'd only talked to Rex a couple of times since they'd been back from Peru, and honestly, he hadn't really missed the adrenaline-inducing missions. After getting hurt on this last one, and he and Black having such close calls, he was ready for a change.

He and the guys had met at The Pit a couple of times since they'd been back, and everyone agreed that while women and children would always need help, they couldn't help *everyone*. Once he and Black were completely healed, they all agreed to have a talk with Rex and ask him if he might be willing to contain their missions to the continental United States. To work closer with the FBI on cases so they'd have more official backup in case the shit hit the fan. With the birth of Darby, and the imminent birth of Arrow's little girl, things had changed. None of them were on their own anymore.

And the longer Meat spent with Zara, the more his willingness to put his life on the line waned. She needed him. He didn't want to be another person in her life who left her. Even if it was through no fault of his own.

How long he sat on his back porch with Zara quietly sleeping on his chest, Meat didn't know. But by the time he got up and carried her inside and up the stairs, placing her on her bed, he'd made a decision.

He'd do whatever it took to convince Zara to be his. If she wanted to date other men, he'd try to be okay with it, but ultimately, he hoped she'd choose him.

It was crazy how fast life could change. One day you could be lying in the dirt in one of the poorest areas of Peru, thinking your life was about to end, and the next you could be planning on spending the rest of your life with the angel of mercy who'd rescued you.

Meat knew he'd fallen hard and fast, but apparently that was what a Mountain Mercenary did. He'd move heaven and earth to give Zara the life that had been stolen from her, and make her happy in the process.

"It's taking too long to get the money," the man mumbled under his breath as he paced back and forth. "And she's not even using it herself. It's going to waste, just like it has for the last fifteen years!" He turned to his companion and threw an arm out. "She just sits at that guy's house and never goes *anywhere*. Doesn't buy a damn thing! We've sent her a ton of emails, giving her that down-on-our-luck sob story, but she just ignores them all. I *want* that money!"

"So do I, but it's not that easy."

"We need to step this shit up," the man mumbled. "Get this done. I've talked to my contact down in Mexico, and they're ready and waiting for us to get there with the cash. Do you know how much cheaper Black Eagle is down there? Instead of a hundred bucks a gram, we can get double or triple that."

"Speaking of which, do you have any on you?"

"No."

"Then maybe you should go and take care of that, don't you think?"

"Fuck you!" the man said. "I'll take care of the drugs, you take care of the money."

"I will. We'll get it, one way or another."

The man nodded, then pulled out his phone to call his dealer. Things would look better after they'd smoked some dope. Things always looked brighter when they were high.

The thought of getting out of Denver and heading to Mexico sounded better and better with every day that went by. He'd lived in this fucking city his entire life, getting nowhere, and he was more than ready to leave.

He'd done enough waiting for a chance at Zara Layne's inheritance, and he'd be damned if he let this opportunity slip through his fingers.

Chapter Twenty

"Do I look okay?" Zara asked as she wiped her sweaty palms down the sides of her jeans as they stood inside the restaurant.

"You look beautiful," Meat assured her, kissing her on the temple before stepping back.

Something about him was different, and Zara couldn't quite put her finger on it. He'd always been protective of her, concerned about her well-being, but lately he seemed even more so.

She was nervous for this first meeting with Renee, and Meat hadn't exactly done much to assuage her anxiety. She was aware he wasn't all that enthused about her meeting face-to-face with her childhood friend, but when he couldn't find anything in her background to be worried about, he'd relented and tried his best to be happy for her.

But it was more than just worry on her behalf that she'd been noticing. She also found him staring at her at odd times, and when she asked what he was looking at, he'd simply smile and say, "You." When they made out, Meat was suddenly more intense. He still let her take the lead in their physical relationship, but the look in his eyes made goose bumps break out on her arms and her belly do flips. He touched her more often. A caress on her arm here, a long hug there.

And he was *constantly* kissing her. Touching his lips to her shoulder, her temple, the top of her head. Not that she minded . . .

He was acting just like she remembered her father acting toward her mother. Loving. She remembered how her dad always held her mom's hand. Zara had complained about them kissing in front of her when she got old enough to understand it. She hadn't really hated it—it was just embarrassing for a ten-year-old.

She'd never felt for any man the way she felt about Hunter Snow. He was the first person she thought of when she got up and the last person she thought of before she fell asleep. He hadn't pressured her to do anything she didn't want to do. He'd been patient and kind, even when gently urging her to step outside the safety his home represented.

As far as that went . . . the truth of the matter was, she was scared. What had happened to her down in Lima had been a statistical anomaly, and she wasn't ready to test her luck just yet.

Meeting Renee today was the first step in gaining back her independence . . . but the confusing part was, Zara wasn't sure she *wanted* it. She'd technically been independent for most of her life, and it hadn't been much fun. She liked cooking for Meat. Liked when he told her where he was going and when he'd be back. It wasn't that she was afraid to live on her own, exactly . . . she simply didn't want to.

"I'm just going to sit over there at the bar," Meat told her, staring into her eyes. "If anything makes you uncomfortable, all you have to do is gesture to me, and I'll be there in a heartbeat. Okay?"

"It's going to be fine," Zara replied, not sure if she was reassuring him or herself.

Meat kissed her once more, not quite a short brush of his lips against hers, but not a thorough claiming either. "Have fun," he said quietly before turning to head to the bar.

Zara followed the waitress to a high-top table near the bar and settled in to wait for Renee. She felt bad that her friend had to drive down from Denver, but Renee had reassured her that it was no problem.

After ten minutes, Zara slipped off the stool as a tall blonde headed straight for her. Recognizing Renee from the picture she'd sent, Zara was still surprised at how tall she was. She towered over Zara's own five-foot-one height as she gave her an enthusiastic hug.

"You're so tiny!" Renee exclaimed.

Zara laughed and awkwardly climbed back up onto the barstool at the table.

"Shit, do your feet even touch the rungs on the chair?" Renee asked with a laugh, leaning over to see for herself. "They don't! That's hilarious. I didn't realize you were so short! Were you this short in the fourth grade?"

Zara forced a smile. She knew she was petite. Living with someone Meat's size brought that home to her all the time. But Meat didn't harp on it. He'd actually adjusted things to accommodate her height. The bed frame he'd made her was lower. He'd made a stool for her to use in the kitchen so she could reach the cabinets, and he hadn't said a word when she'd scooted the coffee table closer to the couch so she could put her feet on it.

"Probably," she told Renee. "Although I'm sure the lack of proper nutrition over the last decade or so didn't exactly help."

Renee frowned. "I'm sorry, I didn't mean to say something offensive."

"You didn't," Zara hurried to reassure her.

"It's just so surreal to be sitting with you," Renee said. "I mean, no one ever thought we'd see you again. It's a miracle you survived."

Zara nodded. *Jeez.* Things seemed much more natural—and a lot less awkward—when they'd talked on the phone.

"So . . . tell me what you're up to. What are your plans now that you're back? It's good that you don't have to worry about money. I heard your parents left you a trust. That's so lucky!"

Lucky? Zara wasn't so sure about that, but she simply smiled again and took a sip of her water. "Honestly, I've been acclimating. Trying to decide what to do with the rest of my life. I've been reading a lot and trying to figure out when I want to try for my GED. There's a lot I have to study, especially math."

"Girl, school sucked so hard after the fifth grade. I'm kinda jealous you didn't have to suffer through it."

Zara gaped slightly, and Renee seemed to realize what she'd said almost immediately.

"Shit, I did it again. I'm so sorry! I didn't mean that the way it came out. You suffered through your own hell. You would've been glad to be living your old life and going to school, wouldn't you? How about we order and I keep my mouth shut for a while and let *you* talk? Tell me more about the guy who rescued you and was responsible for bringing you home."

Zara was glad for a subject change. She'd liked Renee so much when they'd talked online and on the phone, but things had already gotten off to a rocky start.

She ordered a bison burger and french fries, and Renee ordered a salad.

After their less-than-stellar beginning, Renee didn't ask anything inappropriate, or do or say anything to make Zara uncomfortable. By the time they'd finished eating, she was relieved to find that Renee had stopped being so nervous, and they had an easy conversation about the old days.

"I remember that one kid—Derek, I think his name was—he used to chase you around the playground trying to kiss you. You were a lot faster than he was, though, and he wasn't ever able to catch you."

Zara grinned and said slyly, "Wellll, there might have been one time when I let him catch me."

"You didn't!" Renee exclaimed, laughing. "And?"

"And he kissed me on the lips, and we just stared at each other. I wasn't sure if I was supposed to feel something or not, and apparently he felt the same way, because after that, he didn't chase me again."

They both laughed at the memory, and it felt good to Zara to be sharing such innocuous recollections with someone who'd known her before her life had irrevocably changed.

"I've had a good time," Renee said. "It's good to see you looking so well . . . besides that hair, that is." She chuckled.

Zara laughed with her. "I know, it's kind of a mess."

"The offer to help you out with it still stands."

Zara bit her lip and glanced over at the bar. Meat was still there, and every time she'd looked at him, she'd caught his eye. Instead of weirding her out that he was as attuned to her as he was, it made her feel safe. Which wasn't something she'd felt for most of her life.

"What? You have to check with your watchdog?" Renee asked.

Zara looked back at Renee in surprise. "You knew he was here?"

"I mean, first—he's hot. It would be impossible *not* to notice him. Secondly, he's been staring at our table the entire time I've been here. At first I thought he was checking me out, but then it was obvious he was watching *you*. So I put two and two together and figured this was the Meat guy you told me about."

Zara nodded. "Yeah. I don't drive yet, and he offered to bring me here to meet you."

"And decided to stay to make sure I wasn't going to kidnap you for your money, right?" Renee asked.

Zara shrugged. "It's just that after I stupidly put my email address out there, I've gotten a lot of emails from people trying to con money from me."

"How do you know *he* isn't after your money?" Renee asked.

Zara blinked in surprise. "Because. I just know."

"Because your judgment is so good?" Renee asked gently. "Look, I'm not trying to be a bitch, but it's a tough world, as you already know. You can't trust *anyone*. Not even him. I bet he tried to talk you out of meeting me, didn't he?"

Zara shook her head, but obviously her expression wasn't so convincing.

"Yeah, I wouldn't be surprised. He's probably happy to keep you isolated at his place. To not have you drive. To not have friends. I'm probably overstepping here, but seriously, if you ever need *anything*, you can call me.

"We go way back, Zara. We've been friends for twenty years, and I don't care that we haven't seen each other in fifteen. Whatever you need, I'll be there for you. Want to go shopping? Call me. I'm happy to help with your hair and anything else you might need. I'm not that smart when it comes to investments, but I haven't done too bad for myself, so I can help you with that too. Want boy advice? I'm your girl. Want to go out and let your hair down and have a one-night stand? I can hook you up there as well. I just don't want you to trust him *just* because he rescued you. What is that called . . . Stockholm syndrome?"

"He's not keeping me prisoner," Zara protested, not happy at all that Renee was trying to make her doubt everything Meat had done for her.

"Is he or isn't he sitting over there watching your every move?" Renee asked. "He always keep you on such a short leash?"

"It's not like that," Zara insisted, with more heat than she'd intended. "He's a good guy, Renee. You're *way* off base. He's done nothing but help me since we met, and not once has he asked for anything in return."

Renee patted her hand and slid off the stool. "Call me, Zara. I'm here for you without any strings. You need a friend, and not someone *he's* picked out for you. I'm thrilled you answered my email, because I think you need me."

She fumbled with her purse, and Zara quickly said, "I've got lunch, don't worry about it."

Renee winked and said, "That's right—you're the rich one." Then she took a few steps and awkwardly hugged Zara while she was still

Susan Stoker

sitting on the stool. Her gaze went to her hair. "You'd look great as a redhead."

Zara's thoughts turned to how reverently Meat had fingered her hair, and the nice things he'd said about it. She bit her lip.

Renee shook her head. "Let me guess—he said he likes you just the way you are, right? Of course he'd say that. He doesn't want you to pretty yourself up because you might attract the attention of someone else, and you'd slip out of his clutches. Seriously, Zara . . . wise up before it's too late. I'll send you an email when I get home."

"Okay. Renee?"

The other woman turned after a few steps. "Yeah?"

"Maybe next time you can fix my hair for me? Trim it up and make it more even?"

"Yeah, Zara, I can do that. Later."

"Bye."

Zara watched as Renee walked away, her hips swaying as she went, making most of the men at the bar sit up and pay attention. Apparently she wasn't going to introduce her to Meat, after all.

A hand landed on Zara's back, and she knew in an instant it was him.

"You okay? Things looked pretty intense there at the end."

How did she tell him that Renee had as many misgivings about *him* as he had about her?

She couldn't. She trusted Meat, and she was embarrassed that the woman she was so excited to meet had been suspicious of him. She didn't want to burden him with the fact that her only friend other than Meat didn't seem to like him. Meat probably wouldn't care, but Zara did.

She shrugged. "It was okay."

Meat studied her for a long moment. "You don't look happy," he observed.

204

Forcing herself to smile, Zara shook her head. "No, I'm good. I just didn't realize how many memories meeting with her was going to bring up."

"How about we get home and I run a long bath for you? You haven't tried all the bubble bath scents Morgan brought over for you yet, have you?"

Zara couldn't help but remember Renee's words.

You need a friend, and not someone he's picked out for you.

Was that why Meat had pushed her so hard to hang out with Allye, Chloe, Morgan, Harlow, and Everly? He wanted to choose her friends? She didn't think so. But then again, Renee was right about one thing— she wasn't all that wise to the ways of her new world . . . or men.

Put her in the middle of a slum in Peru, and she could survive just fine. But here in the States, it was a completely different story.

Hating that she was second-guessing everything Meat had done for her, and the things he continued to do, she let him help her off the stool, and they walked side by side to the door and out to his car.

They were silent on the way back to his place. Zara struggled for words, but her mind was stuck on everything Renee had said.

After they'd parked back at Meat's house, he turned to her. "You've been pretty quiet. I don't know what you and Renee talked about . . . but I hope to God she wasn't trying to turn you against me. I swear on my life that I only want the best for you, Zara. If you don't want to stay at my house anymore, I'll bend over backward to find you a safe place to live. I'll ask Everly what apartment complexes have the fewest criminal complaints, and I'll investigate the landlords to make sure they're on the up-and-up.

"But please—don't doubt what we have between us. You're special, and my feelings for you have only grown deeper with every day we spend together. It's not pity. Or gratitude. And I certainly couldn't give a shit about your money. I just . . . You're important to me, and I can't stand to see you hurt.

"Here're the keys to the house. Make sure you put in the code for the alarm within a minute of going inside. I'll be out in my workshop if you need anything."

And with that, he placed the keys in her hand and climbed out of the car, making his way toward the large barn next to the house.

Zara watched him until he disappeared through the door to his workshop.

She knew deep in her soul that Meat wasn't doing anything underhanded. She'd let Renee plant the seeds of doubt . . . but wouldn't she tell her friend to be cautious if their roles were reversed?

She owed Meat an explanation and an apology, but she felt confused, out of her element. Not only that, she felt guilty for letting Renee's words get to her, even a little bit, causing Meat to be unnecessarily concerned. She felt particularly horrible about the latter, as if she'd just kicked a puppy.

She wasn't used to having to make such emotional decisions. In Peru, her hardest tasks were finding something to eat and staying out of notice of anyone who might think she was easy prey.

Feeling confused and heartsick about keeping things from Meat, she trudged to the house to do as he suggested. Take a bath. Later, she'd talk to him, try to explain everything that was going on inside her head.

She entered the house and turned the alarm off. Then she went upstairs and stared at the multitude of lotions, soaps, and bubble baths Morgan had sent over for her. She'd included a short note that said, *When things got stressful for me, I found there was nothing better than a long shower or bath to make me think clearly again. There's nothing like being clean, is there?*

Zara knew the other woman was trying in her own way to make her feel welcome. She hadn't tried very hard to get to know Morgan or the others—another thing to feel guilty about—and regardless of what Renee had insinuated, she didn't think the other women were trying to befriend her for nefarious reasons.

It was time to pull her head out of her ass. She'd been back in the United States for almost a month. It was time to get out of her comfort zone and make some friends . . . other than Meat and Renee. And while she still wanted to talk to and see Renee, maybe it wouldn't be a bad idea to get to know the significant others of Meat's friends too.

Her decision made, even if it made her anxious, Zara picked out a scent called "spiced gingerbread" and poured a liberal amount into the running water of the bath.

Chapter Twenty-One

One week later, Zara listened as Meat made arrangements to pick up Arrow in about forty-five minutes. He'd called him to make sure they were still set for their trip to Castle Rock that morning. They were headed up to the small town between Denver and Colorado Springs to visit a friend of theirs who had previously been a member of the Mountain Mercenaries.

Ryder "Ace" Sinclair had moved up to Castle Rock to be closer to his half brothers, and because he'd met and married a woman named Felicity. He'd started working for his brothers' company, Ace Security, and they were currently embroiled in a case that involved what they suspected was human trafficking. They'd asked for a consult with the Mountain Mercenaries.

From what Meat had told Zara after his phone call with Arrow, his friend was reluctant to leave Morgan. She'd encouraged him to go, since it was a work thing and not merely a social visit. Arrow was still nervous, it being only a week from Morgan's due date, but she'd insisted she'd be fine—that if something *did* happen, he'd still be close enough to race back to Colorado Springs to be there for the birth.

Meat tried to ease his mind, pointing out that first children usually took longer to get there anyway, and Arrow had reluctantly agreed. He was still a nervous wreck. Not that it was surprising; after Gray had missed the birth of his son, they were all a little on edge.

Meat explained that none of the other women could hang out with Morgan because they were otherwise busy. Either working or stuck in obligations they couldn't get out of.

It had been just over a month since Zara had arrived back in the United States, and since she'd been living with Meat. She'd needed the time alone to acclimate to her new circumstances. To come to grips with the fact that she could shower anytime she wanted. That she had clean clothes every day and as much food as she could eat.

Renee had insinuated that she was being held prisoner in some way, but in reality that couldn't be further from the truth. She'd been hiding out. Not ready to face the world. Afraid she'd be found lacking. Meat had given her a place to feel safe. Now, she was finally beginning to feel the need to connect with others. To find her place in this new world she was living in.

Renee was trying to be a good friend, and Zara had enjoyed talking to her, for the most part. She'd met up with her again a few days ago, and Renee had trimmed and styled her hair. It was now in what she had called a pixie cut, and Zara loved it. She'd also filled out a bit since living with Meat, and didn't look quite so skinny anymore . . . despite Renee's continued teasing about her size.

All in all, while she liked Renee, the connection they'd had when they were younger wasn't really there anymore. They'd grown into very different people. Zara was still thankful to have her back in her life, but she missed the kind of connection she'd had with Mags and her friends down in the barrio.

The bottom line was that she wanted to try again with Meat's female friends. She owed it to Meat as well. And Morgan was a perfect place to start. She'd been wanting to talk to her about how Morgan had been able to reintegrate back into her old life, and this was her chance.

"I could go with you and stay with Morgan while you guys are up in Castle Rock," she told Meat. "If you think Arrow would be okay with it."

Meat was sitting on the couch lacing up his sneakers, and when he was done, he got up and came straight to her. His hands slid into the hair on either side of her head, and he tilted her face to look at him. "Really?"

She nodded.

"Arrow *and* Morgan would love that."

When he didn't move away from her, Zara asked, "Are you going to call and ask if it's all right?"

"It's all right," Meat confirmed.

Zara rolled her eyes.

"I love seeing you do that," Meat told her.

"What? Roll my eyes?" Zara asked in amusement.

"Yes. Those first few days you were here, you didn't talk hardly at all. You were hesitant in everything you did. You asked permission to get a drink, to sit outside, to do just about *everything*. But you've come into your own quickly. And I love it."

"It's because of you," Zara told him honestly. "You made it so easy to just . . . be me."

"I try. You need to grab anything before we go?"

She shook her head.

"Good. Then we have time for this."

Zara opened her mouth to ask, "For what?" but his lips covered hers, cutting off her question.

Her eyes closed, and she wound her arms around him, digging her nails into his back, trying to pull him closer.

Thankfully, there was still hardly any time they were together when Meat wasn't touching her in some way. Holding her hand, putting his fingers just under her shirt at the small of her back, kissing her. And she loved every second. It had been fun to experiment at first, going slow, but she was already getting impatient.

She wanted more but didn't know how to tell Meat she was ready to move their physical relationship to the next level. Every night, he left her with a kiss at the door to the guest room that made her bones weak, and every night, she couldn't find the courage to invite him in.

But she was quickly losing her shyness. She wanted him. Wanted to know what sex was all about. She just had to find a way to tell him.

Meat pulled back. She could feel his hardness against her stomach, and it made her squirm in his grip. "You're going to be the death of me," he said with a smile, then leaned down and kissed her hard before stepping back. "I wish I didn't have to go up to Castle Rock. I'd rather spend the day here with you."

He never failed to make her feel good. "I'll see you later tonight," she said, then looked at him from under her lashes. "I always look forward to spending time with you."

Meat groaned and reached out to physically turn her toward the door. "If we don't leave now, I might be tempted to haul your butt down on the couch and let you have your wicked way with me."

"And I'd let you," Zara told him, excited that it seemed maybe they were finally on the same page when it came to where things were going between them.

She smiled when she saw Meat adjust himself in his pants before he climbed into his car, but she didn't comment.

As they drove, Meat said, "So Arrow and Morgan recently moved into the new house they had built on a piece of property he bought not too far from us. Morgan used to be a full-time beekeeper in Atlanta, and she's just now dabbling back into the business. They have two hives out at the back of their property. Whatever she says, don't let her talk you into going out there with her. Arrow's been trying to keep her away from them until she gives birth, just in case."

Zara was already fascinated by Morgan. She sounded like the coolest person ever, and Zara hoped they'd be able to find something in common—other than being kidnapped and spending time at the mercy of others outside the United States, of course.

Susan Stoker

"We shouldn't be gone all day. It's been a while since we've seen Ace, and we're looking forward to getting to know his half brothers better. But if you need anything, all you have to do is call . . . You have your phone, right?"

Zara wrinkled her nose as she looked over at Meat and shook her head.

"Zara . . . we've talked about this."

"I know, I know. I'm sorry. I just can't get used to carrying it around. I don't need to have it with me all the time at your house."

Meat sighed. "It's okay. Morgan will have hers. But please . . . try to remember it. I hate the thought of you needing me, or anyone, and not being able to get in touch with us. Besides, I can track it. Not that I think anything will happen to you, but it gives me peace of mind."

"I'll try to remember it in the future," she told him.

They pulled up to a large house surrounded by trees, and Zara couldn't help but immediately love it. It reminded her a lot of Meat's house. She loved the cabinlike feel.

It seemed she had something in common with Morgan, after all. If the other woman could love living in a place like this as much as Zara did, then they'd be okay.

Arrow and Morgan came out to meet them, and the first thing Arrow said to Zara was, "Please tell me you're staying."

Zara smiled and nodded. "If it's okay."

"Hell yeah, it's okay!" Arrow said. "It's *more* than okay."

Zara looked at Morgan. "I didn't mean to simply invite myself over, but I thought you might like some company."

"Of course. I'm thrilled! I've been wanting to get to know you better, but this little bean"—she put her hand on her protruding belly—"has been giving me hell. One day making it seem like she wants to come out right now, and other days sleeping peacefully as if she could stay inside me for another three months."

Zara smiled.

It took twenty more minutes for Arrow to make sure his wife was good. He told her for the hundredth time to call him if she needed anything, and she had to promise not to step foot outside the house.

They kissed so passionately before Arrow left, Zara was almost embarrassed to be a witness to it. But of course, not to be outdone, Meat grabbed her and kissed her with just as much enthusiasm.

Zara knew she was blushing when the men finally left, but Morgan didn't comment. They went inside and turned on the television for background noise while they chatted. They were making small talk when the midday news came on.

There was another segment on Zara's case, this one with a psychologist and a local detective speculating about what Zara had been through and what she might be facing mentally as far as her "recovery from her ordeal."

"They have no idea what they're talking about," Zara complained.

"Unfortunately, they'll continue to say whatever they can think up until you set them straight," Morgan said without judgment.

Zara turned to her. "You think I should give a press conference?" She'd been thinking about it more and more. She hadn't been ready to talk about what had happened to her when she'd first gotten back. Just the thought of getting in front of a bunch of reporters and answering their questions made her feel sick. She'd spent so much of her life trying to fade into the background and *not* be seen that the idea of being the center of attention nearly gave her an anxiety attack.

But with all the interviews and false information about her still circulating on the internet and TV—and getting more sensational—she was feeling the need to tell her side of the story. To set everyone straight.

"I can't tell you if you should or shouldn't," Morgan told her. "You have to do what's right for you. But if you're upset about what's being said, I think you're getting close to deciding."

Zara nodded. "I just . . . When Meat brought me back to his house, it seemed like a perfect place to hole up. To hide from everything. I didn't want to talk about my life in Peru. Or remember. I never really got to grieve my parents, and with everyone wanting to know what I saw and heard all those years ago . . . it's been hard. I still feel some guilt over it. If I hadn't been such a brat at dinner, or if I hadn't been dawdling so far behind them, maybe we would've made it to the hotel faster, and they wouldn't have been at the wrong place at the wrong time."

"You can't blame yourself," Morgan said, leaning forward and putting her hand on Zara's arm. "I asked myself the same questions. Wondered if, had I asked for an escort the night I was kidnapped, if that would've prevented me from being taken. Or if I had fought more when they got me down to Santo Domingo, if they wouldn't have . . . violated me as much. But the bottom line is that we did the best we could in the situations we were in at the time. Don't second-guess yourself." Morgan sat back and shifted in her seat.

Zara wondered if she was uncomfortable with the conversation, and decided that she probably had to be. After all, she herself wasn't exactly thrilled to discuss what had happened to her. "How did you put it behind you and move on? I mean, I don't know what happened between you and Arrow after you came back, but did he . . . did you . . . Shit, I don't know how to ask this."

"You can ask me anything, Zara. What happened to us wasn't fair. We both had parts of our lives stolen. I only had a year, but you had *fifteen years* taken."

"I'm a virgin," Zara blurted. Then immediately closed her eyes and shook her head. "I just mean, I didn't have to go through what you did."

"Just because you weren't raped doesn't mean you weren't traumatized," Morgan said gently. "You missed your entire childhood. You were on your own from the time you were *ten*. I have no idea how you did it. I'm in awe of you, Zara. I don't know what you were going to ask, but if it's about sex, it was hard for me. It took a long time. But Arrow was patient and never once made me feel bad about anything I endured, or anything that happened between the two of us in the bedroom.

"Whatever you went through, I have no doubt you would be an inspiration to so many people, Zara. The world is a brutal place. Humans are unkind. Most people don't experience what we did, but if you can survive that, and still be upright and walking and not in a mental institution, I think others could benefit from hearing what you have to say."

Zara couldn't fathom anyone being inspired by her. Not in the least.

She screwed up her courage and asked what she'd been thinking about earlier. "How did you get Arrow to see you as more than just someone he'd rescued? I mean . . . how did you let him know you would be interested in being more than just friends?"

Morgan shifted in her seat again and grimaced. Then she smiled at Zara. "Sorry, sitting for long periods gets uncomfortable. I'm assuming you're asking because you want Meat to do more than just kiss you like he did before he left, right?"

Zara nodded and tried not to be embarrassed.

"You need to be blunt. Just tell him what you're thinking. How you're feeling. He's probably scared to death to move too fast. If he's anything like Arrow, he wants to give you time to come to terms with what happened, and he's afraid if he moves too fast, he'll scare you."

"I'm not afraid of Meat," Zara said firmly. "I mean, I know how sex works. I may not have done it before, but because of how I lived, I've seen it up close and personal. Not much is private in the barrio. I also helped the doctor birth more babies than I can count. But . . . knowing and doing are two different things, and I'm terrified that I'll mess it up and Meat will ask me to move out."

"Now I get why Meat and Arrow convinced you to come over today," Morgan said with a laugh, gesturing to her belly.

"Oh no," Zara said quickly. "I volunteered. I think I'm done hiding away and licking my wounds. I wanted to talk to you and get to know you better. It didn't have anything to do with the fact you look like you're about to pop." She smiled to let Morgan know she was teasing.

"Good," Morgan said with a laugh. "To answer your question, you aren't going to mess up anything with Meat. He and the other Mountain Mercenaries know what they want and what they like. And what Meat obviously likes is *you*. He couldn't take his eyes off you today. All you have to do is let him know in no uncertain terms that you want to do more than kiss, and he'll take care of things from there."

"My friend Renee thinks I should have a few one-night stands and figure out what I like and don't like when it comes to sex and men. She says that because I've only been living with Meat, any attraction I feel toward him is just because I haven't been around anyone else."

"And what do *you* think about that?" Morgan asked.

Zara took a deep breath. "I think, in some ways, she has a point. I spent the last fifteen years trying to avoid men. But in others, I think she's wrong. I've seen and talked to men in the grocery store, and at a restaurant the last time Renee and I met up. A waiter even slipped me his phone number. Renee was thrilled and encouraged me to call him, but I just didn't feel any kind of pull toward him like I do with Meat."

Morgan nodded. "I get that. I do. I was the same as you in that I didn't want anything to do with men, but there was just something about Arrow that made me feel . . . settled. And it wasn't because he *rescued* me, like some people would say. When he looks at me, it's as if he *sees* me. He listens when I talk and doesn't push me to do anything I'm not comfortable with. I never thought I'd be able to make love again after what happened to me, and I still can't picture letting anyone *but* Arrow touch me. Now we're married—although my dad wasn't happy with the small, quick civil ceremony before Arrow went to Lima. And now I'm having his baby, and I feel as if it's a miracle. Just go with your gut, Zara. It's served you well for fifteen years. Maybe you and Meat won't work out long term . . . but what if you do?"

Zara thought about that, and she knew Morgan was right. "Thanks."

"You're welcome. Are you hungry?"

"Yeah. I've tried to eat just three meals like normal people, but I swear I feel as if I'm *always* hungry. I guess because I went without having food on a regular schedule for so long, my body is always pushing me to stuff myself just in case there's nothing to eat later."

"I know exactly how you feel!" Morgan exclaimed as she struggled to get up from the chair.

Zara helped her up and watched as she leaned over and took a few deep breaths. Then Morgan stood and smiled. "And how about showers and baths? I haven't been able to take any baths recently, but there's nothing like a nice long, hot shower, huh?"

Zara smiled as they walked into the kitchen. "Meat swears he doesn't mind that I take forty-five-minute showers, and even though I feel bad about it, I can't make myself shorten them."

"I'm the same way. Arrow mock-complains about the water bill, but I know he doesn't care. People who haven't been in our situation just wouldn't understand," she said.

Zara inwardly sighed with relief. She'd been silly for staying away from Morgan for so long. She suddenly had the suspicion she'd feel the same way when she got to know the other women as well. She felt as if she could tell Morgan anything and not be judged, simply because she'd been there. She'd lived through some of what Zara had. Not exactly, but close enough.

Maybe that was why she hadn't clicked as well as she'd hoped with Renee.

"Now . . . what do you want to eat?" Morgan asked as she opened the fridge.

"I'm not the best cook, but I'm up for just about anything," Zara said.

They settled on macaroni and cheese, and as they prepared the meal, Zara felt the shields she'd had up for the last month, which Meat had already started to crack, crumble even more.

Two hours later, after eating and chatting about nothing and everything, Morgan excused herself to go to the restroom. When she hadn't returned after ten minutes, Zara got worried and tentatively walked up the stairs to the second floor.

"Morgan?" she called. "Are you all right?"

"No!" the other woman cried.

Alarmed, Zara pushed into the master bedroom and headed straight for the bathroom, where she found Morgan leaning over the counter, resting her weight on her elbows. She lifted her head, and Zara could see she'd been crying.

"What's wrong?"

"I just . . . I've been having pains all day, but assumed it was false labor, just like the other two times Arrow made me go to the hospital. I'm still a week from my due date. It's too early, but I . . ." She paused and grimaced and gripped the edge of the counter hard enough for her fingers to turn white.

"You're in labor," Zara declared, having seen more than her fair share of pregnant women about to give birth.

Morgan shook her head. "I thought I had lots of time! I mean, first babies always take forever! I know how much Arrow was looking forward to seeing his friend. I didn't want him to worry. My water hasn't even broken! I can't have a baby without that happening first, right?"

"It's possible it happened when you were in the shower this morning, or when you went to the bathroom sometime today."

"Wouldn't I have noticed?" Morgan asked incredulously.

"Maybe, maybe not. With this being your first, it's possible you didn't. But let's not panic. I told you earlier that I have some experience with this. Will you let me take a look and see how things are progressing for you? Then I'll go downstairs and grab your phone, and we'll call for an ambulance. I'd drive you myself, but . . ." Zara kicked herself for not getting her driver's license before now.

"Okay."

Zara helped Morgan lie down on the floor of the bathroom. The tiles were probably chilly against her back, but Morgan was in enough pain that she didn't even seem to notice. Zara helped get her pants and underwear off and covered her lap with a towel.

Thinking she'd just see how dilated Morgan was, and that they'd have more than enough time to get to the hospital, she was alarmed when she saw the baby beginning to crown.

"How long have you been having contractions?" Zara asked, standing up and quickly washing her hands in the sink. They weren't going to have time to wait for an ambulance. Hell, she didn't even have time to run downstairs and get Morgan's phone. This baby was coming. *Now.*

"They started last night, but again, I didn't want to worry Arrow," Morgan said, then gasped in pain as another contraction hit. Zara gave her a look. "I know, I know! That was stupid, but he was so excited to see his friend . . . You can yell at me later. I need to push," Morgan groaned.

Zara grabbed some towels and spread them under Morgan as best she could, then got down on her knees and tried to reassure her new friend. "Okay, this is happening now, Morgan. But don't worry, we can do this."

"Shit, Arrow's going to be so pissed!"

Zara figured he'd probably be more relieved that she was all right, but she didn't say anything.

"Whoever gets pregnant next isn't going to be allowed to be alone for their entire last month of pregnancy," Morgan moaned. "With Gray missing Darby's birth and now this . . . we're all doomed."

Smiling, Zara concentrated on what she was doing. "Okay, do you feel the need to push?"

"Not yet . . . Oh . . . wait . . . God, this hurts so bad," Morgan moaned. "I'm pushing!"

Zara watched as the head of hair emerged until she could see the forehead of the tiny baby. She was relieved the birth wasn't breech.

But as Morgan continued to pant and push, Zara noticed the baby's face had a bluish tint.

"*Madre de Dios,*" she muttered. "Stop pushing, Morgan. Right now. Stop!"

"I can't!" Morgan cried. "I just need it out! *Please.*"

Zara put gentle pressure on the top of the baby's head, preventing it from exiting the birth canal. She looked up at Morgan and said harshly, "If you push, you'll kill her. *Stop. Pushing!*"

She got through to Morgan, because the other woman raised her head and looked down at Zara with wide, terrified eyes. "What's wrong?"

Zara took a deep breath. She'd done this before, but always with Daniela at her side. She'd never been solely responsible for a new life like she was right now. "I think the cord is wrapped around her neck. I need to remove it. It's okay. It's not terribly complicated, but you *cannot* push until it's off. Understand? She'll be strangled if she comes out any farther with the cord wrapped around her neck."

"Oh God!" Morgan sobbed, and her head flew back to rest on the bathroom floor once again. "Do what you have to do! Don't let her die! I won't be able to handle it."

Turning her attention back between Morgan's legs, Zara nodded. "Okay, this is going to hurt. There's nothing I can do about it. But if you can hold on for thirty seconds, it'll all be over and you'll have your little one in your arms. Have you and Arrow thought of a name yet?"

Doing her best to keep Morgan's attention off what she was about to do, Zara barely listened to Morgan's answer as she very slowly eased her hand inside Morgan's body as gently as possible. She'd never been so glad for her small hands as she was right at that moment.

She felt for the cord, and sighed in relief when she found it easily. She pulled on it slightly, getting some slack, then eased it over the baby's head at a snail's pace.

Morgan screamed in pain, but she wasn't pushing, which was all that Zara cared about. A woman's birth canal was meant to stretch when birthing a baby, but the process of untangling the umbilical cord couldn't be comfortable.

"Okay, Morgan, the hard part's done. Push. *Hard!*"

With one last scream, Morgan bore down and pushed with all her might. As her body did everything it could to expel the baby from its depths, Mother Nature took over, and Morgan's bladder emptied at the same time the small baby girl slipped from her mother's body.

Not caring that she'd just been peed on, Zara turned the baby and laid her on her arm. She was still a little blue and wasn't crying like she should be. "Come on, baby, come on," she muttered as she did her best to tactilely stimulate the infant. Her heart was beating, but she wasn't breathing very well on her own.

With no way to know how long the baby had been without oxygen, Zara prayed as she rubbed the infant's back and flicked the bottoms of her feet. Using her pinkie, she wiped out the baby's mouth as best she could. Zara knew the longer it took for a baby to cry after being born, the more danger it was in.

Finally, after what seemed like hours but was less than thirty seconds, the little girl took a breath and squeaked.

"That's it, do it again," Zara urged as she continued to rub the baby's back firmly.

She did. One second she was squeaking, and the next, the newborn was flat-out bawling.

Zara grabbed the towel that had been covering Morgan and wrapped it around the newborn, not bothering to cut the cord. She'd leave that for the paramedics.

"Ready to meet your daughter?" Zara asked Morgan, who was propped up on her elbows, staring at her in absolute shock.

"Is she all right?"

"She's perfect," Zara said, as she handed her to Morgan.

"Shit . . . did I pee on you?" Morgan asked as she clasped her baby to her chest.

Zara laughed. "Yup. But I'm impressed you didn't lose your bowels too. That often happens."

Morgan stared at Zara for a second, then her eyes filled with tears and she sobbed in earnest. "Y-You saved her life!"

Zara felt her own eyes tear up, which was crazy. She'd helped birth at least a hundred babies. Some didn't live more than a few minutes, and for at least one other, she'd done almost exactly what she'd just done for Morgan's child. And not once had she cried.

But sitting on the floor of Morgan's bathroom, covered in bodily fluids and blood, Zara felt tears on her cheeks for the first time in years.

"I need to go get your phone," she said after she could talk. "Don't go anywhere, okay?"

Morgan chuckled through her tears. "Right. I'll just be right here."

Zara stood and grabbed another towel that was on a hook by the shower. She gently laid it over Morgan's lap, giving her some semblance of modesty, although she didn't think Morgan even noticed. She quickly washed her hands and turned to race back down the stairs and get Morgan's cell phone.

This would be the last time she went *anywhere* without her own phone. Meat was right. It wasn't smart to not have it in her pocket at all times.

Chapter Twenty-Two

Three days had passed since Zara had saved the life of little Calinda. Meat had never driven so fast in his entire life as he had on the way from Castle Rock to the hospital. Zara had called and informed him that Morgan had given birth and was on the way there, and Arrow had lost his shit. Meat and his friends had, luckily, been able to calm him down while driving like a bat out of hell to get back to Colorado Springs.

Zara had brushed off what she'd done, but Morgan had told everyone *exactly* what had happened, and how Zara had literally saved the life of her baby. Arrow and Morgan had changed Calinda's middle name from Elizabeth to Zara.

Meat had held Zara as she'd cried after hearing that.

Understandably, she and Morgan had become much closer after everything that had happened. But more than that, Meat could tell something else had changed. All the other women had shown up at the hospital, and Zara had gone out of her way to try to be social. She'd sat with them, had actually joined in their conversations instead of just sitting on the outside, listening. She'd seemed far more open to their friendship than she had the last time they'd all gotten together.

Meat truly didn't care one way or another for himself; he was just glad for *her* that she seemed to be finding her way. She'd told him how much she missed Mags and the others, and he hoped her new openness was the first step to lifelong friendships with some of the best women he knew.

Zara had also talked to Renee shortly after the birth of Morgan's baby girl, and the other woman hadn't seemed all that impressed with what Zara had done, just wanted to know when they might get together to go shopping, as they'd talked about recently.

Even though Meat hadn't been able to find anything to be concerned about when it came to Renee, that didn't mean he'd lowered his guard. His gut still felt like something was . . . *off* about the reappearance of her childhood friend. It seemed to him she was trying a little *too* hard to be friends with Zara again. But since Zara seemed to take comfort in the relationship, he didn't have the heart to come between them . . . yet.

But he was admittedly relieved that Zara was making the effort to get to know the other women.

Things between him and Zara had been better than ever . . . and they were hardly bad before. Whatever she and Morgan had talked about before Calinda decided to make an appearance had obviously done Zara good. She'd been a little more forward when it came to physical affection—and last night had flat-out told him she was ready to move their relationship to the next level.

Meat was all for that, but only if she was doing it for the right reasons. He didn't want to be just an experiment for her. Just someone to take her virginity so she could move on to a "real" relationship. As far as he was concerned, theirs *was* a real relationship, and he couldn't imagine being with anyone else after Zara.

At the moment, they were on their way to a big-box store for food and some odds and ends Meat needed for his shop. He held Zara's hand almost constantly now and actually felt bereft when he had to let her go. They walked into the store with their fingers intertwined—and their attention was immediately drawn to a woman speaking in rapid-fire Spanish to a police officer just inside the door.

Zara stopped in her tracks and stared at the duo.

"What's going on?" Meat asked. "What's she saying?"

The police officer looked frustrated and kept talking into his radio, even as the woman spoke to him.

Without answering, Zara dropped his hand and headed toward the agitated woman.

Meat followed right on her heels, his head on a swivel as he looked for an irate husband or anything else that might be of danger to Zara.

She walked up to the woman and said something in Spanish. The look of relief on the woman's face was easy to see. She immediately turned to Zara and began urgently telling her something.

"My girlfriend is bilingual," Meat told the officer unnecessarily.

"Thank God. I've been trying to get another officer here who speaks Spanish, but she's been held up on another call."

Zara put a reassuring hand on the woman's shoulder and turned to the officer. "She says she can't find her son. She was in the boys' clothing section the last time she saw him, and when she turned her back for a second, he'd disappeared."

"How old, and what is he wearing?" the cop asked, all business now.

Zara turned to consult with the hysterical mother, then relayed the information back to the officer. "His name is Joseph, and he's three. He's wearing a red T-shirt and a pair of black shorts. He has black hair and brown eyes. He's also wearing shoes that light up when he walks."

The police officer nodded and immediately relayed the information to his dispatcher. "Can you stay here with her?" he asked Zara. "I'm going to talk to the manager and see if we can get an announcement made."

"Of course," Zara said. "Maybe I can say something in Spanish over the loudspeaker too? I mean, hopefully Joseph is just hiding somewhere, and hearing someone say it's okay to come out, that his mom is waiting for him at the front doors, might help."

"Good idea," the cop agreed.

Meat watched with pride as Zara took the mother by the hand and translated everything that was going on about the search for her son. The look of gratitude on the poor mother's face, that someone understood and was helping her, made Meat swell with pride for Zara.

It took almost thirty extremely tense minutes, but finally the boy was found and reunited with the mother. He'd wandered off to look at toys and quickly got lost, then got scared when he couldn't find his mom. He'd crawled behind a row of stuffed animals on a bottom shelf and hidden.

The mother couldn't stop thanking Zara, and after exchanging phone numbers and promising to be in touch, the woman left with Joseph.

"Thanks for helping out," the police officer said.

"It was my pleasure. I'm just glad I was here."

"Say . . . aren't you Zara Layne? The woman who was rescued after all that time being forced to be a drug runner for the Venezuelan government?"

Meat tensed. It wasn't often that Zara was recognized, since she hadn't done a press conference, but it still happened. A few reporters had gotten some pictures of her getting off the plane when she'd arrived, and they'd spread like wildfire.

"That's me, although I was in Peru, and I wasn't forced to be a drug runner or anything else. I was simply lost and waiting for someone to come and find me after my parents were killed." Her tone was icy.

"Sorry, I wasn't sure on the details. I don't watch a lot of TV. Regardless, I'm just glad you were here today. If you're ever looking for a job, we could use more translators."

"I don't want to be a cop," Zara told him.

"You wouldn't have to be. There are translation services that hospitals and other organizations use. Basically, a number is called, a language is picked from a menu, and a translator comes on and helps communicate with whoever needs the service." The man looked chagrined. "It's

226

not something the CSPD uses, for a few legal reasons. But you could help a lot of others."

Meat's mind whirled with possibilities. He and Zara hadn't talked much about what she wanted to do with her future. With the amount of money she had in her account, she technically didn't have to work, but he had a feeling she would be bored silly before too much longer. She'd found her feet, and now he wanted to see her fly.

"I'll think about it," Zara said noncommittally.

The officer nodded, shook her hand, then strode out of the building.

"So . . . ready to shop now?" Meat asked with a grin.

She didn't return it. "Are you angry? I couldn't just walk by. She was terrified, and it was obvious the cop didn't understand what she was saying."

"Of course I'm not mad," Meat told her. He framed her face with his hands. He loved the feel of her dainty features under his big ol' palms, and if the way she latched on to his wrists and held on tight was any indication, she didn't exactly object. "I'm *proud* of you. I love your big heart. After everything you've been through, you're somehow still able to have empathy and a sense of service toward others. It's amazing. *You're* amazing."

"Thanks." Her eyes dropped from his for a moment before coming back up. She had a look of determination that was sexy as fuck. "Morgan told me that if I wanted something, I should just come out and tell you."

"She's right. Anything I can give you, I will," Meat told her.

"I want *you*, Meat. I remember how amazing it felt to have you sleep behind me, holding me tight. I can't say that I know what I'm doing, but I think I'd like to see if maybe I can sleep on a real mattress. The futon you got me is still great and all . . . but it's missing something."

Meat's heart almost pounded out of his chest. "What's that?"

"You."

"You want to sleep with me, Zar?"

She nodded.

"Just sleep? Because I'm okay with that. I don't want to do something you aren't ready for."

"No, not just sleep. I've dreamed of you. Fantasized about how your hands would feel on my body. About you kneeling over me, taking what I hope we've *both* thought about since we met."

"Shit, sweetheart. Now I have a hard-on in the middle of a crowded store. Not cool."

She grinned.

Meat knew he'd remember this moment for the rest of his life. The moment Zara took back one of the biggest things that had been taken from her. Her sexuality. Her sexual confidence. "There's nothing I'd like more than to take you to my bed," he told her. "We can learn together what we like."

"Okay."

"Okay," he echoed.

"Do we still have to shop?" she asked.

Meat raised an eyebrow and looked at his watch. "It's only eleven o'clock."

She shrugged. "We can only have sex at night?"

"Make love—and no, of course not," he said immediately.

"Then . . ." She let the word trail off.

"I think we can get what we came for another time," Meat agreed, and grabbed her hand and started for the exit.

He heard Zara chuckle behind him—and was shocked when her free hand rested on his ass for a brief moment. He turned to look at her in surprise.

She shrugged. "Morgan *did* tell me I should go after what I want."

"I owe her. Big," Meat said.

As they neared his car, she asked, "Would you have made the first move if I didn't?"

Meat nodded. "Eventually, yes. I like you, Zara. But more than that, I *want* you. There's no way I would've been able to hold out forever." At his car, he turned to her and said seriously, "But if we do this . . . you're mine. I don't want to be an experiment for you. This is the real deal for me. A forever thing."

Zara stared at him. "How can you be so sure?"

"I just am. From the first time I saw you, I knew there was something special about you. And every day we spend together, I'm more and more sure. I want to be in your life, Zara. Not as a friend who's giving you a place to stay until you figure things out, but as a partner. A man you can lean on when you're upset and scared, and one you can laugh with when you're happy. I want to celebrate your accomplishments and support you when things don't work out."

"Do I get the same?" she asked.

"Absolutely. I'm an open book to you, and I promise to never shut you out. We'll be a team, make decisions together, and fumble through whatever life throws our way."

"Deal. Now can we stop talking and get home so I can finally see what all the fuss is about?"

Meat couldn't stop grinning. "Yes, ma'am."

Chapter Twenty-Three

Sex.

Zara was about to experience it for herself. She should be nervous. Instead, she felt as if it were Christmas and Easter all wrapped into one. She remembered the anticipation she used to feel about opening presents or knowing she'd get to search for Easter eggs. This felt much the same, the same sense of exciting anticipation.

Now that she'd decided to go for what she wanted, she couldn't wait to actually see Meat naked. She'd seen him without a shirt, and had felt his erection against her, but now she was going to get to see *all* of him.

When they arrived back at his house, after Meat turned off the alarm, he headed straight up the stairs to the master bedroom. He pulled her inside and didn't even bother to shut the door. Zara wanted to giggle at the single-minded purpose he was exhibiting, but she managed to hold back.

He escorted her to the edge of the bed and turned to sit. Then he wrapped his hands around her waist and held her between his legs as he looked up at her for a long minute.

"Meat?" Zara asked finally. "What's wrong?"

"Absolutely nothing," he told her. "I'm just memorizing this moment. We'll never have another first time together, and I want to remember everything about it."

Gah!

He was so perfect.

There were times when Meat annoyed her a little. Not many, granted, but they were there. Currently, he was saying and doing all the right things, and those little annoyances faded into the background.

There hadn't been too many times in Zara's life that she could remember being truly happy. She'd done the best she could with the hand life had dealt her, but she'd never let herself completely trust someone else. Never let go of control enough to let someone else call all the shots. Not even Mags.

But standing there in front of Meat, seeing his hair mussed from the way he always ran a hand through it, seeing his cheeks pink from anticipation and lust, and feeling his thumbs caress her sides as he stared into her eyes all made her realize that she trusted Meat one hundred percent.

She trusted him to make her first time pleasurable. Trusted him enough to open up about what she wanted to do with her life. Trusted that if she made the first move, he wouldn't embarrass her or make her feel awkward about what they were about to do.

With that in mind, Zara reached down and pulled off her T-shirt.

She stood before him silently, in nothing but her jeans and bra. She wasn't overly large in the boob area, but she'd always been thankful for that because it made binding her chest less painful than it might've been otherwise. She'd worn a bra for the first time when she'd left Peru, and had definitely felt a little inadequate since, after seeing how busty a lot of women seemed to be here in the States.

Meat's gaze went from her face to her chest, and she watched his pupils dilate. He licked his lips and shifted on the mattress.

She loved his uninhibited reaction, the fact that she could turn him on.

Reaching behind her, Zara clumsily undid the clasp of her bra and let it slide to the floor.

Her heart was beating a million miles a minute, and she could feel her nipples pucker in anticipation.

"Damn, Zara. You're so beautiful, I can't even wrap my head around how anyone could think you were a boy for a second."

She opened her mouth to explain it again. How they only saw what they wanted to see, how she purposely did whatever she could to perpetuate the deception—but anything she might've said got stuck in her throat when Meat tightened his grip on her waist and leaned forward.

He nuzzled the inside curve of one of her breasts, and her belly quivered when she felt his tongue flick out for a taste.

"Meat," she groaned, putting her hands on his head, holding on as he continued to explore.

He didn't speak, but one of his hands palmed her lower back, urging her to arch into him. The move thrust her chest out farther, and when she looked down, she watched as Meat's other hand came up to gently plump her other breast, right before his mouth covered the nipple.

Zara'd had *no* idea how sensitive that part of her body was. None. She'd never touched herself, except to wrap the binding around her chest. Hadn't played with her nipples. The sight of Meat with his eyes closed as he obviously enjoyed sucking her, his jaw moving back and forth, was the most erotic thing she'd ever seen.

He shifted to her other breast, and every time he sucked on her nipple, she felt it between her legs. Zara writhed in his hold, and an almost desperate whine escaped her lips. Meat nipped at her, and that ratcheted her arousal even more.

He lifted his head and looked up at her as his thumb lightly flicked at her now-throbbing and erect nipple. "You're very sensitive," he said with a predatory grin.

"Am I?" Zara asked, not really thinking about her words.

"Yeah, Zar, you are. And I can't fucking wait to see how you react when I suck on your clit the way I just did your nipples. I have a feeling you're gonna buck like a wild filly."

She had no idea what he was saying, but the look in his eyes made her want to tear off the rest of her clothes and fling herself down on his bed and beg him to do whatever he wanted. Especially if it made her feel as good as what he'd just done.

"I want to make you feel good too," she told him uncertainly.

"You will," Meat said without a shred of doubt in his words. "Watching you come into your own is a huge turn-on. You gonna be comfortable in here on my mattress? Or do you want to go to your room and the futon?"

Zara wanted to melt at how considerate he was being. A part of her wanted to go into her room, just so she could have his smell on her sheets, but she didn't want to stop what they were doing long enough to change rooms.

"What was that thought?" he asked, his thumb still caressing her nipple.

"Nothing. Here is fine."

But Meat was having none of her prevarication. He pinched one of her nipples between his thumb and forefinger and said, "Tell me, Zara."

She went up on her tiptoes but didn't try to pull out of his grip. She was so wet between her legs and practically panting with lust. "I w-wanted my bed to smell like you, so later I could fall asleep with your scent in my nose."

Meat lessened the pressure on her nipple, and instead of feeling relief, the blood coursing through her sensitive nub made everything throb all the more. Dear God, she had no idea her breasts were so sensitive.

"You *are* going to fall asleep with my scent in your nose, and all over your body, Zar. If you think I'm going to make love with you, then kick you out to go sleep in the guest room, you're insane. From here on out, we're sleeping in the same bed. It might be mine, if you can get used to it, or it might be yours. Hell, we can sleep on the floor, for all I care. As long as you're in my arms, I'll be satisfied."

That was an amazing answer, and all Zara could do was smile at him and put a hand on the side of his face.

Meat smiled up at her, then leaned back to take off his own shirt. He kept his eyes on hers as he reached down and undid the button on his jeans. He lifted his ass and pushed them off, along with his boxers, shoes, and socks.

Zara could only stare at him with wide eyes as he revealed himself to her inch by delicious inch. He didn't seem self-conscious in the least about his nudity. And why should he? He was absolutely gorgeous.

His thighs were muscular, and he didn't have an ounce of fat on him anywhere. His stomach rippled with what she now knew was called a "six-pack," and he had a light dusting of dark chest hair. She couldn't keep her eyes from straying between his legs—and swallowed hard at seeing the most intimate part of him for the first time.

He was long and hard. His cock was curved upward slightly, and there was a bead of precome on the tip.

Meat leaned over and opened a drawer next to the bed and pulled out a box of condoms. He opened it and placed a small packet near the edge of the table. Then he scooted backward until he was lying flat.

His eyes seemed even darker than usual as he held out a hand. "Join me?"

He didn't pressure her to undress any more than she already had. In fact, he had made himself vulnerable by stripping first. Everything he did made her fall harder.

Hands shaking, Zara tried to be as brave as Meat. She toed off her shoes and undid the button and zipper on her jeans. She pushed them down, but couldn't make herself remove her underwear and expose herself completely.

"Come here," Meat said, sitting up and reaching for her.

Putting her hand in his, Zara let Meat guide her onto the mattress. But instead of laying her down and crawling on top of her, he pulled her astride him. Even though she had on underwear, the intimate position made her feel naked.

She knew if she looked down, she'd see a wet spot on the light-gray panties she was wearing.

She didn't want to be embarrassed, yet she still was. Zara was sitting on Meat's stomach, and his hands were resting on her thighs. The heat coming off his palms almost burned her skin.

"Look at me," he ordered.

Zara lifted her gaze and bravely met his own.

"You're beautiful. Every inch. And like I said earlier, I'm a lucky son of a bitch to have you choose to be with me. Whatever happens between us here in our bed is natural and right. You humble me, Zara. You make me want to be a better man. And just to throw it out there . . . I'm nervous as hell."

That surprised her. "You are?"

"Absolutely. I'm not a small man, as you saw. This is your first time. I would rather cut off my right arm than do anything to hurt you. But I know that no matter how gentle I am, no matter how aroused you are, this is probably going to hurt."

Zara knew the basics of sex. She was a virgin, but not all that innocent. And strangely enough, knowing that Meat was nervous made her feel a lot better. "Women's bodies are meant to stretch," she said, trying to control her blush. "I've seen that for myself firsthand when I helped birth babies. I trust you, Meat."

He closed his eyes for a second, and when they opened again, Zara could tell he was back to his usual confident self. It was hot as hell and made her squirm on his stomach.

"Come here," he ordered, lifting a hand to the back of her neck and pulling her down to him.

How much time they spent kissing, Zara didn't know, but without her even realizing it, she found herself on her back as Meat slowly made his way down her body. He kissed and caressed every inch of her skin, making goose bumps rise in his wake. He knew it, if the grin on his face was anything to go by, but he didn't comment, simply continued making his way between her legs.

He finally settled there, lying on his stomach, his face right above her pussy.

He inhaled deeply and nuzzled the wet cotton as he licked his lips. Zara hadn't thought much about oral sex. She'd seen men getting blow jobs, but hadn't really thought about how it worked in reverse. But with Meat practically salivating above her, she couldn't think of anything *but* how it might feel to have him touch her there.

"May I?" he asked as his finger traced the edge of her panties along her inner thigh.

Zara nodded, not sure how this was going to work, as her legs were splayed around his body.

But Meat easily solved the problem of how he was going to get her underwear off.

He leaned over to the drawer in the bedside table, the same one the box of condoms had been in, and pulled out a knife. He flicked it open with one hand and brought the sharp tip to the material at her waist.

She didn't even flinch. Zara knew Meat wouldn't hurt her.

Between one breath and the next, he'd sliced through the cotton on both sides, and the knife made a clattering sound as it landed back on the table.

Zara felt the cooler air of the room waft over her soaked pussy before Meat was once more hovering over her. He inhaled deeply again, and Zara closed her eyes, not sure she wanted to watch what he was doing.

She felt one of his large, calloused fingers slide along her seam, and she groaned at even that light touch. She wanted to open her legs wider at the same time she wanted to slam them closed.

"So beautiful," he murmured, more to himself than her . . . and then Zara felt his tongue replace his finger.

She jolted at the first touch, then moaned. It felt good. Not overwhelmingly, just . . . nice.

He continued to lazily lick at her folds, and Zara got brave enough to open her eyes and look down her body at the man lying between her legs. He was looking right back at her as he licked her lightly over and over. As if he'd been merely waiting for her to open her eyes.

The second her gaze met his, he very slowly used one finger to penetrate her.

Zara inhaled but didn't take her eyes from his. It was intense, staring at each other while he did such intimate things to her, but it also felt right.

Then, as she continued to watch, he scooted up a bit and licked her clit.

She jolted in surprise. While what he'd done before felt good, *that* was unbelievable!

He grinned and licked her again.

Zara moaned loudly. God, she'd had no idea this would feel so wonderful.

As she watched, his eyes shut, and he closed his lips around her clit and got serious about pleasuring her.

Zara whimpered and thrashed in his grasp as he licked, sucked, and nipped at the extremely sensitive bundle of nerves. All the while, his finger lazily pumped in and out of her. At some point, he added a second finger, but she was too lost in the way he was manipulating her clit to even think about anything else.

She loved what he was doing, but it wasn't quite enough to push her over the edge. Zara writhed in frustration, not sure how to tell him what she wanted. What she needed.

But he seemed to know. His head lifted, and she almost cried at the loss of stimulation, but before she could say anything, he began to strum her clit with two fingers. He now had three fingers pushing in and out of her sheath, while he rubbed hard and fast over the most sensitive part of her body with his other hand.

It didn't take long, only fifteen seconds or so of the direct stimulation, before stars danced behind Zara's eyes and she began to shake. It was as if her body belonged to someone else; she couldn't control her thoughts or actions. Her fingers dug into the sheets under her, her ass lifted off the mattress, and she cried out as an orgasm consumed her.

She vaguely realized that Meat had moved, but with pleasure still coursing through her veins, she couldn't concentrate on anything other than how she felt.

When she could finally open her eyes, she looked up to find Meat hovering over her. One hand was propping himself up, and the other held his condom-covered cock as he used the tip to continue to stimulate her clit. He wasn't touching her anywhere but between her legs, and Zara couldn't tear her eyes away from the erotic sight. He slid his hard-as-nails cock through her folds, caressing her clit with each pass.

She shuddered and opened her legs wider.

She wasn't scared. Not of him. Ever. "Do it," she whispered. "I want you inside me."

His nostrils flared at her words. "It's not too late to say no," he countered, his voice throaty and deep. "Just say the word and I'll back off."

The thought of him leaving her now was repugnant. She reached around and dug her nails into his buttocks. "Fuck me, Meat," she said.

He groaned and notched the head of his cock between her legs. He was big—there was no doubt about that—but he'd stretched her with his fingers seconds ago, so she felt pressure but no sting when he slowly pushed inside her body.

It felt amazing. So foreign, but not in a bad way.

He pushed in a little farther, and Zara did her best to hide her wince. The farther he got, the more her body seemed to protest.

He stopped, and she looked down to see he wasn't even halfway inside her yet.

For the first time, she had doubts that this would work. After all, she was only a little over five feet, and he was a full foot taller. Maybe they wouldn't fit. Maybe—

Her thoughts were cut off abruptly when Meat suddenly slid all the way inside her.

She stiffened abruptly and tried to pull away, but Meat wouldn't let her budge. He also stayed stock-still. "I'm sorry," he said into her ear as he lay over her. He'd fallen onto his elbows, and she felt surrounded by him. He was over her, in her, and she was completely overwhelmed by her thoughts, the feelings rushing through her.

On one hand, her body was still humming in contentment because of the monster orgasm he'd given her, but on the other, there was pain.

"Give it a second," Meat said. "Don't move, we'll just lie here until it doesn't hurt as much. I'm sorry, Zara. So sorry."

She inhaled deeply, and Meat's scent filled her entire being. For a tense second, she felt as if she were being ripped apart . . . and then the pain slowly faded. Her fingers had dug into his butt cheeks so hard, she knew he'd probably have marks. She consciously relaxed her fingers and brought her hands up to hold on to his biceps.

She tentatively moved her hips . . . and her eyes widened at how full she felt.

"I'm okay," she whispered.

"Give it another minute or two," Meat said, not lifting his head.

He sounded weird, and Zara had no idea what was going through his brain. She tugged on his hair. "Look at me."

When he lifted his head, she was stunned by what she saw.

Tears. He wasn't actually crying, but his eyes were red, and he swallowed hard. "Yeah?"

"What's wrong?"

"That was both the most beautiful moment in my life and the fucking worst," he told her. "Beautiful because knowing you trusted me enough to let me be the first inside your body is humbling and amazing at the same time."

"And the worst?" Zara asked, not sure she wanted to hear the answer.

"Because I knew I'd have to hurt you in the process of getting inside you. I don't like to see you flinch away from me, and I *really* don't like to see you stiffen in pain because of something I've done," Meat said. "I swear it won't hurt like that again. I can't promise it won't be uncomfortable for a while, since you're so tiny, but I'll do everything I can to make sure you're completely ready for me before I come inside you again."

Her heart stuttered. If she hadn't loved Meat before, she certainly did now. "I'm okay. Is that it?"

He smiled, and some of the angst cleared from his eyes. "No, Zar. That isn't it. I'm going to move now. If it hurts, let me know. I can read a lot of what you're feeling on your face, but I also know you're good at *hiding* your feelings. So tell me if it hurts. I'll pull out right now and go run you a bath if you want me to."

She shook her head. "No. I mean, I wouldn't mind a bath . . . after . . . but I want to finish."

"Brave as fuck," Meat whispered, then slowly pulled out of her body, and just as slowly pushed back in.

He felt foreign inside her, but it didn't hurt . . . at least not like it had the first time he'd thrust inside. She felt full and her inner thighs strained, using muscles she hadn't used before as she kept her legs open wide for him. He gently glided in and out of her a few more times before Zara let out the breath she'd been holding.

"Okay?" he asked.

Zara nodded.

She had no idea how long Meat slowly and tenderly made love to her, letting her get used to his body, before she began to get . . . antsy.

"What do you need, Zar? Never be afraid to tell me anything."

"I don't know," she said. "I just . . . it feels good, but it's not enough."

Meat's hand went under her and lifted one of her butt cheeks. The movement made his thrusts go just a little deeper, and she cried out. She looked down and saw his cock was shiny with her juices as he continued to make love to her.

Not able to stop herself, she reached down and caressed the part of him that wasn't inside her.

He moaned loudly.

Feeling braver, she moved her hand until she was cupping his balls. They swayed each time he pushed inside her body, and his head went back, and he groaned as she caressed him. Zara liked that she could affect him in the same way he did her.

Before she knew what he was up to, his hand dropped from her ass and came around to where they were joined. He flicked her clit—and she jumped.

"Still sensitive, huh?" he asked.

Zara nodded.

"All right, then I have a feeling this is gonna get intense really quick. Hang on."

Before she could ask what he meant, Meat began to strum her clit much as he had earlier. It felt just as good, but so different with his hard cock inside her. Her muscles clenched down, and they both moaned.

"Fuck, Zara . . . you're so tight. That's it, let go. Come all over my cock, let me feel it."

She was only vaguely aware of his dirty talk, more concerned about chasing the intense sensations of an impending orgasm. Her body began to shake once more, and she heard Meat say "most beautiful thing I've ever seen" before losing all track of what was going on around her.

She flew over the edge in another intense orgasm. Meat's easy, lazy thrusts changed, becoming more powerful and fast, and it wasn't long before he pushed inside of her as far as he could go and held still as he groaned long and low.

Then he practically collapsed, immediately turning them so she was lying on top of him. They were still connected, and Zara would swear she could feel his heartbeat through his cock deep inside of her. She was sweaty, and wetness coated her inner thighs and between her legs, but she didn't care. Meat was surprisingly comfortable, and she had no problem laying her head on his shoulder and snuggling into him.

She felt him slip out of her body and whimpered, but still didn't move.

"Zar?"

"Mmmm?"

"You okay?"

"Mmmm-hmmm."

She felt more than heard him chuckle. "Let me guess, you're gonna want to use me as a mattress from here on out, aren't you?"

"You mind?" she asked.

"Hell no," he said without hesitation as his arms came around her. They lay together in the middle of the afternoon, naked as the day they were born, and neither seemed uncomfortable.

"You're mine," Meat whispered after a few minutes had gone by. His hand was lazily tracing the line of her spine up and down, and Zara had almost been asleep.

She didn't have the energy to complain about his over-the-top alpha declaration, or to agree. So she simply turned her head a fraction of an inch, kissed the warm skin of his chest, then immediately fell asleep.

"You know the plan, right?" the man asked his companion.

"Yes. We've only gone over it a hundred times, you don't have to keep reminding me."

"Good. Soon we'll be sitting pretty in Mexico, smokin' all the dope we want without having to worry about the police, your parents, or anyone else interfering."

"It's pissing me off that I'm living in this fucking cheap-ass place while she has all the money in the world. She's not even spending it! I heard she set up some scholarship for the brat one of those bitches just had. A *baby*. Who won't even touch the money for years! She's so stupid."

"Speaking of which, how'd she get so tight with them all out of the blue? I thought she didn't have any friends, just sat in that asshole's house all the time?"

"I don't know, but *that* pisses me off too."

The man smirked. "Sounds like someone's a little grumpy."

"Fuck you. Maybe if you'd gotten more than a fucking gram to smoke, I wouldn't be in such a bad mood."

"Eh . . . soon we'll be swimming in the stuff."

"This better work."

"It will," the man said. "We've got it all planned out. She's too stupid to go to the cops . . . and when we tell her what'll happen if she does, she'll be even more willing to do exactly what we want."

His partner nodded. "You hear she decided to hold a press conference, after all, to tell her sob story to the world?"

"Yup. But it doesn't matter what bleeding-heart story she tells, we stick to the plan."

"Yeah, right."

"What's that mean?"

"Nothing. Just that I think you're right."

"You better not be double-crossing me."

"I'm *not*. I'm with you all the way to the bank."

They smiled at each other.

"To a brighter, sunnier future in Mexico," the partner said, lifting a bottle of beer in toast.

"To Mexico," the man agreed, tipping his own bottle back.

Chapter Twenty-Four

"Are you *sure* you want to do this?" Meat asked Zara for the tenth time.

A week had gone by since their relationship had officially changed from friends to lovers. He couldn't be happier with how things were progressing between them, but he also couldn't help but be concerned about how quickly she'd gone from content to sit alone in his house to wanting to take charge of every aspect of her life at once.

It was as if a light had been switched on after the incident at the big-box store with the Spanish-speaking woman and the police officer. She'd decided she *did* want to be a translator for those who needed it. And she was suddenly desperate to set the record straight when it came to what had happened to her and her parents so long ago in Peru.

The decision to talk to the press seemed to come a little out of left field, but Zara had reassured him that she'd been thinking about it for a while. She was sick of the news getting everything wrong, and all the incorrect information being spread. They'd recently learned her uncle had been responsible for spreading some of the worst rumors via social media. He was apparently done with being subtle and trying to charm her out of her money. He'd gone onto various news pages and made comments about how he'd "heard" that she'd worked as a prostitute, that she hadn't been seen since arriving back in the States because she was a drug addict and going through rehab, and, most absurd, that she'd actually been working with her parents' killers all these years.

And the sickest thing was that people believed that crap. Articles were written for bogus "news" sites and shared all over social media.

The last straw for Zara had apparently been when the police officer at the store had genuinely believed she was a drug runner for a cartel.

She'd talked to Rex and asked if he would arrange for a press conference. Before Meat could discuss the entire situation with her more in-depth, Rex had called the local Colorado Springs news outlets and had talked to Everly about security, and the date was set.

Instead of just local news personnel being present, it had blown up, of course, and there were correspondents from several different countries and all the major networks and shows. *Everyone* had applied for one of the coveted fifty slots that were being allocated to the media.

"I'm sure," Zara said confidently, answering Meat's question after a long pause.

Meat couldn't ascertain any nervousness or concern in her tone or her facial expression. It made him realize all over again how incredibly tough his Zara was. It shouldn't surprise him—she wouldn't have survived what had happened to her if she wasn't. But he still wanted to wrap her up and hide her away from the cruelties of the world.

They'd decided to hold the press conference in the courthouse in one of the large meeting rooms. It was big enough to house everyone comfortably, and would feel less like an interrogation for Zara. The plan was for her to explain in her own words what had happened, then take questions.

Morgan had tried to talk her out of the questions part, but Zara wouldn't budge. She'd decided that if she didn't let the reporters ask what they wanted, more rumors would follow, and she had nothing to hide since she'd done nothing wrong.

Meat couldn't really argue with that logic, but that didn't mean he had to like it.

Zara had moved into his master bedroom the same night they'd made love the first time, and the question of whether she'd be comfortable sleeping on his soft mattress had been a moot point after she'd discovered how comfortable she was sleeping on top of *him*. It had taken some getting used to on Meat's part, but not for long. He enjoyed being able to hold her close as they fell asleep. By morning, they'd usually moved in their sleep to lie next to each other, but she was always touching him in some way. Reaching out for him even in slumber. It made him feel ten feet tall.

"It'll be fine," Zara said, putting her hand on his arm.

Meat nodded and pulled her close. "I know it will. Because you're one tough cookie," he told her proudly.

Zara smiled up at him. "I need to do this to move on," she said. "I hope you understand."

"I do. Did you talk to your grandparents or uncle and let them know you were planning on doing this?"

She sighed. "I called my grandparents, but I never heard back from them. I left a message on their voice mail and invited them to come down, but I doubt they'll be here. They made their feelings about me clear enough the last time I saw them."

"It's their loss," Meat told her, and kissed her briefly on the forehead.

"It is," Zara agreed. "I mean, I don't miss them exactly, because I never really knew them, but I miss the thought of having relatives that give a shit."

Meat hated the Harpers. How they couldn't care about their only granddaughter was beyond his comprehension. Zara was amazing . . . brave and resilient. They should've been ecstatic to have her back. "And your uncle?"

Zara scrunched her nose. "He's still being an ass. Leaving me obnoxious messages on my phone and whining about how if I cared about my mom at all, I'd give him money so he wouldn't be destitute."

Meat growled. "I *hate* that your grandparents gave him your number. They had to know he'd harass you for money. I know you said you didn't want to deal with the hassle of changing your number, but I think it's time."

Zara nodded. "If you think I should, fine. I don't really want to talk to my uncle again. Ever. And after he spread those rumors about me, any chance he might've had of getting part of Mom and Dad's inheritance is pretty much out the window. Do you think I look all right?"

Meat recognized a change in topic when he heard one, and he went with it. "You look beautiful." And she did. She'd invited Harlow over to help her figure out what to wear. Meat had been a little surprised that she'd reached out to her instead of Renee, but happy all the same. She'd continued to make an effort to get to know the other women since the life-altering experience with Morgan and the birth of her daughter.

Zara had on a pair of khaki pants instead of her usual jeans, and a light-yellow blouse that dipped low in the front, showing off a modest bit of cleavage—not too much, since she'd be on camera. It was a feminine and delicate ensemble, and not something she'd normally wear. She'd been coming out of her shell more and more, willing to show off her femininity just a little. Meat couldn't give a shit what she wore as long as she was comfortable, but he couldn't help admiring her. He was as proud of her as he could be, and thankful every day that she was with *him*.

"Okay, it looks like it's about time," Zara said. "Wish me luck."

"You don't need luck," Meat told her. "Just be yourself. I'll be right here watching you, and the other guys will be situated around the room just in case. Everly's here with some of her most trusted friends on the CSPD, and they'll take care of things if the press gets unruly. Chloe and Harlow are in the crowd as well, and Allye and Morgan will be here after it's over, waiting for you with their babies. I think I even saw Renee in the crowd as well. You've got this. You aren't alone."

Zara took a deep breath and nodded. "Here goes nothing." Then she turned and walked through a side door into the large room, onto the platform that had been set up for her. The second the reporters saw her, a hush descended on the room, and it was quiet enough to hear a pin drop.

Meat slipped into the room when all the attention was on Zara, and watched with both dread and pride as the woman he loved held her head high and addressed the crowd.

Zara thought she was going to puke. She wanted to do this. To set the record straight. But that didn't mean she wasn't scared out of her mind.

Her eyes skimmed the crowd staring at her, and it made her feel ten times better to see the people she could now call her friends there supporting her. Renee gave her a little thumbs-up, and Zara nodded at her briefly before she began speaking.

"Thank you all for being here. I apologize for not setting this up before now. I've had a hard time adjusting to life here in the States. It's very strange to go from having literally nothing to having everything—running water, food whenever I want it, money to buy clothes and whatever other odds and ends I need. I also wasn't ready to tell my story. Maybe I'm still not. But because of all the false rumors and ridiculous accounts being made up about what happened to me, I want to set the record straight."

It seemed as if no one in the room even breathed. As if they were holding their breaths waiting for her to spill secrets about where a buried treasure was hidden or something. It was crazy. Red lights from cameras blinked steadily, reminding Zara that what she said would be transmitted all over the country, and possibly the world. She had to be careful not to say anything that would put her friends back in Peru in danger, put del Rio on their trail.

Taking a deep breath, she began. "When I was ten years old, my parents told me they were taking me on vacation to a wonderful country called Peru . . ."

Twenty minutes later, Zara felt as if she'd run a marathon.

She could feel the sweat dripping down her back, and her voice was hoarse from speaking. She'd been completely honest, down to the way she'd been scared to come out of the hole in the wall she'd found to hide in, and how day after day, she kept thinking someone would find her.

She explained how, eventually, she'd stopped expecting to be rescued and concentrated on making it from one day to the next without getting beaten or raped. She did her best to downplay the Mountain Mercenaries' role in her rescue, not mentioning them by name, simply saying that when a group of Americans who were on a joint task force with the Peruvian military had happened to find her, she'd told them her story, and the rest was history.

She felt raw and vulnerable and wanted nothing more than to walk out of the room, now that she'd finished. But she'd promised to answer questions, and that was what she was going to do.

The chief of police was there to help facilitate the question-and-answer period, and he stepped up to explain how the next part of the press conference was going to work.

The first questions were fairly innocuous. Things like, "How did it feel to be home?" and "What was the first thing you ate when you got back?"

But they quickly got tougher after that.

Many people wanted to know about her money, how much her parents had left her, and what her plans were now that she was rich. Zara did her best to deflect those, not wanting to get into her financial situation. She had enough people emailing—and now calling, thanks to her uncle leaking her phone number—wanting money.

She was doing all right until a female reporter stood up and asked, "Why didn't you do more to find help when you were first dropped off in the barrio? I mean, there had to be *someone* who spoke English who you could've gone to. Or who could point you in the direction of the US embassy. You could've been home years ago."

The question didn't surprise her. The FBI had asked the same thing, and she'd read comments online from people wondering the same. But it was annoying as hell that no one thought she'd done anything to try to help herself.

"Do you have children?" Zara asked in a surprisingly calm voice.

"Yes," the reporter confirmed with a nod.

"How old?"

"I'm not sure that's relevant," she said uncertainly.

"How old?" Zara insisted.

"Five, eleven, and thirteen."

"What's the first thing you taught your kids to do if they're lost? Like if they go on a hike and get turned around and don't know which way to go?" She didn't wait for the answer. "You tell them to stay where they are. That someone will find them. The worst thing they can do is wander around, because that makes them even harder to find.

"My parents taught me the same thing. So when those monsters dropped me off in that barrio, I did what I thought was right—I hunkered down and waited to be found. But the kicker was that no one was really looking for me. Everyone thought I was dead.

"Think about your *own* child being in a situation like I was. How well do you think he or she would do? Did you teach them what to do if they get lost in a huge city they've never been in before? Have you taught your kids how to communicate with people who don't speak the same language? Have they experienced hunger so intense they would literally eat dirt just to have something in their bellies?" When the reporter shook her head silently, Zara continued.

"There I was. *Ten* years old, not able to speak the language, hungry, dirty, and traumatized from seeing my parents killed before my eyes—and I did what I was taught. I waited. And waited. And *waited*. But no one ever came. When I had to come out of my hiding place, I was terrified. No one could understand a word I said, and I couldn't understand them. I got chased away from trash cans by men shouting at me in a language I didn't know, and other children threw rocks at me to keep me from getting scraps of food.

"You want to know why I didn't continually approach people and ask, in English, where the US embassy was? Because the few adults I tried to talk to ignored me. Or they looked at me with a bit too much interest . . . if you know what I mean. And the one policeman I approached took a swing at me with his baton. I didn't know where I was, what direction the embassy might be in. When you're ten, the world is a scary place, and even scarier when you're all alone.

"You might be thinking, okay, but what about *after* you learned Spanish? After you got older? Why didn't you ask for help then? Because by then, I was too busy trying to stay alive. To eat. To avoid the people who wanted to prey on a defenseless child.

"But what I *really* hear when I'm asked that question—or any question that starts with 'Why didn't you . . .'—is blame and judgment. I'm being judged for my actions. The actions of a horrified little girl. Let me tell you something: if I could go back and do things differently, I would. I wouldn't have been a brat to my parents at dinner. I would've walked faster so we could've been at the hotel before those men crossed our path. I would've screamed as loud as I could when they first pulled out a knife. I would've run. I would've walked the miles and miles from where they'd dropped me off back to the hotel where we were staying, or at least tried. I would've learned Spanish faster. I would've befriended people sooner. I would've been more assertive and begged someone to help . . .

"But I can't go back. And you have no right to sit there and judge me for what I *did* do. I did the best I could when I was ten. And eleven. And fifteen. And twenty. I pray to God that you are *never* in a situation like I was. One where you're scared out of your mind, lost, terrified that everyone who crosses your path is out to hurt you. There is literally no way you can ever possibly understand why I did what I did unless you've lived through the same situation, and I hope for your sake that you *never* understand. But until such time, you have no right to judge me for my actions. To blame me for the situation I was in and what happened."

The room was silent after Zara stopped speaking, and for a second she thought the woman was going to cry. But she simply nodded and sat back down, her eyes trained on the pad of paper in front of her.

Zara took a deep breath, ready for the crowd to turn against her. For them to ask an inappropriate or downright ridiculous question. But before someone could ask how she'd dealt with her period while she was living on the streets, or if anyone had ever figured out she wasn't a boy and raped her, the chief of police politely wrapped up the press conference, thanking everyone for coming.

He took Zara's arm and gently led her to the side door, whisking her away from the reporters and the cameras.

Before she could take a breath, Meat was there. He wrapped his arms around her, and Zara buried her face in his chest, happy to be able to escape the real world for just a second. Standing in his embrace, inhaling his unique woodsy and pine scent, she could almost forget everything that she'd been through.

Almost.

"You were fucking phenomenal," Meat whispered in her ear.

She'd expected him to be upset on her behalf. When she lifted her head, she saw that he *was* pissed, but she saw the pride he had for her as well.

"You could've just refused to answer her question and moved on, but you put her in her place and explained exactly how her question was rude as hell."

"I did, didn't I?" Zara asked.

"You sure did."

Then they didn't have any more time to talk privately, as they were surrounded by all their friends. They moved to the room where Allye and Morgan were waiting for them, and even though the day had been hard, telling the world exactly what had happened to her and how she'd felt as a kid, hoping against all hope someone would find her, only to be crushed when they didn't, Zara couldn't help but feel lucky.

She'd survived. Her parents would be proud of her, she had no doubt about that. And she had good friends who would do whatever it took to find her if she ever disappeared again. Most had been through their own hell. Even Renee, who had lived a quiet, normal life in Denver, had been nothing but supportive.

The plan was for everyone to go to Gray and Allye's house to have a late lunch and decompress. Meat leaned down and asked, "You still want to go to Gray's house? It's okay if you'd rather go home."

Zara thought about it but shook her head. "No, I'd like to go. I admit that I was nervous, but now that it's over, and I've set the record straight, I want to celebrate. I'm alive. And I want to get to know my new friends better."

Meat got a peculiar look on his face, and she frowned and asked, "What?"

"I just . . . I'm in awe of you, Zar. Every day you surprise me. In a good way."

"I'm just me, Meat. I'm nobody special."

"You're wrong. But that's okay, you can think what you want, and I'll stand by your side, secure in the knowledge that no asshole will ever get another chance to dim the light inside you."

Zara shook her head and smiled. "You're crazy."

"Yup. You continue to live in your delusional world," Meat said with a grin.

She reached up to pull him down to her, but Meat didn't make her work for what she wanted. He leaned over and she kissed him. "Thank you for being here with me today."

"No place I'd rather be, Zar."

"I know that even though I've told my story, people will still gossip. They'll take my words and twist them. My uncle will probably continue to harass me and beg for money, but I know what's really important."

"Yeah?"

She nodded. "Yeah. Friends who'll stick by you no matter what."

"Try to pry me away," Meat said with a snort. "Come on. Let's see if we can't get everyone out of here and back to Gray's. I'm sure you're hungry."

"I'm always hungry," Zara said with a laugh.

Meat pulled a protein bar out of his pocket and held it out to her. "That's why I brought this for you. To tide you over."

The sight of the small bar in his big hand made Zara want to cry. Meat was always looking after her. Even when he was seemingly lost in his computer, researching something for his reclusive handler, Rex, or when he was elbow deep in wood shavings in his workshop, he'd always respond to any question. Or do something surprising like this . . . pulling a snack or piece of chocolate out of his pocket and handing it to her without a word.

But instead of crying, Zara took the food and smiled up at him. She held on to his hand as they walked out of the courthouse to his car. She was well and truly on her way to being the best person she could be, and Peru, and what she had gone through, may as well have been a million miles away.

Chapter Twenty-Five

"Are you sure you don't want me to come with you and hang out at the back of the bar?" Meat asked as Zara entered the kitchen.

"I'm sure. Are you still worried about my uncle?" she asked.

"Zara, Alan's a douchebag, and I'm about ready to lose my shit with him," Meat said.

Zara was severely disappointed in her uncle. He was her mother's brother, and she wished they had a better rapport, but that ship had definitely sailed. It was a week and a half after the press conference, and he still wouldn't stop harassing her and spewing empty threats, now insisting that if Zara didn't give him half of her money, she'd regret it.

Ball and Everly had gone up to Denver just two days ago to personally deliver a threatening message of their own, which hopefully would shut him up.

Technically, Everly had gone to serve him with a restraining order that forbade him from contacting Zara on the phone, in written form, *or* in person.

But when Everly had gone back to the car, Ball had delivered a message of his own . . . telling Alan in no uncertain terms that if he dared even *breathe* in Zara's direction again, he'd lose everything. They knew all about his drug activity, and Ball made sure Alan knew that if he sent one more email, or got in touch with Zara in any way again, the man's dealer would learn how he'd passed information to the local PD in return for cash.

"I'll be fine," Zara insisted. "Everly will be there tonight, and if anything happens, she'll take care of it."

"Who else is going?" Meat asked.

"Harlow and Renee. Allye can't come. She's been exhausted lately because Darby has been fussy. And Morgan can't tear herself away from Calinda yet, but I don't blame her, because she's so adorable."

"No Chloe?" Meat asked.

Zara shrugged. "She said she'd try to come if possible. She's doing an analysis of someone's retirement account and apparently gets super jazzed up about that sort of thing and doesn't like to stop until it's done."

"You'll call when you need a ride home?"

Zara shook her head. "No. There's no need for you to come all the way to town to get me. Renee can drop me off on her way back up to Denver."

"Make sure she doesn't drink," Meat said sternly.

"Yes, Dad," Zara said with an eye roll.

"I'm serious. I don't know what I'd do if anything happened to you."

"Nothing's going to happen to me. I'm just going out for dinner with my friends. I was surprised Renee said she'd come at all. I think she's been feeling a little jealous that I've been getting closer with the others, and I hate that."

Meat frowned. He didn't like the little things he'd heard here and there from Zara. Renee *did* seem jealous, but it was more than that. He couldn't put his finger on it, and he could only hope their friendship would either grow stronger as a result of Zara coming into her own, or it would fizzle out.

"Okay, but call me if you need anything."

"I will."

They heard a horn outside, and Zara turned to grab her purse. She had on a pair of jeans and a fitted T-shirt. Both hugged her curves, and Meat did his best not to stare at her with lust in his eyes. She turned and smirked at him. He hadn't exactly hidden his need for her.

She stood on her tiptoes and kissed him, then turned to walk toward the door. "Meat?" she said before heading out.

"Yeah, Zar?"

"I'm wearing a new, matching fire-engine-red bra-and-panty set that I picked up the other day. Maybe I can model it when I get home."

Meat growled and had already taken a step toward her before even realizing he'd moved.

Zara giggled and disappeared out the door.

Meat headed to the window and watched as she climbed into Renee's car, and they headed down his long driveway. It dawned on him that he'd never actually heard her giggle since she'd moved in.

As hard as his dick hurt, thinking about taking her against the wall as she wore nothing but the red bra and panties she'd bought, he loved the fact that she was comfortable enough, and felt safe enough, to tease him.

"You gonna tell us what had you smiling so big when I picked you up?" Renee asked when they were seated at the restaurant.

Everly and Zara were drinking lemonade, and Renee and Harlow each had a glass of wine. They'd ordered a plate of cheese fries as an appetizer and were chowing down on the fries while they waited for their meals.

"Yeah, you do seem awfully chipper tonight," Harlow commented.

Zara tried to hide her grin by taking a sip of her lemonade, but knew she wasn't successful.

"Spill!" Everly said as she put her elbows on the table and leaned forward.

Zara shrugged. "It's just . . . things are going really well with me and Meat."

The other women all smiled huge.

"Let me guess . . . you either got some right before you left the house, or you teased him mercilessly, and he's gonna jump you the second you get home," Harlow said with a knowing grin.

Laughing outright now, Zara didn't answer the question, but instead said, "I had no idea."

"About what?" Everly asked.

"That being in a relationship could be so . . . satisfying. I mean, yes, the sex is great, don't get me wrong, but Meat just *gets* me. I honestly never thought I'd find anyone who would be so encouraging and understanding about my entire situation. We've also had a few long and helpful talks about what I want to do with my future, and the money my parents left me."

"What *are* you going to do with all that money?" Renee asked.

Zara wasn't sure what was up with Renee tonight, but she'd been a bit . . . harsher than she'd been in the past. On the way to the restaurant, she'd seemed upset that it wasn't going to be just the two of them, even though she'd known from the start that Harlow and Everly would be there. And the more she and Renee hung out, the clingier Zara's old friend got. It was as if they really were still ten years old, and she was jealous that Zara had any friends other than her.

Zara had been through too much to want anything to do with petty shit like that. But since they were already on the way to the restaurant, she'd let her attitude go, telling herself she'd discuss it with Renee later.

"I'm not exactly sure yet," Zara said, "but I'd like to do something to help families of missing children." She looked at Everly as she said, "The police do as much as they can, but their resources only go so far.

259

Sometimes a private detective can be much more effective in finding clues, especially after a lot of time has passed."

"I think that's a great idea," Everly said with a huge smile and nod.

"And I'd also like to see what I can do to help the people living in barrios back in Peru. There's a ton of corruption, so it's a little trickier. But, for instance, I know firsthand what the situation is like for pregnant women, so maybe I could build a clinic or something so there's better health care for those who need it."

"That's awesome!" Harlow enthused.

"You're going to give your money away to the very same people who oppressed you? Who basically held you hostage?" Renee asked, incredulous. "It seems to me there are a lot of people right here in the States who could use the money."

The response wasn't exactly a surprise. Zara knew some people wouldn't understand why she'd want to help the poor in Lima. But she *was* disappointed someone who was supposed to be her friend was so skeptical right off the bat.

"The people I lived with and interacted with on a daily basis weren't the ones who killed my parents. And they weren't holding me *hostage*. There are evil people everywhere, and I never said I wouldn't help people here in the States as well. I want to use the fact that I'm bilingual to help others in some way, maybe by working for that translation service that police officer told me about. I'm just trying to figure out the best way to help as many people as I can."

"I think all of it sounds amazing," Harlow said. "I know the women in the shelter I used to work for could've used all the help they could get. But honestly, it's about more than just money; it's about knowing someone cares. And I think you've got that in spades, Zara."

"Thanks."

The waiter arrived at their table with their meals, and the talk turned to how good the food looked and whether they could finish everything.

Zara silently counted her blessings yet again. A few months ago, she couldn't have imagined she'd be where she was right this second. Sitting in front of a huge plate of food with more money than she knew what to do with. She would've been sitting in the dirt in one of the huts made out of corrugated metal or cardboard boxes, wondering where her next meal would come from.

After they ate, Renee excused herself to use the restroom, and Harlow, Everly, and Zara were alone in the booth.

"I know you and Renee were friends a long time ago," Everly said with a frown, "but you seem like you're complete opposites now."

Zara sighed. "Yeah. I was so happy to reconnect with her right when I came back, but lately she's been kind of tiresome."

"You don't have to keep hanging out with her," Harlow pointed out.

"I know, but I feel . . . obligated? That's not really the right word, but she was there for me when I really needed a familiar face. My whole world had changed, and I wasn't sure how to deal with it all, and she called and visited and even helped me with my hair. It would be a shitty thing to drop her now."

"I'm not saying you have to drop her," Everly said. "But people change. Neither of you are the same people you were when you were ten. Our experiences change us. You can still be friends, but you don't have to hang out all the time."

"She's bitched a lot tonight about the drive from Denver to Colorado Springs," Harlow said. "If she hates it that much, why does she come visit you so often?"

"I think she's lonely," Zara said, looking around to make sure Renee wasn't coming back to the table yet. "She doesn't talk much about any other friends she has, and she seems almost desperate to be my friend at times. I feel bad for her."

"Well, if you ever need us, we're here," Everly said. "No strings attached."

"Thanks. I appreciate it," Zara told them. She was lucky to have found a group of women she did connect with as well as she did with the significant others of the Mountain Mercenaries. She should have given them a chance earlier.

The waiter came back to their table with the bill, and Zara quickly grabbed it before either of the other two women could. "Tonight's on me," she told them.

"No," Harlow protested. "We can get our own."

"Nope. Besides, I've got all this money now and no way of ever spending it in this lifetime, so you'd be doing me a favor by letting me pay." Zara grinned.

"I'm okay with that," Renee said with a smile as she came back to the table.

Zara saw Everly and Harlow frown at each other, but she silently sighed in relief when neither said what they were obviously thinking.

The waiter took Zara's credit card and returned within a minute or two with the slip for her to sign.

"You need a ride home?" Everly asked.

"She's good," Renee said. "I'm going right by Meat's house on my way back to Denver, so I can drop her off."

"Text when you get home," Harlow said.

"You think I'm gonna wreck or something?" Renee asked with a frown.

"No, I'm just naturally a worrywart," Harlow explained.

"Besides, it's all the *other* people you have to be careful about on the roads," Everly threw in. "You could be doing everything right, but all it takes is one drunk driver to cause a huge crash. Believe me, I've seen it."

"Sorry, you're right. I'll be careful. I'm sure Zara will let you know when she's inside. You ready to go?" Renee asked.

Zara nodded and finished signing the credit card receipt, making sure to leave a generous tip for their attentive waiter. She grabbed her purse and slipped out of the booth. She'd managed to put off thoughts of what would happen between her and Meat when she got home, but now all the carnal things she wanted to do to him came rushing back.

She waved to Harlow and Everly and headed out of the restaurant with Renee. The sooner she got home, the better. She had plans for her boyfriend.

Meat was watching television but having a hard time concentrating on anything he saw because he couldn't stop thinking about Zara. He'd gotten so used to her being around all the time that he missed her terribly when she was gone. Even when they weren't in the same room, he at least knew she was nearby, and it soothed him. He loved when she accompanied him to his workshop, whether she chatted with him about nothing in particular or sat in a corner and read a book. Just having her where he could see her every time he looked up was comforting.

But tonight, he couldn't wait for her to get home because of what she'd told him right before she'd left. She may have been a virgin, but she was now wholeheartedly embracing her sexuality. She was no longer content to let him take the lead all the time either, and it was hot as hell.

He was going to make her strip for him right inside their front door, until all she had on was her new matching underwear, then he was going to take her hard and fast while she was wearing it. Then maybe, if he could control himself, he'd carry her upstairs, where she could practice sucking cock some more.

She really didn't need any practice, she was a fucking expert already, but he loved to tease her . . . or maybe she was teasing *him*?

Meat was lost in his fantasies about the woman who had seemed to take over his every waking thought when his phone rang. He looked down and recognized Renee's phone number. Alarmed, he quickly answered. "Hello?"

"Hey, Meat, it's Renee."

"What's wrong?"

"Nothing. Well . . . not really *nothing*. Zara's had a bit too much to drink tonight, and she's gotten it in her head that she wants you to come and get her."

Meat frowned. First off, it was odd that Zara would get drunk. She'd told him once that she'd seen too many men in Peru blow their money on booze, and she didn't like the way people acted when they were drunk. So her imbibing enough to get that way herself was seriously out of character.

"Is she all right?" Meat asked.

"Yeah," Renee told him, and Meat couldn't hear any real concern in her tone, which made him feel a little better. Her voice lowered as she continued. "She's . . . well . . . she's horny. Said that she wanted to try something new on the way back to your house, if you know what I mean. Everly tried to tell her that was dangerous, but you know Zara . . ." Her voice trailed off suggestively.

Meat's cock twitched as he thought about Zara going down on him when he was driving. Everly was right, it *wasn't* safe . . . but that didn't mean Meat didn't like the image. "Okay, I'll be right there."

"Thanks. I'll tell her you're on the way," Renee said. "See you soon."

"Later." Meat hung up and immediately stood. It only took him a few minutes to put his shoes on and grab his wallet. He put in the code for the alarm and left the house, knowing it would turn on two minutes after the front door shut. He headed for his car and started down his long driveway.

Within seconds of pulling onto the sparsely traveled road leading to the street that would take him to the interstate, Meat glanced in his rearview mirror in alarm. A truck was gaining on him—very quickly.

He hadn't seen any vehicles when he'd made the turn onto the road, but now there was a truck right on his ass.

Before he could do anything more than brace, he was rear-ended.

Meat struggled to keep his car on the road, with no luck. He spun in a complete circle before careening toward the trees. He missed two by the skin of his teeth, but wasn't so lucky when he plowed right into a third.

The airbag went off in Meat's face, disorienting him and making him see stars. His head spinning from the impact, it took him a moment to get his wits about him. When he was finally able to pull the airbag away from his face, he opened his door to get out and see what the damage was to his car, and to exchange insurance information with the asshole who'd run into him.

But the second he stood up, he froze.

A man was standing by his door with a gun aimed right at his head.

Meat slowly lifted his hands. "Easy, man. You can take whatever money and cards I've got in my wallet."

"I don't want your money," the man said. His pupils were dilated, and he looked jittery. If Meat had to guess, he was definitely on something. "Where's your phone?"

Meat shrugged. "It's probably on the floorboard of my car. It was on the seat next to me when you hit me."

"Okay, good."

"What do you want?" Meat asked, getting more pissed by the second.

"You're going to come with me," the man said.

Meat couldn't help it. He laughed. "Like hell I am," he said.

"You'll come with me willingly or Zara will die."

At that, Meat's eyes narrowed, and every muscle in his body went tight. "What?"

"You heard me! We've got Zara, and if you don't do *exactly* what I say, she'll be killed. And don't think you can overpower me. I mean, you can, but if you do, and my partner doesn't hear from me in twenty minutes, Zara's dead."

Meat was pissed. *Beyond* pissed. He could take this asshole easily. If it were just his life in danger, he would've already done it.

But he couldn't risk Zara. No way.

The guy could be lying, but if there was even a slim chance he wasn't, Meat wouldn't risk it. "What do you want me to do?" he asked between clenched teeth.

The man pulled something out of his pocket and lobbed it at Meat as he said, "Catch."

Instinctively, Meat threw out a hand and caught the small plastic bottle the man had thrown at him.

"Drink that."

Meat's first thought was *Fuck that.* Then he decided maybe he could pretend to drink whatever it was, and then overtake this drugged-out asshole once they were on their way to wherever he was going to take him.

"*All* of it," the man said.

"What is it?" Meat asked, trying to stall.

"Just a little something to make you sleep. It won't kill you, that's not in our plans. But if you decide to be a hero and do anything stupid, I *will* shoot you."

Meat hesitated. He didn't want to drink *anything* this guy gave him. The man could be lying, and he could die in seconds if the contents were poisonous.

And he had to give it to the mysterious man; he was playing this kidnapping the one way that would guarantee his compliance. By threatening Zara, he had the upper hand. And by not getting anywhere close to Meat, he was ensuring he couldn't be taken by surprise and have the gun ripped from his hand.

"I'm not going to drink this," Meat told him finally.

"I told my partner you wouldn't," the man said—then pulled the trigger.

Pain shot through Meat's shoulder, and he gasped and fell back against his car, clutching his arm as fire raced through him. He clenched his teeth and hung on to consciousness by sheer force of will.

"Drink it!" the man yelled, waving the gun around. "If you don't, I'll do the same to Zara. I'll shoot her in the shoulder, then the knee. Then the other knee. Then I'll climb on top of her and fuck her in every hole before I wrap my hands around her throat and slowly squeeze the life from her body . . . while making sure she knows it was *you* who made me do it!"

By some miracle, Meat was still clutching the bottle in his hand. Not taking his eyes from the man, he tore the top off and lifted the bottle to his mouth. He swallowed the fruity-smelling liquid down without further hesitation. If he was going to die, so be it—but he'd be damned if he did anything to get Zara harmed.

The man's lips lifted into an evil grin. "Good boy. Now you need to walk over to my truck. Slow like. Don't try anything funny."

Meat threw the bottle on the ground, hoping against hope that one of his teammates would find it and his vehicle sooner or later, and figure out what the fuck was going on.

He stepped away from his car . . . and instantly swayed on his feet. Between the accident and whatever it was he'd ingested, he wasn't too steady.

They walked the short distance out of the trees to the truck sitting half on and half off the shoulder. One of the truck's front headlights was busted out, and the plastic was lying in the road.

"Get into the back seat," the man ordered.

Meat did as he was told. He opened the door and clumsily climbed into the back seat of the beat-up old pickup. When the asshole didn't immediately get into the driver's side, he asked, "What are you waiting for?"

"For you to go nighty-night," the man said with a smirk. "The midazolam should take effect any minute now."

Meat swore. That shit was dangerous, especially in liquid form. But it was too late now to change anything he'd done.

His shoulder was throbbing like a son of a bitch, and his eyes were feeling extremely heavy. The man with the gun might be a junkie, but he wasn't exactly stupid. He'd been smart enough to make Meat get himself into the truck, because it would've been impossible for this guy, who was several inches shorter and at least fifty pounds lighter, to get Meat's deadweight body up and into the vehicle.

"If you hurt Zara, there's nowhere you can hide where I won't find you and kill you," Meat swore.

"I don't think you're in any position to be issuing threats," the man told him. "I hold all the cards here."

Meat opened his mouth to respond, but nothing came out. His eyes closed, and he felt himself falling sideways, but he couldn't do anything to stop it. One second he heard the man laughing, and the next, everything went dark.

Zara waved at Renee when she got to the front door of Meat's house. She'd shot Everly a text when they'd gotten close to the house, letting her know she was home, not wanting to have to stop anything Meat might have planned for her when she got inside. Renee waved back and started down the driveway on her way home.

The house was quiet when she entered, and Zara quickly turned off the alarm.

"Meat?" she called, but there was no answer.

Frowning—because she'd envisioned Meat meeting her at the door and demanding to see her matching underwear she'd teased him with before leaving—she called out his name again.

Once more, she was greeted with nothing but an eerie silence.

Zara quickly searched the downstairs. No Meat. She jogged up the stairs and went straight to the master bedroom. It was dark, and Meat wasn't there either. She took a few seconds to check the rest of the rooms upstairs, with no luck.

Pulling her phone out of her back pocket, Zara clicked on Meat's name and brought it up to her ear. It rang four times before Meat's voice mail started. She left him a message.

"Meat? It's Zara. Where are you? It's about nine o'clock, and I'm home from dinner with the girls, but you aren't here. Call me when you get this."

Worried now because it wasn't like Meat not to pick up his phone, especially after all the lectures he'd given her about always carrying her own cell, she shot him a quick text, asking him once again to get in touch with her.

She wandered back downstairs and tried to think. She checked the garage, noting that his car was indeed gone. The alarm had been set when she'd arrived, so he'd obviously left to go somewhere. But why hadn't he left her a note? Or answered her call or text? They hadn't been a couple for very long, but everything she knew about Meat made her think he'd never just leave like this and not let her know where he was going.

Just when she was debating calling Gray or one of the other guys, her phone pinged with a text. Sighing in relief that Meat had finally gotten back to her, Zara pulled her phone out of her pocket and unlocked it to read the text.

But it wasn't from Meat.

It was from an unknown number.

We have Meat. If you want to see him alive again, you need to bring one million dollars to the rest stop south of the Pikes Peak International Raceway on I-25. At the far end there's a trash can. Park in front of it, put the cash in the can, and leave. You have twenty-four hours starting now. If you don't show, we'll kill him. If you call the cops, we'll kill him. If you call his friends, we'll kill him. Text this number when you leave for the rest stop.

A picture popped up seconds after she finished reading the text.

It was Meat. He was lying on his side on a car seat—and there was blood all over his shirt.

Zara's entire being froze. For a moment, she had absolutely no idea what to do.

Yes, she had a bank account, and had more than enough money to get the million dollars for the kidnappers. She'd retroactively received all the stipends she would have gotten since the age of eighteen, and it was just sitting in the bank until she could figure out how to invest it properly.

But she wasn't sure how to go about getting it out. She'd spent her entire life living off whatever money she could beg for on the streets. She was still figuring out checks—tonight was only the second time she'd used her credit card. She *did* know that the banks were closed at the moment . . .

And she only had twenty-four hours.

Zara had no idea if that was enough time to get the money from the bank. Maybe there would be holds on the money due to such a large withdrawal, or the bank wouldn't be able to give it all to her at one time. She simply had no clue—and not knowing scared her to death.

She looked back down at Meat's pale face in the image . . . and a sound somewhere between a moan and a scream escaped her lips.

She didn't give a shit about the cash. As far as she was concerned, whoever had Meat could have every penny. She'd proven without a doubt that she could get along just fine without money, but she couldn't get by without Meat. Not now. Not after falling in love with him.

She'd get the money, drop it off, and get Meat back. Every other option faded to the back of her mind.

She typed back a text as fast as she could. She wasn't that skilled at typing on the small buttons yet, but she did her best.

Don't hurt him. I'll get the money and I'll be there.

There was no response, but Zara wasn't going to sit around and wait for morning to arrive.

Feeling like a lost ten-year-old all over again, she tried not to panic. She still had no idea what to do, only knew that she had to do something *now*.

Trying desperately to think, she paced back and forth. Her palms were sweaty, and she was breathing way too fast. She needed to somehow start getting the money together.

She ran over to her purse, opened it, and grabbed her wallet. Looking inside, she saw she had a measly thirty-five dollars.

Shaking her head, she sighed at herself in disgust. As if she'd magically expected to find a million bucks in her wallet. *Get it together, Zara!*

Then she pulled out the brand-new automatic teller machine card she'd received upon opening her account. Zara had never used it before, but she knew it was connected to her account.

How much money could she get out *that* way instead of waiting almost twelve excruciating hours for the bank to open?

Feeling relieved that maybe she could do something, *anything*— because she sure as hell wasn't going to be able to sleep anytime soon— Zara grabbed the set of keys to Meat's old Honda Accord that he'd had forever but couldn't bear to get rid of, especially when it drove just fine, and headed for the garage. She didn't have her license yet, but she'd risk it. Luckily, Meat had given her a few driving lessons around his property. She'd figure out what she didn't know about driving as she went.

Perhaps if she'd been thinking straight, she would've called one of Meat's friends, no matter what the text said. They would know what to do.

But Zara had all too easily reverted back to the lonely, scared little girl she'd been fifteen years ago. Alone and on her own, with no one to rely on but herself.

"Hang on, Meat. I'm comin'," she muttered as she straightened her spine and vowed to do whatever it took to get him home safe and sound.

Chapter Twenty-Six

The next morning at breakfast, Ball frowned when he checked his email.

"What's wrong?" Everly asked.

"I'm not sure," Ball said, continuing to scroll through the email alerts he'd gotten. "Did Zara seem . . . off last night?" he asked.

Everly sat up straighter in her chair and slowly shook her head. "Not really, why?"

"She and Meat are still okay?" he asked.

"Yes," Everly answered. "In fact, Zara was all excited to get home to show him some new lingerie she'd bought. *Why?* Talk to me, Ball."

Glancing over at Everly's sister, who wasn't paying the least bit of attention to them and was sitting on the couch staring at her phone as she texted back and forth with her friends, Ball sighed.

"I've gotten a few alerts from the bank Zara has her money in. Meat used some kind of program he developed to track any large debits from her account, because none of us trusted her uncle as far as we could throw him. He made me a backup on the alerts, just in case—and I've gotten two notifications that were triggered sometime last night, late. The first was after fifteen hundred dollars was taken out of her account via ATM, and the second when another withdrawal was attempted, but because of the daily limits, it was denied."

"She didn't mention anything about needing money last night," Everly said. "She *did* talk about what she wanted to do with her inheritance. Things like giving it to charity and starting some sort of clinic in Peru, but that's about it."

"God, Meat is a fucking genius. There's even video from the ATMs that came through with the notifications. I have no idea how he does it. I definitely need some more lessons," Ball muttered as he clicked on the video that was attached to the first email notification.

The grainy film showed Zara pulling up to the drive-through ATM. She seemed to struggle with the machine, jabbing the buttons almost frantically. She also looked stressed.

Very stressed.

"Shit," Everly said as she watched over Ball's shoulder. "Something's wrong. First of all, she shouldn't be driving, and secondly, she looks worried."

Ball agreed. As soon as the video stopped, he clicked on Meat's number. The phone rang, but Meat didn't pick up. He then tried to call Zara herself, but she didn't answer either. "Come on. Let's get Elise to school, then we'll stop by Meat's house and see what's going on."

Everly nodded.

Within forty minutes, they were pulling up in front of Meat's house, except it looked like no one was home. After ringing the doorbell and not getting any answer, and calling both Meat's and Zara's phones again, Ball really started to worry. He called Rex.

"What's wrong?" Rex asked in lieu of a greeting.

"Meat and Zara aren't answering their phones. They aren't home, and Zara took fifteen hundred dollars out of her bank account late last night," Ball said without hesitation.

Ball could hear Rex's fingers tapping on a keyboard in the background, then he asked, "You're sure it was Zara who pulled the money?"

"Positive," Ball told him. "Meat set up a special alert on her account and added my email just in case. Saw a video of her at the ATM machine."

"Okay, I'm tracking Meat's phone right now. I'll start with him. I'm assuming he wasn't with Zara when she got the money out?"

"Not that I could see."

"Okay . . . Hmm, that's weird," Rex said.

"What?" Ball asked.

"He's not far from his house. The phone is pinging a few hundred yards east of his driveway, out on the road."

Ball immediately headed for his car, Everly right on his heels.

"You're sure?"

"Positive. I'll wait while you check it out."

Ball put the phone on speaker as he started his car and informed Everly of what Rex had said. He didn't know what to think. Maybe their friend had been in an accident, but that didn't explain why Zara would be taking money out of her account in the middle of the night.

Ball turned right out of Meat's driveway—and almost immediately saw pieces of plastic in the road and a skid mark. He slowed down and could just see the back end of a car in the trees. "Rex, looks like we found his car. There was some sort of accident, I think."

"Let me know what you find," Rex ordered.

Ball grabbed the phone and got out. Everly immediately hopped out as well. He would've told her to stay put, but since she was a CSPD officer, *he* was probably the one who should stay in the car, and that wasn't going to happen.

They walked toward the vehicle—and Ball tensed when he saw a fine spattering of blood on the roof of the car near the driver's side.

Meat wasn't lying injured or dead inside, which was good, but Ball *definitely* didn't like that blood spatter.

He leaned over and used a stick to pick up a small plastic bottle from the ground near the driver's side of Meat's car. He smelled it and frowned. "Found something that could be nothing," he told Rex.

"What?"

"An empty bottle that smells kinda sweet," Ball said.

"Keep it so it can be analyzed if necessary," Rex said. "Have you checked the trunk?"

Ball swallowed hard and reached inside the car to pop the trunk. "Empty. His phone's on the floor of the passenger side, but Meat isn't here."

"Well, fuck. All right—hold on. Call coming through."

Less than two minutes later, he was back on the line. "I'll keep seeing what I can find out—but you need to get to the Bank of America pronto," Rex ordered.

Ball and Everly were on the move before Rex had finished speaking. "Why? What's going on?"

"Zara's there—trying to withdraw a million dollars from her account. In cash."

"What the fuck?" Ball exclaimed. "And how do *you* know?" he asked.

"That was the manager. I'm well acquainted with almost *all* the managers of the area banks. I've made it a point to be. You never know when it might come in handy. And when Meat was helping Zara set up her account, he put my name down as a secondary contact, just in case. I'm guessing he already tried Meat. Ultimately, it doesn't matter *why* he called, just that he did.

"I'm getting in touch with the rest of the team. It's going to take them quite a while to get that money together, so I don't think there's any danger of her leaving before you arrive, but I still asked the manager to make sure she doesn't leave before someone can get there to escort her."

"We're on the way," Ball said.

"I don't know what the fuck's going on, but whatever it is, it isn't good," Rex said.

"No shit," Ball said with a shake of his head as he climbed back into his car. "We'll be in touch. Let us know if you find anything else of interest."

"Will do. I'm going to hack into both their phones and see what I can find. Drive safe."

Ball clicked off the connection and turned to Everly. She reached over and kissed him hard before gesturing with her head. "Let's go see what's wrong so we can fix it."

Ball peeled away from the side of the road and drove as fast as he dared to get to Zara. Hopefully she'd have information about where Meat was—and what the hell was going on.

Zara paced back and forth inside the small office where she'd been asked to wait while the bank employees put together the money she'd requested.

She had no idea how badly Meat was hurt. He'd had a lot of blood on his shirt in the picture that she'd been sent. She didn't know if someone had bothered to patch him up or if they'd hurt him even further. She hadn't gotten any additional texts or pictures, and the not knowing was *killing* her.

"Come on, come on," Zara muttered. She didn't have any idea how long it took to get a million dollars together, but it felt like it had already been forever.

She heard someone at the door and eagerly turned, thankful that she was finally going to get the money and be able to leave.

But instead of the manager she'd expected to see, Gray and Ro walked through the door.

Zara immediately panicked. "No! You guys can't be here. You have to go!"

"We aren't going anywhere," Gray said sternly.

"And you're going to tell us exactly why you need a million dollars in cash so bloody quickly," Ro added.

Zara felt dizzy, and she swayed on her feet. One second she was standing, and the next, Gray had taken her arm and eased her onto one of the plush chairs in the room. He gently pushed her head between her legs and ordered, "Long, slow breaths, Zara. Breathe."

How could she breathe when she'd failed Meat? Whoever had him strictly said no cops and not to get his friends involved. But here they were! They'd want to know everything.

Just as that thought went through her head, Arrow, Black, Ball, and Everly pushed their way into the room. It was quite crowded now, but no one seemed to care.

Zara sat up, closed her eyes, and did her best not to pass out.

Everly kneeled in front of her and took hold of her hands. "You haven't known the Mountain Mercenaries very long—I haven't either, really—but the one thing you have to understand is that they will *always* have each other's backs. No one hurts one of their family, man or woman, and gets away with it. Now take a deep breath and tell us what's going on."

Zara shook her head. "I can't," she whispered. "Please, can't you all just *go*?"

Everly shook her head. "Unfortunately, no. You need to talk to us. Where's Meat?"

Zara couldn't look away from the woman holding her hands, giving her silent strength. She couldn't believe she'd been scared of her at one point. Yes, Everly was a police officer, but she wasn't anything like the corrupt men Zara had known in Peru.

"I don't know!" she finally wailed in despair. "They have him."

"Who?"

"I don't *know!*" Zara repeated. "I got a text."

Just then, five phones belonging to the men standing in the room vibrated at the same time. All five pulled them out and looked at the screens.

"Fuck," Black swore.

Four similar curse words followed.

Zara closed her eyes. She guessed Rex had already found and emailed to the others the same picture *she'd* received. "I don't care about the money," she told Everly. "I'd give up my entire fortune if it means getting Meat back. He got hurt because of me!"

"No, he didn't," Arrow said sternly. "Someone hurt him because they're a greedy asshole."

"Do you know who has him?" Black asked.

Zara shook her head. "I'm assuming it's my uncle? He's gotten more and more angry. I don't know who else it could be."

"It could be any one of the people who have been emailing you, begging for money," Gray said. "Didn't you have someone recognize you just the other day in a store, and they had to be forcibly removed because they got obnoxious about asking for money?"

Zara nodded.

"Rex is on this," Gray continued. "He said the number the text came from belongs to a burner phone, but there are still ways to track it. He can find the serial number and where the phone was sold, then check the surveillance cameras to figure out who bought it."

"There's no time!" Zara said with a frenzied shake of her head. "I was only given twenty-four hours. You guys saw the text!"

"So you were going to . . . what? Just drop off the money and hope to get Meat back?" Ball asked.

Zara winced. "That's what they said," she whispered.

"If they get a million bucks out of you, what do you think they'll do next?" Without waiting for her to answer, Ball went on. "They'll decide they want more. It'll never be enough, Zara."

Frustration filled her. "What was I supposed to do, then?"

Ball leaned over until he was almost nose to nose with her and said in a low, steady voice, "Call. Us."

"But the note said if I got anyone else involved—"

He cut her off. "That's what they *always* say. But, Zara, I don't think I know *anyone* who's ever gotten their loved one back safely without help."

Zara just stared at him for a long moment. Then she stood and took a deep breath, her eyes downcast. "Fine. I screwed up. But all I want is to get Meat back. What should I do?"

No one spoke for a heartbeat—and then it seemed as if everyone started talking at once.

They threw out ideas left and right, discarding them or tabling them for a later discussion. It was fascinating to watch and confusing as hell.

Everly pulled Zara in close and said softly, "This is what they do. They'll talk through every option before deciding on the one that will most likely work. I know it's hard, but you have to trust them."

"I do," Zara said with a tired sigh.

After what seemed like forever, but was probably only around fifteen minutes, Gray left the room to talk to the bank manager.

Ro turned to Zara. "If you agree, here's the plan. You'll get the money and text the kidnapper that you'll be on your way to the rest stop by five. That will give us plenty of time to set up around the perimeter. Rex will also monitor the burner and see if he can track it by following the towers it's pinging off of. You'll drop the money and leave."

"But what about Meat?"

"After you put the money in the trash can, you'll text and ask where you can find Meat," Ro said.

"And if he won't tell me?"

"It's not going to matter, because we'll be there to grab whoever shows up to collect the money," Ball said matter-of-factly.

"But if he doesn't have Meat with him, he could just refuse to tell you where he is," Zara argued. "Or he could have an accomplice!"

"Trust me, when we're done with him, he won't refuse to tell us *anything*," Arrow said in a tone that made Zara shiver.

It was a better plan than Zara had come up with on her own. She just hoped it worked.

Meat felt horrible. His head was throbbing, and his shoulder was on fire.

He stirred, and someone lifted his head and held something to his mouth. He smelled roses, and the body his head was propped against was definitely female.

"Zara," he mumbled.

"Drink," the feminine voice said harshly from above him.

His mouth dry, Meat opened and swallowed what he hoped was water.

But the second the syrupy-sweet liquid eased down his throat, he realized what was happening. He tried to throw off the woman's hold, but was too weak and disoriented.

"That's it, drink it all down," the woman purred.

Choking, Meat fought as best he could. Most of the liquid ended up spilling over his chin, onto his shirt, but enough slid down his throat that he knew he'd be knocked out again before too long. He realized he was still in the back seat of the truck he'd willingly climbed into, and he cracked his eyes open and stared up at the woman who'd just forced another dose of midazolam down his throat.

After a few seconds, he was lucid enough to recognize her.

"Renee," he spat.

"Yup, it's me," she said cheerfully.

"Where's Zara?" he asked, trying desperately to force his muscles to work . . . with no luck.

"She's hopefully at her bank right now, getting us the money we want. You should be flattered that she didn't even hesitate to agree to our terms to get you back. You're cute, but besides that, I have *no* idea what she sees in you."

Meat wanted to say the same about Renee, but couldn't. The drug was already taking effect, and he knew he was going to lose consciousness once more. But he had to know one thing before he passed out again. "Who's the guy?"

"Oh, him? He's my boyfriend." Renee chuckled. "I know you looked into me. I'm not an idiot. But I also knew you wouldn't find out anything about John. He's more my fuck and drug buddy than anything else, but he's loyal, which is something I can't say for many men. We'll have our money and be south of the border before anyone's the wiser. You'll never find us. We're going to disappear and live happily ever after with the money stupid Zara doesn't even want!"

Meat opened his mouth to tell her there was no way she and this John guy were going to get away with kidnapping and extortion.

Not to mention, if they were both using drugs, any money they'd get wouldn't last more than a year. Tops.

"Me . . . ?" he asked, wanting to know as much of their plan as possible before he once more succumbed to the drug.

"If your heart doesn't stop and your lungs keep working after all this midazolam, you'll be just fine."

She slapped him not so gently on the cheek, but Meat didn't even feel it. He'd already passed out.

Chapter Twenty-Seven

Zara was as nervous as she'd ever been. She had a million dollars in the car, and she was going to the rest stop to make the drop. She'd argued with the guys about driving herself to the meeting spot, but they'd categorically refused, citing her lack of a license. So Everly was driving her. She wasn't wearing her uniform but had a weapon on her, so the guys felt comfortable enough leaving the two of them to make their way to the meeting point on their own.

Zara hadn't realized how heavy and bulky a million dollars would be. It wasn't like the movies, where it all fit neatly into a duffel bag. She had *three* bags full of money.

Also worrying her was the fact that she still had no idea who was behind Meat's kidnapping. She hoped it wasn't her uncle, but honestly wouldn't put it past him. He was more than upset with her. But was he pissed enough to hurt Meat just to extort money from her? Would whoever it was decide to keep Meat and demand more?

She'd give every last dime if she could get Meat back safely. Sometime over the last twenty-four hours, Zara had realized just how much she loved him. Irrevocably, unconditionally, and with everything she had. If he was taken from her, she'd never recover. She'd eventually been able to go on without her parents, but she had a feeling she wouldn't survive losing Meat.

He was everything she'd ever dreamed of in a man. Patient, kind, funny, considerate. He was also bossy, a bit too stuck in his ways, and didn't want to say or do anything that might upset her. But she could work with those last three . . . as long as he was alive to work with.

"It's going to be okay," Everly said as she tapped her fingers on the steering wheel impatiently.

They were stuck in slow-moving traffic around downtown Colorado Springs, and Zara wanted to scream in frustration.

She nodded, but didn't verbally respond.

Zara's phone ringing scared the crap out of both of them. Looking down, Zara saw that it was Renee calling. She didn't really want to talk to her, but she clicked on the green button to answer anyway.

"Hey."

"Hi, girl! Where are you?"

Zara frowned. "Why?"

"Just wondering. I was headed down to the Springs to see a client, and I thought I'd stop by."

"I'm not home," Zara told her.

"Oh. Doing anything fun?"

Zara wanted to scream. "No."

"No need to be so short, jeez," Renee complained.

"I'm just stressed. Sorry," Zara said.

"You know what cures stress?" Renee asked. And without waiting for an answer, she went on, "Shopping! You should go and spend some money! You've got enough of it."

Zara was done. "I have to go," she said.

"Oh, all right. I guess I'll talk to you later."

"Bye."

"Bye."

Zara clicked off the phone and leaned back on the headrest. "God. I hate to be a bitch, but she's driving me crazy."

"That was Renee, right? I could hear her side of the conversation from here."

"Yeah."

"Hmmm. Can you dial my phone for me?" Everly asked, telling her next who to call.

Zara was surprised, but she picked up the phone, went to Everly's contacts, and hit the number she'd asked her to dial, putting the phone on speaker.

"This is Rex."

"Rex, it's Everly. Can you check the pings on someone's phone for me?"

"Who?"

"We're on our way to the meet, and Zara just got a call from Renee Heller. She sounded way too . . . chipper. I mean, Zara answered, and she was obviously stressed way the hell out, and Renee started blabbing about spending money—which seemed super odd to me. I have a hunch. I thought maybe you could check her location."

"Where did she say she was?" Rex asked.

Everly looked at Zara.

"She didn't say exactly," Zara told Rex. "She said she would be down in Colorado Springs and wanted to know if I was home."

"Okay, should be simple enough. Hang on . . . Well, that's interesting," Rex said.

"What?" both Everly and Zara asked at the same time.

"She's headed south all right—but she's just now passing the racetrack."

Zara inhaled sharply and turned wide eyes to Everly.

"Seriously? That's the same direction we're headed," Everly told Rex.

"Yeah, I know," Rex said. "Look, be careful out there, okay? I need to look something up before you drop that money. Just watch your back. I'll be in touch." Then he hung up without another word.

"Do you think *Renee* is behind this?" Zara whispered.

"I don't know."

"But she was at dinner with us when Meat disappeared," Zara insisted.

"She was, but that doesn't mean she doesn't have someone helping her. She's always been a bit too interested in your money."

That was true. Zara hadn't really noticed until recently, but almost every time they were together in the last few weeks, Renee had made some sort of remark about how rich Zara was and how it must be nice to not have to worry about money.

The anger that had been pushed down by fear began to rise. If Uncle Alan had been behind this, Zara could almost have understood it. He'd been up front from the start about telling her he deserved some of his sister's estate. But Renee . . .

She'd been there for Zara from the very beginning. She'd been a friend from her life before . . . Would she really betray her like this? Had she only pretended to be her friend to get her hands on Zara's money?

The rest of the ride was quiet as both women were stuck in their thoughts. As they neared the rest stop, Everly said, "Remember the plan. Dump the money, get back in the car, and we're out of here."

Zara nodded . . . but as they drove slowly through the lot, a car parked behind a tractor trailer on the other side of the rest stop caught her attention.

And now that Everly had planted the seed of doubt about Renee, Zara couldn't get it out of her head.

She knew the guys were around the rest stop, watching and waiting, but upon seeing that car, anger rose within Zara so fast and with such intensity, she could barely breathe.

Everly pulled into the last parking space, right in front of the trash can, and Zara got out with one of the bags. She stuffed it into the can and went back to the car for another, since she couldn't carry all three at the same time.

When she'd finally shoved the last bag in the trash can, she started back toward Everly's car . . .

Then Zara abruptly turned and started running as fast as she could toward the car that had caught her eye earlier.

She was pissed. *Beyond* pissed. She was enraged.

This wasn't fair! Not after everything she'd been through for fifteen damn years.

And it definitely wasn't fair to Meat, who hadn't done a thing wrong. All he'd done was help her, love her, and she'd be *damned* if Renee was going to take him away from her.

Zara wasn't even halfway to the car when Renee and a man Zara had never seen before swiftly jumped out. She heard Everly yelling her name from behind her, but Zara didn't stop. She was going to wring Renee's neck with her bare hands. Force her to tell her where Meat was!

"Stop right there!" Renee shouted, pointing a pistol in Zara's direction.

That finally made Zara think twice about what in the hell she was doing. She skidded to a stop—but didn't get a chance to say anything before a shot rang out.

Flinching and taking a step back, Zara expected to feel pain.

But she wasn't the one who'd been shot.

Renee screamed as she dropped the gun she'd been holding. Zara saw Ro and Ball materialize out of the surrounding woods and begin to make their way fast toward where Renee was standing by her car, gaping, holding her hand.

The man with her, seeing that their plan had obviously gone to shit, turned tail and ran for the nearby trees. Zara didn't worry about him getting away. She knew the guys would catch him.

Everly had reached her side and grabbed her arm, urging her toward her vehicle, but Zara refused to back away from the scene.

Renee wasn't going anywhere, not with half her hand missing and blood pooling on the asphalt at her feet. She stood right where she was by the open car door, clearly in shock, staring at her hand as if she couldn't believe what had happened.

With Everly at her side, and Ball and Ro facing Renee with their guns drawn, all Zara could think about was Meat.

And how her oldest friend, together with an accomplice, had most likely kidnapped him.

"I thought you were my friend," Zara cried as she approached Renee. "I trusted you!"

"Oh, grow up! It's been fifteen years!" Renee screeched back, crying out in pain as Ro ruthlessly grabbed her hands and cuffed them behind her, not seeming to really notice that she was covered in blood.

"You won't get away with this," Zara told her former friend.

"*Wrong.* I already have."

"Where's Meat?"

"Fuck you!"

"Tell me right now!" Zara shouted.

"You'll never find him," Renee hissed evilly. "He'll die right where we stashed him—and it'll be *all your fault!*"

Zara stared into Renee's eyes and tried to see the girl she used to know. The one who'd run around the playground with her. Who'd swung giddily on the swings for hours at a time.

But she couldn't find her. In her place was a greedy, selfish, soulless woman.

Zara felt as if she were watching the scene from above, and she moved without thinking.

She balled up her fist and hit Renee as hard as she could in the face.

It hurt like hell, but Zara didn't even feel the pain in her hand.

She leaned in to Renee, ignoring the way the woman's nose was bleeding, and said softly, "It doesn't matter where you've put him. We'll find him."

Renee scoffed and hawked a loogie, preparing to launch it at Zara's face. Ro reached out and clapped a hand over her mouth so she couldn't spit.

"I feel sorry for you," Zara told her. "You have no idea what you've done, to what lengths these guys will go to find their friend."

Renee closed her eyes and turned her head to the side. At a commotion to their right, they all looked over and saw John being hauled back toward the parking lot by Gray and Black.

"I'll collect your money," Arrow told Zara. "You and Everly head out, we've got things under control here."

Zara kept her eyes on Renee as long as possible as Everly took hold of her arm and led her away.

It wasn't until Zara was back in the car that she broke into tears. She cried as she'd never cried before. Huge sobs that shook her whole body. She had no idea where Everly was taking her, but it didn't matter.

Meat hadn't been at the rest stop, and she had no idea where in the world he might be.

They'd figured out who was behind his kidnapping, but they still didn't know where he was or if he was alive. Zara knew the guys would do what they could to get the information out of Renee and John, but what if they were too late?

Doing her best to get herself under control, Zara picked up Everly's phone and hit "Redial." When Rex picked up, she said two words. "Find him."

Chapter Twenty-Eight

Meat tried to blink. He didn't open his eyes fully, trying to get his bearings before he let anyone around him know he was once more awake. He had no idea how much time had passed since he'd been taken by gunpoint, but instinctively he knew it had been hours. Possibly days. His mouth was as dry as cotton, and he hurt all over.

His memories were also extremely foggy. He knew midazolam was used as a sedative, and it had been very effective in taking Meat completely out of the equation. He was physically incapable of doing anything while under its effects, and Renee and her boyfriend had done their best to keep him knocked out.

The last time Renee had tipped the bottle up to his mouth, he knew she'd been trying to kill him. The first two times, he'd only been given a small bit of the syrup when he stirred, but the last time, Renee had tried to force him to ingest several times what he had previously. Luckily, he'd been lucid enough to fight her, albeit weakly, and most of the drug had run down his face rather than his throat.

He lay there for what seemed like a very long time, until he was certain that no one was nearby. Cursing a blue streak, Meat used his good arm to push himself up on the seat. He was still in the truck he'd been kidnapped in, but when he looked out the window, he saw nothing but darkness. There were no lights anywhere, no matter which way he turned his head. He had no idea where he was, or if he was even still in Colorado.

He forced his blurry eyes to focus on his watch.

Two in the morning. And more than twenty-four hours since he'd left to pick up Zara.

Zara!

Meat's adrenaline kicked in. Where was she? He'd gone with the man because he'd said they had Zara. Had they drugged her too? Hurt her?

Groaning, Meat forced himself to sit completely upright. He peered over the seat in front of him, hoping to see keys in the ignition of the truck . . . to no avail. Didn't matter—Ro had taught them all how to hot-wire a car, just in case.

He leaned farther and turned the knob on the side of the steering wheel to turn on the truck's headlights. Wincing at the bright beams that shone through the darkness, he swore once more.

All he could see were trees. Everywhere he turned were trees. No roads. No people. No houses. And again, no keys. This was going to be harder than he'd hoped. But Meat wasn't a former Delta Force soldier for nothing. He'd get back to Zara or die trying. Since he hadn't already died from the gunshot to the shoulder, Meat figured he was good to go.

He pushed open the door next to him, and the second he stood, the world tilted, and he landed practically flat on his face on the hard ground.

Okay, so maybe he wasn't so good to go. He'd just rest there for a minute and get his bearings, then he'd get up, hot-wire the truck, and get the hell home.

One minute turned into two, and two turned into four. He was getting up . . . as soon as the world stopped spinning and his shoulder stopped throbbing.

Zara paced impatiently. Allye, Chloe, and Harlow were all watching her, clearly concerned. Morgan was dozing on the couch, and both Darby and Calinda were fast asleep in a portable crib on the floor. Everly had called in the cavalry and stayed at Meat's house with her until the other women had arrived, then she'd driven off to go help look for Meat.

Zara had called Rex four times, but he didn't have anything else to report, other than he was "working on it." Ball had called shortly after she'd gotten home, giving her the bad news that, just when they'd been ready to take off with Renee and John—to force them to confess where they'd left Meat—the police had arrived. Someone had seen Renee pull her gun and called the cops.

So now Renee and John were in the custody of the police . . . so using more *creative* ways to get them to talk was out.

The fact of the matter was, Meat was as lost as Zara had once been . . . if he was even still alive.

And that was what was so hard about this. He couldn't be dead. He just *couldn't*. She hadn't told him how much he meant to her. That she loved him.

Zara didn't want to think about the statistics. About how people disappeared all the time, their bodies buried in the wilderness surrounding the city and never found. There were literally millions of acres where John and Renee could've dumped Meat. It was a depressing thought, but Zara vowed to never stop looking.

She'd do whatever it took. She had the money. She'd hire private detectives, scent dogs . . . she'd hike every inch of the wilderness if it meant finding Meat.

She'd gone past tired hours ago, now she was simply running on fumes. It was five o'clock in the morning, nearly twelve hours since the scene at the rest stop.

"Please stop pacing and come sit down," Allye begged.

Zara shook her head. She had too much to do to relax. Too many people to contact, too many lists she was making in her head to even try to sleep.

"The guys'll find him," Chloe reassured her.

Zara nodded absently.

She didn't see the worried looks the three women shot each other.

Zara appreciated that they were there. That they wanted to help. She'd been so *stupid* to not be able to see through Renee's fake friendship to the evil underneath. She knew Meat had doubted her sincerity, but Zara hadn't heeded his concerns.

Another thirty minutes crawled by, and Zara felt as if she was going to go out of her mind.

When they heard a vehicle approaching the house, all four women turned their heads toward the front door.

"Are we expecting one of the guys?" Chloe asked.

"No. Gray would've texted or called if someone was coming here," Allye said.

"Is the alarm on?" Harlow asked as she stood and walked over to the crib, as if to protect the sleeping babies with just her body.

"It's on," Zara reassured her friends as she walked toward the front door. She peered out the small window next to the door and frowned as a beat-up old pickup slowly drove into view. It was weaving back and forth, as if the driver were drunk.

Meat's house wasn't exactly on the beaten path, and she couldn't think of anyone who would accidentally drive all the way down the long, winding dirt driveway by mistake.

After turning off the alarm, Zara opened the front door. She heard Chloe on the phone, probably talking to Ro, and she felt both Allye and Harlow come up alongside her.

These were the kind of friends she wanted. The kind who wouldn't hesitate to stand by her side no matter what she faced.

Zara flicked on the outside floodlights and waited for whoever was in the truck to get out and tell them what he or she was doing there.

Nothing could prepare her for who she saw when the driver's door opened.

"Meat!" she shouted, sprinting for the truck.

His face was white as a sheet, and his upper body was swaying back and forth as he continued to sit behind the wheel.

"Zara . . . ," he said, reaching for her with one hand, not making any attempt to get out of the truck.

She grabbed hold of his face and forced him to look at her. His arm went around her waist, and he held her as close to him as possible while she stood on the ground and he sat in the truck.

"You're okay?" he slurred. "Not hurt?"

"No. I'm fine. You're the one who's hurt."

"It was Renee," he said, struggling to keep his eyes open.

"I know. We know. What's wrong? Where's all the blood coming from?"

"Gunshot. Through and through. Drugged me. Midazolam. Hard to stay awake," Meat said.

"You *drove* here? From where?" Allye asked from beside them.

Meat shrugged his one good shoulder. "Middle of fucking nowhere. Somewhere along Rampart Range Road."

"Shit, he's lucky he didn't kill himself driving on that road in his condition," Harlow breathed.

Zara didn't care what condition Meat was in. He was here. In her arms and alive. "I love you!" she blurted.

"Love you too," Meat mumbled. "Wanna see that matching bra-and-panty set," he said, before his eyes closed and he went limp in her arms.

Chloe ran outside and informed them that the guys were on their way and would be there soon.

Zara stood next to the truck, holding Meat steady with help from her friends.

She closed her eyes and thanked her parents, wherever they were, for looking out for Meat. She'd come really close to losing him, she knew that. If he'd been half as strong as he was, he wouldn't have been able to drive himself out of wherever Renee and John had stashed him. He wouldn't have survived whatever they'd drugged him with, and she wouldn't be holding him in her arms.

"He's going to be okay," Allye told her.

"I know," Zara said. "I know."

Epilogue

"I can't wait to see this bar you're always talking about," Zara said.

Meat grinned and reached for her hand as he drove them to The Pit.

It had taken him longer than he would've liked to completely regain his wits after being dosed so many times with midazolam. The doctors said that if he'd actually swallowed the last dose Renee had tried to force on him, his lungs would've stopped working, and his heart probably would've ceased pumping as well.

The gunshot to his shoulder had gone straight through, just as he'd thought. And while it hurt, it wasn't life-threatening, and he'd already healed quite a bit in the last three weeks. He didn't remember driving down Rampart Range Road and back to his house, but he did remember seeing Zara for the first time and hearing her tell him she loved him.

He hated what she'd been through, but it had strengthened her friendship with the other women, and for Meat had truly hammered home how extraordinary his bond was with his fellow Mountain Mercenaries.

At the moment, they were on their way to the bar where he and the other Mountain Mercenaries hung out. Where they talked business in the back pool room or simply enjoyed spending some man time together. They hadn't gotten around to talking to Rex about limiting their future missions to the United States, but that was on the top of their agenda . . . *after* today.

"It's nothing fancy," Meat warned her, running his thumb over the back of her hand.

"It doesn't have to be fancy to be special," Zara responded.

That was very true.

Allye and Gray had decided not to wait any longer to get married. They hadn't wanted a huge production, but of course it had turned into a big deal when all the kids Allye taught in her special-needs dance classes wanted to attend. So Dave said they could use The Pit for the ceremony, and then after the children left, when the bar opened for business, they'd use it as a reception hall.

"You okay with everything you talked about with the lawyer yesterday?" Meat asked. He'd gone with Zara to discuss putting most of her money into a trust for charities, keeping only enough to live off every year. The majority would be invested, with portions doled out each year to whatever charities she designated.

She'd also set aside a small portion of her fortune for her uncle, Alan. He was still an ass, but Zara had thought about it long and hard, discussing it with Meat, and had decided she could never spend all the money her parents had left for her anyway. She'd reasoned it might be worth it to get her uncle off her back. She'd explained she felt sorry for him now, more than anything. She had love and friends, and he had . . . nothing. Bitterness and a drug habit that would surely make him blow through the money he was given. But as Meat pointed out, that wasn't her problem.

He'd also made sure Alan understood he'd never get another dime from her after this, and if he ever contacted her again, he'd regret it. Zara had no idea if he'd abide by their agreement after he spent the money, but ultimately, she knew Meat and his friends would handle him if he didn't.

"Yeah," she said. "It feels good to get it off my shoulders, so to speak. I know after word gets out about what I've done, people will think I've completely lost my mind for giving up so much money, but . . . I honestly don't want it. Look at what almost happened to *you* because of it. I just want enough to live on and raise our family, and that's it."

Meat smiled over at her, lifting her hand and kissing the ring he'd put on her left ring finger the night before. "How many kids do you want?"

"Fourteen."

Meat almost drove off the road at her answer, then stared at her in shock.

She held a straight face for about two seconds before dissolving into giggles. "You should see your face!" she said between gasps of air.

"Brat," Meat griped, happy as could be to see her smiling and so carefree.

"I'm thinking two. Maybe three. You?"

"Two or three sounds perfect," Meat told her. "I'm proud of you, Zar."

She tilted her head at him.

"You went through something that would break most people. But you not only *didn't* break, you came out of it stronger than ever. I'm also proud of you for putting the wheels in motion to start a clinic for Daniela. The money you sent will definitely tide her over until we can work through the red tape and get down there to get the building started."

Zara shrugged. "She taught me a lot, and she's helped so many people. You might say *she* saved Calinda's life, because if she hadn't taught me what to do when an umbilical cord was around a baby's neck, the baby wouldn't have survived."

"And you're okay with going back to Lima someday?" Meat pressed. "It won't bring back any bad memories?"

"Oh, I'm sure it will," she said. "But it'll be different because you'll be with me. I won't be alone."

"Damn straight," Meat said with feeling.

Last night, after he'd put his ring on her finger and after she'd agreed to marry him, they'd talked into the night about their future. In addition to the charities she would support, Zara also wanted to write a book about her experiences, with proceeds going to the Elizabeth Smart Foundation, which focuses on preventing crimes against children and providing resources for children, parents, and families alike when needed.

He pulled up to The Pit and found a place to park in the packed lot. He went around to help Zara out of the car and held her hand as they headed into the run-down bar, and they were immediately greeted by choruses of hellos. Knowing they were running late—because he'd caught a glimpse of Zara in another brand-new bra-and-panty set and couldn't keep his hands off her—Meat pulled her straight into the back room.

Gray glared at him, but Allye simply rolled her eyes. Meat kissed Zara quickly before escorting her to stand next to Everly. Then he took his place next to Ball across from where the women were lined up. The wedding wasn't traditional, meaning there would be no walking down the aisle, and no one was wearing anything fancy, but Ro, Arrow, Black, Ball, and Meat all stood next to Gray, while Chloe, Morgan, Harlow, Everly, and Zara attended Allye.

After everyone quieted down, Dave, who was usually standing behind the bar but had gone online and gotten ordained just for the occasion, started the ceremony. Noah Ganter had been manning the bar when they arrived, handing out fruity virgin drinks to the kids and soft drinks to the adults. Once the reception started and the bar was officially open, he'd serve alcohol.

Meat couldn't take his eyes from Zara as Dave went through the traditional words for the wedding ceremony. She seemed to glow. She had on a dress, which she'd sworn she was changing out of immediately after the ceremony, but he'd do whatever was necessary to convince her to keep it on. She'd considered and discarded the idea of growing out her hair, and it was freshly trimmed. She'd even let her new stylist put in a streak of red for the occasion, to match her dress.

Meat had never really understood his friends' almost obsessive attachment to their women, but he got it now. He'd literally do whatever it took to keep Zara safe and happy. She'd been through hell, and it was time she relaxed and enjoyed what life had to offer. He couldn't bring back her parents, but he could make sure she had the family she wanted. Her grandparents were missing out on the best part of life, knowing their grandchild, but that was their problem, not hers.

When Dave got to the part about anyone objecting, Gray growled at him and turned to glare at each and every one of the Mountain Mercenaries. At one point, Meat might've said something just to fuck with his friend, but the thought of anyone doing anything, even in jest, to keep him from tying Zara to him for the rest of their lives was enough to make him break out in a sweat.

"I now pronounce you husband and wife. You may kiss the bride," Dave said with a huge smile.

Gray grabbed Allye and tipped her backward and proceeded to kiss her as if they were alone at home instead of in a public bar.

Meat didn't even wait for his friend to finish his kiss. He strode across the floor and pulled Zara into his own arms. He may not've married her today, but he would soon. And he couldn't wait another second before putting his lips on hers.

Of course, not to be outdone, Ball crossed to Everly and did the same.

Soon, each of the men were claiming their women. Everyone clapped and cheered, and Dave threw up his hands in exasperation and headed back out to the bar in the front room.

Eventually, the men were able to peel themselves off their women, and they all mingled throughout the room. Meat couldn't help but notice how much Zara enjoyed the children in attendance. She paid attention to their every word, kneeling down to their height to talk. She was a natural—and suddenly he couldn't wait to see her belly round with his child. She'd make an amazing mother, probably overprotective, but he didn't mind.

After an hour, the parents with children slowly started to head out, and around three in the afternoon, Dave announced that the bar was officially open.

A cheer went up, and Meat put his arm around Zara. "Want something to drink?"

"Maybe a mimosa?" she asked. "It's kinda healthy because it has orange juice in it, right?"

Meat laughed. "Sure, Zar, whatever you want to think." She would never be a heavy drinker, which he was all right with. He liked her exactly the way she was.

They walked toward the bar and squeezed in between two other couples. Meat stood behind Zara, protecting her from being jostled from behind. She fit against him perfectly. She was tiny compared to him, but somehow they seemed to just work.

"What's with all the pictures?" Zara asked, gesturing to the hundreds of Polaroids tacked up behind the bar.

"I guess it started when Dave first opened the bar. He took pictures of some of the regulars, and pretty soon everyone wanted their picture on the wall."

Zara leaned on her elbows as she studied the many faces smiling down at them—then Meat felt her stiffen in his arms, and he was immediately alert.

Leaning down to speak into her ear, he asked, "What's wrong?"

Dave walked up just as Zara asked, "Why is there a picture of Mags up there?"

Meat frowned. "You have to be mistaken."

"No. I'm pretty sure that's her. She looks a lot younger, though." She turned to Dave. "Can you bring me that picture so I can see it better?"

"Which one?" Dave asked, turning to look where she was pointing.

"It's right in the middle. The woman with the long black hair. She's got her head back and she's laughing at something."

Dave froze—then he slowly turned to stare at Zara. "You know her?"

"Maybe," Zara said. "I mean, she looks like my friend Mags, who I knew from the barrio in Peru. But it can't be her, can it?"

Meat looked from Zara to Dave . . . and blinked in surprise at the instant change in Dave's demeanor.

The entire time he'd known the big, burly bartender, he'd been jovial and easygoing. He was serious about protecting the women who frequented his bar, and he didn't hesitate to kick out anyone who was causing problems, but for the most part, he was laid-back.

But the man standing in front of Meat right now was *anything* but laid-back.

Dave reached for the picture and removed the thumbtack. He put it down on the bar in front of Zara. She picked it up and examined it more closely.

"I *swear* this is her," Zara said, her confusion easy to hear.

"Where did you see her last?" Dave asked in a voice so intense, almost desperate, everyone around them stopped what they were doing to stare at him.

"In Peru. In the barrio. She took me in, and she's kind of the leader of the group of women I was friends with. We saw Meat and Black get beaten up by Ruben and his friend. It was Maria, Carmen, Gabriella, Teresa, Bonita, and Mags."

"Mags," Dave said. "Short for Margaret?"

Zara shook her head. "I don't know. She only went by Mags. Do *you* know her?"

Dave pointed at the picture in her hand. "That's my wife. She went missing ten years ago—and I haven't stopped looking for her since."

The bar had gotten so quiet Meat could hear the person next to him breathing.

"*Rex?*" Gray asked in disbelief, from behind Meat and Zara.

He nodded once. "That's me."

"Holy shit!" Ball exclaimed.

"I can't fucking believe it," Black said.

"Her family nicknamed her Magpie, and shortened it to Mags," Dave said. "I wanted my own special name for her, so I called her Raven, because of her long black hair." He leaned forward and pinned Zara with his gaze. "You're absolutely positive the woman you knew as Mags is the one in this picture?"

Zara nodded. "Yes. She didn't laugh a lot when I knew her, but it's her."

Dave picked up the picture and stuck it into his back pocket. He walked down the length of the bar and lifted the heavy pass-through that led into the room.

"Dave, wait!" Zara called. "There's a lot I should tell you about her! About the situation she's in."

But Dave didn't even slow down. He moved toward the door with a determined stride.

Meat looked around at his friends, who were all staring in disbelief at the man they'd come to respect. It was going to take a while for it to sink in that the bartender they knew and loved was actually Rex, the mastermind behind the Mountain Mercenaries.

"Where are you going?" Gray called out as he neared the front door.

Dave turned his head and said, "Peru," before opening the door and heading out into the parking lot.

About the Author

Susan Stoker is a *New York Times*, *USA Today*, and *Wall Street Journal* bestselling author whose series include Mountain Mercenaries, Badge of Honor: Texas Heroes, SEAL of Protection, Ace Security, and Delta Force Heroes. Married to a retired Army noncommissioned officer, Stoker has lived all over the country—from Missouri and California to Colorado and Texas—and currently lives under the big skies of Tennessee. A true believer in happily ever after, Stoker enjoys writing novels in which romance turns to love. To learn more about the author and her work, visit her website, www.stokeraces.com.

Connect with Susan Online

Susan's Facebook Profile and Page

www.facebook.com/authorsstoker

www.facebook.com/authorsusanstoker

Follow Susan on Twitter

www.twitter.com/Susan_Stoker

Find Susan's Books on Goodreads

www.goodreads.com/SusanStoker

Email

Susan@StokerAces.com

WEBSITE

www.StokerAces.com

NEWSLETTER SIGN-UP

http://www.stokeraces.com/contact-1.html